THE WHISKEY BOTTLE
Conversation

A Father's Legacy to His Son

Karl,
Thank you for stopping by the book signing and taking the time to view & read the excerpts. I hope you enjoy our story.
Dave Leonard

DAVID LEONARD

Copyright © 2017 David Leonard
All rights reserved
First Edition

PAGE PUBLISHING, INC.
New York, NY

First originally published by Page Publishing, Inc. 2017

ISBN 978-1-68409-758-6 (Paperback)
ISBN 978-1-68409-759-3 (Digital)

Printed in the United States of America

CONTENTS

Chapter 1. A Voice from Far Away 11
Chapter 2. There's Just So Much to Live For.............34
Chapter 3. The Whiskey Bottle and the Snowstorm ...66
Chapter 4. Horses, Automobiles, and Planes 88
Chapter 5. I Really Wasn't a Bad Boy 111
Chapter 6. South of the Mason Dixon Line 154
Chapter 7. I Just Wanted to Fight.............................174
Chapter 8. Into the Wild Blue Yonder......................193
Chapter 9. B-26s, 17s, and 24s..................................217
Chapter 10. I Ought to Court-Martial You! 239
Chapter 11. A Journey to the Unknown.....................257
Chapter 12. You Want to Build Runways?..................300
Chapter 13. The Lucky Leprechaun 343
Chapter 14. Freedom, Equality,
            and the Army Latrine...............................366
Chapter 15. I Wanted to See What We Fought For 400

To Kimberly
for bringing him back to tell his story.

Special thanks to the following people without whose enthusiastic efforts in all aspects of this endeavor, it might never have been completed…

Martha Martin
Jean LeClair
Marlene Peru
Susan Keppel
Erin McGivney
Argus Erhardt
And all our friends in Lake Placid

Introduction

When I was growing up, there would be occasions when my father, Richard Leonard, would tell me stories about some of his experiences in World War II. He served as a B-24 low-altitude bomber pilot in the Pacific Theater. As with most men that served in the war, he didn't speak at great length, but what he shared with me, I found fascinating. Years turned into decades.

In 1995, while attending a funeral for the father of a friend of mine that had passed away, I came to the realization that I wanted to know more about my father's life and experiences. I was forty-seven; he was seventy-five. So began our journey, our adventure.

His story takes the reader from 1920, when he was born in Georgia, to the end of 1945, when Japan surrendered. Through his uncanny ability of almost total recall of dates, names, and places, we are given a firsthand look at the experiences of a boy growing up in the early part of the twentieth century. Those experiences act as a blueprint for the man that joined the Army Air Corps to defend his country.

This book is not just Richard Leonard's story. It represents the story of an entire generation—men and women who believed in the ideals and principles that their country stood for. When it came time to defend those principles, they were willing to fight and die for their beliefs. We shall be ever grateful for their sacrifices.

David Leonard

CHAPTER ONE

A Voice from Far Away

I live in a small town that is nestled in the Adirondack Mountains of Upstate New York. The Lyon Mountain winters have an abundance of snow and frigid temperatures. It was a cold January morning, and I was on my way to a funeral at the Catholic church for the father of a friend of mine. He had passed away unexpectedly.

We had received about four or five inches of snow the night before, and the mountains were a brilliant white against the backdrop of a blue sky. The trees looked as if they had been decorated with large puffs of cotton candy, and the snow shimmered as if sprinkled with cut glass.

As I drove down the hill, past the rows of stucco duplex homes, the smoke rose quietly from the chimneys. People were out, shoveling their walks, scraping the windows of their cars, performing the rituals of an Adirondack winter morning.

The Catholic church was a gray stone building that sat on a hill at the far end of town. I could see that the parking lot was already full and people were turning around and parking their cars on either side of the street.

Lyon Mountain had been a mining town literally built from scratch by Republic Steel back in the late 1800s. Its residents were a hearty group of individuals, mostly of Irish or Polish descent. The mines closed in the 'sixties, but the people stayed on and found other forms of work to support themselves and their families. It was a close-knit community of about eight hundred.

Whenever someone died, got married, or baptized, the whole town would turn out to express their condolences or share in the joy. I entered the church and took a seat in the rear pew. The service had just begun. It was a high mass, complete with the ladies' choir singing hymns from the balcony at the rear of the church.

Family members read passages from the Bible. Each one expressed their own personal sentiments about their father. Some of the stories brought forth tears, and others had the whole congregation in laughter. It was more a celebration of life than the mourning of a person's death.

After the mass, the congregation was invited to the American Legion for a brunch. The Legion was about a block from the church and was the center of any social activity in the town. It didn't restrict its members to just veterans. Anyone was welcomed that could behave themselves. Those that couldn't usually ended up face-first out in the parking lot.

The building itself consisted of a large dining room that could seat around two hundred people. The kitchen was adjacent to the dining room, and the bar was on the other side of the building. People would bring a covered dish of some sort, and the legionnaires would make sure that it was served up in proper fashion.

I sat with my friend John and his family. We didn't really talk about his father much. It was more of a conversation about various family members, their children—things of a lighthearted nature. After we finished our meals, John and I excused ourselves to the bar where he ordered us both a shot of Jack Daniels—his father's favorite drink. We raised our glasses in a salute and tossed down the JD.

I motioned to the bartender to give us another round. We raised our glasses then down the hatch. As soon as they hit the bar, they were filled one more time. A relative two seats down nodded. The three of us clicked our glasses and swallowed our third shot. The bartender held his bottle over our glasses, but I waved him off.

I said, "I'll have mine with a little ice this time." John ordered the same.

We retreated to the table a few feet from the bar. John was a tough individual that had grown up on a dairy farm. He wasn't given to expressing feeling or emotions about any aspect of his life, nor was I. We had known each other for twenty years, and I think we had become good friends because our backgrounds and attitudes were similar.

We sat at the table, sipping our Jack Daniels, not saying much of anything. Finally, he began to talk about his father. He told me stories about working on the farm, hauling milk five miles into town with a team of horses.

He talked about working in the woods, cutting down trees and how his father had the horses trained. He could hook a tree to the team, and they would walk out of the woods by themselves to the barn, where one of his brothers would unhook the load. The horses would turn around and walk back into the woods where they were working. His stories went on for over an hour. I didn't say much except for an occasional question, which seemed to keep him talking.

At one point he stopped and sat there quietly for a while, taking an occasional sip from his drink. He had a distant look in his eyes.

Finally, he looked up at me and said, "You know, Dave, I've had all these experiences with my father, but I really didn't know that much about him—what it was like when he was growing up, had he fought in the war, things that I'll never have the opportunity to ask him now."

I didn't say anything. What could I say? It was true. Time had run out for John's father and any further shared experiences.

People were beginning to leave, so we went into the other room to bid them good-bye. After the Legion had cleared out, just the immediate family remained. I once again expressed my condolences and decided it was time for me to go, giving the family some time to themselves.

As I drove back through town, I thought about my own father. We had always had a strong relationship, but how much did I really know about him? When I got home, I picked up the phone and gave him a call.

We were going to Salt Lake City, Utah, the following week to visit my daughter, Kimberly. Our flight was out of Syracuse. Dick lived in Watertown about seventy miles north of Syracuse. I had planned to stop and pick him up on my way to the airport, but I suggested that he come up and meet me in Lake Placid. He agreed and said, "I'll be up Thursday afternoon."

Lake Placid is a beautiful Adirondack resort community that since the late 1800s has been the summer home to some of the country's wealthiest people. The Roosevelts, Rockefellers, Deweys, and the Posts are a few that built sprawling summer mansions on the lake. It was home to the first Winter Olympics in 1932 and again hosted the games in 1980.

The village itself surrounds Mirror Lake, where at any given time, a person staring at the water can see a reflection of the buildings on Main Street and the images of the surrounding mountains.

The permanent residents number about 2,500, but at the height of the summer and winter tourist seasons, that number can grow to several thousand. It's a vibrant community full of activity, and that vibrancy is reflected in the attitude of the local inhabitants.

I think it was best summed up by Sammy, a fellow from Palm Springs, Florida. He was a chef that had come up to spend a summer with one of his friends that was from Lake Placid. We were sitting in the Laughing Loon Cafe on Main Street. He was telling me where he was from, and I asked him how he was enjoying his stay.

He said, "It's a beautiful area, but what has struck me most is how bright everyone's eyes are!"

I own a small construction company and work primarily in the areas of residential painting, automobile, and furniture restoration. About a year ago, I was contracted to do some work for an elderly couple, Bill and Mary Bennet.

They lived in a stately country home at the end of Wolf Pond Road on the outskirts of Lake Placid.

The house sat on 360 acres with panoramic views of the Adirondack High Peaks range. The man who built the home was from Arizona and had a large Adirondack Great Camp on Lake Placid. He used the house primarily for parties, where he entertained his wealthy friends and business associates. It was 150 feet in length. You entered on the south end into a large country kitchen. A door off of the kitchen opened into a formal dining room beautifully appointed with a ten-foot Chippendale dining room table and a large buffet to match. At one end, there were double doors that opened to a formal living room. Mary's father had sold pianos in New Jersey. The centerpiece in the living room was a magnificent Steinway Grand player piano. Mary had over a hundred rolls of music ranging from Bach to Beethoven. She would put a roll in the piano, and I would sit and listen as the keys moved and elegant classical music poured out as if played by the original composers themselves. She told me that there were only five of these pianos left in the world. At the end of the living room, there was another set of doors that opened into the study, my favorite room in the house. There was a large fieldstone fireplace. The walls and cathedral ceiling were done with old barn board with hand-hewed beams supporting the upper structure of the chamber. The study was furnished with a leather couch and recliner, as well as an assortment of wing-backed chairs. The north end of the room opened into a solarium, and there were two bedrooms adjacent to the study. The master bedroom was huge, with a large silo room. (On the north side a hallway ran the entire length of the house. There were two bedrooms upstairs.)

Bill and Mary's Home

During the month and a half that I worked for Bill and Mary, we became good friends. They would fix me lunch each day, and sometimes I would spend two or three hours listening to their stories.

They had led colorful lives—involved in politics, teaching, and eventually, organic farming. They raised beef cattle in Pennsylvania. Their crops were only fertilized with organic substances, so they had a selective market for their beef. In 1986, they decided to sell their farm and move to Lake Placid.

At one point, I suggested that if they needed someone to look after the house and their three dogs while they were away, I would be more than happy to accommodate them. They called me a week before Dick, and I was scheduled to go to Salt Lake and asked if I could watch the house for five days while they were in Pennsylvania. I was delighted.

I arrived at Bill and Mary's early Wednesday morning. They gave me the particulars of the house. Bill took me down in the cellar and showed me where the relay switches were on the three furnaces in the event they kicked off. At the top of the stairs was a switch, which operated a diesel generator in case of a power failure. It would provide supplemental power for up to three days.

After a brief conversation, I bid them a safe trip and went to work at an old hotel in town that was being renovated. I had been painting there a couple of weeks. That night I returned to "my estate" and immediately built a fire in the study. I poured myself a glass of Scotch and sat in a big leather recliner, staring into the fire, enjoying the splendor of this beautiful home.

Dick arrived the next day at about three in the afternoon. I was working in the lobby of the hotel, and he greeted me as he always does, with a handshake and a hug.

"How's my boy?"

"Good, Dick. How about yourself?"

"Oh, I'm fine." He didn't look very well. He was pale and seemed very tired.

"How was the trip?" I asked.

"It was a nice drive, but I got stopped by a trooper."

I laughed. "No shit! What happened?"

THE WHISKEY BOTTLE CONVERSATION

"Well, I was just driving along outside of Saranac Lake, enjoying the scenery, when I saw these flashing red lights in my mirror. I pulled over, and the trooper pulled up behind me. He asked me for my license and registration. I gave him my license. He looked at it then looked at me.

"'Do you know why I stopped you, Mr. Leonard?'

"I said, 'No, sir, I don't.'

"'You were speeding.'

"'I'm sorry, Officer. How fast was I going?'

"He looked at me and said, 'How old are you?'

"I said, 'Seventy-five.'

"He said, 'That's how fast you were going!'"

I laughed again. "Did he give you a ticket?"

"No. We just had a little visit, and he told me it would be much safer if I kept it at fifty-five. I assured him that I would, and off I went."

"Well, after that, you could probably use a drink."

Dick smiled. "I think that's a good idea!"

We went down to the Laughing Loon Cafe, one of Dick's favorite spots in Lake Placid. Angie, a beautiful, young girl was bartending. When she saw Dick walk in, she came out from behind the bar and gave him a big hug.

"How's Papa?" she asked.

"I'm fine now that I've seen you."

She giggled and gave him a kiss. Angie picked up a glass and said, "You want your usual, Dick?"

"Yes, ma'am, J&B Scotch on the rocks."

My father is a tall, slender man with piercing blue eyes that, depending on his mood, change to gray or green. When he looks at you, there is a sense of warmth, like being wrapped in a big quilt. I've often heard his friends or associates refer to him as a gentleman's gentleman. The girls, no matter what age, love him!

One time we walked into another bar in town (called PJ's), sat down, and ordered a drink. I went down to the end of the bar to say hello to Kathy, a friend of mine.

She said, "Who's that man that came in with you?" I told her it was my father.

"I've got to talk to him," she said.

She got up, went over, and introduced herself, and they talked for about an hour. Before we left, she told me that she had invited Dick to a staff party at the Hilton.

"Oh, by the way, you're invited too!"

As we walked out, I said, "Jesus, Dick! I can't wait until I'm seventy-five so I can get all the babes!" He didn't say anything. He just smiled and winked.

We talked with Angie for a while, finished our drinks, and went over to Bill and Mary's house. Dick went straight to bed.

I woke the next morning to the smell of bacon emanating up the stairs into my room. I got up, took a shower, and walked down to the kitchen. Dick was mopping the floor. I took notice again that he didn't look very well.

"Are you feeling all right?" I asked.

"Yeah, I'm fine. How about some eggs and bacon?"

He put down his mop, went over to the stove, and cracked two eggs into the frying pan. I sat down at the table, and in a couple of minutes, he served me my breakfast. He went back over to the stove and popped two more eggs in the pan.

THE WHISKEY BOTTLE CONVERSATION

I finished eating just as he was sitting down. I took my plate over to the sink and went back upstairs to get my wallet that I had left on the nightstand. When I returned, Dick was sitting at the table with his head down. It wasn't unusual for him to sit down and take a little snooze.

I walked over, gave him a gentle shake, and said, "Come on, Dick. Eat your breakfast. It's getting cold!"

He didn't respond. I sat down next to him, lifted his head, and his eyes were wide open. They were a cold gray. I grabbed his wrist and felt for a pulse. There was none. I held his head up, and there seemed to be a faint flicker in his eyes.

I started shouting, "Move your eyes, Dick! Look at me! Move your eyes!" Nothing.

I grabbed the phone, and on it was a sticker with an ambulance number. I dialed and told the dispatcher that I was at Bill and Mary Bennet's house on the Wolf Pond Road.

"My father's heart has stopped! Please send an ambulance!"

I ran back to the sink, grabbed a towel, and soaked it with cold water. I lifted Dick's head up and began stroking his forehead with the wet towel and talked to him.

"Hold on, Dick. The ambulance is on its way."

My mind was racing. I thought to myself, *Please, God! Don't take him now! Not now!*

I continued rubbing his head with the towel, talking to him. I looked at the clock. Five minutes had passed. By this time, I was screaming, "Dick, hold on! Hold on! You can't die now! We've got to get on a plane and go to Salt Lake to see Kim! There are things I want to know!"

Just then, his eyes began to blink, and I could hear the fluids in his body begin to circulate. It was a strange, eerie sound. He began to choke.

I yelled, "Spit it out! Breathe through your nose!" I tried to open his mouth, but his jaw was clenched.

I shouted, "Spit it out, Dick! Spit it out!"

He began to cough and spat up some mucous. Just then the ambulance pulled up. I continued to rub his head and talk to him.

"You're all right now. You're back. The ambulance is here. I'm going to let them in."

He said, "I'm okay. I don't want to see anybody."

"I know," I said, "but I think they should check you out."

Tears were streaming down my face as I let them in.

There were three paramedics, two men and a woman. They were volunteers dressed in street clothes, carrying a stretcher and their medical equipment. I led them into the kitchen, explaining what had happened as we walked. I had all I could do from breaking down completely.

When we got into the kitchen, the woman immediately took out an oxygen mask, hooked it to the cylinder, and put it on Dick's face. One man took Dick's wrist to check his pulse.

"I can't get a pulse!" he said.

"Check his blood pressure!" the other paramedic said. He seemed to be in charge.

They wrapped his arm, pumped up the rubber ball, and slowly released the pressure. The needle dropped to zero without making a beat.

THE WHISKEY BOTTLE CONVERSATION

"I don't get any reading!" the man administering the test said.

Yet there was Dick, sitting in the chair, talking with the paramedics. I was pacing back and forth, still trying to keep it together.

The woman said, "Mr. Leonard, do you think you can get up and lie down on the stretcher?"

Dick nodded and, with some help from the woman, did as she asked. They administered an IV and covered him with a blanket.

The head paramedic looked at me and said, "We're going to put him in the ambulance and take him over to the emergency room. You can meet us there."

I put my boots and coat on and went out to the car. It was a very cold morning. I pulled around to the front of the house and waited for the ambulance to head out the driveway before I left. The hospital was about a mile away.

By the time I got my car parked, they already had Dick in the emergency room, hooking small circular tabs to his chest. There were about six of them, and they had wires running from each tab to a machine located right next to the bed. I assumed it was some type of heart-monitoring equipment, A physician's assistant was hooking him up. I told him who I was, and he introduced himself as Bill.

He said, "You need to go down to the front desk and fill out the necessary paperwork. I am going to run some tests on your father. The doctor will be here shortly."

The Lake Placid Hospital is a small facility having mostly an outpatient service. People who need overnight or extended care are sent to the Adirondack Medical Center in

Saranac Lake, a hospital about ten miles away. As I walked down the hall toward the front desk, the three paramedics were walking toward me. I stopped and shook each of their hands and thanked them for all they had done. My eyes began to well up, and the older fellow put both his hands on mine and said, "Your dad's going to be okay." I thanked them again and wiped the tears from my eyes and went to the front desk.

When I returned to the emergency room, the machine that Dick was hooked up to was printing out a graph. Just then the doctor walked in. Dr. Patnode was a young attractive woman probably in her early thirties. I introduced Dick and myself as she was looking at the graphs.

She put the paper down and leaned over Dick with her face about six inches from his and said, "Can you tell me what happened, Mr. Leonard?" She had a great bedside manner.

Dick said, "Well, I was up early this morning and was mopping the kitchen floor when my son came into the kitchen. I fixed him some breakfast and then fixed some for myself. When I sat down at the table, I felt very lightheaded. The next thing I remember is hearing a voice from far away. I thought it was a woman's voice, but it must have been my son's. Then I was back in the kitchen with Dave rubbing my head."

The doctor stepped back and took another look at the graph. She said, "Well, Mr. Leonard, this heart monitor doesn't show anything wrong. Your heart rate is normal, your blood pressure is a little low, but other than that, everything seems to be okay. I would suggest having you spend the night at the hospital in Saranac Lake. There we

THE WHISKEY BOTTLE CONVERSATION

can run an EKG on you and just keep you under observation for the night. If nothing shows up on your EKG, you can go home tomorrow."

The doctor told me that they would transport Dick in the ambulance and that I should give them about an hour and a half. Then if I wanted to drive to the hospital, he would be all settled. I thanked her for her efforts and went over to Dick and said, "I'll meet you at the hospital in about an hour."

He took my hand and said, "Don't tell anybody. Don't call home. If they find out, they won't let me go to Salt Lake."

I said, "It was the trip to Salt Lake to see Kim that brought you back. If I have to throw you over my shoulder and carry you on the plane, you're going."

"Thanks, Dave."

I left the hospital and went to the Laughing Loon. I needed a drink. Angie was bartending, and I ordered a double vodka and orange.

She said, "Where's Dick?"

"He's over at the house, taking a nap." I didn't feel like reliving the experience just yet.

The bar was quite busy. I had two more doubles and just kept to myself. The drinks seemed to help me unwind a little bit. I got ready to leave when Angie came over and said, "You're awfully quiet, Dave, are you okay?"

"I'm a little tired."

As I was walking out, Angie called out from behind the bar, "Dave, tell Dick I love him."

I gave her a thumbs-up, walked out onto the street, took a deep breath, and smiled. Dick and his babes.

The hospital in Saranac Lake sat on the side of a hill overlooking Lake Colby. The lake was small as most Adirondack lakes are, and it was surrounded by dark, majestic mountains. There were about eight or ten shanties out on the ice, where some of the locals drank their beer and, on occasion, caught a fish.

When I walked into to Dick's room, he was sitting up in bed. His eyes had regained their deep blue, and his color was better. His room was on the third floor, with a picture window looking out over the lake and mountains.

"You're looking better," I said as I walked into the room.

"How's my boy?" he said as Dick extended his hand. We shook hands, and I gave him a hug.

"Pretty nice accommodations, Dick. Did you have to book this room in advance?"

He laughed.

"This is beautiful, isn't it? And, boy, do they take good care of you here! The nurses are fantastic!"

Just then this cute little gal brought in Dick's dinner. "Hey, Joan," he said. "This is my son, David. Isn't he handsome?"

"Why, yes, he is very handsome, Mr. Leonard—a chip off the old block, I'd say!" As she leaned over to set his tray on his bed, she stared at him for a moment.

"Do your eyes change color?" she said. "When you came in this afternoon, they were green, and now they're blue."

THE WHISKEY BOTTLE CONVERSATION

Dick said, "I've never noticed, but if you say they do, honey, then, I guess they do!"

She turned and began to walk out. "If you need anything, Mr. Leonard, I'll be on all night. Just buzz. Nice to meet you, Dave."

Dick looked at me and said, "See what I mean?"

I went over and sat on the bed. "You want some pudding, Dave?"

"No, thanks. You eat your dinner. I'm going back to Bill and Mary's. It's been a long day."

Dick said, "It sure has!"

"I'll come back in the morning, and if everything is kosher, we'll get out of here and go over to the ski jumping complex. They're having the aerial acrobatic jumping. Should be a good show!"

I didn't know if he would be up to it, but I thought he would enjoy thinking about it.

"Sounds good, Dave." I gave him a kiss and drove back to Lake Placid.

When I got to Bill and Mary's house, I went into the study and built a fire. My next stop was the liquor cabinet, where I poured myself a glass of Dewars White Label Scotch and then sat down in front of the fireplace. As I gazed at the burning logs, I thought about John and the conversation we had after his father's funeral. I was suddenly overcome with emotion. I began to weep and sob uncontrollably. The dam had finally burst. I cried for a long time. After I had collected myself, I pushed back the lever on the side of the leather recliner I was in. The footrest came up, and the backrest reclined. I sat there looking at the fire, sipping my Scotch, and eventually fell asleep.

I woke up about seven thirty the next morning. The sun was streaming in through the solarium windows. The Oriental rug seemed to be alive with its brilliant colors and patterns. The room, as large as it was, provided a warm, secure feeling. Getting up from my chair, I found that I was stiff from sleeping in that position. I walked out into the solarium and looked at the mountains. There had been a light snow that night, so the pine and fir trees were covered in a white dust that glimmered in the sun. It was a beautiful day, and I thanked God he hadn't taken my father from me.

I went up to my room and took a long, hot shower. The hot water felt good on my shoulders and back that were still stiff from my night in the recliner. The shower seemed to renew me, not just physically but emotionally. I felt happy, relieved. I put on a new sweater that Dick had given me for my birthday, went downstairs into the kitchen, and fixed myself a bowl of cereal. After cleaning up, I let the dogs out for a while, filled their bowls, and got them back in the house. By now it was nine thirty. Time to go get Dick.

I took my time driving to Saranac Lake. Whenever driving through the mountains, the beauty of the scenery always captivates me. As I pulled into the hospital parking lot, I noticed the number of fishing shanties on the lake had increased to about twenty. The Saturday morning sunshine had transformed the quiet spot into a bustling center of outdoor activity. There were snowmobiles and four-wheel

THE WHISKEY BOTTLE CONVERSATION

all-terrain vehicles racing across the frozen lake. Very near the road was a man set up to give dog sled rides. I was sure Dick was enjoying the show from his third floor suite.

When I entered his room, sure enough, he was sitting in a chair next to the window.

"Good morning," I said. "How are ya feeling?"

"Fantastic!" was his reply. "I've been watching those snowmobiles and the fellow with the dog sled. He's got a fine-looking group of Huskies." I thought he still looked pale.

As we were watching the activity on the lake, a nurse came in. I introduced myself and asked her if they had done the EKG. She said they had and Dr. Patnode was scheduled to make her rounds in about fifteen minutes. I sat down on Dick's bed.

"Did you buzz that little nurse last night and ask her for a massage?"

"How'd you know?" he asked. "The only problem was, I grabbed the wrong button. When I pushed it, my bed went to the flat position, and before I could find the nurse's buzzer, I fell asleep."

I laughed, and a big smile came to his face.

"Nice to have you back, Dick."

"Nice to be back, Dave."

Within a few minutes, Dr. Patnode walked in and greeted me with a warm handshake. She went over to Dick and said, "How are you feeling this morning, Mr. Leonard?"

"Now that you're here, I'm feeling better by the minute!" he replied.

"I've looked over your EKG, and everything seems to be normal. Your blood pressure is back to an acceptable level, so I don't see any reason why you can't go home. I wish I had an explanation for you as to why this happened, but I don't."

Dick shrugged his shoulders and said, "Just one of those things, I guess!"

Dr. Patnode put her arm around him and said, "Now, I want you to take it easy for a couple of days. No more mopping floors."

I said, "You know, it's just like those gray panthers. You give them a little job to do, and they drop dead right in the middle of it."

The young doctor gave me a strange look, but as Dick and I began to laugh, so did she.

The doctor said she would prepare the paperwork and would send a nurse in with it shortly. She wished us both good luck and left the room. Dick got dressed and read a magazine as I paced around the room and up and down the hall, waiting for the nurse. I had never been a patient in a hospital and always felt uncomfortable when I was in one.

Finally, the nurse arrived with the forms. She told us to take them to the front desk and the woman there would help us filling them out. I had brought a one-piece CarHart suit that I wore when working outside in cold weather. I wrestled Dick into it and gave him his fur-lined leather mittens and a wool ski hat. It was sunny but cold. While he filled out the forms, I went out and pulled the car up to the front of the hospital. As I was getting out to get him, he came out the front door. He walked slowly and seemed to

THE WHISKEY BOTTLE CONVERSATION

be taking deep breaths. Before getting into the car, he stood there and watched the activity on the lake.

"It's a great day, Dave!"

We didn't talk much on the way back to Lake Placid. Dick seemed to be content just taking in the scenery. As we approached town, he said, "Is the acrobatic ski jumping still going on?" I told him that it started about noon and ran until three.

He said, "Let's take a ride over there. I'd like to see that!"

I drove over to the jumping complex, which is on the outskirts of town. We didn't go into the parking lot because there was a large crowd and I felt the walk into the facility would be too much. Instead, I drove down past the hill, turned around, and parked the car on the side of the road. You could see the competition from there. We stood on the bridge, watching the contestants come off the jump, going fifty to sixty feet into the air while they spun, flipped, and did any other gyration that seemed humanly impossible.

Dick stood there and shook his head. Every once in a while, he'd say, "Jesus! How in hell do they do that?"

We watched in awe for about fifteen minutes, then he said, "I am ready for a warm fire and a little Scotch and hot water!"

We walked back to the car and drove to Bill and Mary's, which was about a mile and a half away. When we arrived, the dogs greeted us with barks, jumps, and hand licks. I helped Dick get out of his suit, and we both went into the study. I got a roaring fire going as he sat in his favorite leather chair, covered in a blanket.

"You sit here, and I'll make us some lunch."

He was staring into the fire and didn't respond.

"Dick, I'll make us some lunch," I said in a little louder voice.

He looked at me and said, "I'm sorry, Dave, what did you say?"

"I'll get us some lunch."

"Good, but how about that Scotch with some hot water first?"

I went to the kitchen and got the Dewars out of the liquor cabinet. I put about half a shot in a big coffee mug and filled it with hot water. I took it back to him. He raised the glass to me, took a sip, leaned back in the chair, and said, "Boy, does that taste good!"

I returned to the kitchen, which is about a hundred feet down the hall from the study. I decided to make some chicken noodle soup and a grilled ham and cheese sandwich. When I returned with lunch, Dick was asleep in the chair. I pulled the blanket up around his neck and took his lunch back to the kitchen. He slept until about four. When he woke up, he walked into the solarium and stood there, looking out at the mountains.

"I've got a grilled ham and cheese with some chicken soup. You interested?" I asked.

"Sounds good, Dave! I'm feeling a little empty."

I heated up his lunch and brought it to him. He sat back down by the fire and ate his meal slowly.

"How about a glass of milk, Dave?"

"Sure!" I said.

So back to the kitchen I went. Five or six trips down to the kitchen and back, I was getting a little tired myself. He finished his meal and sat quietly, staring into the fire.

At six, I turned on the TV, and we watched the evening news. Afterward, he said, "I'm going to bed, and I suggest you do the same!"

I gave him a hug and said, "See you in the morning!" I took his advice.

CHAPTER TWO

There's Just So Much to Live For

Sunday morning I woke up around nine. Dick wasn't up yet, so I went to his room to check on him. He was sleeping soundly. I built a fire and then took my morning stroll to the kitchen. I let the dogs out and put on a pot of coffee. It was a gray morning, but the temperature had warmed up and there was a light show falling.

The coffeemaker had begun to percolate, filling the kitchen with that distinctive aroma.

Dick walked in and said, "Boy, does that smell good! I'll take mine with just a touch of cream."

"Good morning," I said. "How are you feeling?"

"I feel good, Dave." Then he gave a quick bob and weave as if he were shadowboxing. He looked rested.

"How about some ham and eggs this morning, Dick?"

"Sounds good. I'll take my coffee and be in by the fire."

"One ham and eggs… comin' up!" I said. "It will be about five minutes."

Dick retreated to the comfort of the warm fire and his leather chair while I sliced the ham and cracked the eggs.

THE WHISKEY BOTTLE CONVERSATION

Just then the phone rang. It was Bill. He and Mary were in Albany and would be home in a couple of hours. He asked how everything was, and I assured him that Dick and I were enjoying ourselves to the utmost. I had no intention of sharing the past two days' experiences with them. I finished cooking Dick's breakfast and took it to him.

He had put a couple more logs on the fire and was reading the newspaper.

"Bill called," I said. "He and Mary are in Albany and will be here about noon."

"Let's not say anything about what happened," he said. "I don't want to upset them."

"My sentiments exactly, Dick."

I returned to the kitchen. By this time, the dogs were barking at the back door, so I let them in. There was still food in their dishes from yesterday. I went back to fixing my breakfast. I ate in the kitchen, figuring by the time I walked to the study, the food would be cold. I did the dishes and cleaned everything up in preparation for Bill and Mary's return.

I decided to call my friend John to ask if Dick and I could stay with him and his wife, Joyce, that night. It was SuperBowl Sunday, and I thought Dick might enjoy the time with our friends. We had to leave for Syracuse Monday and had planned to stay with my cousin, Curt, who would take us to the airport Tuesday morning.

Joyce answered the phone. She seemed excited about having our company and said, "I'll fix a nice pork dinner." I thanked her and said we should arrive around three or four.

Dick brought his dishes into the kitchen and offered to help finish cleaning up.

"Remember what the doctor said. You go back, sit by the fire, and finish reading your paper."

Then I told him about going to John and Joyce's for a SuperBowl Party… complete with a pork dinner. A smile came to his face.

"Fantastic!" he said. "I forgot about the SuperBowl today." He liked John and Joyce. "Real people," he always called them.

I worked my way from room to room, making sure everything was in order. I changed the sheets on our beds, vacuumed and dusted where necessary.

Bill and Mary arrived about twelve thirty, much to the delight of Mort, Sheeba, and Mazy—the three dogs. I went out and helped them with their bags and a few articles they had picked up in Pennsylvania.

"Where's Dick?" Mary asked.

"He's in by the fire… waiting for you."

They both laughed.

"Nice to be home," Bill said.

"You two go in and sit down, and I'll take your bags to your room. Tea or coffee?" I asked.

Mary said, "I'll have tea and honey, Bill will take his coffee black."

I fixed their drinks, got a plate of cookies, and delivered it to them on a little wooden tray.

Mary said, "Boy, this is service! I think I'll keep him, Bill!"

"I'm available for adoption," was my response.

I put another log on the fire and sat down to listen to the story of their trip. They had visited two of their children,

THE WHISKEY BOTTLE CONVERSATION

and of course, Mary told of her grandchildren with great pride. Mary usually occupied most of the conversation.

Finally, Bill chimed in, "You must be pretty excited about going to see your granddaughter in Salt Lake, Dick?"

"I can't tell you how much I am looking forward to it!" he said. Then he told some stories about Kim. I just sat there, enjoying them enjoying themselves.

Mary invited us to spend another night. I thanked her but said we had made plans to go to John and Joyce's house. I excused myself to get our suitcases. When I returned, the three of them were still swapping stories about their families.

I looked at Dick and said, "I guess we're ready!"

He replied, "Okay! Boy, if you're ready, I'm ready!"

Bill and Mary walked us to the kitchen and thanked us for taking such good care of their home and pets. Mary asked when we would return.

I said, "We'll be back a week from Wednesday."

"Bill and I are going to New Jersey that Friday to visit my sister," Mary said.

"We'll be gone for five days. Would you and Dick mind coming back and staying here?"

Before I could open my mouth, Dick said, "Hell, no! We'd love to come back!"

I looked at Bill and said, "You'd better cut a few more cords of firewood the way Dick goes through it!"

Bill smiled. "I'll have the boys put another three cords on the porch."

We bid our final farewell, got in the car, and drove out the tree-lined driveway.

John lived about sixty miles north of Lake Placid in Chateauguay, a small town near the Canadian border. It was a quiet drive. Dick seemed rather distant as he looked out the window at the mountains and the winter landscapes.

"This truly is God's country," he said at one point.

We stopped at my house in Lyon Mountain to make sure the heat was still on and everything was okay. I grabbed a few more things for the trip then drove to John's, about another fifteen miles away.

Joyce greeted us at the door with a warm hello and a hug. There was a tantalizing smell of roast pork that filled the kitchen and a plate full of homemade cookies on the table.

"John is out in the barn, feeding the horses," Joyce said. "Why don't you go out and tell him dinner will be ready in about twenty minutes."

John had four Appaloosa horses. Three were stallions; one was a mare. We walked into the barn, and he had the mare in crossties, brushing her down.

"How's it going, men?" he said when he saw us. "Want a beer? Or I've got some Jack Daniels just outside the door in the snowbank."

Dick said, "I think I'll wait until after dinner."

I said, "I'll do a shot if you will."

"Get the bottle!" he said.

I went outside and looked around for the Jack Daniels. I finally found it buried behind the barn door in the snow with just the cap exposed. When I got back inside, John was showing Dick the rest of the horses. He would bring them out one by one, make them stretch out, back up…

THE WHISKEY BOTTLE CONVERSATION

do whatever he wanted them to do. He was always getting kicked or bit by one of them.

He'd say, "That son of a bitch Sonny kicked me the other day—right in the shin. Then I went to give Domingo his water, and he kicked me in the same spot! Jesus, that hurt!"

He'd lift his pant leg and show the battle scar. He looked the part of a horseman... thick, full beard, black hair, and blue eyes, with a husky build. When he wasn't riding his horses, he was riding his Harley Davidson.

I handed him the bottle, and he took a healthy swig. He handed it back to me, and I did the same. I gave a short, breathless cough, trying to maintain my composure as the Jack Daniels burned its way down into my stomach.

"Joyce says dinner will be ready shortly," I said.

"We've got a pork roast," John said. "The neighbor on the next farm over just butchered a pig. Been feeding it corn and apples. Should be pretty tasty."

John checked to make sure all the stalls were bolted shut and the doors closed. We walked out the door, and he stuck the bottle of Jack Daniels back in the snowbank.

"Makes the chores a little more enjoyable," he said with a smile.

When we got back to the house, Joyce had the table all set, and she was pulling the roast out of the oven.

"John, wash up and come slice the roast," she said. "The potatoes and gravy are ready. Dave, why don't you fill the salad bowls. The dressing is in the refrigerator. Dick, you sit down at the head of the table."

John and I did as she asked, and in no time, we were all sitting down to an excellent meal. After dinner I told the three of them to go in the living room and watch the pregame show and I would clean up. There weren't any objections.

By the time I finished the dishes, the game was about to start. I decided to take drink orders before I sat down. Joyce and I had wine. John had a beer, and Dick had Scotch and warm water. I've never really had much interest in watching sports on television. To me the SuperBowl was more about some creative, entertaining commercials than two teams fighting it out on the gridiron.

During the second quarter, I could see Dick was starting to fade. So at halftime, I suggested he hit the sack. He agreed. After Dick had retired for the evening, I decided to tell John and Joyce about the events of the previous two days. I felt like I needed to share my experience with them to get it off my chest.

Joyce had gone into the kitchen to get us all another drink. When she sat down, I said, "Dick's heart stopped Friday morning for about five minutes."

A pained look came over both their faces. John's father had died a few weeks before, and Joyce's dad had passed away a year and a half ago.

Joyce said, "I didn't think he looked very good."

I told them about the whole episode. They both listened intently. After I finished, we all sat there in silence for a while.

Joyce finally said, "It seems you never really think about your parents being gone, then all of a sudden, they are, and it just seems like there was so much left unsaid or undone."

Those sentiments were similar to the ones John had expressed to me at the American Legion after his father passed away.

I said, "I'm thankful I've been given some more time with Dick, and I'm going to make the most of it."

We watched the rest of the game in relative silence… each of us lost in our own thoughts. After the game, I felt very tired. I thanked them for dinner and excused myself to my room.

I woke up about nine the next morning. I had had a restless night's sleep. I'm not sure if it was the strange bed or the circumstances of the past few days. Dick and Joyce were in the kitchen, having coffee. Joyce was a teacher, and she was telling Dick about her class. They had already been for a walk up to the neighbor's farm and back. John was in town, getting some feed for his horses. Joyce cooked up some fresh bacon from the same pig that had provided the roast the night before and some scrambled eggs. John walked in just as our breakfast was being served. He seemed to have built-in radar when there was food to be had.

I told our hosts about our itinerary and how much I was looking forward to seeing my daughter. They had known Kim since she was about four and were like second family to her.

Dick offered to do the dishes, but Joyce said, "You've got a long drive ahead of you, and they are predicting some snow. You'd better get on the road."

I went to our room, picked up our bags, and went out to start the car to let it warm up.

Dick's circulation hadn't been good for years, so he liked his environment as hot as anyone with him could stand it.

We both thanked them for their hospitality. They extended their best wishes to be relayed to Kim and bade us a safe trip.

"Get in touch when you get back," John said as we climbed in the car.

"Keep that Jack Daniels on ice," I said. He smiled as we pulled out of the driveway.

Syracuse was about a four-hour drive from Chateauguay. We talked about Kim and Salt Lake. I had been there in 1979 on a trip I had taken around the country. I told Dick how impressed I had been with the deep blue of the Great Salt Lake. I asked him when was the last time he had been on a plane.

"I guess it was two years ago when I went to California. There was a bankers' convention in San Francisco."

Dick had served on the board of directors for thirty years at the Oswego County Savings Bank. He had been a B-24 bomber pilot in World War II and had his own plane after the war. He loved to fly. I thought to myself, *That's probably what brought him back... the mention of flying to see Kim.*

There had been occasions when he would tell me about some of his experiences during the war. He had been operations officer for General Clair Chennault of the Flying Tigers fame in Kunming, China, before joining a B-24 combat outfit. He flew with a group of low-altitude Bombers that dropped their bombs at three hundred feet above enemy ships. They flew out of Okinawa up into Japan.

"Do you ever think about the war?" I asked.

"No, Dave, I really haven't thought about it much. I mean, it was fifty years ago. I don't have any regrets, in fact, I really enjoyed my wartime experience."

His statement caught me off guard. I would think that spending three or four years away from home facing death at every turn would be anything but enjoyable.

"When we get back from Salt Lake, I'd like you to tell me some stories about the war and your life."

He looked at me for a moment and then said, "Sure, Dave, I'd like that."

For the rest of the trip, we were both quiet. We never seemed to talk much when we were in the car, so it wasn't unusual.

We arrived at my cousin's house around four thirty. Curt was my godson—a really nice guy. His wife, Mary, and their two beautiful children, Katie (who was four) and Kevin (who was two), were all happy to see us. We were glad to be there after our long trip. We had stopped in Watertown and called so they knew when to expect us. Curt had ordered two large pizzas, which arrived shortly after we did. Mary had made a big salad, and we spent about an hour at the kitchen table, eating and catching up on what was going on in each of our lives. Our plane was to leave at seven the next morning, so Dick excused himself after dinner and went to bed.

I spent the next couple of hours playing with the kids, reading them stories, and looking at all the items they pulled out of their toy box. About eight, Mary took the kids upstairs to bed, and Curt and I sat in the living room, talking. I told him about Dick but asked that he not say anything to the rest of the family. I had planned to do that after we returned.

Curt fixed up the fold-out couch in the den and said he would get me up at five thirty. I told him Dick would probably be up by then, but setting the alarm as a backup wouldn't hurt.

At quarter after five, I awoke to a gentle shake by Dick.

"Come on, boy, we've got to catch a plane."

He had already taken a shower and was raring to go. I lay there for a few minutes, trying to put it all in perspective. After some effort, I managed to climb out the valley in the center of my fold-out bed. I hadn't had a good night's sleep since last Thursday, and it was beginning to take its toll. I made it upstairs to the shower.

When I got down to the kitchen, Dick had a pot of coffee brewing. He and Kurt were sitting at the table, drinking their orange juice.

"Want some scrambled eggs, Dave?" Curt asked.

"I think I'll just have a bowl of cereal and some toast. Those four slices of pizza I had last night are still with me." We ate our breakfast and left the house about ten after six.

We arrived at the airport at six thirty. Curt helped us check our bags at the Delta ticket counter. I thanked him for his efforts and said, "I'll give you a call next Tuesday evening to reaffirm our arrival time."

Dick and I had our tickets validated and walked up to the departure area. We boarded the plane and were in the

THE WHISKEY BOTTLE CONVERSATION

air by seven fifteen. Our route was to take us to Detroit, Minneapolis, St. Paul, and then on to Salt Lake.

Dick took the window seat right behind the left wing. I had picked up a copy of *Newsweek* and began reading soon after we took off. It wasn't long before I fell asleep. The next thing I knew, Dick was nudging me.

"You're missing a nice flight, Dave. We're going to land in Detroit in about fifteen minutes."

The flight attendants were walking the aisles, checking to make sure everyone had their seat belts on. As we made our approach to land, there was some turbulence, which made the plane buck and drift from left to right. We touched down with the usual bounce and the roar of the engines shifting into reverse. We had to change planes, and our next departure point was on the other side of the airport. A half an hour was all the time we had to get there.

The Detroit airport is a massive complex. We hurriedly followed the signs and hopped on the moving escalators whenever possible. I had Dick by the arm, helping him maintain the pace I thought was necessary to make our destination on time. The airport was very crowded, and despite our pace, I think we both enjoyed the activity and the myriads of different people. Whenever I have traveled, I've always liked to take stock of the people in different parts of the country—their clothes, hairstyles, accents… just an observation or overview of what's going on in America.

We arrived at our gate ten minutes before our departure time, only to find out that the plane had been delayed for twenty minutes. I could see Dick was tired from our cross-terminal dash, but all the seats in the waiting area were taken. A young lady apparently could see my situation, stood up, and offered Dick her seat.

"Oh, no," he said, "I'm fine."

She took his hand and said, "I insist. I've been sitting all morning."

We both thanked her, and Dick, much to his relief, sat down.

"Can I get you anything?" I asked.

"No, thanks, Dave," he said.

"Okay. I'll be back in a few minutes."

It was ten forty-five, and the bar was open, so I thought a drink might be in order. I sat down and ordered a vodka and orange juice.

The bartender said, "It's five bucks for a single shot, six fifty for a double."

"I'll take the double," I said.

It never ceased to amaze me how much a drink costs in an airport. Regardless of its price, it tasted good. I ordered a second.

Back in the waiting area, Dick was in deep conversation with a woman sitting next to him.

"Ellie, this is my son, Dave," he said.

I exchanged greetings with her. She was, I'd guess, in her late thirties, blond and quite attractive.

"Ellie is going to Minneapolis to visit her mother," Dick said.

Then he proceeded to give me a brief rundown on her life. In the middle of her life story, they announced the boarding was to begin according to seat assignment. Ellie was called before us, and we bid her good luck.

"Nice gal," Dick said with a smile.

THE WHISKEY BOTTLE CONVERSATION

Our seats were near the back of the plane, and Dick offered me the one next to the window.

"I'm going to take a little nap," he said. "You enjoy the view."

It was a bright sunny morning, and I always enjoyed the scenery from above. After takeoff, Dick reclined his seat. I had asked the flight attendant for a pillow and a blanket. I put the pillow under his head and covered him to the neck with the blanket.

"Comfortable?" I asked.

"Thanks, Dave. I really like this service."

In no time he was fast asleep and looked so peaceful. I thought about the events of the past four days. Once again, I thanked God for giving this good man more time to enjoy the experience of life he had always seemed so happy to be a part of.

I turned my attention back to the window, looking at the blue sky and the ground so far below. I thought about how Dick loved to fly and tried to imagine what it might have been like being in a B-24 bomber over Japan. What did he think about when he opened his bomb bay doors and made a dive from ten thousand feet to three hundred, skimming across the water at three hundred miles an hour, and dropping his bombs just above the deck of an enemy ship? A sense of urgency overcame me. I wanted to know about his life—not just the war part, but his whole life. When we returned from our trip, I would hear his story, and Bill and Mary's house would be the perfect setting.

We arrived in Minneapolis, Saint Paul, about one thirty. Dick slept most of the way. As we were exiting the plane, the pilot was standing by the hatch, thanking everyone for flying Delta. We were the last to get off.

The pilot thanked us, and I said, "This fellow behind me was a B-24 bomber pilot in China and Okinawa." Dick introduced himself.

The pilot shook his hand and said, "Ah, yes, CBI [China Burma India]. My dad flew C-46s over the hump from Bombay into Kunming."

Dick said, "I was operations officer at Kunming Base."

"No shit!" the pilot said. "For Chennault?"

"Yes, sir!" Dick said with a sense of pride. "Once we got the runways built, we had up to four hundred planes a day landing at our base. A good portion of them were C-46s bringing in supplies from India. The hump was a real bitch to fly. You never knew what the plane would do with the turbulence, down drafts, and temperatures. Those C-46s didn't have any heaters. Some of the boys would tell me it dropped down to thirty below in the cockpit flying over the Himalayas!"

As I understood it, the Himalayas were referred to as "the hump" by the pilots. The Delta pilot was enjoying the firsthand account immensely.

He walked us out to the terminal and said, "My dad's gone now, but I want to tell you, Mr. Leonard, how much I respect you men who flew in World War II. It took a lot of guts to fly those planes under those conditions. I have to catch another flight now, but I'd like to thank you for all you did for this country."

He stepped back and saluted Dick. Dick gave him the thumbs-up and saluted back. I thought to myself how appropriate that this coincidence should happen now.

THE WHISKEY BOTTLE CONVERSATION

We had an hour layover before catching our plane to Salt Lake. Dick said he would like to get something to eat and have a drink. He had slept through the meal on the plane. We went to the lounge, where he ordered a hot roast beef sandwich and a J&B Scotch on the rocks. I had a vodka and orange.

I said, "Well, another two and a half hours, and we'll be with our little Kim."

"Hallelujah!" Dick said.

I hadn't seen Kim since she moved from Boston about a year ago. Her mother was working on her PhD at a university in Salt Lake. Kim had grown tired of big-city life and decided to move out West.

When Dick finished his meal, we made our way to the departure area and boarded the plane. It touched down in Salt Lake at a little after four. I was standing by the baggage claim, looking for our luggage. Dick had gone to the bathroom. All of a sudden, someone jumped on my back.

"Hey, Dad!" then a big kiss.

"Kim, you shouldn't be sneaking up on people like that!" and gave her a hug and kiss.

Kim was a beautiful girl about five two, light-brown hair, blue-green eyes, and very fine features.

"Where's Dick?" she asked.

"He went to the men's room. Why don't you go over and surprise him when he comes out? Don't go jumping on his back, though!" I said. "I'll get our bags."

Within a few minutes, our luggage came around on the circular delivery belt. As I collected them, I saw Kim and Dick arm in arm, coming around the corner. Dick was grinning from ear to ear.

"See you found him," I said.

Kim smiled. "Hard to miss this handsome guy."

"She stood behind a big plant next to the bathroom door and jumped out, scaring the shit out of me!" Dick said with a laugh.

Kim had a bit of the devil in her.

I picked up our bags, and we walked out of the terminal. She had parked in a "No Parking" zone, right in front of the door. It was a green Toyota station wagon.

"Whose car?" I asked.

"It belongs to a friend of mine who's a pilot. I'm taking flying lessons, Dick. I've got fifteen hours in," she said. "We flew up to Logan the other night, and it was my first time flying on instruments. The instructor pilot told me I was a natural. I said, 'I should be, my grandfather flew 24s in the 'Big One.'"

"Kimberly, Kimberly," Dick said, "you never cease to amaze me!"

It was about a fifteen-minute drive into Salt Lake. Kim described her job as one of the mangers of a new restaurant that was the first microbrewery in the city. We arrived at her apartment, which was a few blocks from the downtown area.

The apartment was compact and sparsely furnished. It had a living room with hardwood floors, a couch, and a table. The kitchen was about six feet wide with a breakfast booth on one end and a stove, refrigerator, sink, and two cupboards on the other. Off the kitchen was a small bedroom with a bath. There was a futon for a bed.

THE WHISKEY BOTTLE CONVERSATION

"I have to go over to the restaurant for a little while," she said. "I'll come back about six thirty and take you to dinner." She gave us both a kiss and said, "I'm really happy you're here!"

Dick went into the bedroom and lay down. I decided to take a walk and get some fresh air. It was fairly warm outside, and some exercise would seem good after the long flight. I took a stroll around the neighborhood, stopped at a convenience store, and bought a newspaper and then returned to the apartment. I woke Dick up about six. We each took our turn in the shower and dressed for our dinner engagement.

Kim walked in about six thirty.

"I'm going to change, and then I'll give you the five-cent tour before we go to the Red Rock."

That was the name of the restaurant where she worked. She emerged from the bedroom, wearing green lizard-skin cowboy boots, jeans, a black turtleneck, and a brown leather vest. She had small silver hoop earrings dangling from her lobes.

I said, "You sure look like a Westerner, Kim!"

"When in Rome…" was her reply.

We walked out to the car, and she drove us through the downtown area around the Mormon Temple, which was lit up with green, blue, and red lights. It looked more like a Disney creation than a house of worship. A few blocks away, we went past the sports Coliseum.

"This is where the Utah Jazz NBA team plays," she said. "My boss has season tickets. There's a game tomorrow night, and he has offered his seats to you and Dick. They're in the seventh row."

I had played basketball in high school and college but had never seen a professional game in person.

"That's great, Kim!" I said. "You'll have to introduce me so that I can thank him."

"He'll be there tonight," she said.

After a few more quick turns, we were in the parking lot behind Red Rock. It had been an old warehouse that had been converted by the three partners. The front was all windows, which opened out with booths next to them. There was a long bar, and all the cooking was done in the open. A big wood-fired brick oven was the centerpiece of the kitchen area. The ceilings were open, just as they had been in the original warehouse, and there were lots of plants and pictures hanging everywhere. It could accommodate about a hundred people.

As soon as we entered, waiters and waitresses were coming over, introducing themselves to us.

"Kim has really been looking forward to your arrival," one of the gals said.

"That's all we've heard about for a week," another waiter said. "I'm glad you're finally here!"

Kim blushed. "Come on, Dad, there's Bob, one of the owners."

She brought Dick and me over to him. He was in his midthirties, a nice-looking man.

"This is my dad, Dave, and my grandfather, Dick." We shook hands.

"Kim has been really excited about you two coming," he said. "We're very happy to have her here. She keeps things running smoothly."

THE WHISKEY BOTTLE CONVERSATION

I congratulated him on his opening and said how impressed I was with the renovations.

"Oh, by the way," I said, "thanks for the tickets for the Jazz game."

"No problem," he said. "You folks enjoy your meal. It's on me."

We thanked him again, and Kim took us to our table.

After dinner she asked what we wanted to do. We both said, "Go to bed."

It had been a long day, and Dick was showing the signs of our cross-country adventure. On the way out, I went over to Bob and complimented him on the food and service. When we got back to the apartment, Kim told us to take her room and she would sleep on the couch.

The next morning, after a night on the futon, the first thing I did was pick up a newspaper and begin looking for a furniture store. I was going to buy a bed because I didn't plan on suffering for the rest of the week. Kim and Dick weren't around, so I assumed they had gone for a walk. The sun was out, and it was about forty-five degrees. Utah averages about 250 days of sunshine a year. We're lucky if we get a hundred in the Adirondacks.

I went into the kitchen, whipped up some eggs, and sliced some cheese. I thought an omelet would be appreciated after their walk. They arrived shortly thereafter, and both were pleased to see breakfast was soon to be served. After we ate, Kim said she had some errands to run then had to be at the Red Rock by noon. She was going to work a double so she could have the next two days off.

"I'll come back and leave you the car. The Jazz game is at seven, so why don't you come over to the restaurant afterward? Tomorrow we'll go up to Park City. It's a ski resort, but the town has kept the Old West flavor."

"Sounds like fun," I said. "We'll see you tonight!"

I picked up the newspaper, renewing my search for a bed, while Dick did the dishes.

I found a place called Murray's New and Used Furniture. I called to get directions and was told that they had a large selection of what I was looking for. When Dick had finished his kitchen chores, I said, "Let's go explore Salt Lake. Murray's New and Used Furniture and good time emporium awaits."

Dick laughed. "I'm ready!"

The downtown area of Salt Lake is only about ten square blocks, then the rest of the city runs for miles in every direction. The streets are very wide, and most of the buildings are single-story. Murray's was about four miles from Kim's apartment, so we got to see a good part of the city in the northeast direction.

We found the warehouse without much problem. It was stacked to the rafters with anything and everything you could possibly imagine. Murray came out and fit the image of his store perfectly. He was, I'd guess, in his early seventies, bald, potbellied, and wearing polyester pants and a shirt that had a few buttons missing.

He walked up to us, extended his hand, and said, "Murray Cohen, at your service. What can I do you for?"

"I called for a box spring and mattress," I said.

"Ah, yes. I've got quite a selection in the back of the store."

THE WHISKEY BOTTLE CONVERSATION

As we wound our way through the aisles, stepping over this and tripping over that, I commented about the variety of items he had.

"Yep," he said, "been here for forty-five years. Brought up in Brooklyn, New York. After the war, I met a gal from Salt Lake, married her, and moved out here."

I asked Murray what branch of the service he had been in.

"Merchant Marines, hauling war supplies from the States to Britain. Saw a lot of ships go down!"

I said, "Dick flew 24s in China and Okinawa."

"Fly Boy, huh? Must have been hell over there," he said.

I left Murray and Dick to swap war stories while I looked for a mattress set. When I returned, the two of them were laughing and enjoying each other's experiences.

"I found a set that looks pretty good, Murray," I said. "How about giving me a price?"

Dick piped in, "Let's not forget the World War II veterans' discount."

Murray threw his head back and laughed. "You Fly Boys are all alike! Always on the make!"

Murray pulled his pencil out and scratched some figures on his little pocket notepad.

"Here's what I'm gonna do," he said. "The price for this set is usually $175, but I'm gonna give it to you for $135 and throw in free delivery. Don't tell anyone about this good deal, though. I've got a reputation, you know."

We agreed, gave Murray the directions to Kim's apartment, and paid him.

"Nice to meet you, fellas," he said as we were leaving. "Now, if your daughter needs anything else, send her to Murray. I'll do right by the little lady."

As we stepped out of the store, you could almost taste the fresh air. Murray's Furniture Outlet had the scent you experience in your grandmother's attic.

As we left, Dick said, "Now there's a real character!" I nodded my head and rolled my eyes in agreement.

We returned to the apartment, and I made us some lunch and afterward Dick went into the bedroom for his nap. I took a walk down the street to a convenience store to get a fresh newspaper. It was about fifty degrees, and the warmth of the sun felt good. I sat down on a bench outside the store for a while, soaking up the rays.

I began to doze off, sitting there, so I decided to go back to the apartment and take a nap before we went to the basketball game. I got up about five thirty. Dick was in the kitchen, making some soup, and asked me if I wanted anything to eat.

I said, "I'm going to take a shower and get dressed. Then I'll have something."

We arrived at the coliseum about fifteen minutes before game time. The Jazz were playing the Orlando Magic. This was the game where if Dave Stockton got seven assists, he would break Elgin Baylor's all-time assist record. The place was packed, and the hometown crowd was pumped! You could feel the electricity in the air!

Our seats were seven rows up from the court just to the right of the basket. Each time Stockton would make an assist, the crowd would go wild, doing the wave and shouting his name. In the third quarter, he made his seventh assist, and they stopped the game. The TV cameras came out, and the head of the NBA gave him an award.

We decided to leave about ten minutes into the fourth quarter in order to beat the rush. As we left the coliseum, attendants at the door gave us a certificate stating we had been at the game where a new NBA all-time assist record had been established.

It had been an entertaining evening, but now it was time for a nightcap at Red Rock. We walked in the restaurant and sat down at a table next to a front window. I could see Kim was busy, so a wave and a smile would serve to acknowledge our arrival.

When our waitress arrived, we ordered two beers and a deluxe cheeseburger for each of us. Kim brought us over our beer and asked about the game. I told her we had a great time, and we showed her the certificates they had given us. I could tell she was happy we were enjoying ourselves.

"As you can see, we're very busy," she said. "So I've got to get back to work. If you need anything, Beth, your waitress, will take good care of you." She gave us both a kiss and disappeared into the crowd.

It wasn't long before Beth brought us our burgers. We ordered two more beers, and when she returned with them, I asked her to leave the check.

"That's all taken care of," she said with a smile. I thanked her, and when we finished, I left a generous tip.

Dick and I found Kim and told her we were going back to the apartment.

"I have to work until eleven thirty," she said, "and some of us are going out afterward, so I'll see you in the morning."

The next morning after breakfast, we left for Park City, which was about fifty miles from Salt Lake. It was a sunny, warm day, and the ride through the mountains was very pleasant. We stopped in different places and took pictures of each other against the panorama of the Rockies.

As we approached Park City, in the surrounding countryside, there were numerous homes being built. There seemed to be a construction boom everywhere we went. The houses were large and fashionably built in a chalet or contemporary style. As we entered the town, however, it was like stepping back in time.

The main street was very narrow, and the buildings and shops were mostly single-story dwellings built around the turn of the century. Kim had accurately described the town. It definitely had an Old West flavor.

Most of the shops and restaurants had Western themes and offered a wide variety of items for the shopper. We strolled up one side of the main street, stopping in stores that interested us, then down the other side doing the same.

My cousin Curt's wife had a brother who worked in Park City. We decided to stop in a restaurant, have some lunch, and give him a call. Unfortunately, he wasn't home.

Most of the afternoon was spent taking in the sights but even more so enjoying each other's company. I bought Kim some earrings, and we got Dick a Park City hat. Being with my daughter and my father made me very happy. We arrived back at Kim's apartment in the early evening.

THE WHISKEY BOTTLE CONVERSATION

Dick made himself a cup of tea and went to bed. After he had retired for the night, I decided to tell Kim what had happened.

"Last Friday, Dick had an episode where his heart stopped for about five minutes," I said. "We were taking care of a friend's house in Lake Placid."

I could see a horrified look come over Kim's face. I explained what had happened, including the part where I was screaming, "Dick you can't die now! We've got to go to Salt Lake to see Kim!"

"Then he came back," I said.

A little smile came to her face, and then she began to cry. So did I. She came over to the couch and sat next to me. I put my arm around her.

She said, "It would have been so terrible if he had died. I love him so much."

"Well, Kim, it was coming to see you that brought him back," I said. "It was his love for you that I feel gave him reason to hang on."

She cried some more then gave me a kiss. "Thanks, Dad, for telling me. It means a lot!" She went into the bathroom to wash her face.

When she came out, her eyes were puffy, but she was smiling. "Well, Dad, I think I need a drink," she said. "How about you?"

"Count me in darlin'! How about a vodka and orange?"

"You've got it. I just have to squeeze some oranges."

She emerged from the kitchen with two glasses. "Here's to Dick!" she said as we raised our drinks.

"Here's to you, Kimberly," was my reply.

We sat quietly for a while, listening to a jazz tape she had played. Finally, she said, "We have a big day tomorrow. A friend of mine works at Snow Bird, a ski resort up north. He got us a discounted room for the night. It's a beautiful hotel with a heated outdoor pool and Jacuzzi on the top floor. We can take the tram to the top of the mountain Sunday."

"That's fantastic, Kim!" I said. "You're a great host."

The next morning I woke to a knock on the door. It was two men, with the bed we had bought at Murray's. I had forgotten all about the delivery.

"What's this?" Kim said.

"Oh, it's just a little gift from Dick and me. We want to be comfortable, I mean, we want you to be comfortable."

She gave me a kiss. "Thanks, Dad!"

After eating breakfast and packing an overnight bag, we were off. Snow Bird is a sprawling resort that sits twelve thousand feet above sea level. It has the facilities to move nine thousand skiers an hour. The road up through the canyons is treacherous. There are fallen rock zone and avalanche signs every few miles.

The hotel is a magnificent eight-story building with a fifty-foot-high glass atrium facing the mountain. On the south side is the world's highest manmade climbing wall. We checked in and were given a room on the fifth floor facing the mountain. Dick decided to take his nap, so Kim and I were off to the steam room and then the pool.

The steam bath was located on the seventh floor in the health club. It had a eucalyptus scent and was very relaxing as well as therapeutic. From there we walked up a flight of stairs, out a door into the pool area. There was a Plexiglas wall that provided a wind break but allowed the swimmers a view of the mountains. There was no roof.

The pool was quite large and maintained a temperature of about one hundred degrees. Next to the pool was a large hot tub. Kim and I swam, floated, and sat in the warm water as snowflakes fell around us. We probably spent an hour going from pool to hot tub and back.

When we returned to the room, Dick was up reading the brochures about the resort. I gave him a rundown on our activities, and he said, "I'm ready if you want to go again."

I said, "Sure, I think I could stand another round."

Kim decided to go exploring. Dick got his bathing suit, and I told him to bring his overcoat as the walk to the hot tub was outside. We made our way to the health club and into the men's locker room. Once changed, we joined some other resort guests in the steam room. It was a real treat for Dick.

After about twenty minutes, I suggested we go up to the Jacuzzi. I helped him with his overcoat and draped the towel over his head. He looked like a retired boxer after a long workout. Judging from the looks of the people in the hot tub as we walked across the deck, they had the same impression.

When I helped Dick into the tub, a big smile came to his face. There were about fifteen people in there with us. The sun was shining, and light, fluffy snowflakes had begun to fall. A waitress came out to take any drink orders, so we requested two strawberry daiquiris.

I was sitting next to a woman who introduced herself as Jill. I'd guess she was in her late fifties.

She said, "My daughter and I are from San Francisco. We're here skiing for a week." She asked if that gentleman with me was my father.

I said, "He is. In fact, he was in San Francisco a couple of years ago at a bankers' convention."

"Isn't that a coincidence?" she said. "My husband was a banker. He passed away three years ago. What's your father's name?"

Dick leaned over, "If you don't mind, Dave, I'll introduce myself."

"Be my guest," I said. "I'm going to the pool to swim for a while, anyway." As I stepped out, Jill slid over.

I spent about a half an hour in the pool, just swimming, floating, and taking an occasional sip of my daiquiri. I could see Dick and Jill were enjoying their conversation. I didn't want to leave him too long in the hot tub, so I walked over and said, "I think we should hit the showers."

He took the last swallow of his daiquiri. "Whatever you say." He gave Jill a kiss on the hand.

"I've enjoyed meeting you."

"Likewise," was her response.

He extended his hand, and I yanked him out of the hot tub, put his overcoat on him, and draped the towel over his head.

We took our showers and returned to the room. Kim was there, and she suggested we go down to the atrium and grab a sandwich. After having our dinner, we strolled around the hotel, visiting the shops, and spent some time sitting in the lobby, taking in the sights.

THE WHISKEY BOTTLE CONVERSATION

Dick began to nod off in his chair, so with a gentle nudge, I said, "I think it's time for bed." He agreed. We returned to our room, where he immediately climbed into bed and soon was sound asleep. Kim and I watched TV for a while then went down to the piano bar for a nightcap.

The next morning, we were all up early. I felt rested, and Dick was looking better each day. We went down to the restaurant and enjoyed a fine breakfast buffet. Afterward we walked over to the tram that would take us to the top of the mountain. Each car held about twenty people, and we were the only ones without skis. The scenery on the ride up was spectacular. The summit was twelve thousand feet above sea level with a 360-degree view. There was a small lodge at the top, so I went in and bought three hot chocolates while Dick inspected the building, which provided power for the tram. Kim had brought her camera, so we enlisted the help of two men with accents to take pictures of us.

One of the fellows, Jim, was from England, and the other, Scott, was from South Africa. Dick had a good friend in Johannesburg and had made several business trips to South Africa over the years. He and Scott struck up a conversation about how he happened to come to America and what had attracted Dick to South Africa.

We spent about an hour on the summit. Kim had to work that night at Red Rock, so when the next tram arrived, we took it back down. On the return to Salt Lake, we stopped to take some pictures of the mountains and each other.

We arrived at Kim's apartment late in the afternoon. She hurriedly prepared herself and then left for work.

Monday and Tuesday were quiet days. Kim had to work a double on Monday and the noon-to-six shift on Tuesday. Dick and I took walks, read, sat outside in the afternoon sun, and went to the movies to see *Legends of the Fall*.

Tuesday night Dick made his famous heart attack stew, which consists of pork chops, potatoes, sauerkraut, brown sugar, and other elements he won't reveal. Actually, it isn't bad. The only problem is if you don't eat it all in one sitting, any leftovers bind together and become petrified by the next day.

I called Kurt and told him we would arrive in Syracuse at 3:00 p.m. I said, "If Mary could follow you to the airport, we would head home from there."

The next morning, we were up at dawn. Kim made us breakfast and drove us to the airport.

We checked our bags, and she gave us both extended hugs and said, "Now you take care of yourself, Dick. I don't want anything happening to you!"

"Don't you worry, Kimberly, I'll be around for some time yet."

I thanked Kim for showing us such a good time and said I'd call tomorrow morning to confirm our safe arrival home. We bid our final good-byes and made our way to the departure area.

Our flight back home was more direct. We flew from Salt Lake to Chicago, changed planes, and then on the Syracuse. Kurt and Mary were at the terminal when we arrived. We went into the bar, ordered a drink, and told them about our trip.

THE WHISKEY BOTTLE CONVERSATION

Afterward, Kurt said, "I'll go get your car and pull it up front."

We picked up our bags, and Mary helped get them to the car.

She said, "You're more than welcome to stay tonight."

I thanked her but said, "After two weeks of travel and strange beds, I'm feeling the need to be home."

She smiled. "I understand."

It was cold, but the weather was clear and the roads were bare. The four-hour trip back to Lyon Mountain seemed to go by fast. When we got home, I told Dick to get a fire started in the wood stove and I'd get our bags. In no time he had a roaring fire going and was sitting in the chair next to the stove. I poured us both a glass of Scotch and raised my glass to him.

"Well, Dick, it's been quite a week."

He took a sip and just sat there for a moment Then he looked up at me and said, "You know, Dave, there's just so much to live for!"

I looked into his deep blue eyes and said, "There certainly is, Dick."

As I took a drink, I felt a tear roll down my cheek.

CHAPTER THREE

The Whiskey Bottle and the Snowstorm

I slept late into Thursday afternoon. When I got up, Dick was on the couch, reading.

"How're ya feeling?" he said.

"Like a zombie. How do I look?"

He just laughed.

"That was a tremendous trip, Dave. I've been thinking about it all day."

"We'll take the film to Lake Placid tomorrow and have it developed," I said. "That reminds me, I'd better give Bill and Mary a call."

Mary answered the phone. She was happy to hear from me and asked about the trip. I gave her a brief rundown on some of the highlights.

"Sounds like you and Dick had a good time," she said. I agreed and told her we would have pictures for them to see by the time they got back from New Jersey.

THE WHISKEY BOTTLE CONVERSATION

"We're planning to leave by noon tomorrow," Mary said. "If we've gone by the time you get here, you have a key and know where everything is."

I told her we would try to be there before they left but if we missed them, to have a good time and we would see them on Wednesday.

I made Dick and me some dinner, and we spent the rest of the evening watching television. After Dick had gone to bed, I thought about my request for him to tell me stories about his life. Then I began to think about my grandmother.

As a boy, I had spent a lot of time with her, and as an adult, whenever the opportunity presented itself, I would stop by and visit. About a year before she passed away, she called me one afternoon and asked if I could come by when I had a chance. I went to see her the next morning.

Mimi, as all the grandchildren called her, was a wonderful woman. She was soft-spoken, very kind, and always showed a genuine interest in people and their lives. I can't ever remember her speaking a negative word about anyone or anything.

Mimi greeted me warmly and asked if I would like some cookies and milk. The cookie jar on the kitchen counter was always full of home-baked delights. We sat in the living room and talked about what was going on in my life and, of course, how her first great-grandchild, Kim, was doing.

On the coffee table was a box that had "Dick" written on the side. So I asked her what it contained.

"Well, that's the reason I called you here," she said. "Over the years I've collected and saved items of your father's—his high school yearbook, all the letters he wrote home to us during the war, pictures, articles he has written, and other memorabilia, which I'd like you to have, Dave. I know you'll take good care of them and at some point will share them with the family."

I opened the box and found several folders. Three contained letters, which I would guess numbered around one hundred pages. Dick's yearbook looked like it could have been printed that year instead of 1938. There was a folder of pictures from childhood through his military career. Another folder contained articles he had written, Army discharge papers, and other military memorandums.

Mimi made us some tea while I was looking through what I considered to be a family treasure. Before I left, I thanked her for entrusting me with these items that she had so painstakingly sought to preserve. I assured her that I would follow her good example.

As I sat there, thinking about my grandmother, I decided to take the letters and other information to Bill and Mary's with us. Dick might enjoy reliving some of the experiences he had shared with his family. I went upstairs and got the box. I spent the next few hours reading letters. For the most part, they were written as stories. Some even had titles.

The next morning, while Dick fixed us breakfast, I got the car started and our bags loaded. It was cold and overcast. On our drive to Lake Placid, I thought about how beautiful the Adirondacks were with the thousands of lakes and ponds and, of course, the wilderness atmosphere. The Rockies had always seemed so barren and cold to me.

THE WHISKEY BOTTLE CONVERSATION

We arrived at Bill and Mary's about twelve thirty, and much to my surprise, they had already left. As a rule, they ran an hour or two behind schedule. Mary had left a big pot of beef stew on the stove and a container of homemade oatmeal raisin cookies on the table.

I took the luggage to our rooms while Dick started a fire. As I walked past the study, Dick said, "Bill left us about four cords of seasoned wood on the porch."

"Well, I guess I'll know where you'll be for the next five days," I said. "I am going into town to get a few things. You're in charge of keeping the home fires burning. Later on this afternoon, we'll go downtown and catch happy hour."

"Sounds like a good plan, Dave. See you later."

When I returned, Dick was asleep. The leather couch on the other side of the room looked very inviting. I decided a nap might be a good idea. It was six when Dick woke me up.

"You going to sleep all day?" he asked with a smile. "We don't want to miss happy hour!"

"I can see you're getting back to normal," I responded.

I went into the bathroom and splashed some water on my face, trying to emerge from the postnap syndrome. Dick had let the dogs out and filled their bowls. He was sitting at the table, drinking a cup of tea.

"Where are we going to go?" he asked.

"I thought we'd go down to ZigZag's... on Main Street."

It was a new bar opened by Brett and Dave, two friends of mine. The name came from one of the curves at Mount

VanHoevenberg, the Olympic bobsled run. The inside was decorated with old bobsleds and memorabilia from the Thirty-Two and Eighty Olympics.

When we walked in, I heard, "Dick's here!" and two of our friends, Theresa and Chris, came over and greeted him with hugs and kisses.

"When did you get back?" Chris asked.

"Wednesday night," Dick said.

"Well, come and sit down. Let me get you a drink. I want to hear all about your trip," she said.

I took his coat, and they took him. The bar was crowded, and there were several "Helios" and handshakes as he walked by the patrons.

I sat down with Theresa's and Chris's boyfriends, who both happened to be named Dave.

Dave, the owner, was bartending and said, "Four Daves rule," which meant that whenever the four of us were together, we had to do a shot of Jagermeister. I guess it was as good an excuse as any. Dave lined up our glasses, and with a salute and a quick toss, they were all empty.

Just then Brett and his girlfriend, Mary, walked in. "Hey, Dave! How was the trip?" Brett asked.

"We had a great time! Nice to see my daughter again."

Mary asked where Dick was.

"He's down at the end of the bar, filling Chris and Theresa in on all the details of our journey."

"I think I'll go down and say hello," she said.

Brett walked behind the bar and filled all our glasses again. "Welcome back, Dave."

For the next couple of hours, we shot pool, swapped stories, and talked with other friends who came in.

THE WHISKEY BOTTLE CONVERSATION

Adirondack Bob and his wife, Nancy, who owned a guide business; Joe, the painter; Al, who bartended at ZigZag's; Cindy and Marlene, both bartenders in town; Jerry, a contractor, and his girlfriend, Lisa, who worked for a publishing company; Big Tom, the manager of the Northwoods Inn; and my good friend Greg, a builder in town, all filtered into the bar. It turned into a real party!

The main topic of conversation was the snowstorm predicted for Saturday. There was always a sense of excitement when a big storm was coming. It meant more skiers, better snowmobiling, shoveling roofs, and plowing driveways. A good snowstorm provided a boost to the Lake Placid economy. The local forecast said possibly two feet would fall by Sunday. It would be a good time for storytelling.

About eight thirty, after extended good-byes, offers of snowmobile rescues if we got stranded, and other inebriated ramblings, Dick and I departed ZigZag's for a warm fire and a movie, *The Hunt For Red October.*

Saturday morning, I looked out the window to find that about four or five inches of light, fluffy snow had fallen overnight. It wasn't really snowing hard, but it was steady, and there were dark gray clouds that loomed above the mountains. I went downstairs and found Dick at the kitchen table, reading the paper and drinking coffee. There was a plate of warm cinnamon buns in front of him.

"Good morning," he said. "Hell of a party last night."

I smiled and said, "This town is a never-ending party! Looks like the predictions of a big storm are right on, Dick," as I looked out the window over the kitchen sink.

"Nothing like a good snowstorm, especially in a house like this!" he responded. I made myself a cup of hot chocolate and sat down to enjoy a couple of cinnamon buns.

"This would be a good day to just sit by the fire, and you can tell me stories."

He agreed.

"I'm going into town to get us a bottle of Scotch. Can you think of anything else we need?" I asked.

"I'd say that was the most important item, but why don't you get some more milk and ice cream… chocolate marshmallow, if they have it. I'll get the fire started."

I drove into town to pick up our provisions. By the time I got back, the snow was really beginning to come down. The mountains were barely visible in the distance.

I put the milk and the ice cream in the refrigerator, grabbed another cinnamon bun, and walked down the hall to the study. Dick was standing in the solarium, looking out at the falling snow.

The scene reminded me of those crystal balls that you shake and the snow inside swirls around in a simulated storm. The fire was crackling with an occasional pop—sounds always created by well-seasoned wood. Dick had two stacks of logs on both sides of the fireplace. It looked as if there was more than enough wood to last the day.

I walked into the solarium and put my arm around him.

"Beautiful, isn't it?" he said. We stood there for a few minutes, taking in nature's wonder.

"Well, Lieutenant Colonel Richard P. Leonard, how about spinning some yarns for me on this fine Adirondack day?"

He looked at me and saluted, "Yes, sir! Whatever you say, sir!"

We walked back to the fire and sat down. He took the leather recliner, and I sat in the Morris rocker.

"Where do you want me to start?" Dick asked.

"Start at the beginning. Tell me about growing up. Tell me the story of your life."

He sat there for a while, staring into the fire. It was an unfocused gaze, and then he began.

* * *

My first recollections as a boy are of Millan, Georgia, where I was born in 1920. Millan was a small farm community with a general store, barber shop, hotel, town hall, and a Baptist church. The streets were dirt and consisted of either boot-sucking mud in the rainy season or nostril-plugging dust in the summer.

Your grandfather, Harsey King Leonard—or HK, as he preferred to be called—and your grandmother, Harriet, moved to Millan from Ithaca, New York. HK had attended Cornell University where he met Harriet. She was studying journalism, and he obtained a degree in veterinary sciences.

After graduating, HK took a job with the state of Georgia, vaccinating hogs. Most of the transportation at the time was by horse and wagon. However, HK had one of the few cars in the area that didn't belong to a bootlegger. His car had a long engine, two bucket seats, and a large trunk strapped on the back, where he carried his supplies and equipment. There was no roof.

HKs first car Georgia 1921

HK, Harriet, and I would ramble off through the Georgia countryside, stopping at farms, vaccinating hogs. Most of the farms were small enterprises with ten to twenty hogs and perhaps a few dairy cows to provide the family with milk and cheese. It was a tough job, wrestling the hogs all day, but HK was a tough, unforgiving man.

His father, a medical doctor, died of a heart attack at an early age. HK, about fourteen at the time, had to quit school and get a job in the coal mines of Virginia to support his mother, three sisters, and a younger brother. Apparently, he was quite a scholarly boy who loved school. The sudden change from a fairly comfortable life to the backbreaking, dirty work of coal mining forged a rugged, uncompromising individual. That attitude dominated his entire life and on many occasions was a point of conflict between us.

THE WHISKEY BOTTLE CONVERSATION

After a few years, HK bought a twenty-acre farm outside of Millan. About half of the land was rolling meadows that were divided into small fields by stonewalls. The rest of the property was wooded, consisting mostly of Georgia Pine. There were a few apple, plum, and peach trees in the front yard.

The house wasn't much to speak of. It was a four-room structure with unpainted clapboards on the outside. The roof was covered by wooden shingles. Inside there was a small kitchen with a hand pump next to the sink. There were no cupboards, only open shelves. An old Home Comfort wood-fired cook stove served the dual purpose of cooking and providing heat and hot water. The living room had pine floors with plaster walls. There was a trapdoor that led to a small root cellar where Harriet stored her preserved and canned goods. We had a garden in back of the house where we grew corn, peas, potatoes, tomatoes, beans, and squash. The care of the garden was my responsibility. When it was time for harvest, I helped Harriet cook and can the vegetables.

There were two bedrooms. Mine was so narrow I had to stand on the bed to open the door. The outhouse was in the backyard.

The barn was in tough shape. It had old pine boards for walls, full of cracks and holes, and the roof leaked. Inside were two straight stalls for our milk cows and a pen for the chickens. The hogs had a large pen attached to the outside of the barn.

We had about ten hogs, two milk cows, three beef cattle and a few chickens. The beef cattle were allowed to roam in the pasture. Harriet and I were responsible for the daily chores. Every day before he left, HK made sure I knew what my duties were.

He'd say, "Dick, you make sure those hogs and chickens get fed. Milk the cows, and get the barn in order!"

I was only five or six at the time, so Harriet did most of the heavy work. I basically took care of the chickens and milked the cows.

Dick age 5 in Georgia

A few years after HK bought the farm, his financial situation got tough. He had a hard time making ends meet, so he sent Harriet and me back to Ithaca, New York, where her family lived. It was quite a change for me—leaving the

THE WHISKEY BOTTLE CONVERSATION

back roads and farms of Georgia to the beautiful stately homes with paved, tree-lined streets of Ithaca. Most of the women wore long dresses, floppy hats, and carried parasols. The men wore suits with bowler derbies.

Your great-grandparents, Pop and Leaura Pressure, lived quite comfortably in a two-story home that had a large front porch complete with rocking chairs and a swing. Pop had his own construction business, which consisted primarily of finish plaster and painting of both residential and commercial buildings. Leaura took care of the home. They had three daughters: your Great-Aunts Helen, Betty, and your grandmother.

Pop would often take me with him to his jobs. He would give me small tasks to perform, such as, mixing plaster or paint and carrying lathe to put on the walls before plastering. His favorite saying was, "Dick, always do the best job you can possibly do. It doesn't matter if anyone notices. What matters is that you know you've done your best."

Soon after we arrived in Ithaca, your grandmother took a job with the local newspaper. She was a very intelligent, soft-spoken woman with a quiet determination that she applied to whatever task was at hand. Her job was supposed to entail covering local social events—such as, ladies' tea parties, entertainment, college functions—however, her interests as a reporter extended far beyond social events.

On her own initiative, she began writing stories and articles she felt were newsworthy. Her articles ranged from local and national politics to commentaries on different areas of local interest. She apparently got to be quite a correspondent. The editor was so taken with her, the only woman on his staff, that he gave her more and more responsibilities. In a relatively short time, she became a well-known and respected journalist.

HK remained in Georgia during this time, trying to maintain his farm and the job with the state. We didn't see him for about a year and a half. As I understand it, my grandmother finally wrote him a letter and told him if he didn't get home and take care of his wife and child, he would be in big trouble. He sold his farm and came back to Ithaca.

Harriet the journalist

THE WHISKEY BOTTLE CONVERSATION

After spending some time exploring different areas in upstate New York, HK took a job at a milk factory in Adams, New York. Adams was a small farm community near the eastern end of Lake Ontario. We lived in a two-story house, which was owned by the milk company and was provided for us at a reasonable monthly rate.

HK was in charge of inspecting barns and cattle, making sure that the standards of the milk company were being met. When he was inspecting the barns, he got to know the farmers. If they had a problem with their livestock, they would contact him and he would make calls on his own time, usually at night. When he heard of a veterinarian retiring, he would buy his books and do his own study and research, keeping up with the latest techniques.

His job with the milk company took him into the surrounding areas. After two years, he decided that Mexico, New York, about thirty miles west of Adams, would be a good place to set up his own practice. Mexico was a prosperous town of about 3,500 people. It had been home to the Union Free Academy, a military school established in 1895. It remained in operation until 1928, when the State condemned the building and the New Mexico Academy, a public school, was built.

The town itself was a bustling little community. It had its own newspaper to give its readers the news of the world as well as the local gossip and concerns. The economic base in town relied on two milk plants and a canning factory. Trains arrived twice daily, bringing visitors, businesspeople, and supplies for the local stores. On the social side, the barber shop and the local men's club provided the opportunity for the men of town to conduct their business. There were three churches: Methodist, Presbyterian, and Catholic. We belonged to the Presbyterian church. Your grandmother was involved in many different organizations affiliated with both the church and the town.

Beck's Hotel was located in the center of the village. John Beck, a large, robust, friendly man owned the establishment. John always provided a good meal, a clean, reasonable room, and a relaxed atmosphere for his guests.

At the north end of Main Street was the town hall where meetings, community events, and election day voting took place. The school, a large brick building, was on the south end of Main Street. Two doors down from there was the three-story house that HK bought. It was a real mess!

Many of the windows were broken, some of the doors were off their hinges, and much of the plaster was falling off the walls and ceiling. It had been part of the old military academy buildings that the State had condemned. Most of the inside had to be gutted.

* * *

"Did you help with the renovations?" I asked.

"Oh, Christ!" Dick said. "I spent every day after school and weekends shoveling plaster, pulling nails, puttying windows, and following whatever other orders HK gave me."

Dick sat quietly for a minute.

"Your grandfather was always on my back about something. I wasn't working hard enough, or I didn't do this or that right. He could be a real prick if he wanted to."

I didn't say anything. I was surprised to hear him say that.

* * *

We lived in an apartment that HK had rented in town until the house was finished. It took about six months before we moved in. The downstairs was complete, but the upstairs still needed work. HK spent a good deal of his time during renovations establishing his new practice.

He had gotten to know many of the farmers in the area during his tenure at the milk factory and enjoyed a respected reputation. It didn't take long for his business to prosper. When I wasn't in school, he expected or, shall I say, demanded that I assist him on his calls and in his office.

Although automobiles were becoming more prevalent, most transportation in the summer was still horse and wagon and in the winter, horse and cutter. For winter transportation, HK had fashioned a stripped-down Model T Ford with four wheels in the back, cleat tracks around them on both sides, and wooden skis for runners in the front. It was cut down so the skis could fit into the horse cutter tracks. There was a makeshift windshield to protect the driver from the wind. The poor bastard that rode with him, usually me, would sit in the back on a jump seat and freeze his ass off. It was brutal.

He would use this Model T snowmobile to make his calls because you usually couldn't get through with a car. Mexico, being near Lake Ontario, got lake-effect snow. It wasn't unusual to get two to three feet in one storm.

The mornings, when the temperature was way down, HK would go out, pour some hot water on the carburetor, and then crank the engine by hand until it started. He'd load his supplies, and off we would go, heading out of town, following the horse cutter tracks. Most of the time, I would ride up in the jump seat.

When we got into the countryside, the roads were often drifted. As we'd approach a large drift, HK would pick up speed and try to break through. Sometimes we would make it, and other times we would tip the damn thing over. Being up in the jump seat, I would usually end up a few feet away in a snowbank. We always brought along a pole with us so we could get it back up on its tracks. I used to get so damned cold.

Once we got to a barn, I would stand between two cows or horses, using their body heat to warm up. Sometimes I would take off my mittens and put my hands on the animal's belly, which always seemed to be the warmest spot. After HK had finished his work, we'd get back in the Model T and go to the next call. Some days we would travel twenty miles before making it home.

There was one occasion that I'll never forget. I was probably twelve or thirteen at the time. It was a bitter, cold winter night about twenty to thirty degrees below 0. HK got a call from a farmer, Ralph Schmidt, who lived about ten miles outside of town. Ralph had Holstein cattle, and one was ready to deliver, but the calf was turned crossways inside the cow. We took HK's car. It was snowing hard, and the wind was blowing. The roads had drifted, but we made it to Ralph's farm without incident.

When we got to the barn, HK immediately went over to the cow and began pushing on her stomach and sides. He stripped down to his sweater, which had the sleeves cut-off, and pushed his arms up inside the cow. He worked for a good half hour, trying to move the calf into the proper position. We had the cow's back legs tied so she couldn't kick. It didn't stop her from bellowing, though!

Once he had the calf in position, he took a canvas strap that had a ring on one end, pushed his arms back inside the cow, and hooked it around the calf's hind legs. He hooked a long chain to the strap and told me to wrap the other end around a beam that was behind us. Then he told me to stand on the chain.

I put one foot on it and pushed down.

HK yelled, "Stand on the goddamned thing!"

"I don't want to hurt the calf," I said.

"Just do what I tell you, boy!" he shot back.

So I held on to a beam above me and jumped on the chain, madder than hell.

* * *

I looked at Dick and couldn't help but laugh. I could just picture him. Then he began to chuckle.

"What happened then?"

"Well, the chain went slack, and we could see the calf's hoof. She was coming out. HK told me to take up the slack on the chain and jump on it again. So that's what I did. This time, the back legs were exposed. He wrapped his arms around the calf's hind legs and shouted, 'Pull on that chain, Dick! Pull that damn calf out of there!' The mother was making all kinds of strange sounds.

"I pulled with all my might, leaned back, and using my weight, slowly she began to come out. I took up the slack, pulled again, and with a sudden lurch, she popped out and I fell backward in a pile of manure! HK had the calf in his arms."

Dick and I both laughed. He shook his head and said, "You know, that damn little calf was alive! Mr. Schmidt was very happy."

* * *

HK was covered in sweat, and I was covered with cow shit. There was a hand water pump in the room where the milk was stored. We went in there and cleaned up as best we could.

While we were delivering the calf, the storm outside had gotten worse. It was a hard driving snow and the wind was blowing. There were times when we couldn't even see the hood of the car because of the whiteouts.

HK told me to put my head out the window and hold on to the steering wheel with my left hand. He had his head out the window with his right hand on the wheel. We did pretty well, keeping the car on the road, until about six or seven miles from home when the road took a sharp right. We went off into the ditch on my side.

THE WHISKEY BOTTLE CONVERSATION

HK started yelling, "Goddamn you, Dick! Son of a bitch! I told you to watch the road!"

I got out and shoveled and pushed until finally, we got the car back on the road. The snow continued to blow and drift. Visibility was zero at times. We drove a few more miles and went into the ditch again on my side. I got out and shoveled while HK swore and cursed at me. When we managed to get it out of the ditch, I opened the door to get in.

HK said, "You run in front of the car, Dick. We're not going in the ditch again. You run in front of the goddamn car!"

I slammed the door and began running. I could see the road in places and not in other spots because of the driving, swirling snow. I ran all the way to Mexico, probably four miles. I fell a few times and stopped on occasion to catch my breath. Every time I stopped, HK would lay on the horn so I'd keep going with that big car right on my heels.

When we got home, I made it into the house and collapsed. Harriet wanted to know what happened, so HK told her. She was furious! She helped me up and into a hot bath. I soaked for a long time then went to bed. HK didn't say a word to me the next day. Not a word.

HK and his car that he made Dick run
in front of during snow storm

* * *

Dick sat quietly for a few moments, staring into the fire. I felt sad.

Finally, I said, "That sounds like some of the stormy rides home we had from Oswego."

I had gone to high school in Oswego, New York, which was about fifteen miles from our house. Dick was part owner of a boiler manufacturing company, whose plant was in the city, so I used to ride to and from school with him. We experienced similar situations where, because of the driving snow and whiteouts, I would have my head out the window, looking for telephone poles as a point of reference.

He was still staring into the fire.

THE WHISKEY BOTTLE CONVERSATION

"Why do you think Gramp was so hard on you?" I asked.

He looked over at me and didn't say anything for a minute. Then he said, "I'm not really sure. I suppose it could be because he had such a hard life as a boy. He had to quit school to support his family. I told you, he worked in the coal mines as a teenager. That had to be tough. He sacrificed and put every one of his sisters and his brother through college. Maybe he felt I needed to have the same kind of discipline so that I could succeed like he had. I'd like to think that was the reason." Then he looked down and shook his head. "I don't know, Dave. I really don't know."

We sat quietly until I said, "Well, Dick, there's one thing I know, I am sure as hell thankful you never made me get out and run in front of the car!"

He looked at me, and a smile came to his face. "Why don't you go and get the bottle of J&B? Let's have a drink."

He stood up and walked to the solarium.

"The wind is picking up, Dave. Looks like it's going to be a hell of a storm!"

CHAPTER FOUR

Horses, Automobiles, and Planes

I went into the kitchen and got the bottle of J&B, two crystal rocks glasses, and an ice bucket. I put them on a silver tray and returned to the study. Dick was still in the solarium, watching the storm. The fire had died down, so I threw on a couple more logs and joined him.

"Boy, it's really coming down, Dave," he said. "Watch the veranda."

I looked out on the long slate veranda that wrapped around the front of the house. A gust of wind would come up and create these mini white funnels of swirling snow that would move back and forth before disappearing into the storm.

The house sat in a meadow that was like a plateau surrounded by the mountains. The wind would come out of the north and roar down over the plateau, swirling and, sometimes, driving the snow almost in a horizontal direction. Then it would pass and the flakes would resume their slow floating descent to the ground. A few minutes later,

THE WHISKEY BOTTLE CONVERSATION

another gust of wind would roll through and repeat the event.

"Are you ready for a drink, Dick?"

"I was born ready."

We returned to the comfort of our chairs. The fire had come back to life and was making that familiar crackling sound as I poured us both a glass of Scotch. Dick took a sip, sat back in his chair, and closed his eyes.

"That's what I needed," he said. "Now where were we?" He pulled the lever on the side of his chair, transforming it into the reclining position.

"You had just finished telling me about your race to beat Gramp home in the snowstorm," I said.

Dick laughed.

"When you weren't working for Gramp, what other kinds of things did you do?"

"Well, let's see…" he said as he took another sip of his Scotch.

* * *

When we first moved to Mexico, HK bought me a pony. Probably 80 percent of the transportation at the time was by horse: horse and carriage or a team of horses pulling a wagon. Whenever I wanted to go someplace, visit a friend, or just get out of town for a while, I'd saddle up CoCo. He was a paint and a miserable little prick that threw me almost every time I rode him.

Sometimes a group of boys would get together and race. There was an old abandoned farm behind the school that had a big pasture. We'd set up a course, get five or six horses together, and have races. Other times we'd see who could do the best tricks, like standing up in the saddle or running alongside the horse and swinging yourself up on his back. It was a lot of fun, but my real love was automobiles. I was fascinated by them.

My first car was a Model T Ford. I was about eleven and paid seven dollars for it. To me a Model T was like a gift from heaven. I would buy one, fix it up, and swap it for something else.

We had a small barn behind our house, and I made a shop down in the basement. It had a garage door on the back side so I could bring my cars in and work on them. Whenever I had a free moment, I would be out in my shop, tinkering with my Model Ts. I had seven of them by the time I was fourteen and never paid more than eight dollars for one.

My first few cars I just took apart, labeled, cleaned all the parts, and put them back together. They were pretty simple, and I seemed to have a knack for mechanics. You didn't need a license back then, and gas was only ten cents a gallon. Once I got one of my cars running in good order, off I would go, putting around the back roads, seeing the sights. It was the best eight dollars I ever invested.

When I was fourteen, I traded two Model Ts for a Chrysler touring car. It was quite a step up from the Ts. The car wasn't running when I got it, so I had it down in my shop. A friend of mine, "Sneezer" Babcock, lived on a farm on the outskirts of town. He was a tall, gawky kid that walked with a limp. One of his legs was a little shorter than the other. Sneezer would stop by the shop whenever he could and help me work on my cars.

It was a Saturday morning in November, and I was working on the Chrysler when Sneezer walked in.

"Where'd you get the touring car?" he asked.

"I swapped my two Model Ts with Freddie Jones," I told him.

Freddie was the local junk dealer. I had pulled the carburetor off and was cleaning it. I told Sneezer if he wanted to help, to take the spark plugs out and sand down the tips. We worked for a couple of hours, cleaning and reassembling the various parts. Sneezer got in and turned the engine over while I poured some gas in the carburetor. The car fired up for a minute and then stalled. I pulled the distributor cap off and adjusted the points.

"Hit her again," I said.

Sneezer turned the key, and the car started. It wasn't running smoothly, but it was running.

I had the barn door closed as it was a cold morning. We let the car run for about a half an hour. Sneezer stayed inside, giving it gas whenever I instructed him to. I adjusted the carburetor and set the timing. I finally got it so that it was idling smoothly, and I told Sneezer to rev it up.

I had my head under the hood, and when the engine remained idling, I called out again, "Rev it up, Sneeze."

There was no response.

I stepped back to see what the problem was, and there was Sneezer, slumped over the wheel.

I thought to myself, "Shit! Carbon monoxide!"

I opened the car door, pushed him back in the seat, and said, "Sneezer, wake up! Come on, Sneezer! Wake up!" He was unconscious.

I pulled him out of the car, threw him over my shoulder, and carried him outside. He was turning blue. I laid him on the ground, held his nose, and blew into his mouth.

"Come on, Sneezer! Breathe, breathe!" I shouted. I performed the maneuver several times. I slapped his face and shook him. "Come on, Sneezer! Come on, breathe!"

My heart was pounding. I was terrified. Finally, I pushed hard on his chest a couple of times, and he began to cough. He opened his eyes and continued to cough and spit.

I rolled him over on his stomach and told him to breathe through his nose. After a few minutes, his color began to come back. He lay there for some time. Then he sat up.

"What happened, Dick? The last thing I remember is being in the car. How did I get out here?"

"I carried you. You passed out from the fumes. How do you feel?"

"I've got a terrible headache," he said.

"You should have. You scared the shit out of me, Sneezer!"

I pulled him up, put his arm over my shoulder, and walked him around in the pasture behind the shop. Then I took him home. He didn't want me to say anything to his parents or anyone else. I respected his request.

* * *

THE WHISKEY BOTTLE CONVERSATION

Dick picked up his glass, swirled his ice cubes, and took a sip of Scotch.

"You know, Dave, Sneezer was Canaan's grandfather."

Canaan was my sister Mary's son. She married a fellow by the name of John Babcock right out of high school. After having Canaan, they split up, so I never really got to know John or his family.

"That's quite a coincidence," I said. "You save Sneezer's life, and forty years later, his son and your daughter have a child."

Dick swirled his ice cubes and took another drink. "Yes, it is," he said. "Yes, it is."

I poured some more Scotch in my glass, topping it off with a couple of cubes. I took Dick's glass and said, "Let me freshen that up for you."

He smiled. "Good idea, Dave."

I sat back down and rocked in my chair for a few minutes.

"How did you pay for cars, Dick?"

* * *

It was about the time when I had the Chrysler that I began to take on part-time jobs. I went to work for R. Austin Backus, a successful man who lived in Mexico. In fact, he was the town. R. Austin was president of the Board of Education and proprietor and publisher of the *Mexico Independent*, the town's newspaper. He was also the owner of the *Holstein Pedigree Review*, which published an individual record of cattle. He owned several large Holstein breeding farms in the area and the Earlville Auctioneer

Barn, where he could auction off his herd. He was a man of means and distinction.

R. Austin lived in a stately three-story home at the end of Church Street. The house was surrounded by large maple trees with a beautiful rock and flower garden in the backyard, complete with a fountain of a child pouring water into a wishing well. He was a tall, slender man with his hair always combed straight back. He had small round glasses with wire frames, wore double-breasted suits, and smoked long, thick cigars. I got to know R. Austin through my friendship with one of his sons, Richard.

One day I stopped by to see if Richard was home. R. Austin answered the door.

"Ah, Dick! Come on in! Richard isn't here, but I'd like to talk to you about going to work for me part-time on one of my farms. Would you be interested in something like that?"

"Yes, sir, Mr. Backus! I'd be grateful for an opportunity to work for you."

"All right then, Dick," he said as he chewed on his cigar. "You report to my brother, Jay, out at the farm on the Spellman Road. He will tell you what to do. The pay is twenty-five cents an hour. Mark down each day you work, the time, and what you did. Give it to Jay at the end of the week, and he'll pay you."

I stood up and shook his hand and thanked him.

"I'll do a good job for you, Mr. Backus."

He walked me to the door and said, "I know you will, Dick."

I left R. Austin's house feeling elated. The most prominent and successful man in the county wanted me to work for him! I hopped in my Chrysler and drove out to the farm. I had been there before with Richard, so I knew Jay. There was a big white barn and a two-story white farm house. The barn could accommodate about sixty cattle. Both buildings were well kept and cared for.

I found Jay outside, repairing a set of harnesses for his team of horses. I explained that R. Austin had hired me and I was to report to him. Jay looked a lot like his brother, but his demeanor was much different. He was a farmer—low-key, soft-spoken, and patient.

"I could sure use a strong fella around here!" he said.

Jay took me around the barn and showed me what my immediate duties would be. I had to tend to equipment, do basic chores of cleaning and organizing the barn, and help with the milking whenever possible. After about a month, Jay and I would take a truck and go around to different farms in the county and pick up cows that were just skin and bones. I couldn't understand why R. Austin would buy such animals.

As the number of cattle on the farm grew, so did my duties. I had to tend to the new animals, making sure they were fed with a special mix of grain, corn, and alfalfa hay. I trimmed their hooves, groomed, and generally cared for them.

* * *

"What was the point of buying these death row cows, Dick?" I asked.

"Well, Dave, first of all, R. Austin paid little or nothing for the animals. Giving them that high-grade mix of feed within a month, they began to put on weight, give milk, and take on the shape of a real healthy animal. We kept a file on each cow, giving it a pedigree number. R. Austin published the *Holstein Review*, which acted as a registry of Holstein cattle, their bloodlines, and backgrounds. This could be used as a point of reference for farmers when buying cattle."

* * *

R. Austin would establish a pedigree for these cattle and put them in the *Review*. Once they were healthy, we'd take them to his auction barn, where he could sell them and make a nice profit.

About a week before auction, R. Austin stopped by the farm in his new Cadillac. He stepped out with that big cigar in his mouth and took a look at his cows. He and Jay reviewed the paperwork established for each animal. Then he came over and complimented me on the fine job I had done. He got back in his Cadillac and was gone.

I was impressed with R. Austin's approach. His belief in his fellow man and his ability to get the job done with just a word of encouragement. This word of encouragement turned into action around the farm, and all his men seemed to understand and respect him for it.

When it came time to take the cattle to auction, I was given the job of working the cattle, putting them on a truck, and driving them to Earlville, where they would be auctioned off. Each cow was "a celebrity," with his or her name in the pedigree book.

THE WHISKEY BOTTLE CONVERSATION

Pulling into the Earlville area, I could feel the activity: other trucks loaded with cattle, farmers with wagons, food stands… almost a carnival atmosphere. I was directed to an area to unload the cattle and place them in a barn that was assigned to R. Austin. I could feel the pulse of the action with its realm of activity, and I was one of its participants.

The cows were given a day of rest then put in the "beauty parlor," where they were washed, groomed, and their hooves were cleaned so they shined. Each cow was placed in a box stall with its history on the front gate. Buyers came to look and ask questions. Being in charge, I explained their attributes, elaborating somewhat as any good cattle salesman does. My self-esteem rose to the highest level I had ever felt.

As a prospective buyer approached, I greeted him with a handshake and, "Hello. I'm Dick Leonard. I represent R. Austin Backus and these fine cattle that will be auctioned off today."

I had all the records on each stall and would review them with the interested party. Almost everyone in the cattle business knew of R. Austin Backus, and I was proud to be associated with him. From that point on, when R. Austin called, I worked and was paid well for my duties.

On another occasion, he called and told me he had a small farm in Texas—a little community just outside of Mexico. It didn't have any cows yet, but he wanted me to get the hay in.

He said, "Dick, go down and survey the farm for equipment and do the job. If you need anything, just charge it to me."

It didn't take long to survey the equipment. There was a hay mower, a hay rake, and a couple of wagons. The barn was equipped with a hayfork hooked to a rope. At that time hay was put in loose.

The first thing I did was take the mower to a nearby farmer and have him sharpen the blades, grease it, and generally check it over. The hay rake basically needed a little grease. Now these pieces of equipment had to be pulled by something. There were no horses, so I went to a junkyard and bought an old Buick touring car. I paid twenty dollars and drove it down to the farm. I made a hitch that was to the left of center so I could see what I was towing.

I hooked the mowing machine to the car and got Hoppy Smith to ride on it. When we made a turn, he would have to pull a rope and raise the sickle bar. In no time we had a system. The Buick ran great with a quart of oil every hour or so and plenty of gas. It took us three days to mow the two fields. Next we had to rake the hay into piles.

The hay rake had two wheels with half-moon-shaped forks about three inches apart. It was pulled with the forks down until it was full of hay. Then we had a rope run through the back window of the Buick, where Hoppy—sitting in the backseat—would pull it to tip the rake up and release the hay. Once the hay was all in rows, we had to pitch it on the wagon by hand with pitchforks.

When we had a full load, I'd pull the wagon into the barn, where a large pronged fork would drop down from the ceiling into the loose hay. The hayfork was hooked to a rope on a pulley, which was hooked to a track that ran the length of the barn. I hired a farmer with a team of horses to pull the hayfork up and across the barn where it was released. Our system worked well. It took us five days to complete the job. R. Austin came down to the farm and was very pleased. That night he put on a picnic dinner for me and "my crew."

I learned a great deal working for R. Austin. His willingness to give me the responsibility to accomplish a job on my own initiative is something I have always been grateful for.

* * *

"It must have been a welcomed change from working for Gramp," I said.

Dick drank the rest of his Scotch and said, "Yes, it was. R. Austin treated me as a man. He never scolded me, only offered advice or words of encouragement."

"Did you have any other jobs?" I asked.

* * *

I worked for Harry Vorice. He was the sheriff and had a farm just outside of town. A few nights a week, I would go to Harry's. He had about ten cows and for my efforts would give me milk for our family. Harry was about sixty—a big, burly man that had been a farmer all his life. His family had a farm when he was a boy, which Harry eventually took over after his father died. He ran it until he was about fifty then sold the entire concern, except for a few cows, which he kept. He took his cows and bought what I call a hobby farm not too far from my house. He gave most of the milk away.

Harry loved to talk. He'd always start out a conversation with, "Dick, have I told you about the time…"

And even though he probably had, I'd say, "No, Harry, I'd like to hear about that."

He would then ramble on for about an hour about how tough he had it as a kid or some story about life on the farm. I'd be there, sitting on my stool, pulling teats, and Harry would be a few cows over, doing the same. We didn't really see much of each other. There were just voices and stories floating around in the barn with an occasional bellow from a cow.

I was still driving the Chrysler at the time. Harry's farm was at the bottom of this steep hill, and sometimes I would take some friends out to the farm with me. I'd drive up past the barn, maybe a mile over the top of the hill, turn around, and push the pedal to the floor. We would break over that hill and pass Harry's farm, going like hell. The kids would be hooting and hollering, and the dust and stones would be flying.

Every so often, Harry would be out in the road and stop me.

He'd say, "Dick, I don't think you should be driving the car down the hill at that speed. I'm either going to have to arrest you or tell your father."

I said, "I'd appreciate it if you wouldn't tell my father."

He never did, that I know of, nor did he ever arrest me. I enjoyed my evenings with Harry. Even though he was the sheriff, he was a kind, gentle man.

* * *

THE WHISKEY BOTTLE CONVERSATION

"Sounds as if you spent a lot of time around cows, Dick," I said as I put some ice in his glass and poured him some more Scotch. "Between working with Gramp, R. Austin, and Harry, you were a real farm boy!"

Dick had gotten up and was walking around the room. I could see that he was stiff.

"I didn't mind the farm work," he said. "I got to be outside, and it was hard physical labor. I just liked to be doing something where I had a sense of accomplishment."

He came back and threw another log on the fire then sat back down.

* * *

Not all my jobs were on the farm. There was a fellow by the name of George Young who had a garage not too far from my house. When I began buying and working on Model Ts, I would often go to his garage to ask him questions or swap for parts that I needed. If I didn't have money or something to swap, he would have me do some small task for payment.

Our relationship grew, and when I was about fifteen, he said, "Dick, why don't you come to work for me? You know, when you have some free time."

George was a real nice guy but a bit on the crazy side. He was about six feet tall, skinny, and walked with a limp. He had thick, straight black hair and always wore a black T-shirt and black mechanic's hat with brim turned up. His garage had two bays, and he kept it neat and clean. He made sure that I always cleaned and put the tools back in their proper place.

George would save all the used parts that he replaced on the cars. Much of my time there was taken up with rebuilding them.

He'd say, "Take that starter over there, break it down and let's see what's wrong with it."

I'd take it apart and see if I could figure out why it wasn't working. If I got stuck, George would show me where the problem was. I'd go in the back room, where he kept all his used parts, find what I needed, and replace it.

One day he had finished working on a Harley Davidson and took it for a ride to check it out. Everything seemed to be all right until he put on the brakes and the back wheel locked up. The motorcycle skidded off the road and into a ditch. When he hit the ditch, it threw George off the bike onto a stonewall about ten feet away.

I was working at the garage, and when he didn't return after an hour, I decided to go look for him. I had noticed which way he had headed out of town, so I took my car and went in the same direction. About three miles outside of town, there was the Harley in the ditch and George unconscious on the stonewall.

He had a cut over his right eye, and his face was bloody, but it didn't appear that there were any broken bones. I dragged him into the car and drove him to Dr. Pulsifer's office. The good doctor came out and helped me get him inside. He used some smelling salts to bring George back around, stitched up the cut over his eye, and sent him home with instructions to take it easy for a few days.

The next morning George pulled up to the garage. He had some difficulty getting out of the car.

I said, "What the hell are you doing here?"

THE WHISKEY BOTTLE CONVERSATION

"I've got a headache, and my back's a little sore, but I've got to fix the Harley back up," he said. "Thanks for coming after me, Dick. I appreciate it."

He spent the next few days trying not to show the pain he was in.

Not too long after that, George decided to buy an airplane.

He said, "I've been thinking about buying a plane and learning how to fly. What do you think about that, Dick?"

I told him I thought it was a great idea. I had always had a keen interest in airplanes. I read all the stories about the World War I aces: the German, "Red Baron," and, of course, Charles Lindburg, who was my hero. I began building model airplanes when I was about ten, and I had quite a collection in my room. When George told me he was going to buy a plane, I could hardly control myself.

After shopping around for a while, he found a single-wing, two-passenger plane. Two or three days a week for a couple of months, he would go and take flying lessons from the previous owner. During this time we built a runway in a field behind his house. George borrowed an old grader that we pulled behind a truck. I would raise and lower the blade with a big hand crank, leveling off some of the high spots and smoothing out the rough areas. A lot of stones were dug up by the grader, so we had to pick those off the runway. We used most of them to fill in low spots and then cover the area with dirt. When we had it where George felt it was level enough, I drove the dump truck back and forth, towing a big piece of wire mesh fencing. The weight of the truck packed the newly excavated runway, and the wire mesh helped make a smoother surface. Finally, George decided it was suitable to land on.

I had asked him if I could go with him when he brought the plane home.

He said, "I had better be sure I know what I am doing before I take a passenger along."

I was disappointed, but I knew he was right. George went the next day to get the plane. I waited at his house, watching the sky, listening for the sound of an engine. All of a sudden, off in the distance, there was a plane. In no time it was making a low-level pass over the house with George at the stick.

His landing was, let's say, less than perfect. He hit hard when he first touched down. As a result, the plane took a couple of healthy bounces, but he managed to keep it under control and bring it to a stop.

When he climbed out of the cockpit, I said, "That was great, George, but I think you were right about not taking anyone with you for a while." We both laughed.

After a few more flights, he decided to take the engine apart and rebuild it. We pulled it off the plane and took it over to his garage. George didn't have any books or manuals. He just seemed to know what to do. As we tore the engine down, he explained what the various parts were and what their function was. When it was finished, we put it back in the plane. I gave the propeller a spin, and it fired right up.

I had a sudden surge of pride, and I knew George was pleased. He smiled and gave me a thumbs-up. He taxied the plane up and down the runway for a while, making sure that it was running properly. Then he took off.

THE WHISKEY BOTTLE CONVERSATION

George was gone for about an hour as I waited patiently on his front porch. He made a pass over the house then circled and landed.

* * *

"Were his landings getting any better?" I asked.
Dick just chuckled.

* * *

During the next week, he took the plane up almost every day.

Finally, he said, "Dick, I think it's time you learned how to fly. Meet me tomorrow morning at seven, and we'll take her up."

I was there at six thirty.

George was in the house, having his coffee, and I am sure he could sense my excitement.

He said, "You know, Dick, flying a plane is a lot different than driving a car, not only in style, but more so, in risk. You make a mistake in a car, and usually you can correct it or perhaps end up in a field. You make a mistake in a plane, well… I think you know what I mean."

When he finished his coffee, we went out to the plane. As I had on other occasions, I helped him with his preflight check—making sure the rudder, flaps, tires, fuel, and oil were all in working order.

Finally, George said, "Okay, spin the prop, and let's go for a ride."

I gave the propeller a whirl; the engine came to life with a roar that sent a chill down my spine. I don't know if it was the sound of the engine or the anticipation of flying for the first time. I do know the butterflies in my stomach had already taken off.

I climbed in, fastened my seat belt, and George taxied down to the end of the runway. He spun the plane around and pushed the throttle forward. As we started down the runway, the plane bounced and made sounds that were unfamiliar to me. It was louder in the cockpit than I had expected. It wasn't like being in a car at all. When we neared the end of the runway, he pushed the throttle all the way forward, and we lifted off the ground. What a feeling! I was excited. My heart was pounding, and there was this sensation of being light, almost weightless, for a minute.

From all the books I had read and the models I had built, the expectations could not have prepared me for the actual feeling of flying. I loved the sense of freedom. Something about being off the ground with everything seeming to be so small down below. It was overwhelming. I asked George if he had felt the same way.

His response was simply, "It's a whole different world up here, Dick."

It was a different world. We flew over the town, out over the lake, and back again. I was impressed with how ordered and geometric everything seemed. The fields of corn and hay divided by roads and the streets of Mexico paralleling each other all seemed to be so well-thought-out.

George showed me the basics of flying the plane. He had me put my hand on the stick. As I pulled backward, the nose of the plane tilted up and we began to climb. As

THE WHISKEY BOTTLE CONVERSATION

I pushed it forward, the nose dropped and we began to descend. A movement to the left, and it banked in that direction; to the right, it did the opposite.

I was surprised at how sensitive the control stick was. George kept his hand on it during my instruction, protecting us from any untrained move that might spell disaster.

After about fifteen minutes, he said, "That's enough for one day, Dick. Time to take her down."

As we circled the runway and made our approach, I began to get nervous. I felt a queasiness in my stomach as I thought about George's rough landings. The closer we got to the ground, the more the plane seemed to drift right and left as George made alternating moves on the stick. I could feel my body tense as we touched down. The plane made one long hop then coasted to the end of the runway, spun around, and stopped.

* * *

Dick laughed.

"My heart was beating like a base drum, Dave. What a tremendous feeling it was! It's really hard for me to put into words."

He sat there for a minute, sipping his Scotch, staring into the fire with a little smile on his face.

"George took me up several times after that and let me handle the plane on my own. I asked him once if I could fly it solo."

Dick took his eyes off the fire and looked at me. His smile was gone, and he seemed sad. "He didn't think that would be a good idea.

"Several years later when I was training in the Air Corps, George crashed and was killed in a fire, trying to save his passenger. I thought about him often when I was flying in the service. He had taught me many things, but most of all, I thought about how he introduced me to 'that different world' above the ground. For that reason alone, I will always have fond memories of him."

Dick stared back into the fire, and his eyes seemed to get a little misty, but there were no tears. He was too proud to show that much emotion even to me.

After a few minutes of silence, he got up out of his chair and said, "I think I'll have a dish of ice cream. Dave, you want some?"

"No, thanks. I'm fine," I said as he left the room.

I walked into the solarium and looked out at the mountains. The snow was still falling, but the wind had died down. A thick white blanket covered the ground and the trees. As I stood there, I thought about how some of my childhood experiences had paralleled his.

I grew up on a dairy farm, which my father owned and my grandfather managed. I assisted in the delivery of calves and helped with the milking. I listened to the stories of Richard Crandle and Pearl Dawley, two hired hands who ran the daily activities of the farm.

After the war, Dick bought an airplane. It was a five-passenger Canadian-made Stinson. Just about every Sunday, when the weather cooperated, he used to take my mother, my brother Rick, my sister Kathy, and me flying. At the age of five, I often wondered how the airport made

THE WHISKEY BOTTLE CONVERSATION

all those little toy houses and moving cars I looked down on.

Dick kept the plane at a small airport about fifteen miles from where we lived. When I was about eight, he decided to build a hangar and runway on the farm. He borrowed an old grader much the same as the one he and George had used. We pulled it with one of the farm tractors, leveling a strip of land for his runway.

Once that was finished, we built a hangar. It was a Sunday morning when Dick said he was going to get the plane.

Of course, we all wanted to go with him, but he said, "I had better get a feel for landing at this new airport. We'll go for a ride after I land."

The farm sat on a hill overlooking Lake Ontario. To land Dick had to approach facing the lake and then drop in over a group of tall pine trees that stood about one hundred yards before the runway. We all waited anxiously for the sound of his plane.

About an hour had passed before we heard the sound of a distant engine. In no time Dick made a treetop pass over the runway. He pulled up and circled around to make his approach. I watched with anticipation along with my mother, brother, and sister and some of the neighborhood kids.

As he came in over the tall pines, the engine sputtered and stalled. The plane, having lost its power, dropped, and hit a stonewall about fifty feet before the runway, causing it to cartwheel—wing over wing—three times. Rick and I ran to the plane as my mother screamed and cried.

I said, "He's all right! He's okay!"

The plane was upside down with Dick still strapped in his seat.

"Get away from the plane! Get back!" he shouted.

Rick and I backed up.

I saw him reach for the buckle on his seat belt. When he released it, he fell out of the seat. He tried to get the door open, but it was jammed, so he kicked the front window out and crawled through it. By this time, my mother was there, still crying. We all ran over and hugged him.

"I'm all right," he said. "Just give me a minute."

He went back to the plane and walked all around it. Then he walked down the runway by himself. Every once in a while, he'd stop and kick the dirt, and we'd hear him shouting. That ended our flying experience and his. He never bought another airplane.

Dick had joined me with his dish of chocolate marshmallow ice cream.

"What are you thinking about?" he asked.

"Oh, I was just reminiscing about the runway we built on the farm. Just like you and George had done."

"Yeah, very similar circumstances," he said. "The big difference is I survived the crash and George didn't!"

I put my arm around him. "Thank God for that, Dick!"

CHAPTER FIVE

I Really Wasn't a Bad Boy

Watching Dick enjoy his dish of ice cream, I decided a little snack might be a good idea. I was beginning to feel the effects of sipping Scotch for a couple of hours and didn't want to pass out just when things were getting interesting.

I went to the kitchen and ate the last cinnamon bun. The dogs were standing at the side door, so I let them out. It looked as if about a foot of snow had already fallen.

It was twelve thirty, but I wasn't really hungry enough for lunch. I made two cups of tea with honey and got a plate of the oatmeal cookies Mary had left for us. I let the dogs back in before I returned to the study. Dick was reclined in his chair, looking relaxed and comfortable.

"How about some tea and cookies for a second course, Dick?"

"Nothing like a little dessert after ice cream," he said. "It doesn't get much better than this, Dave!"

After we finished the cookies, I said, "What were your years in school like?"

Dick laughed and shook his head. I could tell he was really beginning to enjoy reminiscing about his life.

* * *

My years in school seemed to focus on two areas: sports and getting into trouble. When I was in the sixth grade, I wanted to play soccer. I went to the coach and asked him if I could try out for the team.

He said, "You can try out, and if you show potential, I'll give you a chance."

After school the next day, I was on the soccer field. The coach put us through running drills, like forward and backward sprints. We had to kick and throw the soccer ball and run down the field, dribbling as we went. I was a good athlete, and it seemed that I could run circles around the older boys. I made the high school team.

That season we won the league championship. The older boys were tickled to death to have me on the team. I played right wing, and my job was to try and center the ball so the halfback could get a kick on the goal. We had two fullbacks that could kick the ball practically the length of the field. I was fast and could dribble the ball well enough, so the other team had a tough time getting it away from me. I loved the game, and even though I was in the sixth grade, I wasn't afraid to mix it up with the older boys. I played on the varsity team in the seventh and eighth grade too.

In eighth grade I wanted to run track. The team would start their practice runs going by my house. I would run

THE WHISKEY BOTTLE CONVERSATION

out of the house and join them on a route that took them a good mile and a half around town. When we got back to school, I was right up in front. The coach wanted to know where I joined the team.

I said, "When they went by my house on Main Street."

He asked me if I wanted to run for the varsity team.

I said, "Yes, sir!"

I ran the 220 and the 440, and the last leg of the 880 relay. It just seemed that anything I wanted to do, I did well. I loved the competition of sports. I hated to lose.

I received quite a bit of recognition as well in the classroom, but it wasn't for my scholastic aptitude. I apparently had a reputation in the earlier grades for being sort of a wise guy.

* * *

"Why, Dick. What would you do?"

He sat there for a moment, looking at the fire. Then a smile came to his face.

* * *

Living next to school, I would wait until the last bell had rung and then make a run for it. When the teacher wasn't looking, I'd sneak into class. As she was ready to send the attendance slip to the office, she'd notice that I was in my seat.

"Mr. Leonard, I've got you marked absent," she said.

Then she would have to make out another attendance report.

I apparently was—I don't want to say—smart, but I seemed to be ahead of the teachers, so I would do certain things to irritate them. For example, sometimes I'd take my toothbrush to school. When the teacher would write on the blackboard, I'd stand up and brush my teeth and pretend to spit in my desk. The whole class would start laughing. As she turned around, I'd sit down and act like I was paying attention. Once she resumed her work on the board, I'd get back up and comb my hair or pretend to gargle, getting the class into an uproar. She'd turn around and want to know what was so funny. I'd be back in my seat, trying to look as innocent as possible.

My eighth grade teacher was Ina B. Stone. Ina was a short, stocky woman who had a reputation of being tough on her students. She lived with another woman named Dorothy Wilson, a history teacher. I think they were in love. The first day I walked into her class, no sooner had I stepped inside, Ina grabbed me with both hands and pinned me up against the wall.

Ina B. looked me right in the eye and said, "Nice to have you in my class, Mr. Leonard. I just want to advise you that when you are in my class, I am the boss!"

I said, "I'm sure everything will be fine, Ms. Stone. No matter what class I'm in, I'll pay strict attention!"

She let go of me and straightened out my shirt.

"That's good, Mr. Leonard. I'm glad we understand each other. Now take your seat!"

As she turned around and walked to the front of the room, I followed her doing a gorilla walk. There were a few snickers from the class but no real laughs. Everyone was afraid of Ina B. It seems the teachers did plenty of talking about my behavior—with good reason, I suppose.

One day, in October, I was sitting in my eighth grade biology class when I got the bright idea to steal the human skeleton that we were studying at the time. I got Hoppy Smith and Charlie Tylerton, two friends of mine, to help me.

I had met Hoppy when I first moved to Mexico. He was a strong, well-built kid who was a hell of a tackle on the football team. His mother was Polish. She and Hoppy's stepfather, Kurt Pond, owned a restaurant about five miles outside of town. He practically lived at my house when he was playing sports.

Charlie was a tall, handsome boy. His parents were Seventh Day Adventists and very religious people. He was smart in school, but he couldn't really look out for himself. I mean, he couldn't fight, so I kind of looked after him in that respect.

I met Charlie and Hoppy at lunch and told them of my plan.

"I'll fix the lock on the back door so we can get in the school tonight," I said. "You can stay at my house, Hoppy. Charlie, why don't you meet us behind Earl Dexter's barn around seven thirty?" Earl's house was next to ours.

We met that night, and the three of us sneaked back into the school and took the skeleton out of its glass case.

Hoppy said, "What the hell do we do with it, Dick?"... something I hadn't really given any thought to.

I said, "Let's put it in Mr. Dexter's barn!"

He had a feed business, and in his barn were these big bins where he stored grain and oats.

We carried the skeleton across the school yard, over Earl's fence, and quietly sneaked into his barn. Charlie opened a grain bin and began pushing the grain to the sides so we could bury our guest.

Hoppy said, "If Earl comes out here for grain and finds this skeleton, he'll have a heart attack!"

We all laughed!

Once our friend was completely covered, we closed the bin and sneaked back out of Earl's barn. We took a walk uptown, laughing and congratulating ourselves on our accomplishment.

A few days later, a fellow by the name of John Mahar, a janitor, overheard either Hoppy or Charlie telling some of the other boys what we had done.

Mr. Mahar came to me and said, "Dick, I understand you have a skeleton in Earl Dexter's grain bin."

I said, "Well, I can't say I do and I can't say I don't."

He said, "I'd suggest that you get it back to school. I am not going to tell anyone, but I think it might be a good idea to get the skeleton and put it back in the classroom."

I wasn't going to argue with his size or his rationale—especially if it meant I wouldn't get caught. When school was over that day, I got the skeleton out of the grain bin and put it in my shop under our barn. That night I went back to school where I had unlocked one of the doors before I had gone home. Skeleton in hand, I sneaked into the biology lab and put him safely back in his glass case.

About two nights later, I went back to see if the skeleton was still in the case, and much to my surprise, he was

THE WHISKEY BOTTLE CONVERSATION

gone… and so was the case! I started looking around and finally found him in a storage room under the stage in the auditorium. The next night I sneaked back in school and took him out of the case and put him in our barn. Nobody missed him. They thought he was well taken care of.

The following week was Halloween. I got Hoppy, and late the night before Halloween, we took the skeleton, hooked him to the rope on the flagpole, and pulled him all the way to the top. Hoppy shimmied up the pole and tied the rope off. The next morning the whole school was out on the front lawn, laughing and cheering.

Of course, Mr. Mahar knew who did it. He called me aside and asked me how we were going to get the damned skeleton down.

I said, "What do you mean? How did he get up that flagpole?"

We both laughed, and he said, "I'd say we have a real problem."

I said, "Maybe I could get one of the boys to shimmy up and get the rope, and we could let him down."

I got Hoppy to go up and unhook the rope, and to the wild cheers of the students, the skeleton made his descent to earth. We gave him to Mr. Mahar, and he put him back in his glass case. Safe at last.

Dick Charlie and Hoppy the skeleton crew

* * *

I was smiling through this whole episode as Dick relished in his story. When he finished, I began to laugh.

"You really were a pain in the ass," I said.

"I was just having a little fun," Dick said with a wink.

* * *

In my freshman year, I continued with the sports program. I played soccer and joined the basketball and baseball teams for the first time. Our teams didn't do all that well, but I enjoyed the challenges of the new sports.

As far as my academics, my lack of interest continued. For example, in history class, the teacher would give us our daily lessons, and it seemed that everybody took notes except me. I guess I had what they now refer to as a photographic memory. I seemed to be able to recall just about anything I had read or had been explained to me.

At the end of the semester, the teacher wanted to see our notebooks. I went to a girl by the name of Janet Leary and asked if I could borrow hers. She agreed, and for the next few nights, I went through and read her notes. She was very smart. After reviewing her work, I sat down and composed my own notebook, referencing hers and reflecting on my own recollections of the classroom instruction. I turned in my notebook on the day of the final exam and got a 90 for my history grade.

It was during my freshman year that HK bought an old sanitarium that had been used for the treatment of tuberculosis patients in Parish, which was about fifteen miles from Mexico. It was a large three-story structure about forty by sixty. He was interested in building houses to sell, and he figured he could build two or three houses from the lumber.

For the next year and a half, on weekends and vacations, Harry Tomlin and I would drive to Parish and work dismantling the sanitarium. Harry was an older gentleman who was a carpenter around Mexico. We started by tearing off the roof. We scraped the shingles off, removed the boards and rafters. Each night before we finished, we would pull all the nails out of the boards and stack them. Once the roof was off, we dismantled all the partitions and pulled up the maple hardwood floors. I used to get so sick of prying up boards and pulling nails. After the partitions and floors were up, we would take out the floor joists and move to the second floor, repeating the same process.

* * *

"Did Gramp pay you?" I asked.

"He paid Harry, and when he felt like it, he'd give me a few bucks. I worked because I was told to… It wasn't a matter of choice. By the time I graduated from high school, HK had built and sold three single-story houses out of that lumber.

"My sophomore year, the school burned. They figure the fire started in the boiler room. The fire department was only equipped with the old hand pump water wagons pulled by a team of horses. There wasn't much they could do except protect the houses around the school. They just let it burn. It took two weeks before it burned itself out completely."

"So where did you have your classes, Dick?"

* * *

They set up classes all over town in church basements, the town hall—wherever there was space available. We spent most of our time traveling from place to place. I didn't have much interest in either chemistry or physics, so consequently, I didn't do my homework and the teachers would get upset with me. A couple of days before the test, I would study for several hours and always pass with high marks.

THE WHISKEY BOTTLE CONVERSATION

They kept the sports program going after the school burned down. I continued in the baseball, basketball, and soccer programs. I loved the competition and the personal determination required to excel in the various sports.

One day after class, I was coming out of the town hall. The principal's office, administration, and some classes were being housed there. On the corner there were a group of boys gathered, and I could see one of the boys was shoving and pushing someone around. I went over to see what was going on.

Benny Burke, whose father was a bootlegger and owned the men's club in town, was taunting my friend, Charlie Tylerton. Benny was a big, husky kid, and it seemed he was always picking on somebody. He would push Charlie and say, "Come on, you sissy, fight me! What's the matter, sissy? Afraid to act like a man?" Then he pushed him again. Charlie didn't say anything.

I stepped in between them, grabbed Benny by the throat, and pushed him backward.

I said, "You want to fight someone, Benny? Fight me!"

Benny took a swing. I ducked and came across with a right hook that caught him in the nose. The fight was on. Benny charged at me, and I hit him in the stomach with another right. As he doubled over, I came down on his face with a left. He spun around and hit me in the face, knocking me back a couple of steps. That really pissed me off! His nose was bleeding. I hit him with a couple of left jabs in the nose and then caught him on the side of his head with a roundhouse right. His knees buckled, and he went down. I jumped on top of him, pounding his face. Some of the boys watching pulled me off when they saw he was practically unconscious. It took three of them to hold me down until I was finally calm enough to be let up.

Benny had a broken nose, two black eyes, a few cuts, and a big lump on his chin. I had a swollen jaw. During the fight, quite a crowd had gathered, cheering for either Benny or me. Apparently, all the commotion attracted the attention of the principal, who was in the town hall. He came out and, of course, gave me hell.

He said, "Leonard, you shouldn't be fighting in school!"

I said, "I'm not in school! I'm out here on the street!"

Mr. Perkins was a short, miserable man that always seemed to be on my case about something.

He said, "I'm going to have to inform your father about this, Dick!"

At that time HK was on the Board of Education.

I said, "Go right ahead. Tell my mother too. My grandfather lives on Dobbs Street. Why don't you give him a call?"

* * *

Dick and I both cracked up. Dick picked up his glass and took a drink and laughed some more.

"I had had several run-ins with Mr. Perkins. He had suggested to HK that I go to military school. I think he thought the discipline of a military academy was just what I needed."

"From the sounds of it, I don't think he was too far off the mark," I said.

Dick looked at me, took another drink, and smiled.

THE WHISKEY BOTTLE CONVERSATION

* * *

After the fight, Charlie walked home with me.

He said, "Thanks, Dick, for helping me out. I would have fought Benny, but he would have killed me."

"It's okay, Charlie. Benny's a bully, and he's had a good ass-kickin' coming to him for a long time."

When we got to my house, Charlie said, "My grandmother is baking bread on Saturday. Why don't we take the horses and ride out and see her."

"Sounds like a good idea," I said.

As Charlie walked away, he turned and said, "Thanks again, Dick!"

Saturday morning, we saddled up and rode out to his grandmother's. She lived about five miles outside of town. We would follow the roads, then go off in the woods, gallop through the fields, playing tag or racing each other. We worked up an appetite on our horses and arrived just as the first few loaves were coming out of the oven. There's nothing like the smell of freshly baked bread to two hungry boys!

We spent most of the day helping his grandmother around the house, doing whatever chores needed to be done. We ate all the nice, warm bread and butter we wanted and, after our stay, rode back to Mexico.

On the way back, we were racing through the field, and a pheasant spooked my horse, and he threw me. I landed on a tree stump and broke my wrist. I got back on and rode home. I went to Dr. Pulsifer, our neighbor, and he set my wrist and put my arm in a cast.

About a week later, a bunch of us boys were playing soccer before school in Earl Dexter's front yard. Earl had a large home with a big yard that was between my house and the school.

A fellow by the name of Orsie Guile, who was a real character, lived in Butterfly—a little community outside of Mexico. Orsie's father had a big wagon that he converted into a school bus. A team of horses pulled the wagon as it made stops along the way from Butterfly, picking up students coming to school in Mexico.

This morning the boys riding the "school bus" came over to Earl's and challenged us to a quick game. At one point, Orsie was dribbling the ball, and I took it away from him. He got mad and tripped me. So I got up with one arm in a sling and tore right into him. I gave Orsie a pretty good beating and, as a result, ended up in the principal's office again.

Mr. Perkins said that he was going to tell my father in no uncertain terms that I should go to military academy because until my attitude changed, I wasn't welcome in his school.

I said, "It's not your school, Mr. Perkins! It belongs to the taxpayers!" I think that really made him mad.

HK didn't say much to me for the next couple of days. I tried to avoid him as much as possible. It was on Sunday morning, just before we left for church, when HK called me into his office.

He said, "Dick, I'm fed up with reports from the principal and your teachers about the trouble you cause at that school! I am on the school board and a respected man in this community, and all I hear is what a troublemaker you

THE WHISKEY BOTTLE CONVERSATION

are! You don't do your assignments! You're never on time for class! You're going to military academy in Syracuse!"

I said, "I'm not going to any military school! I'll stay right here. They can't kick me out. It's a public school!"

HK pulled off his belt and took a swing at me. "You'll do what I tell you to do or else!"

I said, "You don't scare me!" and out the office door I went.

I got into my car and took off. I didn't want to go to a military academy with all their rules and regulations! Hell, I had a tough time accepting the standards in public school. How long could I last in a military institution?

I stayed out that whole day. When I returned home that evening, HK was out on a call, but Harriet was up waiting for me.

She said, "Dick, I know you don't want to go away to school, but under the circumstances, I think it's the best thing for you. Your father's upset, the principal's upset, and I think if you stay, things can only get worse. So for me, go to this military academy just for a year until the new school here is finished. Then I think things will be such that you can return and graduate with your classmates from Mexico."

My mother had a way of making what seemed to be a bad situation turn into something that would be all right.

* * *

"You know what kind of woman she was, Dave. On many occasions, she intervened on my behalf with HK, or anyone else that was having a problem with me."

* * *

The week before Labor Day, my parents drove me to Manlius, a suburb of Syracuse, where Manlius Military Academy was located—my new home for the next year, or what I thought would be the next year.

As we pulled through the gates, I was a little nervous, but I was also impressed with the expansive manicured lawns. All the buildings were large brick structures. There were three barracks: A, B, and C, which housed about fifty boys in each. The dining hall and lounge were adjacent to the dorms. Across the quad from the dining hall was the gymnasium. Next to the gym was the building where classes were held and the administrative offices were located. Colonel Verbeck, the school commandant, had a two-story brick home across the street.

All the cadets were in uniform. I had been fitted for my military clothing at a tailor shop in Syracuse that handled all the needs of the school. We drove up to the administrative building where HK and Harriet accompanied me into the office. There I registered and was given my barracks assignment. I was told to report to Robert Smith, the master sergeant in charge. HK reminded me that this would be good for me, that I should work hard and above all, behave myself.

My mother started to get a little weepy, gave me a big hug, and said, "Be a good boy, Dick."

I went to my barracks, and they went to a luncheon for the parents at Colonel Verbeck's house.

When I got to the barracks, I was met at the door by Sergeant Smith, whose nickname was Trigger. He was

THE WHISKEY BOTTLE CONVERSATION

a senior and had been at the military academy practically all his life. His uncle was Secretary of State, a well-known man in the US government. Trigger and I seemed to hit it off almost immediately. He was a tall, clean-cut, handsome boy with blond hair and a good build. He ran the barracks, and if you didn't do as he ordered, he could make it tough on you. For example, he'd call bed check at nine thirty then check every bed. If your lights weren't off, he'd assign you latrine or KP duty.

About two weeks into the term, Trigger came in for bed check and asked me to come to his room.

We sat down, and he said, "I'd like to give you some advice about military life, Dick. There are certain things you need to do in order to move up in a military situation. First, you always address an upperclassman or instructor as 'sir.' I know, some of them don't deserve that respect, but it's expected. Always keep your uniform clean and pressed, your shoes shined, and try not to make waves. Discipline is the key."

We talked for about an hour, and when I left, I thanked him for his advice and said I would do my best to follow the military code.

There were many nights when I went to his room and we'd talk.

Once he said, "What's it like to have a family?"

Although I never asked him about it, apparently, he hadn't had any type of civilian or family life. I got the impression that he might have been the illegitimate son of the Secretary of State, the man he referred to as his uncle. Our conversations would sometimes run late into the night. I told him about my life, and he told me about his. It was a good exchange.

About a week after school started, I tried out for the football team. I didn't play football at Mexico, so I thought it might be fun to try a new sport. I made the team and was a receiver on offense and a linebacker on defense. I hated to get tackled. It wasn't that it hurt; it was the fact that someone could grab hold of me and bring me down. I did like tackling other people, though. Our team didn't do all that well, but I enjoyed playing. Near the end of the season, I twisted my knee, which sidelined me for the remaining few games.

Our classes, as far as academics, were the same as public school. Life on campus was definitely military! Each morning before breakfast, everyone assembled by barracks and had to stand at attention on the quad while the flag was raised. Our physical education classes consisted mostly of military drill. We would have to run in cadence around the campus. Behind the administration building was an obstacle course, which had a wall you had to climb over. We had to crawl under wire fencing that crisscrossed about two feet above the ground. There were ropes that you had to climb and ring a bell at the top. The classes were broken up into teams of ten cadets. The losing team through the obstacle course had to do some extra duty. Sometimes it was additional marching, or depending on the cadet in charge, some cleaning duties might be involved.

I found that I enjoyed the discipline, the standards, and the challenges that had to be met in a military environment.

* * *

THE WHISKEY BOTTLE CONVERSATION

"From what you've told me about your years at public school, that surprises me, Dick," I said.

"To be honest with you, it surprised me, Dave. It just goes to show, no matter what your preconceptions are, you never know what opportunities a new situation will offer!"

"So did you manage to stay out of trouble?" I asked.

Dick took a sip of his Scotch, smiled, and said, "Well, not entirely."

* * *

One day at lunch, some of the boys were bullshitting about their prowess at drinking and bars. You know how boys like to brag! Finally, one of the "big shots" asked me if I would like to take them down to one of the bars since I was from the area and knew my way around. I said if I could get Trigger to cover for us, I'd be happy to.

Trigger said, "I'll do my best, but if you get caught, you're on your own!"

That night after bed check, we gathered outside the dorm and I took four boys to a bar in downtown Manlius. We walked about a mile into town and went to this tavern. There was no age limit back then. If you had money and could reach the bar, they'd serve you. The four boys started drinking beer, and after a few bottles, they challenged each other to see who could do the most shots of whiskey. They all got roaring drunk. I stayed sober to make sure they got back in one piece.

After a couple of hours, they were beginning to get pretty sloppy—singing songs, spilling their drinks, basically becoming a nuisance to the other patrons.

I said, "It's time to go, men."

The walk back to school was quite a show. There was a full moon, so they decided to start howling and barking at it. One of them, right in the middle of one of his howls, threw up all over himself.

I tried to keep them all moving and was getting a little nervous about getting them back in the barracks. Just before we got to school, the kid who threw up decided to climb a tree, apparently trying to regain some of his pride. He got about six feet up and fell, landing on his back. The other boys were rolling on the ground laughing.

Finally, we got to the gates of school, and I stopped them.

I said, "You've got to shut your mouths, now. No noise! I don't want to get caught."

They all saluted me and said, "Yes, sir, General Leonard!" I got them all in their respective rooms without incident and went to bed.

I didn't give much thought to the episode until the next week when I was told to report to Colonel Verbeck's office. The colonel had apparently found out about the drunken night out and felt that I instigated the whole affair. I walked into his office, which was a walnut-paneled room with a big desk and a bookcase behind it. There was an American flag on a pole in the corner and World War I photos hung on the wall. The colonel was about sixty—short, heavy, and had a thin, manicured moustache.

I sat down in the chair in front of his desk.

"I didn't give you permission to sit down, Cadet Leonard!" he said. "Stand at attention!"

I stood up and saluted, "Yes, sir!"

THE WHISKEY BOTTLE CONVERSATION

He started in... "You've been kicked out of your local high school, and if you're not careful, you'll be booted out of here! This is a military academy. We expect discipline, and the rules and regulations are to be followed to the letter!"

He went on to say that my father had spent hundreds of dollars to send me here, and I obviously didn't give a damn. He lectured me for quite some time then dismissed me. It wasn't anything that I hadn't heard before.

This all happened just before Thanksgiving. I hoped that over the vacation, the colonel might relax a little bit. I asked Trigger if he would like to come home with me, and he was thrilled. The folks picked us up, and of course, they welcomed him with open arms. We had a ball. I wasn't home for five minutes and was out of my uniform. Trigger brought some civilian clothes with him. We both put our military uniforms away and went out on the town for Thanksgiving dinner.

Every Thanksgiving, Hoppy Smith's stepfather, Kurt Pond, put on a dinner of wild game. Kurt's bar and restaurant served a free feast of deer, rabbit, duck, and pheasant for all his regular customers.

Trigger had spent practically his whole life in a military institution, and for him to be able to do things that we took for granted was a really thrilling experience. Hoppy had filled his parents in on Trigger's life, so when we arrived at the restaurant, they made him feel like one of the boys. Trigger couldn't get over that. In fact, the whole experience of being in my home and the hospitality of the people in the community was just overwhelming to him.

When we returned from Thanksgiving vacation, I had been assigned to kitchen duty for my part in the drunken cadets' experience. I was to work breakfast and lunch every other day for a month.

Before each meal, we had to stand at attention and enter as a group. One day I wasn't scheduled to work, so I was out with the other cadets. An upperclassman, Sergeant Massiano—an Italian boy who was about six three and weighed about 220—came over to me and asked why I wasn't on KP duty. I told him I wasn't scheduled to work that day. He had the reputation of being a prick for harassing underclassmen, so nobody really liked him.

He said, "I don't care! You get into the mess and start scraping trays!"

I said, "Yes, sir!" As I began to walk in the building, he kicked me in the ass.

That was it! I turned around and punched him two or three times in the face. He backed up, surprised, and then took a couple of wild swings at me, and I ducked them. I swung at him and missed, and he hit me right square in the forehead. The punch picked me right off the ground, and I landed on my ass a couple of feet back. I could tell by the way he was swinging, he didn't know how to fight; but I knew, if he caught me with a couple of good blows from those pile-driving arms, I'd be in trouble.

I got up and squared off with him. He took a roundhouse swing that I ducked under and got behind him. I put my arm around his neck and gave him two good shots in the kidney before he grabbed my arm and threw me over his shoulder. He outweighed me by sixty pounds.

I got right up, and he charged, grabbing me in a bear hug. Our feet got tangled, and I fell straight backward, and he landed on top of me. That 220 pounds felt like two thousand when we hit the pavement. It knocked the wind out of me. He put his hands around my throat and started choking me.

He said, "I'll kill you! You bastard!" I tried to pull his hand away, but he was too strong.

I cupped my hands and smacked both his ears as hard as I could. He let go of my neck and grabbed his ears. I pushed him off and got up, still trying to catch my breath.

By now all the cadets were cheering, "Come on, Dick. Kick his ass! Give him a taste of his own medicine!"

I was madder than hell that he had tried to choke me! When he got up, I hit him right square in the nose. Blood gushed out. Then I hit him with a hard left and two quick rights. He started to stagger. So I gave him a roundhouse right that caught him over his right eye. There was another gush of blood, and he dropped like a ton of bricks. He was out cold.

All the boys were cheering and patting me on the back as I stood bent over with my hands on my knees. I was tired, and my back hurt, but I felt good. I ran my hands across my face to see if there was any blood, but there wasn't.

* * *

I was laughing and said, "Jesus, Dick! You were a tough son of a bitch! Maybe Gramp had a good plan for you after all!"

He looked at me but didn't say anything.
"What happened next?"

* * *

Well, Massiano was still on the pavement, unconscious, with blood running out of his nose and over his eye, so I told some of the boys to drag his sorry ass into the infirmary. I went into the mess and had lunch.

Just as I was finishing my meal, one of the upperclassmen came over and said, "Colonel Verbeck wants you in his office now, Leonard!"

I finished my meal then went to his office, walked in, and sat down in the chair. I still had blood all over my shirt.

He said, "I didn't give you permission to sit!"

And before he could say another word, I said, "I don't care, Colonel. I'm in the chair, and that's where I'm staying!"

He bristled, pointed his finger at me, and said, "You are a disgrace to the military establishment. You're a loner. You can't follow rules and regulations. I'm calling your father to come and get you because you are not fit to stay in this school!"

I said, "How would you know since you're not fit to run this school, *sir*!"

That "sir" really pissed him off! His face got red.

"Get out of my office, and pack your bags!" he shouted.

I never took any shit from anybody. I think that's why I always seemed to get in trouble.

I went back to my room, packed my bags, and told Trigger what had happened.

THE WHISKEY BOTTLE CONVERSATION

"I'm sorry you're leaving, Dick, but Massiano got what he deserved."

I told him he could come to Mexico anytime he wanted.

"I'd like that," he said.

A cadet came in and said that HK was on his way to get me.

* * *

"Were you nervous about seeing HK, Dick?"

"No. I didn't think I had done anything wrong. If that guy had come to me after formation was dismissed and told me to get into KP duty, there wouldn't have been a problem. But no, he had to make a scene and kick me in the ass. If I hadn't fought him, everyone would have thought I was a coward." Dick seemed almost angry as he was telling me this.

"What happened when Gramp got there?"

"He came up to the room and said, 'Get your bags and get in the car.'"

* * *

On the way home, he didn't say anything for about twenty minutes. Every once in a while, he'd give me a cold stare. I just turned my head and looked out the window.

Then he started in... "What in the hell is wrong with you, Dick? You've been kicked out of two schools in one year. I've spent all this money. I'm a respected man in the community."

I cut him off right there. I said, "It's always about you, isn't it? What about me? That guy kicked me in the ass for no good reason. What did you want me to do… turn tail and run? Do you want a coward for a son? Is that what you want?"

HK didn't say another word the rest of the way home. It was a long ride.

I was on restriction the rest of my junior year. All I could do was go to school and come home. No sports. That really hurt. HK told me if I didn't straighten up, more drastic measures would be taken. I got the impression a little time in jail might not be out of the question.

I really wasn't a bad boy. I just did things that I wanted to do, or if someone else had some wild idea, I would always volunteer to go along. We just seemed to get in trouble.

I managed to stay out of harm's way for the rest of the year. The new school wasn't completed yet, so I got to go around town because our classes were still in different buildings. I passed all my courses with high marks.

I worked for George and R. Austin that summer. A big event on town during the summer months was when the Mexico Band had concerts on Thursday evening. Glen Smith, the postmaster, was the band leader as well as the music instructor in the community. A group of the community volunteers would wheel out the band stand into the middle of Main Street. The band members were all decked out in their best dress.

It was a night when the farmers and the townsfolk would gather and the merchants kept their stores open.

THE WHISKEY BOTTLE CONVERSATION

Givos' Candy Kitchen, the A&P market, in fact, all the merchants were hustling their wares. The Ramsey's—with their men's and women's clothes—in fact, just about anything in household accessories were available at his store. Crandall's Pharmacy was always ready to serve its customers or give them good advice on medical problems. In fact, it was a good night for all.

Glen Smith, in his white band leader's outfit, would announce a song and then direct the band in its rendition. They would play until 9:00 p.m., and then the crowd would start to break up.

Harry Vorice, the town sheriff, always parked his car on the corner of Main and Church, right near the bandstand. He'd sit in his car usually for the entire performance. Earl Brown and Fuzzy Moore were the two barbers in town, and the barber shop was the place where things happened. They would think up little tricks that would take the town by storm.

One night, as the music played on, we carefully shoved a jack under the rear wheels of Harry's car and jacked the back end up so the car couldn't move. Then one of the barbers' friends told Harry about a fight down at Beck's Hotel. He started the car, put it in gear, and of course, it didn't move! The boys in the barber shop roared; in fact, it was the hit of the concert. Harry was embarrassed as hell.

Another time, there was this old gentleman that lived about a block from the barber shop. He had an outhouse. About the same time each day, he'd go and visit his little abode. Well, one day when he was nicely settled, a couple of the barbers' friends—myself included—sneaked up and pushed a piece of wood through the handle so he couldn't get out. Between the four of us, we had two poles that we put the outhouse on and carried it to the corner where the band usually sat. Needless to say, the gentleman inside his privy was in a rage. After a few minutes, we pulled the stick and let him out. The boys in the barbershop went wild. It was just a little fun on a summer's eve.

My senior year was full of activity. I was off home restriction and allowed to play sports again. I played soccer, basketball, and baseball. I was captain of the team in both soccer and basketball and named to the county all-star basketball team. I also served as president of the student council.

The new school wasn't finished yet, so we continued to take our classes at various places around town. Our English teacher—Tiger Lil, as we called her—put me on the committee to raise money for the yearbook. I had a '31 Chevy Coupe, so she would give me and some of my classmates time off to go sell advertisements. Our sales pitch was that the new school was still under construction and any money left over from the yearbook expenses would be donated to the school fund. We raised over two thousand dollars, which was a lot of money in 1938.

THE WHISKEY BOTTLE CONVERSATION

Dick taking a break from selling advertisements for the yearbook

For the most part, I managed to stay out of trouble. There was an incident with Bobby Bracy, who was a good friend, a little crazy but generally a nice guy. His father, Fred, owned a meat market and always gave you the choicest cuts of meat. Fred was a good six feet three and, according to rumor, had put a few men who crossed him in the hospital.

One New Year's Eve, Bobby asked him if he could take his car because we had dates in Parish, a neighboring town. Fred gave his permission but told us to drive carefully because it was snowing and the roads were slippery.

We started for Parish with Bobby driving. There were times when the snow would blow across the road so we couldn't see for a couple of seconds. As we were going down a hill just before coming into Parish, the wind whistled across the road in a whiteout. Bobby was driving carefully but got too far to the left and hit a snowbank. We went into a skid, and the car tipped over on its side! We slid down the road about twenty or thirty feet before it stopped! Bobby was scared to death—not because we tipped over, but because he had to go home and face his father, who would probably kick the shit out of him.

We climbed out of my side of the car and started to look over the situation. Neither of us were hurt—just scared! The car didn't look too bad, but we couldn't see the side it had tipped on. A few minutes later, another car came along with two men in it. They offered their help, and the four of us tipped the car back up on its wheels. It was banged up, but Bobby started it, and it seemed to run all right. They followed us into Parish.

Bobby got some oil and put it in the engine; the gas was okay. We drove to pick up the girls, but when they saw the car and we told them what had happened, they said they couldn't go with us. We decided to find someone who could help us straighten the car up. Needless to say, it was a futile effort, so we ended up in Kirk Pond's restaurant.

Many of our friends were there to offer their condolences and to go out to see the condition of the car. Of course, we got all kinds of advice, which didn't help one bit! We stayed around, had a couple of beers, and decided to head for home and probably a good thrashing from Bobby's father.

THE WHISKEY BOTTLE CONVERSATION

I told Bobby I would stand outside with a ball bat, and when Fred started to give him a beating, I'd try to protect him. Bobby went inside and told Fred what happened. He grabbed him, and instead of beating Bobby, he gave him a hug and started crying. Mrs. Bracy was crying, so I sneaked off the porch and walked the three blocks to my home.

The next morning I went to see Fred and got the same treatment. He called me Lucky Teeter, a well-known race car driver in those days. Fred gave me a hug, and then I told him what had happened. He said he didn't care about the car—just that the two of us were all right. I wish HK had had a little of Fred's compassion.

Near the end of the year, when graduation was rapidly approaching, Tiger Lil decided that because I was president of the student council, I should write the class prophecy. The school wasn't quite finished, but the Board of Education felt that the graduation exercises should be held in the new auditorium.

Graduation night, the auditorium was full of parents and townspeople interested in seeing the new school. After some lengthy speeches by dignitaries, board members, and the principal, I was introduced to read the class prophecy.

* * *

I told Dick to hold that thought for a moment and I would be right back. I went up to my room and got the box of letters and other memorabilia my grandmother had given me. I brought it back to the study and set it on the coffee table between us.

"What's that?" he asked.

"It's your life."

I had never told him that Mimi had given me these treasures. I opened the box and pulled out his yearbook.

"Does this look familiar?"

"Where did you get that, Dave?"

"That's another story I'll tell you about later."

I got up and put some ice in Dick's glass and poured him some more Scotch. I handed it to him and said, "I think you're going to enjoy this."

He said, "Going to? I've been enjoying this ever since you opened that bottle!"

We both laughed… laughed really hard. The Scotch was beginning to work its magic. I sat down, opened the book, and found the class prophecy that he had written.

I began to read…

Class Prophecy of 1938

> Swiftly and steadily the houseboat moves down the river of time and progress, carrying with it the lucky and ambitious but alas, leaving behind the failures and unfortunates. As visitors let us hop aboard the houseboat, we observe the success and failures of the members of the graduating class of '38.
>
> Let us start the journey with a roar of laughter, for the first person or persons we see are Mr. and Mrs. Charles Homer Ames. Mrs. Ames is the former Eloise Wood. "Charles, Black-Boy, life of the party," Ames is now a noted comedian who is praised for his

natural acting. We learn that the credit for his great success should be given to his beautiful wife.

Continuing on down the river we are attracted by a large but cozy home. In the front yard we notice a sign which reads "Dr. R. C. Backus, Surgeon." Through all these years Charles has remained single. We wonder if that is why he gets so much business.

As the current carries us onward, our attention is drawn to a large new public library, which we are told is dedicated to those three capable librarians—Miss Beatrice Bellinger, Miss Dorothy Southworth, and Miss Estella Fravor. It was through their combined efforts that the library was built in Mexico. We take off our hats to these notable citizens.

Moving on down the deep, blue highway of the future, our ears are blessed with the irresistible rhythms of that well-known swing master, Robert Bracy and his Wonder Band. We also wonder! It had been reported that the rhythm king plans to wed his famous piano player and singer Grace Moore. Congratulations!

Progressing down the eternal river we come upon a fine prosperous looking farm. The name on the mailbox reads Mr. and Mrs. James LiCourt. Mrs. LiCourt is better known to us as Lois Loucks. On this farm they specialize in raising pigs.

Moving down our waterway of life we are confronted with a small but comfortable looking bungalow, where we learn Richard P. Leonard lives with his wife. We don't wish to say anything out of the way but we have heard Richard lives on his *wife's earnings. He claims to be a clever speaker and occasionally he bluffs some club into paying him a few dollars for an after dinner speech. Poor Richard, he met his downfall in History C.*

Oh, but let us move on away from this spot. Next we come upon a beauty shoppe where we find that coiffure stylist Robert Bourlier massaging the face of a lovely woman. (I guess he hasn't lost that certain touch.) Well, well, if it isn't Jeanette Kellogg. Jeanette inherited her father's monument works and is making quite a success of it. Jeanette always could slay 'em.

Leaving the beauty salon we came upon a very fine-looking billiard parlor. Entering, we find Cornelius Leary, the owner. As I remember, Cor was pretty clever with the cue, especially in prize speaking.

Next we see on our journey down the river a first-class shoe repair shop and lo and behold if Lilly Tagliareni isn't running it. She must have learned the trade from her father. Well, the job just fits Lilly because she always had a good time shooing away the men.

It certainly beats all how these women have taken over the men's work. For example, here we find a law office and believe it or not inside is Margaret Row, one of the best women lawyers in the country. We remember back in History class when she used to evade answering questions so cleverly the teacher thought she was good in the subject.

THE WHISKEY BOTTLE CONVERSATION

We have not gone far when we see a very shy but pretty school marm ringing the old country bell to call the children to class. As we come closer we see that this girl is none other than Pauline Harmes. We wouldn't mind being pupils ourselves, would we boys?

Leaving the country school we behold a large white hospital. Who is in this building that we know? Well, if it isn't Virginia Henry, a nurse. What's that you say fellow? Oh, you feel sick?

Dusk is starting to fall so let tie our houseboat up and stay at a hotel for the night. Here this looks like a suitable place. You all wait here a minute and we will make reservations with the manger. Opening the manager's office door who should we see sitting there with his feet on the desk, but Gerald Moot. And to think "Gramp" started out here as a mere bellboy.

Arising bright and early we board our faithful houseboat and again start on our way down the river of tomorrow. Gliding swiftly and smoothly along the water we notice a large herd of handsome cattle and stopping to inquire we find that these belong to our good friend Donald Row. We are glad Donald made a successful farmer.

Our journey is nearly over and it is nearly time for us to leave our houseboat and our river of time and progress. But before we go let us visit Bob Jones, at his super service gas station where he is working under a car. "Why Robert, you shouldn't get so mad.

Let's see that smile that makes all the girls trade here. That's better."

Mexico—slow down to two knots per hour—and here we are back in our home town. Now our journey is at an end, so our undertaker, Newton Miner, can bury it! Here we shall leave the houseboat. But even though we do get off, the boat still follows the tide of life, picking up the lucky and ambitious and leaving behind the failures and the unfortunates.

Richard Leonard

Dick had been staring into the fire with a slight smile on his face while I read the class prophecy.

"Those were some pretty insightful thoughts for a bad boy troublemaker," I said.

"They were a good group of kids," Dick said. "I think there were twenty-five in our graduating class. After the ceremonies we had a party."

"Tell me about that," I said.

* * *

Well, after receiving our diplomas, numerous handshakes and hugs, the whole class came over to my house for a party. HK and Harriet agreed to spend the evening with friends, so we had the place to ourselves.

We rolled up all the rugs in the living room and had a dance band that played through the night. It was quite an event, having a ten-piece band at our party. The girls baked

THE WHISKEY BOTTLE CONVERSATION

cookies and made ice cream. We didn't have any alcohol in the house because I promised my folks we wouldn't. Some of the boys brought some booze and got a little high. Everybody in the class came and danced. Some of them went out to the cars and had a good time. It was a typical graduation party.

That summer I continued with my part-time jobs and basically just relaxed and enjoyed myself. Sometimes I would spend an evening in the men's club. Benny Burke's father was a bootlegger and owned the club in Mexico right across from Beck's Hotel. It was a house that Mr. Burke had converted. There was a bar, one pool, and two billiard tables. It was a big open room with tables and chairs around the outside walls. You could get any kind of sandwich you wanted. Club members would shoot pool, play cards, smoke their cigars, and generally fraternize with each other. No women were allowed.

One Saturday, when Mr. Burke was out making one of his runs, a group of us got together at the club. We spent the afternoon drinking, shooting pool, and playing cards. As the afternoon wore on into the evening, one of the boys suggested we go to Sandy Pond and go roller-skating.

Sandy Pond was a summer hangout on Lake Ontario that had beautiful white sand beaches. There was a roller-skating rink there that opened after Memorial Day and stayed in operation until Labor Day weekend. We took a couple of bottles of booze and drove to the rink. It was a large rectangular building with hardwood floors. There was a mirrored ball in the center of the rink that reflected the different-colored lights on the floor as the resident organ player would give his rendition of the popular tunes of the time. We spent a couple of hours skating, talking, and occasional hit off our bottles of whiskey.

Across the road from the rink was a bar called Pete's Pavilion. There was a long bar with tables and chairs scattered around the room. At the end of the room was an open doorway that went into the pavilion. Pete used this for dances, covered dish suppers, and on Saturday nights, he'd set up a ring and have wrestling matches. The boys and I decided to go over and watch the wrestling for a while.

This particular night the place was packed. There was good down-and-out wrestling. We sat on the right-hand side, more or less at ring level. We had been drinking most of the day, so all of us had a good buzz on. Benny would take some of his bootleg whiskey, pour it in our beers, and we'd throw it down. We were cheering and hollering for whomever we wanted to win.

Every match would have a house wrestler that would challenge anyone who wanted to come up and wrestle. This fellow Rusty Scranton came out and got in the ring. He was probably six or seven years older than me. He had a nice build. Rusty would walk around the ring, flex his muscles, and challenge anyone to take him on.

Benny stood up and yelled, "We've got someone to fight you! Leonard will take you on!"

I pulled Benny back down in his seat and told him to shut his mouth.

After Benny's drunken declaration, all the boys started shouting, "Leonard, Leonard" and soon the whole crowd joined in. Before I knew it, some of the boys picked me up and threw me into the ring.

I told the referee I didn't have any trunks.

THE WHISKEY BOTTLE CONVERSATION

The owner said, "Don't worry, son, we've got trunks for you."

Of course, I was pretty well looped myself. They took me out into the back room and gave me a pair of shorts. I had boxer underwear on that hung down below the shorts, and I was barefoot.

I came out to the ring, and all the guys thought it was hilarious.

Benny called out, "Nice underwear, Leonard! Where are your slippers?"

They had the whole crowd cheering and hollering. So I walked around the ring and flexed my muscles, just like Rusty had. The more I flexed, the more they cheered.

When I was in high school, we had this athletic instructor, Ed Louis, who had won the National Wrestling Championship in college. He gave lessons to any of the boys in school who were interested. I took maybe a year or more of lessons, so I had some knowledge of the sport.

The referee got into the ring, called us over, and gave us the rules—which were basically, "Don't kill each other!"

We started wrestling, and I figured the best thing for me to do would be to stay away and kind of feel him out. I just moved around a little when he grabbed me, picked me right up over his head, and started to spin. He threw me down on the mat and knocked one of my front teeth out. Of course, everybody was screaming and hollering.

One of the boys yelled, "Tie him up with your boxers, Dick!"

I spit my tooth out and yelled back, "Thanks for the support, fellas!"

When I got up from the mat, he grabbed me again and spun around and threw me down for the second time. Suddenly, I realized this guy was serious! When I hit the mat the second time, I got pissed off. I got up, walked up to him, spit in my hand, and slapped him across the face. He went crazy and charged at me. I sidestepped and threw him right out of the ring. He climbed back in while I retreated to the other side. When he charged again, I pulled the same move, and out of the ring he went.

After the second time, he just lost all his senses. I knew that if he ever got ahold of me, it would be curtains. The minute he stepped back in the ring, I grabbed him, got him to the mat, and pinned him until the referee made the count of 3. I got up, shook Rusty's hand, and paraded around the ring, flexing my muscles, smiling with a gaping hole where my front tooth used to be.

The boys all started chanting, "Champ, champ, champ!"

When we got into the back room to change, Rusty was complaining of his side hurting. I said I'd see if there was a doctor in the crowd. There wasn't a doctor, but a fellow that had some medical training checked Rusty over and said we should take him to the hospital. The owner of the bar got someone to drive him to Oswego. A few days later we found out he had a rupture. A couple of us went to see him, and we became good friends.

When I got home that night, the Burgesses were visiting my parents. They saw I was missing a tooth, and HK wanted to know what had happened. I told him the story and said that I was now the champ and was going to take Rusty's place.

THE WHISKEY BOTTLE CONVERSATION

He said, "Like hell, you are!"

Dr. Burgess, the family dentist, volunteered to put a false tooth in. That was the beginning and the end of my professional wrestling career.

* * *

"You are really something, Dick!" I said. "Did you ever lose a fight?"

He looked squarely at me and said, "Never!"

"Well, all this fighting has made me hungry," I said. "How about you?"

"Starved!" he said. "You know, I've got to keep my strength up just in case I have to kick somebody's ass!"

He stood up and made some boxing moves, shuffled his feet, which caused him to lose his balance. He fell back in the chair. Maybe it was the Scotch, not the shuffling, but in any event, his display was comical. I just shook my head and laughed.

"I'll go heat us up some of Mary's stew. You just take it easy, Champ."

I walked out of the room, down the hall, laughing all the way to the kitchen.

I turned on the stove and got some bread and buttered it. I poured us two glasses of milk, figuring if we were going to last the day, we had better get a good base to absorb some of the J&B. when the stew was ready, I filled two bowls, put them on a tray with our bread, milk, and the four remaining oatmeal cookies, and returned to the study.

When I walked in, I saw that Dick had moved from the chair to the leather couch. He was covered with a red fleece blanket and was sound asleep. He had fed the fire, so I sat there and enjoyed my lunch. When I finished, I went back to the kitchen, put Dick's stew back in the pot, and left the stove on simmer. I covered the bread and put his glass of milk in the refrigerator. While he slept, I decided to take the dogs for a walk.

I put on my CarHart suit, Dick's mittens, and his ski hat. As I was getting ready, the dogs were anxiously jumping at the door. The storm seemed to be at a lull. The sky was dark, and the large flakes were still falling at a slow steady pace.

When I opened the door, the dogs bolted out on the porch and down the steps, barking and playfully chasing each other around. The snow was almost up to my knees, but it was light and fluffy. As I walked around the house and down the driveway, the tall cedar trees, covered in white, looked like giant ice cream cones.

The dogs would run ahead, then turn around, and race back, barking as if to say, "Come on, Dave. Let's play."

Mort was a little poodle-sized mutt that had to follow in the trail of Sheeba and Maisy. If he went off on his own, all you could see were a set of ears occasionally popping out of the snow.

The four of us walked about a half a mile down the road to the neighbor's farm. The scenery was spectacular with the trees, mountains, and ground covered in a blanket of white.

On the way back, we left the road and walked through the meadow. At one point, I lay down in the snow, staring up at the dark gray sky. I had always enjoyed the sensation of lying in deep snow. There was something very serene about it. I opened my mouth and tried to catch flakes as they fell. Sheeba, the collie, came over and licked my face then lay down next to me. Mort and Maisy soon joined her. I felt happy and fortunate to be spending this day with my father, reliving with him the stories he was sharing with me. I lay there quite some time until the snow began to fall at a much faster rate and there were gusts of wind coming out of the north. The lull was over.

When I got back in the house, Dick was in the kitchen, eating some stew.

"How is it out there?" he asked.

"Beautiful, Dick. The dogs and I walked down to the next farm then lay in the snowbank for about a half an hour."

He smiled.

"The wind is beginning to pick up," I said. "I think the storm is ready for round 2. Pretty good stew, isn't it?"

"I didn't realize how hungry I was," he said. "This is my second bowl."

I sat down at the table and had a couple of cookies while he did the dishes.

When he finished, he said, "Well, after a little nap and a good meal, I'm ready to get back to my story."

We returned to the study, the comfort of our chairs, and the warmth of the roaring fire.

CHAPTER SIX

South of the Mason Dixon Line

"So, Dick, had you given any thought about what you wanted to do after high school?"

* * *

I decided I wanted to take a trip to Florida. I had heard about the beautiful beaches and sunshine. It seemed like a good destination that would take me along the entire East Coast. I wanted to get away from home and see the world, so to speak.

I had a V8 Model A Ford with a rumble seat, but I needed a trailer for supplies and a place to sleep. Your great-grandfather, Pop, had moved to Mexico and had a little farm outside of town. He raised chickens and did light carpentry work. I used to visit him quite often. Once I had made my decision, I went to him and asked if he could help me build a trailer.

He said, "Get me an axle and a set of wheels, and I think we can put something together."

I went to Freddie Jones's junkyard and found the frame from an old wagon. It was about six feet wide and eight feet long with a wooden floor. I got an axle with wheels off an old cattle truck. Freddie let me borrow his truck to take them back to Pop's house. We took some long U-bolts that I had taken off the cattle truck and bolted the axle to the wagon frame. It fit perfectly.

Then Pop built a wooden frame, which was about five feet high and the same size as the wagon bed. We bolted it on and covered three sides with pine clapboards to keep the weight down. The roof was wooden boards covered with canvas that we painted to keep it nice and dry inside. It was big enough for a mattress and shelves for supplies. The back door was the width of the trailer, and when you raised it up, two wooden poles on hinges dropped down, which then acted as a canopy. It was a pretty neat trailer. In fact, I was thrilled, and Pop was delighted as well. George Young helped me build a hitch and attach it to the car.

I licensed it and drove around, taking short trips to get the feel of how it handled. I decided that I'd like to have someone go with me. A friend of mine, Bingo Keno, was an Italian boy that had a barbershop in town. He was a couple of years older than me. Bingo was short and stocky with black hair that he parted in the middle and combed straight back. He always had some type of oil or tonic in his hair, so it was nice and shiny.

Bingo was from Oswego, and I had met him before he set up his shop in Mexico. Some Sundays I would go to the Italian section of Oswego and roll dice or play cards with the boys. Even though I wasn't one of the locals, I got along fine with them. Bingo had served as an apprentice to his uncle, a barber in that section of town. One Sunday he told me that he wanted to set up his own shop. I told him the barber in Mexico was going to retire and maybe he should check into it. Bingo and Mr. Moore struck a deal, and in a few months, he was running his own shop.

One afternoon I stopped by to get my hair cut. As he was trimming away, I said, "I'm going to take a trip to Florida, and if I could get someone to go, I'd take them along."

Bingo said, "Sounds like fun! When are you going to leave?"

I said, "I'm not sure, but why don't you think it over? If you decide to go, we'll set a date."

When he finished, I went to pay him, and he said, "This one's on me. I'll let you know in a few days."

Now that there was a good chance someone was going along, I began to get excited and anxious about leaving. I picked up a map and studied the route we would take. I had worked pretty steady for R. Austin and George that summer, so I had maybe twenty-five or thirty dollars saved.

* * *

I interrupted Dick. "You were going to Florida with thirty dollars?"

He said, "That was quite a bit of money back then. Gas was only ten cents, and I filled the rumble seat with headlights and parts off cars that I figured I could swap for food or gas."

THE WHISKEY BOTTLE CONVERSATION

"You were an enterprising soul, Dick. I'll give you that!"

* * *

Two days later, Bingo stopped by the house.

"When are we leaving?" he asked with a smile.

We made plans to leave in a week. It was the end of August. The next day I drove Bingo into Oswego to see his parents and tell them of his plans. While we were in town, we ran into a buddy of his, named Sam Christafolie. Bingo told Sam about our trip to Florida, and he wanted to know if he could go. That made three in the front seat.

I said, "It's going to be a little crowded, but if you want to go, get your things together and we'll pick you up Friday morning." Both he and Bingo were delighted.

Harriet and the mothers of Sam and Bingo gave us all the canned goods we could carry in the trailer. They each had about the same amount of money that I did. We picked Sam up early Friday morning and headed south.

We took our time because the roads were dirt and gravel. Fifty miles an hour was the top speed for towing the trailer. We'd drive for a couple hundred miles, find a field to park for the night, make a fire, and cook dinner. We took turns sleeping in the trailer. Two of us could fit fairly comfortably on the mattress, and the third would curl up in a sleeping bag under the awning. We bought some mosquito netting to wrap around the awning to keep the bugs out. It worked pretty well.

The first major town we stopped in was Philadelphia. Bingo suggested that we go to the Italian section. We found that part of town without much trouble. Bingo, Sam, and I walked around the streets, and they would speak to people in Italian. I didn't have a clue what they were saying, but after a few introductions, Bingo said, "We've got a place to park our trailer, Dick."

This older fellow walked back to the car with us and rode on the running boards, giving Bingo directions, which he translated for me. In no time, we were behind a big tenement house that had clothes hanging on lines strung from the fire escape to windows. Bingo and Sam went inside with the gentleman, while I set up the trailer. A number of curious kids and some adults came around back and started asking me questions. At least, I assumed they were questions. They spoke in Italian, so I couldn't understand a thing they said!

Bingo and Sam returned and told me their newfound friend, Marco, had invited us for dinner.

"You're going to get a real Italian meal tonight, Dick!"

I said, "Home cookin' will be a welcome change from our campfire dinners!"

"Amen!" Bingo said.

After we got the trailer situated, we walked around the neighborhood. Bingo and Sam would introduce themselves. The people were very friendly. Every once in a while, amidst the flowing Italian, I would hear my name. I was glad they were including me in their discussions.

We went up to Marco's apartment about five thirty and entered to the tantalizing smell of spaghetti sauce and garlic. Sam introduced me to Marco, his wife, and their four children.

THE WHISKEY BOTTLE CONVERSATION

I just shook their hands and said, "Hello," and smiled a lot. It was a small two-bedroom apartment that was very cramped but also very clean.

Marco, Sam, Bingo, and I sat at the table while Anna served us. She put a plate of spaghetti and meatballs in front of me that looked like Mount Everest. There were three loaves of bread and two bottles of wine on the table. Sam, Bingo, and Marco spent the next two hours talking, laughing, tearing off chunks of bread, and soaking it in their sauce before devouring it.

I had all I could do to finish my plate of spaghetti. As soon as I was done, Anna put another in front of me. I smiled, put my hands on my stomach, and shook my head.

She said, "Mangia, Mangia. Eat! You, skinny!"

I couldn't insult our hosts, so slowly but surely, I managed to finish what she had brought me.

After dinner, Marco brought out those short Italian cigars and offered one to each of us. Sam and Bingo took theirs, but I politely said no. Marco shrugged his shoulders.

They talked for a while when Bingo said, "We're going to play some cards. You want to join in, Dick?"

I said, "I'm feeling a bit heavy. I think I'll go for a walk and get some fresh air."

Both he and Sam laughed. I got up, shook Marco's hand, and went into the kitchen to thank Anna. I left and walked around the neighborhood for a while then returned to the trailer.

The next morning I told Bingo and Sam that I wanted to go see the Constitution and the Liberty Bell. They said they had made plans to spend the day with Marco. I went into the center of town and found the museum where the Constitution was kept. It was in a glass case.

I remember thinking, "What a magnificent-looking document!" The handwriting was beautiful, and I got goose bumps as I read the signatures.

I spent the rest of the day taking in historical sights of Philadelphia. When I returned to the trailer, Sam and Bingo were on the front steps of the tenement, talking to some girls. I told them I wanted to get back on the road tomorrow. I could see that they were enjoying themselves, but I didn't want to get bogged down in one place too long. The next morning we hooked the trailer back up and headed out of town. Sam and Bingo talked all that day about their newfound friends.

We kept a steady pace for the next few days, taking turns driving and camping out at night. Whenever we saw a pond or some body of water, we would stop and swim, wash up, and be on our way. It wasn't until we were in the Blue Ridge Mountains of West Virginia that we made an extended stop.

We were driving along, enjoying the scenery, when I saw a farmer out in his field cutting hay. In the barnyard, there were some chickens, pigs, and a few milk cows. I pulled into the yard.

Bingo asked, "Why are we stopping here?"

I said, "See those pigs and chickens? That means ham and eggs! Maybe we can help this guy with his hay and get some good grub for a few days."

Bingo smiled. "You're always thinkin', Dick."

THE WHISKEY BOTTLE CONVERSATION

I walked out in the field and introduced myself. I told him with my best Southern accent that I was raised in Georgia but had been up North for a few years.

"Damn Yankees!" he said.

I repeated his words, "Damn Yankees!"

The farther South we got, the more apparent it became that most of the folks south of the Mason Dixon line were still bitter about losing the Civil War.

I said, "My two friends and I are on our way to Florida. We would be glad to give you a hand with your hay in exchange for a few good meals and a place to park our trailer."

He looked over at the car and then looked me up and down. He stuck out his hand.

"Josh is my name, and I could sure use a hand. Ain't got no sons… just two daughters. Park your trailer over there on the other side of the barn."

I walked back to the car and said, "Well, boys, you're gonna be farmers for a few days. I told him we all grew up in Georgia, so no Italian. Whenever he asks you something, say, 'Hell, yes!' or 'Hell, no!' and try and talk like this." I gave them my Southern drawl. We all laughed.

As we set up the trailer, I could see someone peeking out the window at us. When I would look, they would move their heads back. As soon as we got settled, I took Sam and Bingo out in the field and introduced them to Josh.

He said, "You boys ever done any farmin'?"

"Hell, yes!" they both said at the same time. I had all I could do to keep from laughing.

Josh told Bingo to go to the barn and get three more sickles. He was a rugged man, probably in his fifties, with curly brown hair and a weather-beaten face. His hands were about twice the size of mine, and his shoulders were stooped—definite evidence of what life on a West Virginia farm was like.

Bingo came back with the sickles, and we began swinging our blades, cutting the tall grass. It was a hot day, so it wasn't long before the three of us had our shirts off, sweating under the West Virginia sun. It felt good.

* * *

I wanted to ask Dick where in West Virginia he was, but he seemed to be enjoying his recollections and the story was flowing smoothly, so I didn't interrupt him.

* * *

At one point I stopped to catch my breath, and I saw two teenage girls on the front porch, watching us. It looked like they were whispering to each other, then they would laugh.

We worked alongside Josh until about four.

He said, "That's enough for today. There's a pump in front of the house if you boys want to clean up. My wife will have dinner at five. Put your sickles back in the barn."

We put our blades away, went to the trailer, and got a bucket and some soap.

I filled the bucket with the cold water and poured it over my head. It felt great! Bingo and Sam took turns doing

THE WHISKEY BOTTLE CONVERSATION

the same. After washing up, we went back to the trailer to dry off and change our clothes.

At five we went up to the house and knocked on the door.

"Come on in, boys."

When I walked in, Josh was sitting at the table, and his wife was cooking at the stove. It smelled like pork. I didn't see the girls. His wife turned around as we entered.

"This is my wife, Sarah," Josh said.

She said, "Hello," in a sweet Southern voice. "Come on out, girls. I don't want to have to introduce everybody twice."

The bedroom door opened, and out came two lovely girls. They both had on sundresses that looked to be handmade.

"These are my daughters, Emma Jane and Billie. This is Dick, Sam, and Bill."

"That's Bingo," Bingo said.

"Bingo! That's kind of funny name, ain't it?" Josh asked.

"Hell, yes. It is!" Bingo retorted. "I don't know what my Maw was thinkin'!"

The girls giggled.

I could see that spending the day listening to Josh, Bingo's accent was improving.

* * *

"Both Emma and Billie had long, thick curly brown hair with blue eyes and shapely figures," said Dick with a smile.

"Nothing like those West Virginian farmer's daughters!" I said.

He continued…

* * *

We sat down at the table, and Sarah brought over a pork roast, a big bowl of potatoes, and a fresh pitcher of milk. During the course of our dinner, I asked Josh how long he had been on the farm.

"I was born right here in this room, just like those two youngins there. This was my Pappy's place. He fought with the Blue Ridge Mountain Boys in '63. My Maw died when I was born, and Pappy passed on in '21 from consumption."

I told Josh how I was brought up on a farm in Georgia. Once in a while, my accent would slip and he'd look at me.

I said, "That's what happens when you spend a few years with those 'damn Yankees.'"

Bingo chimed in, "Damn Yankees!"

After our meal, we thanked Josh and Sarah and retired for the evening.

Bingo and Sam slept in the trailer, and I slept out on the ground. When I got up the next morning, Emma and Billie were out at the pump, filling a bucket of water. They saw me and came over.

"Nice car," Emma said as they walked around it and looked inside. "We don't see many boys come 'round here, especially ones that's got a car! We ain't never been in a car before. Have we, Billie?"

"Sure haven't," Billie said.

THE WHISKEY BOTTLE CONVERSATION

The girls didn't seem quite so shy when their folks weren't around.

Emma said, "Suppose you could take us for a ride sometime, Dick?"

I said, "I'll have to ask your dad, but if he says it's okay, I'd love to take you ladies for a ride!"

They both giggled and went back to their chores.

I got Sam and Bingo up just as Josh called us in for breakfast. Sarah had a platter of bacon and eggs waiting. After eating we went out in the field and cut hay until about noon. Billie brought out some water and smoked ham sandwiches. After lunch Josh hooked up his team of horses to a wagon, and we spent the rest of the day loading the hay and taking it to the barn. I think Josh enjoyed having some males around, and I know he was happy to be getting his hay in.

At dinner that evening, I said to Josh, "Emma and Billie told me they've never been in a car before. Would you mind if I took them for a ride some afternoon?"

He looked at the girls, and they looked down at their plates. Josh sat there for a minute, chewing on his bread.

He was still looking at them when he said, "Well, since there's a car right here, I guess it wouldn't hurt nothin' if they went for a ride."

Emma and Billie looked at each other and smiled, but they didn't say anything.

The next day we followed the same routine: cutting hay in the morning and pitching it on the wagon in the afternoon.

About three Josh said, "Dick, you go clean up, and if you wanna' take them youngins for a ride, the boys and I will finish up here. Bingo and Sam looked like they were going to cry.

I went over to the pump, filled a bucket, and dumped it over my head. After I had dried off, I went back to the house. The girls were on the porch.

"Are you ladies ready?"

They jumped off the porch and ran over to the car and got in. I started it up and took off down the road through the West Virginia countryside. Emma sat next to me. They were like two little kids, laughing and whispering to each other.

"Can you go faster?" Billie asked I pushed the pedal to the floor and got it up to about 65.

Billie had her head out the window. I took Emma's hands and put them on the steering wheel. She did pretty well until we came to a curve and she turned the wheel too hard. Off through the fields we went. I was laughing, and they were screaming.

We drove around the back roads for about an hour. On the way back, Billie and Emma were whispering again.

Finally, Emma moved closer to me and said, "Me and Billie ain't never been with no boys before."

"Is that so? Why don't you two come visit with us by the fire tonight after your folks go to bed?"

Billie said, "Sure! That sounds like fun!"

That night and every night after that, Billie and Emma came down to our fire.

* * *

THE WHISKEY BOTTLE CONVERSATION

"Bingo and I got to know the girls real well," Dick said with a wink. "Sam wasn't so lucky."

"How long did you stay at the farm?" I asked.

"We were there a week. I hated to leave the warm hospitality of those two Southern belles, but I thought Josh was getting a little suspicious. I didn't want to end up looking down the barrel of a shotgun."

* * *

We had out most of the hay and put in the barn. I was getting the itch to be back on the road, so I told Josh we would be leaving early the next morning. That night Sarah fixed a delicious baked-ham dinner. Josh told us what a help we had been to him and he was sorry to see us leave. Emma and Billie got a horrified look on their faces. We hadn't told them yet.

That night after Josh and Sarah had gone to bed, the girls came out to see us.

Emma said, "You don't have to leave now. You can stay as long as you want."

Billie was crying. "You could take us with you. We could ride in the trailer, and we would cook and do all your cleanin'."

I said, "Your ma and pa need you two here. Ridin' in a closed-up trailer ain't no way for ladies to travel." They cried some more. "When we come back, we'll try to stop and see you all again."

Emma came over and sat on my lap and put her arms around me. "I'm gonna miss you, Dick."

"I'll miss you too, darlin'," I said.

I held her for a long time. Billie and Bingo had gone for a walk. We left at sunrise the next morning.

I talked it over with the boys, and we decided our next stop would be Washington. The further South we got, the worse the roads were, so we didn't make very good time. When we arrived in Washington, we found the Italian section. In no time Bingo and Sam found us a place to park our trailer. We decided to stay for a while, so Bingo set up shop to cut hair under the trailer awning, and Sam got a job at the local grocery store. I toured the city.

I spent a couple of days at the Congress, listening to the debates and spending time in the library. I sat in the visitors' gallery, watching our government in action. I was impressed with the respect the men showed for each other. I toured the Lincoln Memorial. Abraham Lincoln was one of my heroes. I had read his speeches and all the books about him. What I admired most was that this simple backwoods farm boy transformed a nation through his determination and a belief in the just causes of freedom and equality for all men. I spent an entire morning there, sitting on the steps, talking with people, and enjoying the warm September sun. During the week we spent in DC, I went to the White House, the Washington Monument, and the Smithsonian. It was a fantastic city filled with the history of our country, the struggles of the past, and the promise of a future fueled by democratic ideals.

Bingo and Sam were content to stay in the Italian section. I did manage to get them out on a couple of days.

THE WHISKEY BOTTLE CONVERSATION

I shamed them by saying, "You're in the nation's capital, and you can't take some time to see what it's all about? That's why your parents came to this country... Freedom, democracy, and opportunity brought them here! We're right in the center of it, boys! Show some pride! You're Americans!"

Just as I finished my little speech, a man came up to Bingo and asked him, in Italian, for a haircut.

I laughed and said, "America, 'The Melting Pot'!"

* * *

Dick raised his glass and took a sip.

* * *

We decided after leaving Washington that because the natives were getting less friendly the further south we went, we would continue straight through to Florida. We took turns driving and only stopped for gas and to sleep at night.

Florida was just small country towns. The roads were built by laying logs down in the sand and then covering them with gravel. It was quite swampy, and this technique helped keep the cars from sinking in. The car, it seemed, was always jumping. Just outside of Palm Beach, the hitch broke off, and we had to leave the trailer in someone's yard. We drove to a small town and found a blacksmith. He put the hitch back on and did a really good job fixing it.

Once we got the trailer fixed, we continued our journey to Miami. When we arrived, we drove around, looking for a place to set up, and after some searching, stopped at a railroad yard. We thought we could get a shower at the facilities for the men who worked at the yard. I went into the station and asked the station master if he would mind us parking our trailer there out of harm's way. He was an accommodating fellow and showed me where to park it.

"Feel free to use the showers, boys," he said.

We got the trailer situated and drove in to town. Miami, at the time, had a population of about thirty thousand. The streets were gravel, and most of the buildings were one- or two-story structures. There were a few hotels that might have been three or four stories. The beaches were beautiful. The white sand extended for as far as the eye could see in either direction.

After driving around for an afternoon, Sam and Bingo wanted to go to the Italian section. We found it, and they immediately struck up conversation with some of the local residents. In a few days, Bingo was cutting hair, and Sam got a job on a produce farm. I didn't work. I went to the beach, swam a lot, and read books I picked up at the local library. I was a Southern gentleman.

We lived out of the trailer with the door propped up and a few chairs we had found. The trains bothered us a little, but we put up with them. Every day the boys would go into the Italian section, and every now and then I would go with them. We got along great. They were both making money, and I would swap some parts I still had when I needed cash. We made enough to keep us living well.

After about a month, the station master came over and told us we'd have to move our trailer. I decided that we should probably head back North so that we could be home for Christmas.

THE WHISKEY BOTTLE CONVERSATION

We didn't do much sightseeing on our return trip. I think we were getting a little road-weary, and the thought of home and familiar surroundings seemed very inviting. When we reached Virginia, our money was just about gone. I parked the trailer at a gas station in Suffolk and began to look for a job.

There was a new grocery store that had just opened, and a young lady owned it. She had a "Help Wanted" sign in the window. I walked in and applied for the position.

She said, "I just this minute hung that sign! You're hired! You can start tomorrow morning."

I went back and told the boys about my job. We were all thrilled.

That night the town sheriff and two of his deputies came to the station and arrested us for vagrancy. They made us take the car and the trailer and drive into the big walled-in compound that surrounded the jail. We were given instructions to park the trailer and the car into an area adjacent to the jail. I told him I had a job and that I was from Georgia. Sheriff Teeter didn't believe me. He was a big, fat, redneck son of a bitch who hated Yankees.

He said, "We don't want no Yankees comin' down here takin' jobs that belong to Southerners!"

They locked us up.

They treated us like real criminals even though we hadn't done anything. We sat in the cell all day except for a couple hours when they let us out to walk around in the yard. They sure didn't like us!

Every time the sheriff would see us, he'd say, "I got to feed you damn Yankees and you two greasy Italians, I ought to let you starve!"

We practically did starve because all they gave us was beans and grits.

After a week we bribed one of the guards with an expensive wristwatch Sam had been given for graduation. He sent some wires to Sam and Bingo's parents. I wasn't about to contact HK. He probably would have called back and told Sheriff Teeter to throw away the key!

Bingo and Sam's folks sent enough money to bail us out. The sheriff and his deputies took us out to the car and followed us to a gas station where we filled it up. The gas station attendant, on the sheriff's orders, charged us double the price and put the difference in his pocket.

He came over to the car and said, "Now get your sorry Yankee asses back up North where you belong."

They followed us to the edge of town. When I got to the city limits, I stuck my arm out the window, gave him the finger, and stepped on the gas!

* * *

It looked like Dick was still mad about the incident that happened over fifty years ago.

I said, "Well, there's another incident where you didn't do anything wrong and got into trouble."

"No shit!" he said, and we both started to laugh. "That was the only place we got into trouble. I mean, serious trouble. Suffolk, Virginia… I'll never forget it. We drove all the way home without stopping because we were sick of no one hiring us.

"All things considered, it was a good trip—full of adventure, new places, and people. However, seeing the sign

'Mexico, NY,' for the first time in three months gave new meaning to the old phrase, 'There's no place like home.' It was good to be back."

"What kind of reception did you get when you got home, Dick?"

* * *

Harriet was thrilled that I was back, and I think even HK was happy to see me. The night after my return, Harriet fixed a roast beef dinner and invited some of the neighbors over. They all wanted to hear details about the trip—where we had stayed and what the different cities were like where we had stopped.

Bingo and Sam's parents had a dinner for all of us, and we relived our experiences again and again. All the boys at Burke's men's club wanted to hear about our adventure. After about a week of retelling the story, the glory aspect of our trip began to wear off.

CHAPTER SEVEN

I Just Wanted to Fight

I had been so engrossed in Dick's story that I lost track of the snowstorm until I heard some creaking noises. I looked out the solarium windows and saw that the snow was almost horizontal in its descent. The wind was howling, and every so often a gust would cause the house to moan.

I got up out of my rocker, put some ice in our glasses, and poured us both a drink.

Dick said, "I was wondering when you were going to get around to that!"

While I was up, I threw some more wood on the fire and got a blanket and laid it over Dick's lap. We sat there for a few minutes, sipping our Scotch as the fire came back to life. Every so often, the ceiling in the study would react to the wind with more moans and groans.

"Think she'll hold?" I asked.

Dick looked up at the beams and said, "I hope so!"

Then he returned to his story. He seemed eager to continue.

* * *

THE WHISKEY BOTTLE CONVERSATION

After I got back, I worked for Austin and George. On occasion, I would fill in at the A&P grocery store. I kept those jobs through the spring and summer. During this time I had been thinking about going to college. Hoppy Smith had received a football scholarship to Syracuse University, so I decided to apply there in the engineering program. I was accepted for the fall semester.

Hoppy and I went to Syracuse in August and found a small furnished apartment a few blocks from campus. I had no interest in living in the dorms. Football practice started about a week before classes.

Hoppy said, "Why don't you come to practice with me and try out for the team? If you make it, they feed you real well."

I went to practice with Hoppy, and after a week of try-outs, I made the team. The coach put me in the halfback position. It irritated the hell out of me to get tackled. They would give me a play to run, and the defensive team, for the most part, couldn't tackle me. They'd make passes or get an arm on me, but I just seemed to be able to get away from them. Hoppy and I were on the freshman team, but one afternoon the coach said he wanted me to run against the varsity squad. I got to be quite well known as the freshman who was running against the varsity. I made the first string. I used to get so excited when I ran the ball, trying to evade the other team.

One game I was making an end run and got hit by one of the tackles, which spun me around, so I cut across center field and got hit again, but I got away. I was so intent on not going down I got my direction mixed up and ran three quarters of the field the wrong way and scored a touchdown for the other team. Jesus! Was I embarrassed about that! The other boys reminded me of it before every game. That was my one year career of football at Syracuse. It was fun, but more importantly, Hoppy was right; they fed us well.

I stayed at Syracuse for two years. The engineering program was tough, so most of my time was spent studying. I had this English professor, who for some reason, didn't like me. Every time I handed in a paper, I'd get a D on it. Even if there were no grammatical errors, I'd get a D. I came home one weekend and explained my situation to my high school English teacher, Tiger Lil.

She said, "I'll write your next paper, Dick, and we'll see what he gives you."

Lil had graduated from Syracuse at the top of her class. She wrote the paper, checked, and double-checked for errors.

The day it was due, I handed it in to Mr. Jenkins. I got it back two days later with a D on it. I took it home that weekend and showed it to Tiger Lil. She was madder than he!

She said, "I think I have to go see Mr. Jenkins and have a talk with him. When is your next class, Dick?"

I told her my classes were Tuesday and Thursday at 4:00 p.m. "They last an hour."

Lil said, "I'll be in Tuesday at quarter to five."

She was standing outside the door when class ended. Lil walked in and introduced herself and said that I had been one of her students in high school.

"Mr. Jenkins," she said, "I graduated magna cum laude of my class, and I wrote this paper and checked for any

THE WHISKEY BOTTLE CONVERSATION

errors. There are none. So I want to know why you graded this with a D!"

Mr. Jenkins got red in the face and said, "I don't understand."

Lil said, "I want you to go over this paper with me."

Jenkins couldn't very well give her a D. After reviewing it again, he said that it was excellent and told Lil that he would work with Richard on some of his "shortcomings." Lil thanked him, and we left the room.

We went to a restaurant a few blocks away from school, and I bought her dinner. I thanked her for the time and effort she had put forth in my behalf.

Lil said, "If you have any more problems with Mr. Jenkins, you let me know, Dick."

I assured her that I would. It was B+ and As for the rest of the semester in English class.

In the rest of my classes, I got along pretty well—at least, I passed them. After my sophomore year, I decided that the engineering program wasn't for me. I transferred to Oswego State College. They had a two-year industrial arts program. It consisted of drafting, metallurgy, and the fundamentals of building. I worked with my hands in areas that I could see almost immediate results for my efforts. I really enjoyed those subjects.

* * *

I said, "It seems like you had always been a nuts-and-bolts type of guy, Dick. You worked on your cars, helped George in his garage, and built your model airplanes."

Dick a sip of his Scotch and said, "I really did enjoy working with my hands, creating or repairing something."

"It was at Oswego State that I met your mother… Jean McGivney, an Irish girl from Fulton, New York, with auburn hair, a freckled face, and blue eyes."

"How'd you two meet?" I asked.

* * *

Janet Leary and Jill Moore, two girls from Mexico, rode to the college with me every day. They were in some of the same classes with Jean. In between classes the three of them, and sometimes more, would come out to my car and smoke cigarettes and, of course, talk. I was on a tight schedule, so I seldom got to enjoy the "women's club." I didn't really get to see much of Jean, but she roomed with another girl, and occasionally, they would ask me for a ride to their apartment.

I learned more about her as time went on, and one night while giving her a ride, I asked her for a date. We set a time on that weekend, and I drove to Fulton, where she lived on South Third Street. That evening I met her family. Richard Gerald, her father, made me feel like a shrimp. He was six four with a hand that wrapped around mine like I was a small child. Jean's mother, Eleanor, was a beautiful petite women. There were six children in Jean's family: Jean, John, Robert, Bruce, George, and Maureen. Jean was the oldest and shouldered the responsibility for her siblings. When she spoke, all the boys jumped.

THE WHISKEY BOTTLE CONVERSATION

Jean and I had many dates. We'd go to dances, roller-skating, out to dinner, or take a picnic lunch somewhere. Her family treated me like one of their own. On one date, we took a ride down to a spot on the Oswego riverbank. It was a warm, beautiful evening, and we sat there, talking and throwing sticks and stones into the water.

At one point I leaned back and put my hand on something that felt strange. I turned around and took a good look. It was a dead body.

Trying to be nonchalant, I said to Jean, "I think we should get going."

She protested, "I don't want to leave yet. It's such a nice night."

I grabbed her hand and pulled her up. She was upset but walked back to the car. When we got to the road, I told her I had grabbed the arm of a dead body and wanted to get her out of there. At first she didn't believe me, but I finally convinced her. I took her home and then went to the police station. I told the desk sergeant what I had seen, so they assigned an officer to go with me. We drove to the riverbank, and I showed him the body.

He said, "I'm going to need some help, so we'll have to go back to the station."

When we returned the officer went to the lieutenant and told him what he had found. The lieutenant asked me some questions and said I could go.

I went to a saloon across the street and had a couple of shots. The next morning I drove to the sight, and it was all fenced off. It had been a hell of a date!

During my year at Oswego, there was more and more news about what was going on in Europe with Hitler and his Nazi party. They had invaded Poland and were working their way through Belgium toward France. I couldn't understand why America wasn't doing something about this man who, I felt, was just a bully on a large scale.

I decided at the end of the semester that I was going to go to Canada and join the Royal Canadian Air Force. I wanted to fight, and if this country wasn't going to join in, I was going to one that was!

One afternoon I was sitting in the men's club, having a beer, and a friend of mine, Raymond Lavoie, came in. I told Ray about my plans to go to Canada and join up. Ray's father owned the bank in Mexico, and he worked there as a teller.

He said, "Dick, if you don't mind, I'm gonna go with you. I'm sick of standing at the counter all day, waiting on people and listening to my father."

He surprised me. I'd known Ray all through school. He was a tall, awkward kid who always had good grades and never got into trouble… something that was hard for me to relate to.

* * *

Both Dick and I laughed his statement.

* * *

He never struck me as the type of boy to do anything adventurous, but I said, "I'd be happy to have you along!"

We decided not to tell our parents… at least not our fathers, anyway. I planned to leave the following Saturday.

THE WHISKEY BOTTLE CONVERSATION

I told Harriet, and she said, "If that's what you want to do, Dick, you have my blessing. It's a terrible thing those Nazis are doing in Europe. They have to be stopped, and I'm proud of you, son!"

We left on Saturday morning and drove to Ottawa. Once we arrived, we asked around and found out that the recruiting office was in the Chateau Laurier Hotel, right in the heart of the downtown area. We entered through the revolving glass doors and saw a sign with an arrow designating the direction for the RCAF Recruiting Center. We followed the sign, and just off to the right of the main lobby was the office.

We went in and were greeted by a British officer named Lieutenant Colonel Jones. Raymond and I introduced ourselves and said we wanted to join up.

"You boys American?" he asked.

We both said, "Yes, sir!"

He offered us a seat and then told us some of the stories of his experiences in the war. He had been shot down several times and shared the things he did to survive. He explained what we could expect in our training, and if we joined, there was a good chance we might not make it back.

"You boys still interested?" he asked.

We again answered, "Yes, sir!"

He gave us the paperwork to fill out and told us to return in two days.

We got a room at the hotel and spent the next two days seeing the sights in historic Ottawa. On Tuesday morning we reported back to the recruiter's office. There were four soldiers standing in front of the door. They wanted to know our names, so we told them.

Two of the soldiers got in front of us and two behind, then they said, "Follow us!"

Christ! I figured we were already in! They took us to see this officer who was Canadian.

He said, "Which one of you is Raymond Lavoie?"

Raymond acknowledged his question. Then he looked at me and said, "Then you are Richard Leonard?"

I said, "Yes, sir! I am."

He said, "Please have a seat, men. A problem has developed that concerns both of you and is an outgrowth of the actions of Raymond's father. I don't know all the details, but apparently, Mr. Lavoie has been up here, making such a stink with the government that I have been instructed to tear up your induction papers. I told Mr. Lavoie that I would report to him. He's here in Ottawa. I didn't, however, say when I would make my report."

He tore up our papers and said, "I'll give you twenty-four hours to get out of Canada before I contact Mr. Lavoie."

I said, "But we both want to fly!"

He said, "You have to get out of the country. When Raymond's father quiets down a little, you can come back and join the best 'goddamned Air Force in the world'!"

* * *

I asked Dick what Raymond's father was like.

"He was a tough little shit that looked down on everyone," he said. "He wanted his two boys to stay home and work in the bank. They lived in a beautiful home on Main Street. His wife, Betty, was an attractive woman who worked

THE WHISKEY BOTTLE CONVERSATION

her butt off to keep the house up to the highest standards. When you went into the house, you entered through the basement door. The cellar was finished off, and that's where they basically lived, and if you went upstairs, you took your shoes off. Raymond Sr. was the king of the basement. He kept his wife, his daughter, Edith, and two sons, Raymond and Jimmy, jumping. I never had much use for the man myself."

* * *

When we left Canada, we decided to go stay with Bill Pond, who had gone to work in Keeseville, New York, located in the Adirondack Mountains. Bill was a friend of mine from Mexico. As we were driving through the mountains, we turned on the radio and heard that the State Police had a warrant out for our arrest. We kept an eye out for the cops and made our way to Bill's without being captured.

* * *

I started to laugh. I said, "There's another incident where you didn't do anything wrong and now you're on the lamb."

Dick laughed and said, "No, shit! See what I mean?"

* * *

Bill had just married a really nice girl with black curly hair and a great body to go with her personality. Bill was a big, husky guy with a robust personality. When we arrived, we told him what had happened, and of course, he got a big kick out of it.

He said, "Well, if the cops are after you, we'd better hide your car! There's a railroad yard on the other side of town. I know the station master and I think he'll let us stash your car in one of the buildings."

We took the car to the station and parked it in a building where they stored heavy equipment.

We stayed with Bill and Ellen for a week. The four of us climbed Pocomoonshine, a nearby mountain, taking a picnic lunch and spending the day reminiscing and taking in the natural beauty of the Adirondack scenery. Another day we went to the beach on Lake Champlain, drank beer, swam, and bullshitted about Mexico and Raymond's father. Each night we would listen to the radio to see if the police were still looking for us. When we felt the heat had died down, Ray and I drove to Vermont, where my aunt and uncle, Betty and Henry Parker, lived.

On the way we decided that if we could find a job, we'd stay and work for a while. Neither of us had much interest in going back to Mexico.

Betty and Henry received us with open arms. I told them about our situation, and Henry said, "I've got a friend at the J&K Turret Lathe Company. I'll take you down there tomorrow, and I think he'll be able to put you to work."

The next morning Henry took Ray and me to the plant and introduced us to Mr. Keppel, the plant manager. He asked us about our backgrounds. I told him I had two years of college engineering and one year of industrial arts.

Raymond said, "I've worked in a bank for four years."

THE WHISKEY BOTTLE CONVERSATION

I was put on a milling machine, and Ray got placed in the stockroom. We didn't want to burden Betty and Henry, so after a week, we got a room with two double beds in a boarding house.

The mill employed about seven hundred men and produced gun turrets for battleships and tanks. The plant itself covered about three city blocks. During my second week, the foremen brought me a set of new cutting blades.

He said, "Dick, I want you to try these out and keep a record of the time saved and how they perform."

It took me a day to break the machine down and replace the blades.

The difference between the two was like night and day. The new blades cut milling time in half, and they lasted twice as long as the old ones. I kept my records, detailing the time saved and the performance on the different types of steel that was being milled. At the end of two weeks, I spent an afternoon with the plant manager, reviewing my data and offering suggestions based on my experiments. For example, with softer steel, running the lathe at a slower speed would reduce the milling time. On the other hand, with harder or denser steel, a much higher rpm was needed for milling. The manager was impressed with my observations, and as the other machines in the plant were fitted with the new blades, he would have me spend a shift with the man on that machine. I would instruct him on the various techniques needed for the lathe to operate at top efficiency.

Our shifts were twelve hours long, seven days a week. Then we had a day and a half off. We got paid seventy-five cents an hour. Ray and I decided to work for a month straight. That way, at the end of the month, we'd have six days off, which would give us enough time to go back to Mexico to get our clothes and see our families.

When we returned home the first time, we found out that Raymond's father had bought a farm with cattle because you couldn't be drafted if you were working on a farm. He also bought Raymond a new Chrysler Highlander convertible and told him to "get his ass on that farm and start taking care of the cows!" Ray came by the house and told me he and his brother, Jimmy, were going to be farmers and he wouldn't be going back to Vermont.

The day before I left, I was in the men's club, having a few beers, talking with the boys, when Leonard Watkins, a friend of mine, walked in. I told him what I had been doing.

Leonard said, "You know, Dick, I haven't had much luck finding a job. Since Ray isn't going back, do you think they might hire me to fill his position?"

I said, "I don't see why not! If you want to go, get your things together, and I'll pick you up in the morning."

When we got back to Vermont, I talked to Mr. Keppel, and he hired Leonard and put him in the stockroom.

Leonard and I continued to work a month straight and then took our six days off and returned to Mexico. I spent most of my time with Jean. We were very much in love and decided that when the time was right, we would get married.

I worked at the turret company for about a year. On one of my trips home, I bought a Packard convertible. I paid five hundred dollars for it. I went to Fulton to see Jean

THE WHISKEY BOTTLE CONVERSATION

and took her for a ride in my new car, had some dinner, and returned to Mexico. The next morning, Harriet and I were listening to the radio as we ate our breakfast.

They announced that Pearl Harbor had been bombed and that the United States had declared war on Japan and Germany.

Dick's Packard convertible

* * *

I asked Dick how he felt about that.

He said, "It made me mad in one sense, but I was also glad that America was finally going to stand up for what was right and enter the war. Now I could join our own Air Corps and fight for this country!"

I could sense his pride as he spoke those words.

"So what did you do?"

* * *

I got up from the table, went next door to Dr. Worboy, and told him to give me a complete physical. Once he finished, I took the paperwork and drove to Syracuse to sign up for the Army Air Corps.

The recruitment center was in the State Tower building on Salina Street. When I pulled up, I saw a line of boys that ran out the front door and halfway down the block. I stood in line for three hours before I got to talk to a recruitment officer. I gave him my physical report and filled out the paperwork.

He asked me my preference, and I said, "Air Corps."

But that didn't mean I was going to be a pilot or bombardier. There were so many boys who joined. They put us on hold, and the date that we were to be called was up to them.

On the way back from Syracuse, I stopped by to see Jean and told her I had signed up to fly. She cried but understood. We decided to get married before I left for the service. The recruiter told me it would be at least a couple of months before I was called, so I decided to go back to Vermont and give them my notice at the plant. I drove back to Mexico and spent the night. I don't think I slept at all. I was excited about joining up, and all these thoughts and the anticipation of being in the war kept running through my mind. I left early the next morning. When I got about ten miles from Springfield, Vermont, I fell asleep, and the car spun around in a skid that woke me up. I was going backward and hit a power pole, snapping it off at the base. The pole and wires came crashing down, just missing the car on the right side. I went off the road, down an embankment, and the car rolled over. I lay down on the seat and held on. I rolled several times and stopped when it hit a tree.

I crawled out and looked at what was left of my beautiful Packard. All the fenders, the hood, and trunk lid were scattered here and there in the field. I walked back up to the road and sat down. I wasn't bleeding, but my shoulder and right leg hurt. It wasn't long when a farmer pulled up in a pickup truck.

He got out, looked at the wreck, and said, "Where did they take the body?"

I said, "They didn't take him anywhere. That's my car."

The farmer helped me in his truck and took me to his house, where I called Leonard. He borrowed a car and brought me back to the boarding house.

The landlady was a nurse, so Leonard told her what had happened. She came up to our room and looked me over as I was getting ready for work.

She said, "Why don't you take these pills and lie down for an hour before you leave."

I took the pills, lay down, and in about five minutes, I was out. I slept for two days.

* * *

"That sounds a lot like the time I wrecked your car, Dick!"

Dick laughed and shook his head. "That was a good one, Dave!"

It was 1966, and I had just graduated from high school. I had been out on a date with my girlfriend, Penny Sterling. I dropped her off about two in the morning and was on my way home when I fell asleep. I was driving Dick's 1963 Olds 98, which was a two-and-a-half-ton luxury car.

When I woke up, the first thing I saw was the speedometer. It registered at 110 mph. I had gone off the left-hand side of the road and was in a field when the car hit an embankment and went airborne. I saw the nose of the car going down, so I lay down on the seat and held on. It flew 150 feet from impact to first landing, then began flipping end over end. Just as this was happening, a fellow by the name of Richard Buckley had stopped on a side road, waiting to make his turn on the main highway. I hit him, demolishing the left side of his car, and flew over the top without leaving a scratch on his roof. My car landed upside down next to his.

To this day I don't know how I got out of the car. The roof was pushed almost flat with what was left of the body of the Olds. I wasn't hurt... not a scratch. Richard was slumped over his steering wheel apparently in shock. The driver's side of his Mustang was perfect. I tried to wake him up to take me home, but he was out cold. I walked around the other side of his car and saw that it was caved in.

I thought, *Shit, I rolled right over him!*

THE WHISKEY BOTTLE CONVERSATION

I saw the lights of a car coming down the main road, so I went out and flagged them down. I told the man to go to my house and get Dick. He arrived in about a half an hour. Dick took Richard and me back home. Then he called the Troopers. I slept for forty-six hours. The doctor called it "psychotic trauma."

Dick and I sat there, reliving the accidents and how similar our experiences had been.

I said, "I think we ought to have a toast to whomever has been looking out for us all these years."

Dick raised his glass, looked up, and said, "Amen!"

We sat there in silence for a while sipping our Scotch.

Finally, I said, "So? What happened after you recovered from the accident?"

* * *

A couple of days later, I went back to work. The boys in the plant gave me a hard time about smashing up my car. I worked until the end of April, when I decided that my time for induction was probably getting near. I went to Mr. Keppel and told him that I had signed up for the Air Corps and would be leaving in two weeks.

He said, "Dick, you don't have to go in the service. Working at a plant, making war materials exempts you. You've done a fine job here, and we'd hate to lose you!"

I thanked him for his compliments but told him that I wanted to fly and fight for our country.

He said, "You're a fine man, Dick, and I wish you the best of luck."

After my wreck, Leonard and I bought a Pontiac convertible. I finished my two weeks, and Mr. Keppel gave me an extra week's pay as a bonus. Leonard drove me back to Mexico, and I told him to keep the car.

Jean and I decided to get married on June 20. It was a big wedding, with all our family and friends there. For our honeymoon, we drove to Vermont and spent a week with Aunt Betty and Uncle Henry. We rode their two horses, went on picnics, and just relaxed.

From there we went to Gorem, New Hampshire, and visited Jean's relatives. Her grandparents had settled there after moving from Ireland. I met her aunts, uncles, and cousins. They were a hearty, fun-loving group of people who made me feel right at home.

After we left Gorem, we drove to Old Orchard Beach, Maine, and spent four days at a hotel on the ocean. We ate our fill of seafood, took long walks on the beach, and swam in the cold Atlantic.

When we got back to Mexico, we stayed at a cottage that HK owned on Lake Ontario. About a month later, I received my orders. I was going to Tennessee for basic training.

CHAPTER EIGHT

Into the Wild Blue Yonder

Two weeks after receiving my orders, Jean took me to the train station in Syracuse. Four sergeants were there, checking names and giving us our seat assignments. There were probably two hundred men going to Nashville. The trip took three days but seemed much longer, I suppose, because of my anticipation about what lay ahead.

When we arrived in Nashville, we were loaded into open trucks and driven to the Nashville Classification Center. It wasn't long after we left the station that it began to rain, and I don't mean a drizzle! It came down in buckets! I had put on a suit in order to make a good first impression. By the time we pulled through the gates, we looked like two hundred drowned rats.

They took us to a building where we were interviewed about our backgrounds and filled out what seemed like endless forms. Then we were issued one blanket, one cot, and given our barracks assignment.

The base consisted of an officers' quarters, mess, a latrine, a building set up with desk chairs for testing, and ten barracks. The barracks were nothing more than a large rectangular building that was completely open except for a cot and a footlocker for each man. There were twenty men to a barracks. Our heat was a wood stove in the center of the room.

Every morning at 6:00 a.m., a private would march in, blow a whistle, and line us up outside. Then we would march down to the mess. For the first week we remained in our civilian clothes and did nothing but take tests, do KP, or clean and mop the barracks and latrine.

In the second week we were given our Army clothes and began our physical training. Every day we would march, run two or three miles, and do obstacle courses. We were given rifles and taught how to disassemble, clean, reassemble, and fire them. I didn't mind the training. Having someone screaming at me all the time was hard for me to take. I bit my tongue, swallowed my pride, and managed to finish my six weeks without incident. It was in Nashville that I received my classification for pilot training.

* * *

"It must have been hard for you, Dick, given your background with authority figures, to keep from kicking somebody's ass down there."

Dick looked at me and said, "You don't know how hard it was, but I had remembered the advice Trigger had given me at Manlius.

"When our training was over, they put us back on the train and sent us home for two weeks before we would be shipped out for our next assignment. I spent my time

THE WHISKEY BOTTLE CONVERSATION

home making preparations to leave for who knew how long. I bought some life insurance and made up a will. We decided, after much discussion, that Jean would live with HK and Harriet in Mexico and continue taking courses at Oswego State. While I was home, Jean found out she was pregnant."

"How did you feel about that?" I asked.

"Naturally, I was thrilled that we were going to have a child! We had talked about a family, but I hadn't really expected it to start so soon."

I said, "Were you at all apprehensive about going off to war with your wife carrying a child you might never see?"

Dick sat there quietly for a minute, looking into the fire.

He took a sip of his Scotch and said, "I suppose I was. I probably felt that if I didn't make it back, there would be part of me that could carry on my name and the heritage of both of our families."

Dick took another drink and turned his gaze from the fire to me.

"Fortunately for you," he said, "that didn't happen."

I was the third child, and obviously, if my scenario had come true, I wouldn't be here.

I said, "You aren't going to get any argument out of me about that, Dick."

He laughed.

"So where were you sent on your next phase of training?" I asked.

* * *

About a week after I got home, I received a telegram telling me to report to the Syracuse train station at such and such a time. I was being sent to Bakersfield, California, to begin my pilot training. The day I was scheduled to leave, I didn't want anyone to bring me to the train station, but they all came anyway. HK, Harriet, Jean, and her parents were all there. It was very painful going away, not knowing if or when I would return.

There was another fellow there in uniform. From the moment we introduced ourselves, we got along. His name was Al Sterns, from Syracuse, and he was going to Bakersfield as well. His parents, brothers, and sisters were all at the station to see him off. We said our good-byes amidst a flood of tears, hugs, and "I love you's." Finally, we got on the train, and both of us were still a bit weepy.

After we collected ourselves, we talked and decided, the hell with it! We were going to war, and that was that! Al was average height, thin, and had brown hair. He wasn't someone you would notice or pick out of a crowd. He had a hell of a sense of humor, though.

Once we were a few miles out of Syracuse, he began to talk about himself.

He said, "You know, Dick, except for basic training, I've never been away from home. I graduated from high school in '39 and immediately went to work at Solvey Process. I lived at home and helped out my parents with my brothers and sisters, buying them clothes and contributing what I could to the family finances. My father's always been a hardworking man, but with five kids, there wasn't much extra to go around. When the Japs bombed Pearl Harbor,

THE WHISKEY BOTTLE CONVERSATION

I didn't really want to leave my family, but I thought it was my duty to fight for our country."

When Sterns finished talking, I told him about how I had gone to Canada and tried to join the RCAF.

I said, "I really wanted the United States to enter the war and put a stop to German and Japanese aggression. No country has a right to dominate or impose their ideals on the people of another nation. That's what our country stands for… the right of free choice, and we should defend those people who can't defend themselves. I joined to do what I can to put an end to what has happened in Europe and the Far East and to seek retribution for the bombing of our forces at Pearl Harbor!"

Sterns and I were very different men, but evidently, we shared the same goal.

For the first part of the trip, we talked some more about our families, our high school careers, and generally got to know each other. We were the only two boys on the train in uniform. Many of the passengers would stop and engage us in conversation about what branch of the service we were in and where were we going. They all thanked us and said we would be in their prayers. We both were very proud to be treated in such a manner, even though we hadn't done anything to deserve it yet.

As our train traveled westward, we really began to enjoy the changes in scenery. For a couple of young fellows, who really hadn't been away from home, the different landscapes through the Midwest out into the Rockies was overwhelming. After our initial conversation, we didn't talk about the war. We were both excited about what we were going to do and wondered if we would make it through pilot's school. Just a couple of young kids on the way to their future. As far as knowing anything about what we were getting into, I don't think we had a clue.

After six days, we arrived in Bakersfield. It was a very comfortable California community of about twenty-five thousand. I say "comfortable" because the people were very friendly. They showed a real interest in the boys in uniform, treating us like heroes.

The base was a beautiful facility that had been a private flying school the Army had taken over for pilot training. They had to build five good-sized barracks that each housed thirty men. There was a mess hall, officers' quarters, a classroom, the control tower, and a large area where we did our physical training. There were two runways and about fifty planes.

When we arrived, we were given our barracks assignments, three sets of uniforms, and a set of textbooks. During the first nine weeks, most of our time was spent in the classroom. We took what would be the equivalent of college math, physics, chemistry, and aeronautics—courses that would be useful in flying and repairing an airplane. A lot of the boys were having trouble with the classes, so after lights-out, I'd meet with whomever wanted help in the latrine. I'd spend a couple of hours going over the material and explaining things that they didn't understand.

* * *

"How many men would be in there with you, Dick?"

THE WHISKEY BOTTLE CONVERSATION

"Oh, it would be different every night. Some nights there might be ten, on other nights, up to twenty-five."

* * *

Aside from the classroom, we had physical training every day. Revelry was every morning at six. We would have ten minutes to get outside for roll call. Then they would give twenty minutes to get dressed. We'd stand in formation in front of the barracks and then be marched to the mess for breakfast. The food was good, and you could have all you wanted. After breakfast we did our physical exercises, like running in cadence, going through a course with high wooden structures that had ropes hanging down on one side. We'd have to pull ourselves up to the top and then jump to the ground. We had to deal with things we might encounter in war: run through a fixed course, jump over ditches, and crawl under barbed wire.

There was also a seventy-five-foot tower that had a cockpit built on top of it. We had to climb up to the cockpit, strap yourself in, and when they blew the whistle, you snapped off your safety belt and dove out headfirst. There was a cable hooked to a parachute harness that every pilot wore. It was quite an exercise and a hell of a thrill when that cable snapped you back upright about five feet from the ground! The rest of the day until six or seven was spent in the classroom.

After nine weeks we began our primary training, which was flying PT-17s. They were double-winged biplanes built for acrobatics. They had two seats, one behind the other, with open cockpits. There were connecting controls, which meant the instructor in front was generally flying the plane. The trainee in the back had his hand on the stick and feet on the pedals, enabling him to feel what the instructor was doing and how the plane would react. It was terrific!

Flight Training School Stearman biplane

My instructor pilot was Captain Bellinger. He had flown stunts and exhibitions around the country before joining the Air Corps. Rumor had it that he had flown stunts in a few movies.

The first time he took me up, I just felt like I belonged there. I had flown with George, but this was different. I could really feel the plane and how it responded when he did different maneuvers. We communicated by speaking through a tube that ran from the front cockpit to the back. Each time we went up, he would do a maneuver, like a slow

THE WHISKEY BOTTLE CONVERSATION

bank to the right or put the plane in a dive. Then he'd let go of the controls and yell through the tube for me to do the same thing. My fourth time up, he told me to shoot a landing—which means, you come in, land the plane, and take right off again. I circled the field, made my approach, and made a smooth landing then pushed the throttle forward and took off again. What a thrill that was!

There were many things I had to learn about flying. Safety in flight is dependent on the pilot's ability to remember all the little things to check before he lines up to takeoff. As an example, when I climbed into the cockpit, I strapped myself in. It doesn't sound like a big thing, but one time I had forgotten, and when Captain Bellinger made a quick turn, I found my body floating and struggling to stay with the plane.

Another was a simple thing like a "preflight check." When the airplane is parked and tied down for its stay on the ground, "the ailerons" have locks on them. Once I overlooked the stay rods that lock the flight controls. I was embarrassed as hell when I tried to take off.

A "flight pattern" was a simple thing to remember. Every airfield had a recommended pattern so you didn't fly into someone's way or come up under another plane and crash into him. A pilot always had to check the pattern before he took off. Generally, a "flight pattern" would be as follows.

The airfield is in a N-S direction, 0 to 180. It's ten thousand feet long and a thousand feet wide. Winds are southern. I should mention the direction of the winds are very important! As an example—when sitting on the end of the runway headed south, the winds are from the southerly direction at twenty miles per hour, and the flight speed, or "takeoff speed," is sixty miles per hour. The runway speed would be forty miles per hour until takeoff.

You now have the picture of a plane, ready for takeoff, and the pilot applies the throttle and the plane starts its run or takeoff time. As the plane reaches its flight speed, it rises from the runway and is in the "takeoff pattern." The plane rises to about seven hundred feet and then turns to the left or right, flying out of the "takeoff pattern." If you're planning to "fly the pattern," after takeoff, you'd climb to seven hundred and then gradually turn to the left, climbing to around a thousand feet. When you're approximately ninety degrees to the runway, there is an excellent view of any traffic coming into the field and can guide your plane accordingly. It being a clear approach, the pilot makes another ninety-degree turn on the "downwind leg" of the pattern. In other words, his plane is flying at "one thousand feet" on the left-hand side of the runway. He holds this flight pattern, or "downwind side," of the pattern to the end of the field. He continues his flight path for about three or four minutes and then starts a ninety-degree turn to "the approach pattern," letting his plane gradually slow down so he's in a descending position on the pattern. When he sees the end of the runway, the pilot lines his plane to the runway, letting down until it's just over the boundary, and then completes the landing!

My first solo flight was quite an experience! Captain Bellinger climbed into the backseat and motioned me to the front seat.

THE WHISKEY BOTTLE CONVERSATION

I got all the preliminaries checked out, and he said, "Okay, start her up, and take me out to the end of the runway."

I had a feeling, you know, a tickling in the pit of your stomach. After a check, I taxied onto the runway and lined up for takeoff.

Bellinger picked up the speaking tube and said, "Take off and fly 'the pattern,' and then bring her back down on the runway."

I did as he instructed, making a nice, smooth landing.

He picked up the tube again and said, "Repeat the same procedure!"

Once we were back on the ground, he told me to take him back to the parking area.

He climbed out and told me to get in the backseat, strap myself in, then said, "Shoot a few landings, and go out into the space where we had practiced, and get the feel of the plane."

Boy! Talk about the feeling in the pit of my stomach! I taxied back out on the runway and took off, shot a few landings, and then headed into the wild blue yonder!

* * *

"What a feeling, Dave! I can't explain the feeling, but it's one I'll never forget!"

* * *

I went out and did "figure eights" at about three hundred feet around some oil derricks, then climbed up to a height where I thought it was safe, put the plane into a dive, pulled back on the stick, and did a loop. After the loop I flew some more figure eights and a few slow barrel rolls before heading back to the field. I taxied into the parking area and parked the plane. I was one happy and proud SOB!

The instructor pilot greeted me with, "Congratulations! Now, tell me about your flight."

I told him about the feeling in the pit of my stomach, my takeoffs and landings, my figure eights, loop and barrel rolls.

He said, "Whoa, boy! Tell me again about after you left the pattern."

I explained about my figure eights. He asked me at what altitude I was doing them.

I said, "About three hundred feet."

Then he asked me again about the loop and barrel rolls. I explained what I had done and how the plane handled.

He turned, saying, "I want to see you the first thing in the morning, ready to fly!"

I didn't sleep well that night but was on the flight line bright and early! Captain Bellinger was already there, had checked the procedures, and told me to get in the front seat. I took special notice that he wasn't as friendly as usual and thought that maybe he was going to give me a flight check, which wasn't usual, but a check meant that your future was on the line!

We were taxiing out, and I thought, "Put all those crazy thoughts out of your mind and do as he tells you!"

He didn't say a word. We took off and headed out of "the pattern" to the flight practice area.

THE WHISKEY BOTTLE CONVERSATION

He then spoke to me through the tube, "Is your seat belt good and tight?"

I checked to make sure and said that it was. He flew up to one thousand feet, did figure eights around the oil derricks, and then he started to climb at a real steep pitch. He climbed and climbed when all of a sudden, he kicked the right rudder as hard as possible, and the plane nosed over into a tight spiral.

I thought, "Boy! This is really something," as I braced myself, holding the sides of the cockpit.

After eight or nine spins, he kicked the left rudder pedal as hard as he could, and the plane started to level out into a diving position, and gradually, he leveled it off into a normal flight pattern. Then he started to climb again. He put the plane in an inverted position, and I was literally hanging from my safety belt! My whole body, including my legs, were dangling with only the seat belt holding me. It was rather a chilling situation, and then *snap*, I was back in an upright position—a little out of breath, but otherwise feeling wonderful!

He pulled back on the stick until we were about eight thousand feet. He leveled off and started a slow descent to get back to its normal speed, when he started doing several barrel rolls, then went into a diving position up and over into a loop. He then picked up the speaking tube and asked me to put my feet on the foot pedals and take hold of the stick just to get the feel of the "aerobatics." He put the plane through every altitude and position possible. What a flight! I know he must have been tired; a couple of hours of that kind of flying was exhausting!

When he said, "You take us home," I knew that we had finished a damned good day's instruction!

We landed, tied the plane down, and then went into the flight room for a soft drink. After a few minutes, Captain Bellinger started talking about my flight the day before and doing figure eights at three hundred feet. He thought it was commendable that I did them; however, at three hundred feet, I was endangering my life and those who might be watching. Just a change of fate at that altitude, a forced landing, and I'd be on the ground with no excuse.

"You have to consider the people on the ground, their property, and what you could do if a forced landing occurred," he said. "Doing a loop with no instruction doesn't make any sense."

He explained what could happen and the possible results. To put it mildly, I'd really screwed up!

He told me that he could write up a report that would put me out to pasture, or he could give me instruction.

That's what today had been about, and he hoped I'd learned a good lesson—end of meeting! I thanked him and from then on looked at flying in a whole new light.

* * *

"Sounds like you were having a ball, Dick!"
"I was having the time of my life, Dave!"
"How long did you have to fly PT-17s?"

* * *

THE WHISKEY BOTTLE CONVERSATION

I think we had to fly ninety hours. Every day at your flight time, you just hopped in your plane and took off. Some days I would have to go cross-country to different places and then return. I really enjoyed the responsibility but more so was the fun of doing different maneuvers and acrobatics, putting the plane and myself to the test.

A lot of the boys were scared to death of the airplane. I'd say maybe 40 percent made it to the next stage of pilot training. Those who didn't were assigned to navigator's bombardier school. Sterns and I made it. Flying had become a serious business, and the balance of my time in the PT-17s was not only fun; I had learned a good lesson in responsibility.

Those of us who made it through the pilot training stayed at Bakersfield for the second phase, which was flying PT-13s. The rest of the boys were shipped to another location for navigator and bombardier training. The PT-13s seemed like a big step in flight training to me. It was a double-cockpit, double-controls, single-wing airplane. The wing was below the fuselage, and there was a 600-horsepower Pratt and Whitney engine.

Sterns and I were lucky enough to make it through phase 1, and although we weren't assigned to the same barracks, we spent most of our free time together. It had been approximately three months since we had left Syracuse as a couple of crazy kids, and now we were pilots.

* * *

"What was the second phase of your training like, Dick?"

"Well, we still had our school assignments, which were tough but interesting, and of course, the flying was terrific! The instructors were friendly but serious, yet very low-key in their approach. They took us in groups of five, walking us through the various aspects of the plane and all the pre-flight checks we had to make. Each of us was taken up by our instructor pilots to get the feel of the plane. After about five hours of flight, takeoffs, and landings, my instructor got out of the plane and told me to take her up and shoot a few landings, then go out in the practice area. I was thrilled, but it still wasn't as great as flying the PT-17 biplane! Each day we had our flight time and were given maneuvers that we had to perform. For example, I'd be in the practice area and pull back on the stick to put the plane in a steep climb. At about ten thousand feet, the stick would get real light. The plane would slow to a stop, one of the wings would dip, and the nose would fall, putting the plane into a dive. I'd be going straight down, and as the plane picked up speed, the stick would start to respond again. At about one thousand feet, I'd pull back, and it would level off at about five hundred feet.

"I'd pull back on the stick again, putting the plane back into the steep climb. This time when I got to the height where it stalled, I'd kick the right rudder pedal and the nose would drop down and I'd be in a slow spin. As the plane picked up speed the spiral would tighten up. When I got back to one thousand feet, I'd kick the left rudder pedal which would bring the plane out of the spin."

"Did you ever get disoriented or dizzy when you were in the spin?"

THE WHISKEY BOTTLE CONVERSATION

"I never did, but some of the boys couldn't pull the plane out of the spin and crashed."

"How many crashed while you were there, Dick?"

"I'm not really sure, but I would guess at least ten."

* * *

During the second phase we were given more free time. Every Saturday night the school would sponsor a dance, and that was a real pleasure. The officers in charge would invite girls from the community about the ages of eighteen to twenty-five along with chaperones who were usually their mothers. It was a wonderful opportunity to relax and have a change from the military environment. Sterns and I went to the dance with our uniforms spit and polished. The girls were beautiful to look at and exceptional to dance with. It reminded me of home and brought back many fond memories.

Halfway through phase 2, I was playing touch football, went out for a pass, and ran into the goal post, fracturing my leg. I was pissed off that my flying time was cut and I figured I'd probably be put back into a new class. Sterns came in to see me that evening. I expressed my feelings about being put back while he would be able to graduate ahead of me. He leaned over the bed and whispered, 'I'll see you tomorrow.' I thought he was going to just stop by and see me, but the next afternoon, in came Sterns being carried on a stretcher. He was moaning and groaning and holding onto his side. They operated and took out his appendix. That crazy bastard faked it! They put him into the bed next to mine.

When he came to, he said, "Well, I guess we'll be starting over together!"

I laughed and said, "You're shittin' me!"

"That's the God's honest truth, Dave."

Then he chuckled and shook his head.

* * *

The following afternoon, the two girls Sterns and I had met at the dance came in to visit us. Loretta, the girl I had danced with, was dressed to kill. She had on a spring dress, wide-brimmed hat, gloves, and high-heeled shoes.

She said, "Well, I guess you two won't be doing any dancing for a while."

I said, "Flying either!"

Loretta looked sad, "I'm very sorry, Dick."

I thanked her, and we talked about my injury and, of course, Sterns' charade.

On the stand next to my bed was a picture of Jean. She asked who the beautiful girl was.

"She's my wife. We were married a few months before I entered the service!"

She looked surprised. "I didn't know you were married."

I apologized for not telling her. Neither of us said anything for a while until Loretta asked if I would mind if she continued to visit me while I was in the hospital.

I told her, "I'd be honored to have you as my friend."

Each day she came by, she'd bring me cookies or something she had baked. Loretta was good company, and I was happy to have made her acquaintance.

THE WHISKEY BOTTLE CONVERSATION

My stay in the hospital was short-lived. I was released in four days with my crutches and cast. Sterns followed two days later. We continued our studies, and when my leg was healed, we continued our training. We would take off in groups of ten planes and get into formation to simulate a bombing run. Targets like Billings, Montana, would be designated. We'd fly to Billings, make our run on the city, and then fly back to Bakersfield.

Sterns and I finished PT-13 school three weeks behind our original class. It was a pleasant experience in a pleasant community, with friendly people and a school that was hard to say good-bye to. Our next stop was Yuma, Arizona.

Ours was the first class to use this new base. It wasn't actually a base, per se. All they had was a runway, parking area for the planes, and tents. There were no buildings. We slept intents in the middle of the desert. I'd wake up in the morning, and my nose and ears would be plugged with sand. The latrine was a tent with several shitters in a row that had pull-out buckets beneath them. I pitied the poor bastards that had to empty them. The showers were outside with a curtain and showerhead. You pulled on a rope when you wanted water.

The planes we were going to fly were twin engine. There were two seats next to each other, for the pilot and copilot. The BT-17 and BT-13 had very limited instruments. These planes, however, were equipped with a full instrument panel. There were gauges indicating fuel and oil pressure, air speed, engine rpm's, and indicator lights for wheels up or down. There was also an altimeter and a compass.

* * *

I asked Dick if there was much difference between flying a twin engine as opposed to a single engine.

He said, "Not much. The main difference was it had a control for fixing the position of the propeller. For example, when preparing to take off, I'd adjust the pitch to a forward position, which would tip the prop down a little. That would cause it to take a big bite of air needed to get the plane off the ground. When I was airborne, I'd adjust the prop back, which would allow the plane to go faster and use less fuel.

"Another difference was the engines had to be synchronized. There was an rpm gauge, but I found it easier to do it by sound. If they were out of sync, one engine would sound different, like, vroom, vroom, vroom."

I had to laugh as he sat in his chair moving his body, making those sounds like he was going to take right off then and there.

He said, "So I would adjust that engine until the two sounded as one."

"Jesus, Dick! For a minute there, I thought you were going to take right off in your chair!"

He laughed and held up his empty glass. "How about another little touch? All this flying is making me thirsty."

I put some cubes in both our glasses and poured us a three fingered shot of J&B.

Dick got out of his pilot's seat and put some more wood on the fire. He picked up his glass and walked out into the solarium. We had both been so engrossed in his

THE WHISKEY BOTTLE CONVERSATION

storytelling we hadn't paid much attention to the storm. I grabbed my glass and followed him.

The windows on the north side of the solarium were covered with snow. Apparently, the temperature had warmed up, so the snow was no longer light and fluffy. It was coming down hard with gusts of wind, pushing it in different directions. The stonewall around the veranda was no longer visible, so at least eighteen inches had fallen.

We sat there sipping our Scotch, watching Mother Nature show us who was in charge. Our feet were up on a bench in front of the window and our heads back on the leather cushion of the small couch where we were sitting. We sat in silence until we heard the sounds of popping and crackling in our rekindled fire.

Dick looked at me and said, "Sounds like our old friend is calling us back to the story."

I smiled. "Sure sounds like it to me, Dick."

We walked arm in arm back to our chairs.

We sat down, and Dick said, "Now, where were we?"

"You were telling me about the differences between the planes."

"Oh, yes."

"These twin-engine planes had two half-moon-shaped steering wheels: one for the pilot another for the copilot. The stick was a thing of the past. On the steering wheels were two buttons that controlled your machine guns."

He made a movement like he was holding onto the wheel, pushing it forward, then pressed his thumb against the imaginary buttons.

"Ra-ta-ta-tat, ra-ta-ta-tat, ra-ta-ta-tat."

Then he pretended to pull back on the wheel. His gestures were comical.

"Boy, that was fun, firing those guns!"

I was in hysterics.

* * *

There were about two hundred of us in Yuma. Most were pilots, except for the mechanics that they had working on the planes. It would get so damned hot in the middle of the day that these electrical landing gear switches would fuse and the plane would collapse on the runway. They had a hell of a time getting that straightened out!

After they got that problem solved, four or five planes crashed. They found that the temperature differential between ground temperatures and altitude-flying temperature caused the engines to cut out. After some analysis, they realized it was necessary to use carburetor heat from the manifold to pass through the carburetor so the pilot had some control over the operation of the engine. After those few problems were straightened out, the planes were a real joy to fly.

The bookwork was now a thing of the past. So now all I had to worry about was my flying. There were pre-flight instructions on flying procedures. For example, we'd meet as a group of, say, ten pilots of five aircraft, and we'd get instruction on formation flying. The instructor would draw on the blackboard the position of the five airplanes—say, three planes at eight thousand feet in close formation. Then he would draw two planes at ten thousand feet behind the three. All pilots were supposed to look for the enemy, and copilots would watch the instruments. At the same time another instructor would be giving a different group procedures on attacking a target.

After the briefing we checked our planes, got in, and were ready for takeoff. When we were given the signal, the plane rumbled down the runway. As we lifted off, I'd give the signal to the copilot for gear up, flaps up, and we were off… into the wild blue yonder. The other planes began to pull into formation, and communication came over the radio. All the planes advised that they were in position and ready, but not for fun. This was combat. We had to be prepared to protect our lives, to think and act as if this was the air battle of the war.

On other occasions we were given instruction in air to ground attacks. This was the use of our machine guns on targets fixed to the ground. We'd be given a pattern to fly and then attack the target, for which you would receive a score on your performance.

* * *

"Did you have any sights to look through before you fired your guns?"

"No, basically, I put the plane in a dive and pointed it at my target. I had to be careful, though. You know, diving down on a target, blasting away with your guns, it was easy to become totally engrossed in hitting the target. Some of the boys weren't watching their altimeters, got too close, couldn't pull out of the dive, and crashed."

* * *

One event that sticks out in my mind about Yuma was the time when near the end of our training, I cut my leg getting into the plane, and it became infected. I went to the medical tent, and the doctor looked it over. He picked up a pair of blunt-nosed scissors, punched them into the infection, and forced it open. I damned near passed out!

He sprinkled some type of powder on it and said, "I'll see you tomorrow."

The cut would drain and begin to close up. I'd go back the next day, and he'd perform the same procedure. In about a week, it healed. I didn't think so at the time, but I guess he knew what he was doing.

We spent eight weeks at the Yuma base, and then we graduated and were commissioned second lieutenants. There wasn't any real ceremony. We were just marched up and given a certificate that said we had passed this course. It had been roughly twenty-seven weeks since Sterns and I arrived in Bakersfield. It had been a hell of an education. Now we had a two-week leave and could go home and see our families.

CHAPTER NINE

B-26s, 17s, and 24s

Sterns and I caught a flight home on a troop carrier that was heading in the neighborhood of Syracuse. We were both excited about going back East and were met with much love by our families. After seven months, it was great to be home!

Jean looked beautiful with her freckled face, rosy cheeks, and protruding belly. It was hard to believe that in about two months, I would be a father. My first night home, Harriet prepared a roast beef dinner with all the trimmings. They all wanted to know about my training—where I had been and the things I had experienced. I think even HK was glad to have me back and seemed proud as I related the stories of military life.

During my two-week stay, Jean and I went for drives in the country, had dinner with some of our friends, and spent a good deal of time with her family. One Friday afternoon I went to the men's club in town and got pretty drunk. All the boys wanted to hear my tales, and the older gentlemen treated me with a great deal of respect. The familiar surroundings felt very comfortable, but in no time my two weeks were over.

While in training I didn't have much time to be homesick. With all the activities of studying and flying, my mind was always occupied. Being home again with my family made it difficult when I had to leave.

Jean and Harriet took me to Syracuse where I was to pick up the transport. We met Sterns at the airport, and after tearful good-byes, we boarded the plane, which took us to Del Rio, Texas, the B-26 flight school.

The base at Del Rio was large by comparison to Bakersfield. There were thirty two-story barracks, four runways, a control tower, an officer's club, a large mess hall, and two administration buildings. A chain-link fence surrounded the base with sentries at all the gates. Del Rio was a Western town of about twenty thousand.

The B-26, or Martin Marauder, was the world's fastest medium-range bomber and was originally designed as a low-altitude bomber. It was built to fly in at two or three hundred feet, strafe the target, drop the bombs, and get the hell out. It had two Pratt and Whitney R2800 Double Wags engines. This gave the plane 3,700 horsepower and speeds of 325 mph. Without a load and stripped down, it could push 400 to 500 mph in a dive. The plane's bomb load was three thousand pounds, and its service elevation was twenty-five thousand feet with a range of a thousand miles. It weighed twelve tons and had up to twelve .50-caliber machine guns, four packaged guns on the fuselage, and three 1000-pound bombs.

THE WHISKEY BOTTLE CONVERSATION

The first plane produced demanded a lot of respect. The instructors told us that there had been numerous crashes. The 26s had the shortest wingspan of any bomber, and that meant your landing speed had to be at least 160 mph, which was extremely fast. A fighter plane like a P-40, for example, had a landing speed of about 60 mph. So when a 26 hit the ground at 160 mph, it was really moving. If the plane's speed dropped below 160, it literally fell out of the sky. Consequently, a lot of pilots thought it was unsafe and were scared to death of the plane. I thought it was a joy to fly, and it handled like a big fighter. The pilots nicknamed them the Flying Prostitutes—no visible means of support.

After about ten hours with an instructor pilot, we were given the planes to fly by ourselves. The crew consisted of a pilot, copilot, bombardier, radio operator, and four machine-gunners. Our training involved formation flying with anywhere from ten to fifty planes. We would make mock-bombing runs on Phoenix, Arizona. We also had target practice with our .50-caliber machine guns. I really enjoyed the target practice: skimming across the Texas desert at about three hundred feet with guns blazing. It made me feel like somebody… with the responsibility for the plane and my crew. It was a real thrill to fly them!

B26 Martin Maurador, world's fastest medium range bomber plane

From the B-26s, we moved on to the B-17s and the B-24s, which were four-engine bombers. The engines produced 7,500 hp. They carried a much larger payload of nine 500-pound impact bombs. The crews consisted of a pilot, a copilot, bombardier, radio operator, navigator, and six gunners. The .50-caliber guns were in the nose, the tail section, one out on top of the plane, another on the belly, and two side gunners. They both had a landing speed of about eighty miles an hour.

* * *

"The 17s and 24s handled a lot differently than the 26s. As I told you, Dave, the 26 had a short wingspan, which gave it a great deal of maneuverability… like flying a fighter. The 17s and 24 had a long wingspan and were like flying a big kite. They didn't respond as quickly and almost seemed like they could fly themselves."

B-24 Liberator

B-24 bomber cockpit

* * *

We continued our formation flying, making runs on Phoenix. The people who lived there must have been awfully tired of having large formations of planes flying over their town day in and day out. There was no air-to-air combat as such. To give the gunners experience in combat training, we would tow targets for them to shoot at. I was assigned to tow targets and was put in charge of the maintenance crews that kept the forty planes in the squadron flying. We had two stripped-down B-26s towing the targets. I was in one, and I assigned Sterns to the other plane. Sterns and I would climb up to the altitude, usually about ten thousand feet, and meet the other planes that were going to shoot at us.

Each of us had an engineer who flew copilot until it was time to let the target out. The target itself was a big strip of canvas with a bull's-eye on it and was hooked to a 2,800-foot cable that the engineer let out. One target was red and the other one, blue. The remainder of the B-26s were broken up into two groups of ten planes, and each group was designated to shoot at one of the targets.

I would fly by one side of the formation, approximately a thousand feet above them, so the side gunners could shoot over the other planes in their formation. Once I had made my pass, I would circle the plane and come back on the other side so that both side gunners got a chance to practice. Then I would circle around and cross behind the planes at one thousand feet below them so that the tail and belly gunners could shoot at the target.

I'd make five or six passes in the various directions, then would fly back over the base, and the engineer would release the target and reel in the cable. The ground crew would retrieve the targets, and after dinner, all the gunners would be called into a classroom where they could see how they had done.

* * *

"Did your plane ever get hit?"

He smiled and said, "Oh, every so often we'd find four or five holes in the plane where one of the boys got a little excited."

* * *

When I wasn't towing targets, I was responsible for keeping all the planes ready to fly. I had a great crew of about one hundred mechanics who worked day and night to keep those birds in the air. When the brass called for a formation, we had to be ready, and if we weren't, there would be hell to pay. My group never missed a formation. I was out there with them most of the day, making sure they got the parts and supplies they needed. I became a pretty good scrounger. On many occasions, I'd work late into the night alongside my mechanics to make sure we were ready. I think the boys really respected me for that, and whenever I asked for something to be done, they worked their asses off to see it was finished on time.

Dick's B26 crews at Biggs Field used for target towing pilots mechanics gunners all on hand

There was this fellow, Captain Grubbs, who was supposed to be in charge of group activity, such as, military protocol and administrative duties. He wasn't a flight officer; he was a paper shuffler as far as I was concerned. Grubbs was a short guy who always had his head shaved and walked with a swagger, like he was somebody important… a real pain in the ass!

I had a run-in with him once when he came to inspect our barracks. I had never had an inspection and told the boys just to do their jobs, not to worry about their bunks or gear. I mean, we had all we could do just to keep the planes flying. So Major Grubbs comes by for barrack's inspection

THE WHISKEY BOTTLE CONVERSATION

one day, and when he saw the condition of the barracks, he went ballistic.

He came out on the flight line, where I was overseeing the maintenance operations, and said, "Lieutenant Leonard, I want an explanation!"

"Explanation about what, sir?"

"I want an explanation on the condition of those barracks. I've never seen such a mess! There are clothes everywhere, the beds aren't made, and I found lipstick on some toilet paper!"

I tried to keep from laughing as the major berated me.

"Is that a smile on your face, Leonard?"

"No, sir! But you know what is required of us to keep these planes flying and to meet our demand for towing targets. These boys have been working night and day on these planes to meet that demand. I told them not to worry about cleaning the barracks, just worry about keeping the planes in the air."

He said, "I'm going to report this to the base commander!"

I said, "Do whatever you've got to do, Major," and walked away.

"I didn't dismiss you!"

I just kept walking.

Major Grubbs made his report to General Tibits, the base commander. Tibits called in Captain Bob Borders, who was the operations officer for the entire base, and told him about Grubbs's report.

Bob acknowledged that he was right. The barracks were a mess, but the boys were working hard trying to keep the planes flying and that Lieutenant Leonard was doing a good job and should be commended, not reprimanded.

General Tibits called me in his office and said, "I've met with Major Grubbs, and he's filled me in on the condition of the barracks."

I expected the shit to hit the fan, but the general said, "When you get the chance, Lieutenant, see if you can get the men to pick up a little. Keep up the good work. You're dismissed."

That was the last I saw of Major Grubbs.

Bob Borders had been a B-26 pilot in Europe. He was the only one to survive out of his squadron. When he returned stateside, he was assigned as operations officer at Del Rio. Bob was twenty-five, tall, handsome, and from South Carolina. His wife, Betty, was a Southern belle. She was prim and proper and looked like she belonged on a plantation. Both of their families were well off.

When he arrived I was operations officer in charge of planes. I familiarized him with what was going on in my area. As far as running the base operations, I don't think he really gave a shit. He was just damn happy to be there. He'd seen a lot of his buddies die and was glad to be out of the war. He never really talked much about it. In fact, he hated to fly. Whenever he had to go someplace, I would always do the flying. Bob and I became good friends.

As time went by, more and more of the officers on base were being transferred to different places. Near the end of my stay in Del Rio, Bob and I basically ran the whole show. I was in charge of scheduling all the flights and continued my duties with the maintenance crew. Bob was in charge of the overall operation of the base, and with two thousand

THE WHISKEY BOTTLE CONVERSATION

men under his command, he had his hands full. It was at Del Rio that I made first lieutenant.

Captain Borders pushed for my promotion, and when it came through, he pinned my first lieutenant wings on me in a small ceremony. Bob was a great man to work for. He would always listen to my recommendations before making decisions on subjects under my jurisdiction. He was a Southern gentleman, a trifle war weary, but projected an air of self-assurance. I felt this was a result of being the only pilot to survive from his squadron in the European Theater.

The day I received my promotion, I called home to tell Jean and my family about my new status. Harriet answered the phone.

I said, "Hi, Mom, how's everything going?"

She said, "Don't you talk to me."

"Why? I just called to tell you I've been promoted to first lieutenant," I said.

Harriet interrupted, "Do you know that you've been a father for seven days and haven't had the courtesy to send a wire?"

"I didn't know anything about it! I hadn't heard a word. I'm terribly sorry!"

Then she began to cry. "You've got a beautiful son, Dick. He weighed eight pounds, seven ounces. Both Jean and Richard Jr. are doing fine."

I asked if Jean was there, and Harriet said, "She's at her mother's in Fulton."

I told Harriet that I would see if I could get a flight to Syracuse. I called Jean and apologized for not calling or sending a wire, but I didn't know. Jean began to cry.

"I miss you so much, Dick. I wish you were here."

"Come hell or high water, I'll get a flight up to Syracuse. How's our son doing?"

Jean said, "He's so beautiful. His face is perfectly round, and his eyes are blue. I was in labor for three hours. Harriet and my mother were with me the whole time. They were a comfort and provided the moral support I needed."

"I wish I could have been there, Jean. I'll call you as soon as I can get a flight."

* * *

I asked Dick how he felt about being a father.

"I was a little sad because I hadn't been there but proud as hell to have a son."

* * *

I went and got Sterns, Bob Borders, and a couple other friends and took them into town for a celebration. We smoked cigars and drank until Bob and Al had to carry me back to the barracks. At least, I think they carried me because I don't remember going back to the base. I was a pretty sad case the next day.

While we were out celebrating, I had asked Bob about getting some leave to go home.

He said, "Let me talk to the base commander. Maybe I can get you a B-26, and I'll set it up as a cross-country training flight."

Bob filled out the paperwork and submitted it to the general, which he approved. I put a notice up on the bul-

THE WHISKEY BOTTLE CONVERSATION

letin board for any boys who wanted to go to Syracuse. About a dozen signed up. Since I was in charge of flight assignments, I had Sterns as my copilot. I was planning on buying a car and bringing Jean and Rick back with me. Sterns could fly the 26 back to Del Rio.

Before we left, I called Jean and Harriet and told them approximately what time I would arrive in Syracuse. I got all the boys on, and we took off.

Once we got airborne, I looked at Sterns and said, "We've come a long way from two hicks on a train to California."

Sterns said, "No shit! In less than a year, we've gone from privates to lieutenants flying our own B-26 on a little vacation! Not bad for a couple of country boys!"

We both laughed as I pushed the throttle forward and put the 26 in a steep climb.

As we flew over Ohio and into New York, seeing all the trees and green fields made my heart pound. I decided to fly over Mexico before landing in Syracuse. We approached from the west. I had the 26 at maximum throttle doing about 350 mph and flew right up Main Street at treetop level. I made a circle out over the lake and came back down Main Street in the opposite direction. We put on a show for the hometown fans. Sterns was laughing his ass off the whole time. After our little performance, we flew to Syracuse, landed, and checked the plane in. We had a soldier stand guard so that no one got in the plane.

When Sterns and I walked out of the control tower, there were Jean and Harriet and HK. Jean ran up and jumped in my arms. She was crying. We embraced and kissed for a long time. Harriet was holding Rick.

"Well, let me see my boy!"

Harriet put Rick in my arms, and I got quite emotional. I said, "Jesus! He's so small!"

Sterns said, "You've got a real handsome boy there, Dick."

He gave Jean a kiss and congratulated her.

Sterns and the boys only had a weekend pass. I had two weeks.

I said, "Now, don't get lost on the way back to Del Rio. I'll see you in a couple of weeks."

We drove back to Mexico, and for the next few days, I just relaxed and spent time with Jean and Rick.

Dick sees his son for the first time

Jean and Rick at 9 months old

THE WHISKEY BOTTLE CONVERSATION

While I was home, I went into Oswego and bought a two-door Chevy coupe. There was a bench seat in the front and no seat in the back—just a small open space. That afternoon, I drove up to Burke's men's club and had a few drinks with the boys.

Old Man Burke said, "You know, Dick, last Friday some crazy bastard flew this war plane right down Main Street! Then he turned around and flew back down the other way! He was so close I could have hit him with a stone. The dogs were barkin', windows rattled, and I haven't seen my cat since then! You wouldn't know anything about that?" he asked with a wink.

"I don't know nothin' about that!"

He said, "The rest of your drinks are on the house, Dick. We're all proud of you!"

Over the next five days, Jean and I made preparations for our trip back to Del Rio. I took one of those baby swings and hooked fasteners to it and attached them to both sides of the car in back of the seat. We filled the trunk of the coupe and strapped a trunk to the roof filled with everything we could fit in it.

Harriet had applied for, and had been given, the job of issuing the rationing cards in Oswego County. Many things, such as gasoline, tires, some types of food, among other items, could only be acquired with a rationing card. It was a very important position. She never took a paycheck. She said that if her son was going to fight, she wanted to contribute. All her pay went into war bonds. She was a wonderful woman.

* * *

I saw some tears rolling down Dick's cheeks. He made a couple of soft sobs then wiped his eyes and sat there quietly staring into the fire. That was the only time I ever saw him cry. I got up, put some more ice in his glass, and poured him a shot.

I handed it to him. "She was a great lady, Dick. Everybody loved her!"

He raised his glass to the fire and said, "Here's to you, Harriet!" threw the shot down, and placed his empty glass on the coffee table.

"Now where were we?" he said.

"You were getting ready to leave for Del Rio."

* * *

Jean, Rick, and I left on a Saturday morning. We had Rick in the swing behind our seat just rocking back and forth. He barely made a peep the whole trip. I only had a week to make it back to the base, so there wasn't much time for sightseeing. Jean and I hadn't had much time together since we had been married. It was great having her by my side, sharing our experiences of the past ten months.

We'd drive most of the day and in the evening find a motel or boarding house and spend the night. In the morning Jean would make sandwiches. She'd put Rick in his little swing, and off we would go. When we got about five hundred miles from Del Rio, I ran out of gas in the middle of the desert.

After about a two-hour wait, a sailor came along, stopped, and asked what our problem was. I told him I was out of gas.

THE WHISKEY BOTTLE CONVERSATION

He said, "Well, I've got a rope. I'll tow you to the next gas station."

So he towed us for two hundred miles through the Texas desert and countryside until we came to a station. I filled up both of our cars and thanked him for his help. We arrived in Del Rio late Thursday afternoon. I got Jean and Rick a room in a boarding house in town. Then I went over to the base to report in to Bob Borders.

Bob welcomed me back and filled me in on what had been going on in my two-week absence.

He said, "I've been transferred to Biggs' Field in El Paso as head of base operations. Biggs is a training facility for B-17s and B-24s. I've requested, and it's been approved to take you along as operations and accident investigating officer. So don't bother getting an apartment here. We'll be leaving in three days."

I asked Bob about Al Sterns.

He said, "Al has been assigned to a B-17 squadron going to Britain. You'll have to get all your paperwork in order and familiarize a Lieutenant Sager about your procedures. I've spent some time with him while you were gone, but he really needs to talk to you. Check back with me tomorrow afternoon and let me know how things are going."

I walked out of Bob's office and went to find Sterns. As I approached his barracks, he came walking out the door.

"Hey, Dick!" he said. "How was the trip?"

"Long, Al. I guess I prefer traveling in the air. I heard you've been assigned to a B-17 group going to Britain."

"That's great, isn't it? I'll finally get to see some combat. I'm getting a little bored towing targets and dropping imaginary bombs on Phoenix."

"Wish I was going with you," I said.

"Your time will come, Dick. Bob said you're going to be operations officer over at Briggs—a man of rank and responsibility."

"To be honest with you, Al, I'd much rather be responsible for dropping five hundred-pound bombs on those Nazi bastards in Germany. When do you leave?"

"Well, I've been given a ten-day pass so I can go home and see my family. Then I have to report back here, and we're flying our squadron of 17s over. I'm catching a transport back to Syracuse tomorrow morning."

I said to Al, "Let's go to the officer's club and have a drink."

We spent the next couple of hours reminiscing about the past year and how far we had come. When we got up to leave, Al gave me a hug, stepped back, and we saluted each other.

"You take care of yourself, Dick, and give Jean and your son a kiss for me!"

I said, "Send me a postcard from Berlin, buddy."

* * *

I asked Dick if he looked up Al after the war. He was staring into the fire.

"Sterns was shot down and killed in a bombing raid over Germany."

THE WHISKEY BOTTLE CONVERSATION

Dick swung around in his chair and looked out into the solarium and the storm outside. I didn't say anything. I felt like I had known Al Sterns, and his death gave me a real sense of loss.

Dick remained with his back to me for about ten minutes. When he turned back to the fire, his eyes were red, but there were no tears visible. He began talking again while looking into the fire.

* * *

After I got my replacement familiarized with procedures, Jean and I drove to El Paso. It was a town of about twenty thousand with a Mexican-American mix. Most of the buildings were wood structures, and some of the streets were paved and others weren't. Personally, I thought it was a real shithole.

We arrived at Biggs's Field, and I took Jean and Rick to a building that had rooms for wives of the servicemen. It wasn't a permanent residence, as such. It just provided a place for a few days until other accommodations could be made in town. There were about fifteen bedrooms, a common kitchen, dining, and living rooms. There were four shared community bathrooms. Once I got Jean and Rick settled, I reported to Bob Borders.

I found Bob in the administration building. He introduced me to the base commander, General Kaska. The general was a big man with graying hair and a bit of a paunch. Whenever I saw him, he always had a long cigar hanging out of his mouth or in his hand. When he talked to you, he used his cigar as a pointer.

Bob and I hopped into a jeep and drove over to the area of the base where the B-26s were. Biggs was a large base that encompassed three to four hundred acres. It was like its own little town. There were barracks that housed roughly three thousand personnel. It had an officers' and enlisted men's club, where you could get a drink, something to eat, or attend social events, like dances. The PX served as a general store where you could get anything from food to clothing to hardware supplies. The base had a control tower and four runways, which crisscrossed so you could take off or land in any direction.

As far as the planes, there were three different areas. One section was for our group, the B-26s. The B-17s and 24s had their own areas. Each section had three or four hangers, which could fit up to five planes in to work on them. Between the B-17s and B-24s, there were about six hundred planes. We had fifty B-26s.

Bob and I arrived in Area A, where the 26s were kept. He took me around and introduced me to some of the pilots and heads of the maintenance crews.

He said, "This is the man you'll answer to. If you need anything or have any problems, contact Lieutenant Leonard."

The main function of our group was to continue to tow targets for the 17s and 24s to practice their air-to-air offense. My responsibilities included scheduling all the flights, making sure the maintenance on the planes was kept up, and keeping all the 201 files on the four hundred men under my command. The 201 files were a person's military records.

THE WHISKEY BOTTLE CONVERSATION

When I was in Del Rio, I became friends with another pilot, Gus Kriesmont, who was from Chicago. His mother was a ward boss for Mayor Daley. She was a big woman who, as I understood it, could really make things happen. Gus was about six three, well over two hundred, and always had a hell of a time fitting into his flight suit. Every so often, when he'd return from a flight, the crotch or back would be ripped open on his suit. Gus had been transferred to El Paso, and I ran into him when I was inspecting one of the hangars.

"Hey, Dick!" he said.

We shook hands. I hadn't seen him since I left to go get Jean.

"Are you ops officer on this show?"

"I'm afraid so! Captain Borders requested my transfer here."

He asked about my trip and wanted to know where Jean and Rick were.

I said, "They're over at temporary housing until I can find a place in town."

"No kidding!" he said. "Marion is over there too! Why don't we see if we can find a place together in El Paso? That way the girls can keep each other company!" Marion was Gus's wife.

We drove over to the quarters and found Jean, Marion, and another girl on the front porch. Marion was holding Rick.

When she saw us, she said, "Gus, come look at Jean and Dick's beautiful son!"

I had met Marion in Del Rio, so when she and Jean began to talk, everything clicked.

Before we could tell them of our plan, Jean said, "Marion and I think we should look for an apartment we can share. That way we can keep each other company while you two are flying."

Gus and I looked at each other and smiled.

He said, "Gee, that sounds like a great idea! Don't you think so, Dick?"

"Sounds good to me!" I said.

The girls spent the next two days looking for a place. Because of the size of El Paso and the number of military personnel, there wasn't much available. They finally settled on a one-bedroom apartment on the first floor of a two-story house. It was furnished with two double beds in the bedroom, a small kitchen, and a living room. There were a set of railroad tracks a couple of hundred feet behind the house.

The girls put a curtain down the center of the bedroom to offer some sense of privacy. Gus and Marion wanted to have a baby. The train would come through every night about eleven.

We would be in bed, and Gus would say, "Hey, Dick. I hear the train coming."

I'd say, "I'm getting ready, Gus."

We'd continue this silly banter until one of us yelled, "Shit! Here she comes!" and then the train would roll through, drowning out any other sounds.

CHAPTER TEN

I Ought to Court-Martial You!

I asked Dick if he still flew much at Biggs given all his other duties. He said…

* * *

Well, at Del Rio we were still in flight training, learning the particulars of flying the B-26s, 17s, and 24s. Our target-towing and air-to-air combat drills were on a limited scale.

At Biggs the flight training was over, and we were preparing for war. My group of fifty B-26s were used almost exclusively for towing targets. It required a lot of effort on our part to keep up with the demands of six hundred B-17s and 24s. Much of my time was spent on the ground, coordinating flight schedules and making sure my mechanics had the parts they needed to keep the planes flying. I was also in charge of investigating and filling out the reports on any accidents involving the planes on the base.

On one occasion General Kaska had a woman copilot, and he was letting her taxi this B-24 out on the runway when she clipped the wing of another plane. I did my investigation, naming him as the pilot, her as the copilot, and submitted my report. A few days later, I was told to report to the general's office. I walked in, saluted, and he pulled out the report and tore it up and threw it in the waste basket.

He pointed his cigar at me and said, "I've filed this report, understand, Lieutenant Leonard?"

I saluted and said, "Yes, sir!"

"You're dismissed, Lieutenant!"

There were some special missions that Bob Borders would assign me to fly. If it required more than one plane, I would pick the other pilots. After a couple of months of target practice and small formation bombing runs, there was going to be a large-scale mock attack on Phoenix. It was a coordinated effort between three bases to join up over the Midwest and make their bombing run. There were supposed to be 750 planes.

About a week before the mission, Bob came to me and said, "I want you to pick six pilots and get six stripped-down 26s. I've got a dozen cameras coming tomorrow that will be mounted where your .50-caliber guns are. You're going to simulate fighter attacks on this upcoming bombing operation. You get your pilots together, and I'll meet you tonight to fill your team in on all the particulars."

I picked Gus and five other pilots.

Bob met with us that night and explained what was going on. On the blackboard he drew diagrams of how the German fighter pilots had attacked his squadron and what type of evasive maneuvers they made.

THE WHISKEY BOTTLE CONVERSATION

He said, "The B-24s and 17s have orders to stay in formation no matter what happens. If someone breaks away, you all go after him. When you push the button for your guns, the cameras will shoot and give us a record for our analysis. Take the next couple of days, take your planes up, and practice your attack procedures. Give 'em hell, boys! Make me proud!"

Before we went up for our practice maneuvers, I'd spend an hour in front of the blackboard, giving the boys our plan of attack. I'd show them the different directions and altitudes we would use. I wanted us to be prepared. With that many planes, one mistake could spell catastrophe.

Two days before the exercise, the major in charge of logistics gave me all the information on the bombing group—where they would meet up, what their altitude and direction would be, and the expected time of the bombing run on Phoenix. The day of the exercise, I decided we would make our attack about five hundred miles before the squadron arrived at Phoenix.

It was a beautiful sunny day with not a cloud in the sky. They were heading west, and we were heading east with the sun at our back, so they couldn't see us.

I got on the radio…

"Gus, you're on my left wing. Bill, you pull up on my right. The three of us will fly right straight at them and pull up over the top of my mark. You other boys break off and come in from the north and go under them."

Gus, Bill, and I put our 26s in a dive, leveled off, and headed right for the lead planes with cameras blazing. Jesus, that was fun!

When we got about one thousand feet away, I'd say, "Pull up!" and we'd fly right over the top of them, scaring the hell out of those lead pilots.

We'd pull up, make a circle, and come in from the opposite direction, doing the same maneuver. After a few passes in formation, I told the boys to break up and make attacks on their own.

"Keep in contact," I said, "so we don't go running into each other."

I was having a ball! I'd fly up behind the squadron, put my 26 in a dive, and come in right over the nose on the lead plane. Then I'd make a sharp left bank and come up on their underbelly. All this time the top tail and belly gunners would be spinning around in their turrets, trying to hit me with their camera shots.

At one point, Gus called over the radio, "We've got one breaking away from the pack at eight o'clock. He's heading in a southwesterly direction."

I got on the radio and said, "Let's go get him, boys!"

I'd let him get about ten miles away from the rest of the squadron to give us room to maneuver. We were above and behind him, so he didn't know we were there.

I said, "We'll take him two at a time. Gus, you and I'll go first. We'll dive and fly right over the top of him, circle around, and come straight for him. At one thousand feet, I'll pull up. You go under. When we've made our run, we'll pull up behind the group, and the next two can have a go at 'em."

Gus and I put our planes in a dive and screamed just over the top of this 24 at about five hundred miles an hour. Gus broke left, and I broke right. We made a big loop and joined up on each other's wing, flying right at him. When

THE WHISKEY BOTTLE CONVERSATION

we got as close as possible, I pulled up, and Gus drove. Our planes were so close they shook as we passed each other. I wanted to give that pilot his money's worth, as Bob Borders had instructed. What I didn't know, but was soon to find out, was that it was General Kaska.

After about fifteen minutes of taking turns attacking the B-24, I said, "Let's form up, take a little run out over the ocean, and head home."

When we got close to the base, I got on the radio and said, "I think we ought to give a little show for the tower. Let's buzz them in formation at about four hundred feet. Then we'll break off and make a two-formation landing. Gus, Bill, and I will land in one group, then you boys touch down in pairs."

At about fifteen miles out, we were up at ten thousand feet. I put my 26 in a steep dive, building up speed. Gus and Bill were on my wings, and the other two were behind us. We leveled off about four hundred feet and went roaring over the base at full throttle. Then we pulled up, circled, and made our formation landing. As I taxied to the parking area, the tower called and said they wanted the pilot in charge of the 26 group to report immediately to Operations.

General Kaska was there, pacing back and forth, chewing on his big cigar.

I walked in, saluted, and said, "Lieutenant Leonard reporting as ordered, sir!"

He took the cigar out of his mouth and began pointing it at me.

"What in hell do you think you're doing, Leonard? I was in that plane that you attacked and risked the lives of all involved. What was going through your mind, flying head-on at me like that? Then on top of that, buzzing the tower at a couple hundred feet! What do you think this is, some type of circus? Well, it's not! This is the Air Corps, where rules and regulations are to be followed! I'm seriously considering bringing you up on charges, and I ought to start court-martial proceedings! You tell Captain Borders that I want to see him! Dismissed!"

* * *

I began to laugh at Dick. I said, "Jesus, it's hard for you to stay out of trouble!"

Dick smiled and said, "Just doing what I was instructed to do."

"I don't remember Bob telling you to buzz the tower!"

Dick said, "That might have been pushing it a little."

I asked Dick if the general brought him up on charges.

* * *

After the general dismissed me, I went to the major who was in charge of the operations and told him what happened.

He laughed about our attack on the general's plane and said, "I saw your formation landing. There's just one thing I've got to say about that, Lieutenant. That was great!"

I breathed a sigh of relief. I thought I was going to get another ass-chewing.

The major said, "I'll get together with Bob Borders, and we'll go see the general in a couple of days. Give him a little time to calm down."

THE WHISKEY BOTTLE CONVERSATION

Three days later, the general sent for me. I arrived in his office, saluted, and stood at attention, eyes forward.

He said, "I'm not going to press any charges, Lieutenant. From what Captain Borders and the major have told me, you did exactly as you were instructed to do, and both of them commended you on your performance. I myself thought it was reckless. You're dismissed!"

I saluted, turned, and walked out.

Before I got to the door, the general said, "Lieutenant." I turned around. He pointed his cigar at me and said, "I don't want to see any more of those formation landings."

I said, "Yes, sir!" and left his office.

* * *

I laughed and said, "You weren't happy unless you got your ass chewed out every once in a while, were you, Dick?"

He smiled and said, "I guess it helped keep things in perspective, Dave."

* * *

About a month after this happened, Bob came to me and said, "I've received orders to assign a pilot to fly Frank Costello, a congressman from California, around to all the women's flying schools in the country. They're going to discontinue the women's flying program, and the congressman has been selected to visit the bases and explain the Army's decision. I want you to take him, Dick. It will be good duty."

I looked at Bob and said, "When do we leave?"

Bob said, "The congressman is flying in tomorrow, and you're scheduled to leave at ten thirty Thursday morning. Get one of your stripped-down B-26s cleaned up, and be ready on Thursday."

I got one of my crew chiefs to polish and clean the plane. I went over to the officers' club and borrowed a big, comfortable chair and had the chief secure it right in behind the cockpit. I picked a good engineer, Sergeant Dubois, who knew the plane well.

That night I told Jean about my orders, and she said, "Don't worry about me. Marion is good company."

The next morning, Sergeant Dubois arrived at the plane at 10:00 am. As we were walking across the parking area, I saw three men standing by the plane. One of them was General Kaska.

I said to myself, "Why did he have to show up?"

As we got closer to the plane, the general called out, "Are you the pilot of this plane?"

I said, "Yes, sir."

Then he recognized me. He said, "Jesus! It's you! Don't tell me you're assigned to this plane?"

Bob Borders said, "General, I recommend Lieutenant Leonard very highly. He's our best pilot."

The general just mumbled something as the congressman came over and shook my hand.

"I'm Frank Costello, and I think we're going to get along just fine." He turned to the general and said, "Don't worry, sir, I'll take good care of Lieutenant Leonard."

The general just shook his head. I saluted him and said, "May I be excused to check the plane over, sir?"

THE WHISKEY BOTTLE CONVERSATION

He pointed his cigar and said, "I don't care what the hell you do! You're excused!"

As I was doing my preflight check, the congressman came over and followed me around, questioning me about what I was checking.

I explained everything to him and said, "In my opinion, this is the best airplane the Air Corps has. Captain Borders flew them in combat. He can tell you what a wonderful plane it is."

Costello went over and talked to Bob.

Bob said, "Yes, sir, I flew a B-26 over in Europe. It's a tremendous plane, especially in the areas of speed and performance." Then he said, "Lieutenant is probably our best pilot, and he will fly you anywhere you want to go."

The congressman got aboard and checked out the inside. He immediately took off his jacket and tie and sat down in the seat we had set up for him. I taxied out on the runway and took off. The congressman was a Scotch drinker. When we were airborne, he brought out his flask and had a little touch.

We flew to all the women's flying schools. I think there were ten schools, mostly located in the Western part of the country. We landed on fields that weren't up to the standards set for the 26; most of them were too short. When we were ready to land, the congressman would put on his tie and coat and pants.

He would say, "We're going into a base of fine women pilots, gotta act like gentlemen."

First we would buzz the field and then make our landing. The commander of the field, usually a woman, would meet us with her staff of officers. Congressman Costello and I would march with the commanding officer and all the women staff into the bar and have a drink just to relax and get to know our hosts. There were some nice-looking officers and students there.

We would stay two days at the most. Initially, we would get a tour of the facilities, which would take half a day. Then the commanding officer would show off her girls by having them fly for us in the afternoon. They were flying PT-13s and AT-6s, which were similar to the BT-13, but the BT-13 didn't have any automatic gear. It was just a little different. The AT-6 was a beautiful plane—single engine with a double cockpit, one in back of the other.

They'd take off, and the girls put on a good show. They took the AT-6 up, and it was so maneuverable they would do twists, turns, and fly in formation. The schools turned out literally hundreds of flyers—not bombardiers, but women pilots and navigators. Most of them knew the airplanes inside and out. I would consider them to be excellent pilots when they graduated.

The congressman would explain to them exactly what was going to happen. These schools were going to be closed down. He told it not so as to offend the pilots.

He'd say, "Based on performance records and my personal observations, your training program is excellent. It's the Army's decision, regrettable as it may be, that these women's facilities are to be closed."

He just told them the way it was, and he told it in a way that when we left the base, we were treated with same respect as when we got there. Of course, the women were really downhearted. The base commanding officer and her contingency had been notified in advance that the school was

THE WHISKEY BOTTLE CONVERSATION

going to be closed down. I think the congressman was sent to soften the blow. I'd say we were gone a month, flying all over the country. Congressman Costello got off at every base with the utmost dignity—nice shirt, suit and tie, and then when he got back on the airplane, he'd strip down. He'd start boozing after we took off, just enough to catch a little buzz. That month was one of the best times in my military career. I'll always remember Frank Costello and the fun we had.

* * *

"It sounds more like a vacation than military duty, Dick."

"It really was, Dave. You know, being in charge of our B-26 squadron, scheduling flights, and seeing that all our planes were kept ready to fly was a lot of pressure. Having a month of no responsibilities except to fly and socialize was a welcomed change. The congressman was a fine man and an excellent traveling companion."

* * *

After our duties were completed, we flew back to Texas. The congressman took Jean and me out to dinner.

He thanked me for the fine job I had done and said, "If there's anything I can ever do for you, Dick, you just let me know."

While I was gone, the pace of the operation at Biggs had slowed down. Much of the training was over for the squadrons, and they were gradually being sent overseas. I spent some of my free time flying B-24s and 17s on bombing runs. On other occasions, I would go along to observe the pilots and spent time with the gunners in the back of the plane. I wanted to see what their general attitude was and how they handled the gun.

One afternoon I got word to report to Bob Borders's office. Bob told me he had received orders to send two pilots in B-26s to Blythe Air Base in California.

"They want two planes equipped with cameras to fly air-to-ground missions for General Patton's tank group training in the desert," he said. "I want you and Gus to get your planes fitted up and fly to Blythe. Operations there will fill you in on the rest."

The next day I had our planes fitted with cameras in the wings where the .50-caliber guns were. Gus was happy as hell to be going along. Friday morning we checked our planes out and took off for Blythe.

Blythe was a B-25 base in the middle of the California desert. B-25s were twin-engine light bombers that were used on aircraft carriers. They were one of the first groups to bomb Japan from carriers before Okinawa was secured from the Japanese. Gus and I landed and reported to a Captain Wilson. He explained that there were five hundred tanks in the desert on maneuvers. We would be given patterns to fly and attack procedures to follow. Each day Gus and I would fly our mock combat missions on the tank group.

* * *

I asked Dick why they called for planes out of Texas to fly these missions if they had B-25s already at the base.

THE WHISKEY BOTTLE CONVERSATION

"Our group at Biggs had the most experience in combat air-to-ground and air-to-air combat training. The B-25s were designed primarily for bombing."

* * *

Each day, usually in the morning, we were given our instructions. We'd fly out in the desert and make low-level passes at about three hundred feet, across the tanks, shooting our camera guns. Sometimes we'd come in behind them, and other times we'd attack from the front. The tanks had cameras in their guns too. They were trying to defend themselves by swinging their big guns around, twisting and turning, trying to shoot us.

That was great fun! I don't think they were hitting us too well. By the time they got swung around to shoot, we would be gone. They'd expect us to come back in the way we went out. I would circle around and come in from the opposite direction. It was a guessing game as far as they were concerned. We'd come in right over the top of them at about four hundred miles an hour, so I'd say it was tough to draw a bead on us. I know I wouldn't want to be in one of those things. A tank would stop a bullet but not a .50-caliber cannon.

When we finished making our runs, Gus and I would get in formation and fly up the coast and meet these P-38s—which were twin-tail, twin-engine fighters. They were patrolling the coast line. Of course, they knew who we were just by vision. We'd spend an hour or so having dogfights. Outnumbered five to one, they would dive on us trying to give us a little scare.

"We weren't supposed to be doing that, but you've got to have some fun," Dick said with a wink. "At night they would show the films of the attacks to the tank crews and explain how they could improve their performance."

"What did you do when you weren't flying your missions, Dick?"

"We really didn't have any other duties or anyone to answer to except when we were scheduled to fly."

Dick and Gus in California mock attacking Patton's tank crews with cameras instead of guns

THE WHISKEY BOTTLE CONVERSATION

* * *

A lot of times, we'd gas up our planes and just take off on a little cruise. One day we flew up to Lake Tahoe. I was practicing a bombing run on the town, when all of a sudden, a Navy torpedo plane was making a run from the other direction. I was watching my instruments when I looked up and there he was, heading right for me! I pulled back on the wheel and went over the top of him. We missed each other by less than a couple hundred feet. I was that close to a catastrophe! It really took the wind out of my sails. I didn't stop shaking until I touched back down at Blythe.

Another time Gus and I took a plane and flew up to the Grand Canyon. I flew, and Gus took pictures. Some of the time, I'd fly right down in the canyon and other times would skim across the top… three hundred feet above the ground. We spent a couple of hours just playing around. Gus got some great pictures.

* * *

"So basically, Dick, you had your own plane and did pretty much whatever you wanted to do?"

"That's right. We didn't have an assignment. We were always Johnny-on-the-spot when they wanted us. Gus and I flew our missions in the desert and then flew up the coast with the P-38s chasing us."

* * *

A few weeks after we arrived at Blythe, Jean and Marion drove up. Gus and I were surprised as hell to see them. We thought they were safe in the apartment back in Texas. I think they got along so well because they were both headstrong, determined girls. They couldn't stay on base, so Gus called his uncle in Los Angeles, and he agreed to put them up. On weekends Gus and I would borrow a car and go see them. We'd tour the city, go out to dinner, sit on the beach—things you would do in any new place. Sometimes we'd take Rick, and other times Gus's aunt and uncle would watch him. He was a good baby.

One weekend while we were in Los Angeles, the captain and a few boys decided to take my B-26 for a ride. Apparently, they flew around for a couple of hours, and when they made their approach, the landing gear wouldn't go all the way down. Being unfamiliar with the plane, they didn't know how to remedy the situation. They did manage to get it back up and bellied the plane in on a grass field. It bent the props all up but didn't do a lot of damage to the plane itself.

When we got back, the captain came to us and explained what happened. There would be an investigation, and he was scared shitless that he'd lose his wings. The day before he had to appear before the investigating committee, Gus and I spent several hours with Captain Wilson, instructing him on the emergency guidelines for a B-26. He went before the committee, and they ruled it mechanical, not pilot error. He was one happy son of a bitch! He took Gus and out for dinner and drinks. For the remainder of our stay at Blythe, whenever we made a request, it was honored immediately.

THE WHISKEY BOTTLE CONVERSATION

When we were nearing the end of our stay at Blythe, Jean decided to return to New York. She wanted to go back to school, and we both felt it would be better for Rick and her to be with family. After a tearful good-bye, she and Rick boarded a train in Los Angeles and headed East.

Gus and I flew back to Texas, while Marion drove. When we arrived, Gus had orders to be transferred to a base in New Mexico. It was a school for training navigators and bombardiers. He was a pilot instructor for crews scheduled to go overseas.

I felt that I had accomplished all I could stateside and wanted the adventure of an overseas assignment, hopefully with a combat outfit.

I went to Bob Borders and said, "I want a transfer."

He said, "Are you crazy, Dick? You and I have it made here! We work well together, and you're ready to make captain. Not only that, we need you! Think it over for a few days."

It was a very convincing argument, and I did give it a lot of thought.

I went to him the next day and said, "I want to thank you, Bob, for all you've done for me, and I've given a lot of thought to what you said. But I joined the Air Corps to give it my all and to fight just as you have done. I sincerely want you to put my name in for a transfer to an overseas station."

He shook his head and said, "You're nuts, Dick, but I'll see what I can do."

Two days later I was told to report to General Kaska's office. Both he and Bob were there, the general chewing on his cigar.

The general said, "Lieutenant Leonard, your transfer to an overseas assignment has been approved even though Bob and I think you're out of your mind! We both wish you Godspeed and the best of luck."

They both saluted, and the general dismissed me.

CHAPTER ELEVEN

A Journey to the Unknown

I looked at my watch. It was six o'clock.

I said, "We'd better have some dinner before we take our journey overseas."

"I think that's a good idea," he said. "I'll go fix us up something."

"There are some chicken breasts in the refrigerator, and the potatoes are in the pantry."

Dick got up from his chair and headed for the hall, staggering a little.

"Are you okay, Lieutenant?" I asked.

"Just have to get my land legs back after all that flying, Dave."

The fire was beginning to wane, so I threw some more wood on it and went into the solarium. The wind had stopped, and the snow was falling at a gentle pace. There was a full moon that wasn't clearly visible, but it provided enough light so I could see the silhouette of the mountains. I sat down and stared at the shadows in the black-and-white winter landscape.

My thoughts drifted back to the conversation John and I had had at the American Legion. The phrase "I really didn't know anything about my father" gave the conversation Dick and I had been having a new perspective. In the previous seven hours, I had relived a part of his life with him, and that life had been an adventure. He approached it with zest and determination, never looking back and always following his instincts no matter where they might lead him. As I looked out into the shadows of the Adirondack night, I felt very happy, but even more, fortunate, to be sharing this experience with my father.

I sat in the solarium until Dick returned with our dinner.

"Come and get it, boy!"

He set the tray on the coffee table. There were two plates with roasted chicken breasts, mashed potatoes, and corn. Milk and a dish of peaches served as complements to our meal.

"You really know how to take care of a guy, Dick!"

He smiled and said, "I do my best!"

We ate in silence, except for the occasional sound of the fire crackling. When we finished, I took our dishes back to the kitchen and fixed two bowls of ice cream. After our dessert, I asked Dick if he wanted an after-dinner drink.

"Sure!" he said.

I put some ice in our glasses and poured us both a little Scotch. Dick swirled his glass for a minute before taking a drink.

"Do you feel like continuing your story, Dick?"

"Hell, yes!" he said. "We're just getting to the good part!"

THE WHISKEY BOTTLE CONVERSATION

I laughed. "After what I've heard so far, how much more exciting can it get?"

He smiled. "You'll see. Where did I leave off, Dave?"

"You had asked for and received a transfer."

"Oh, yes!"

* * *

It took about two weeks after I requested an overseas assignment until I got my orders. I was to report to Kerns Distribution Center in Salt Lake City. Kerns was an Army base used primarily as a last stop before personnel were shipped overseas. I had to fill out a lot of paperwork and was reclassified into an overseas category. There were about five thousand men there, waiting to be shipped out.

The first day there, I've met Don Oaks, another first lieutenant and pilot. Don was a tall, quiet, handsome boy from California. His parents had oil wells on their property, so they were quite well off. Don received a monthly percentage of the profits.

We were the only two officers from the Air Corps at the base, and both of us had been assigned as operations officers. We had no idea where we were being sent. In fact, we didn't know until we reached our final destination. We spent two weeks at Kerns and had a lot of free time on our hands.

The first weekend we were there, Don and I went up into the mountains and stayed at the Rustler Ski Lodge in Alta. The trip up the mountain was beautiful. The road was a twisting, turning trail from sea level at the beginning to eight thousand feet when we arrived at the lodge.

As we went up, the snowbanks became deeper and there were signs of "Beware of Avalanche." The lodge was built into the side of the mountain. It had about thirty rooms, a huge stone fireplace, a large dining room, and a cocktail lounge. There was a deck that wrapped around the front of the building, providing visitors a panoramic view of the Rockies.

Don and I were in uniform and seemed to be the topic of conversation among the patrons. They all wanted to know what branch of the service we were in and where we were going. Most seemed impressed that we were both pilots. Everyone showed us a great deal of respect. In fact, I don't think we paid for a drink our entire stay.

The manager took us under his wing and made a schedule of activities for us. We took the lift to the top of the world, approximately eleven thousand feet above sea level. What a view! You could see for miles in any direction. The next day the manager took us for a ride up the mountain in a snowcat. He explained the use of the machine in emergency operations, like if someone was injured. They carried stretchers and medical supplies onboard. Ski patrol personnel ran the cat. They were persons who were expert skiers and trained in medical emergency techniques.

Don and I were taken around and shown all the duties of the personnel, from general housekeeping to the maintenance of the equipment. Most worked for little or no money. They were compensated with room and board and free skiing. We met many people and enjoyed their company as much as they seemed to enjoy ours. It was a great trip and relaxing time for both of us. The following week we received our orders. We boarded a train with a couple

THE WHISKEY BOTTLE CONVERSATION

thousand other GIs and were taken to Los Angeles to catch a ship headed for the Far East. We sailed out on Christmas Eve with no lights.

There were twin ships with, I'd guess, a couple thousand men onboard. None of us knew where we were going. Don and I had duties consisting mostly of supervising the enlisted men. For example, if we were out on deck, I'd have a certain area to watch to make sure fights didn't break out or keep the boys from getting into trouble. Their sleeping quarters were swinging hammocks. They just stacked them usually three-high. When the men were in there, they had maybe a foot separating on hammock from the one above it. They were horrible. I didn't know how the hell they could sleep in those things! Because Don and I were officers, we had a very small private room with two cots.

We also had a desk down in the enlisted men's sleeping quarters. If any of the men had complaints or just wanted to talk, they would come over, and we'd shoot the shit for a while.

* * *

"What kinds of things did they talk about, Dick?"

"Different ones. They would talk about their wives and kids or spoke about their feelings of going off to war. Some told me stories of how they happened to be in the service. They were all going to war, and I'd say most of them had a positive attitude about it.

"Many of them talked like they were going to win the war single-handedly, but in reality, I think they all knew they'd probably end up as cannon fodder. I would say the average age was about twenty… just a bunch of kids who were lonesome and needed someone to talk to."

I asked Dick how old he was at the time. He closed his eyes for a minute and then said, "Twenty-three."

"What kinds of duties did the enlisted men have?"

"There really wasn't a lot to do onboard. Basically, they had to keep their areas clean and each day would do calisthenics up on the deck. They had a game room, where many of them spent hours playing poker. Some of them never got out of their chairs. They slept there, borrowing money from one another, just passing the time. I used to go in and watch, and sometimes I'd join in."

"What was the weather like?"

"For the most part, it was really nice. There were a few occasions when we got rough seas. The ship would be really rolling. When you hit a big wave, the ship would break up over the top of it, then the bow would drop down, plowing through the next wave. The propellers would come right out of the water. The engines would rev up, and as the bow went up over another wave, they would dig back into the water.

"A lot of the guys were sick, and I tried to help them. We had been given medicine to settle our stomachs, but it didn't have any effect on a majority of the boys. I'd talk to them and say, 'I know this is tough, but you'll pull through. This storm can't last forever.'

"The GIs I'd be trying to comfort would moan, 'I just want to die. Take your gun, Lieutenant, and shoot me, please. I can't stand this anymore.' Then he'd throw up, or if there was nothing left in his stomach, he'd dry-heave.

"Sometimes the storms would last three or four days. I had a crew of boys that went around, cleaned up the vomit, and tried to keep the floor mopped so you wouldn't slip on the slime and puke."

Dick laughed and said, "You know, when there's two thousand men on a ship, and half of them are throwing up, it makes quite a mess!"

* * *

After the storm was over, we were allowed back up on the deck. What a relief that was to get some fresh air! Being locked down below for three days with a bunch of sick boys wasn't my idea of a party!

When the weather was clear, I had a favorite spot on deck. It was up near the front of the ship where the air exchanger was located. There were good-sized vents that sucked fresh air into the ship, and on the stern were vents that expelled the stale air from below deck. It was like a big vacuum cleaner.

Where I sat, it kept the air moving, so it was always relatively cool. I'd sit there in a pair of shorts and read a book or watch the fish that followed the ship. I saw all kinds of fish—porpoise, dolphins, whales, and at night, there were these flying fish that would jump out of the water and create what looked like fluorescent lighting. The spray would just light up! I suppose it was because of the bacteria or the salt solution in the water. When they broke the water and flew fifty or sixty feet, it looked like a trail of different-colored lights was following them. It was really beautiful!

We had a couple of submarine scares. I'm not sure if there were whales or real subs. I never saw anything, but when the alarm went off, we all had to get below. The ship would break to the left or the right, trying to avoid giving the subs a good shot. I don't think we were ever shot at. As far as I was concerned, they were just drills. That was pretty much life aboard ship.

* * *

I picked up the box of Dick's letters and put it on the coffee table. I still hadn't told him what was in it.

I said, "About a year before Mimi died, she called me and asked if I would stop by her house. She had this box sitting in the living room. It contains all the letters you wrote home during the war, pictures, your Army discharge papers, and other items of yours. She wanted me to have them."

Dick opened the box and pulled out the folder with the pictures and began looking at them. One of the letters he had written was about his experience aboard the ship. I pulled out the folders and began leafing through them looking for it.

When I found the letter, I said, "Dick, I want to read you something."

He put down the pictures, and I began…

> *To my Dear Parents, One month ago today, at bayonet's end, I was helped aboard this luxury liner! The grandmothers of the Red Cross were down to see us off, and with a few gentle pats, a flooding*

THE WHISKEY BOTTLE CONVERSATION

eye, and a ham sandwich, they bid us adieu, bon voyage, and farewell.

The Coast Guard band, and a very big outfit it was, played "I'm Dreaming of a White Christmas," "Please Don't Talk about Me When I'm Gone," and "Good-Bye Dear, I'll Be Back in a Year!" So with the bayonet, the Red Cross, the band, and a few other very elite persons, we said good-bye to the fair coast of California.

As soon as we were aboard, they sent us to our staterooms and ordered us to remain below. Already I was becoming an old salt. Just before we left the Port of Embarkation, we were all issued seasick pills and instructed in the use of them. Consequently, a great many of the mentally weak assumed they would immediately become ill. Well, the first night aboard, the latrine or "head" (as we seafaring men call it) was filled to capacity. It was a very cheery sight. As the weather was rather stuffy, the majority had completely disrobed, soooo, as you entered the door to the "head," you saw one long row of chubby, rosy cheeks, and were reminded of that very foolish bird—the Ostrich—except of course, it would have to be a young ostrich of the pin feather variety. I suppose this seasickness, as it was called, seemed very logical to the land lubber, but I noticed the crew walked around with a smirk in their faces. I thought nothing of it at the time, figured they just felt superior, but when after a very smooth night voyage, and we were allowed to go topside, I could fully understand their attitude. We were still tied to the dock! Believe me, those hypochondriacs, or shall we call ostriches really had a silly look on their faces and the comments that went from mouth to ear, by the hearty didn't ease the situation for many a day!

It wasn't hard to see we were in for a wonderful time!

The first few days everyone spent most of their time on deck, breathing deep of the salt air and admiring the white-capped blue of the ocean. And then someone would holler, "Shark!" and for a few dreadful minutes, the ship would list badly. Then everyone would very disgustedly return to whatever they were doing, which was usually nothing, and the ship would right itself and continue merrily on its way. The sharks—or perhaps the figments of someone's mind—seemed to be rather shy because very few people really saw them and they were there with us! We did have the pleasure of witnessing many, many schools of flying fish, and these tiny creatures of the deep are truly an amazing sight! They vary in size from a few inches to a couple feet, have very long batlike fins, and a large fan-like tail. They actually pop out of the ocean and glide fifty to seventy-five feet at a clip. They have wonderful depth perception—but being creatures of the deep—oh, well, I won't say it—pretty bad! Every now and then a school of porpoise put on a show for us; but this was only on special occasions—Christmas, New Year's, etc. One day we saw the spout of a whale—really an occasion! That's about the limit of my fish stories,

THE WHISKEY BOTTLE CONVERSATION

and after thirty days at sea, I'd say they were pretty damn poor!

The food situation, as I have mentioned before, is really pretty good, aside from the fact we only eat twice a day. The evening meal is usually exceptional, fact of the matter is, nine times out of ten, you can actually eat it! Marvelous—of course, I'm only fooling—after going all day without food.

We used to eat at eight in the morning and six in the evening. Now we eat at three forty-five and fifteen forty-five, if you care to be militaristic—I don't. Well, at the six o'clock meal, the ship's Navy officers had a table of their own and from what I have gathered, eating to them is more of an occasion than it is to the average soldier. This seems highly improbable, but I assure you it is true. To prove my theory, I'll give you an example. One night, and this is only one of many, we of the Army elite (officers), were quietly partaking of very fat and greasy pork chops, while at the crews table, with the most elaborate service, equaled only at McCarthy's, sat our competent Navy officers smacking—and I'm not exaggerating—their lips on nice big shrimp cocktails. The rest of the meal was equally as good. Roast beef rare or well done, as their taste desires, baked potatoes which I would gladly have given two dollars for a skin, cauliflower, iced tea, hot biscuits and this was topped off with strawberry shortcake! Well, I had a hard time controlling myself, but I managed down what food I had. Perhaps you have gathered from my above description that I am a little bitter—I assure you, you are right! One thing I am grateful for is, that by watching them eat their delicious meals (and no matter how good ours is, there is always at least a dollar and a half [in the states] better), my saliva glands actually pour out the fluid, thereby digesting my food better than I have ever experienced.

We crossed the equator a couple weeks back, and as I have already told my little wife, we had a remarkable experience. But for you who do not read my wife's mail, I will, in the same words, tell you about it. If this is old stuff, I am warning you, skip a page and a half because it's not worth rereading! (This goes for the censor, too)

In my last letter I mentioned a Christmas party and that soon after we were planning on another celebration. This, of course, was crossing the equator, and as many tradition has it, we had to be initiated into "the ancient order of the deep," thus graduating from a lowly "polliwog" to a "trusty shell back"!

The initiation was well planned and everything was prepared; we all stood breathlessly waiting. Suddenly there was a lurch of the ship, and we all knew we had crossed the equator and that the initiation was to begin. The ceremony consisted of several rather grotesque pranks executed by "Davy Jones" and his gang of cutthroats—who were in reality, persons who on previous occasions had gone through a similar honor and were now full-fledged members of the "Royal Order of Shell Back."

THE WHISKEY BOTTLE CONVERSATION

The initiation started early in the morning and lasted until sundown the same day; but unfortunately, all the passengers did not have the pleasure of the experience. There was always, on this particular day, a line of practically nude figures waiting initiation! Each person had in his hand a summons from "Davy Jones" to appear before him, and on each summons was a charge which the man was to answer. They varied from bigamy to seduction (or is that one in the same). Some had defied "Davy" to cut off his hair, others professed to be notoriously amorous, still others bragged about their ability to fly, sail, steal candy from babies, or fight. Some even claimed they could outdrink "Old Davy" himself, but even I know this would be impossible. All had to plead "guilty" or "not guilty" to their particular charge, but it was soon evident that it was much easier to plead "guilty" because they all had to accept the same punishment which stated something like this...

First, you would get on your hands and knees and crawl through a narrow trough made by the members of "Jones' Court." These members wore various costumes suitable to the occasion, and all had new mops for hair which gave them a really fishy look. As you proceeded through the line, and you didn't tarry longer than possible, you were compelled, by vicious whacks on the ass, to kiss a big fat greasy belly of one, a little toe of another and so it went. Very tasty as you can imagine, and I might add, rather salty as it happened to be a very hot day. All that went through this line were eliminated from taking the daily salt tablet.

When and if you survived this ordeal, you were examined by two doctors who persisted in giving large doses of castor oil (which persisted in coming up), and rinsing the mouth with some vile-tasting liquid composed of saltwater and many other horrible ingredients. Then, as if this weren't already enough, you were compelled, by the same method (a whack on the ass), to climb several stairs and sit in a barber's chair which overlooked a very salty pool.

Here, lovely curly locks were shorn from the cranium of men who, no doubt, thought their profile would equal that of Barrymore, but were soon shown the light on their first glance into a reflector! Here they saw the awful truth, in fact many of them found that unlike Sampson, it was their beauty which was confined in their hair and not their strength! Anyway, they got a very patchy haircut by a very inexperienced barber who didn't even use a bowl; and then to top it off, they were dumped over backward into the pool of very, very salty and after the first hundred men, very smelly water. If, after this ordeal they could still crawl under their own power, they were paddled into unconsciousness!

Note: Those who did not have any hair on their head were clipped under the arms. Those effeminates who had no hair on their head or none under their arms were clipped elsewhere! I daresay more escaped the barber!

THE WHISKEY BOTTLE CONVERSATION

This was the extent of the initiation—neat, eh? For all this we received a certificate—exclamation mark! We also received a certificate which shows us members of the "Imperial Domain of the Golden Dragon." In short, we crossed the one hundred and eightieth meridian thereby donating a whole day to posterity. In other words, we celebrated ten years a day ahead of you and we're listening to a Rose Bowl game on the second instead of the first—ain't it wonderful?

I have a confession to make. In the first page of this epistle, I stated that I had been on this ship one month today. What I neglected to tell you was... once we were ashore for nine hours! Please try to forgive my carelessness. I doubt if the censors would tolerate me naming the place, so I won't. It was truly a beautiful spot and the people were very hospitable. Perhaps it was their curiosity, but let's give them the benefit of the doubt and say they were just nice people. The thing that impressed me most about this beautiful land was the fact that for fifty cents of American money you could get seven beers! One of the seven wonders of the world you'll have to admit! As soon as it's allowable, I'll tell you more, but now my mouth is gagged and my hands are tied.

I have gone on and on and I hope someone has lasted this far, because I'm about to tell you in a very few words how I am feeling—Fine!—a bit lonesome and homesick at times, but this is to be expected. I hope you are all well and are taking care of the Good Old U.S.A.—it's a great place!

God bless you all and may he grant me the privilege of a speedy return to you.

All my love,
Dick

While I read, Dick had stared into the fire with a little smile on his face.

After I had finished, he said, "Boy, does that bring back some memories."

He took a sip of Scotch and kept looking at the fire with a distant look in his eyes.

I asked him when the first time was he saw land after leaving Los Angeles.

He turned back at me and said…

* * *

On the fifty-third day, we sailed into a large river and followed it for a few miles to a port at Hobart, Tasmania. It was supposed to be the deepest natural harbor in the world. We were the first American ships to arrive there. All of us were on deck, and it was a beautiful sight to see land again. As we entered the river, there were big, high cliffs on both sides. Most of the boys stood and gawked at the cliffs and the scenery. Some of them cheered.

We were scheduled to be in Tasmania for the time it took to refuel and restock the ship. The men in groups of one hundred were scheduled for one day onshore. I was in the first group to be allowed off. We all put on our best dress and went ashore. When I first stepped on the dock, I

THE WHISKEY BOTTLE CONVERSATION

almost fell over. Having been on the ship for two months, my equilibrium was way off. It took a few hours before I walked like I wasn't drunk.

We were greeted by about fifty young ladies that ranged in age from about sixteen to twenty-five. Being aboard ship for fifty-three days with nothing but other men, they all looked like Ms. America candidates. The girls took us up to a yacht club where they had tea and crumpets prepared for us.

This one gal came up to me and introduced herself.

She said, "Hello, my name is Tracey. Welcome to Tasmania."

I said, "I'm Dick Leonard, and I can't tell you what a pleasure it is to be here!"

We talked, and I asked her about the island.

She said, "Tasmania was originally a prison colony for Australia. Most of the families that live here now are descendants of the prison guards and officials. A few of the families are relatives of prisoners who were released and decided to stay. My parents and my brothers and sisters were all born here."

All the girls seemed very friendly and were, for the most part, attractive—except their teeth were bad. It wasn't that they didn't take care of them; it was apparently due to some deficiency in their diet. We talked, drank tea, and walked around the outside of the club. About two in the afternoon, Tracy said she had to go home.

I said, "I hope I haven't offended you in any way or said anything improper."

She said, "No, not at all. We girls have a surprise for you."

I said, "Do you mind if I come home with you and meet your family? I'd like to see a little more of the island."

She said, "That would be fine. We've never met any Americans before."

Her parents' home was on the outskirts of town. It was a cute single-story little bungalow. It had a white picket fence around the well-kept yard that was in bloom with a variety of flowers. When we got inside, Tracey introduced me to her parents, two brothers, and three sisters. She was the oldest. They were all really thrilled that I was there.

Her parents wanted to know all about America. Her father asked about the cities and the amount of work available for people.

One of her little sisters asked, "Are the streets really paved with gold?"

Another asked, "Can you go to the movies every day?"

Silly questions. I thought they were silly, but to them, it was an opportunity to talk to an American and see how we lived. Everywhere I went, America seemed to be held in very high regard by the people of different countries.

Tracey excused herself and went upstairs. I continued to talk with her family. I asked her father how the people of the island supported themselves. He said that many of the people have fishing boats, some work on the mainland during the week, and others survive by barter or trade. Boats traveled back and forth on a regular basis.

We had talked for about an hour when Tracey came downstairs. She had a long evening gown on, like a girl might wear to a formal or going out to a nightclub. Apparently, they had seen American movies where the women were always dressed to kill.

THE WHISKEY BOTTLE CONVERSATION

Tracey asked, "Is this how American women dress at night?"

I laughed and said, "Sometimes, but I've never seen one as pretty as you!"

She blushed and giggled.

She said, "We have known for months that the first American ships were going to land here. All of us girls got together with our mothers and made these dresses like the women wear in America."

Tracey said, "I'm ready to go back to the club now. There's going to be a band, so we can dance."

I thanked her parents for their hospitality, and we returned to the yacht club. All the girls had their evening gowns on and looked fantastic. We danced, talked, and drank some cocktails that were made up for us. After being on the ship for that length of time, it was a wonderful experience. We had to be back onboard by twelve. Tracey walked me to the clock. I thanked her for the lovely evening and introducing me to her family. She gave me a kiss and said good night. The next day another group got off the ship and was met by the same girls.

Our ship was in the port for about three weeks. I was assigned a group of boys who had to wash down the ship, do some painting, and general maintenance. Once we were resupplied, we sailed out of Tasmania and in two weeks saw land again. It was Bombay, India.

After docking in Bombay harbor, we were told to get our gear packed in our barracks bags, and on the third day, all two thousand men left the ship. We marched a couple of miles down this dirt road, then climbed up a steep hill. The hike up the hill took about three hours, and believe me, those full barracks bags got awfully heavy. On top of the hill, there were tents set up. The grass was mowed, and it was a good place to get your land legs back and put body and soul together. The tent groups were broken up in squadrons. The officers were in a group by themselves.

Don and I still didn't have a clue what our final destination was.

* * *

"Were you nervous about where you were being sent, Dick?"

"I would say I was curious, but I don't think I really cared. I was on an adventure, seeing the world. My attitude was, whatever happens, happens. Wherever I ended up didn't matter. All I wanted was to do what I could to help win the war."

I remembered reading some of his letters about India. I looked through the folders and found four letters. I thought Dick would enjoy listening rather than talking for a while. I poured him some more Scotch and put another log on the fire.

"I've got some of your letters about India, Dick. Why don't you just sit and listen for a while?"

He pushed his lever on his chair, and it reclined.

"I like that idea," he said.

I began to read...

THE WHISKEY BOTTLE CONVERSATION

Hello Folks:

Well, here's your little boy in India, no less! We embarked from "The Yacht" a few days ago and since that time have visited a city here in India and taken a train ride inland to a recuperation center. It's situated on a small lake and is surrounded by beautiful high mountains. Reminds me a little of Vermont. The weather is perfect: hot in the day time and cool at night with always a cool breeze blowing. All we have to do here is eat, sleep, swim, and drink beer, whiskey, or cokes. Tough life!

We're rationed our candy, beer, cigarettes, and other necessities, but it is a very liberal amount. We get twenty-four bottles of beer a month. Not bad, eh? Especially since it's Budweiser! As our stay here won't be long, we only received eight bottles of beer and so we have one a night just before supper. It sure tastes good!

Another kid and myself searched the shore yesterday and procured about eight logs and proceeded to build a raft. We lashed it together with some old rope and got a long bamboo pole for propelling it. We really had a wonderful time! I found some fishing tackle that someone has abandoned on the shore and so after getting some bread and an old chicken leg from the mess hall, we went fishing. Believe it or not, I never got a bite!

The swimming is wonderful; the water is just cool enough to be invigorating and is clear as a bell. I spend most of my time in the lake. Sure wish I had our little canoe up here; I'd go exploring. We are supposed to be surrounded by all sorts of wild creatures, but as yet I haven't even seen a grass snake.

I would like to tell you about our visit to a certain city here in India, but right now it's impossible. I will say that all the things you have heard about poverty and the cheapness of life here are true. There are millions of beggars and as many deformed and decrepit people struggling through the streets. Not a very pleasant sight, but one that makes you appreciate how much America has to offer!

When the ship docked, everyone was overjoyed to find mail waiting for us! It was the first letter I had received since December ninth. I was on guard duty at the time and still had three hours to go. I was getting pretty fed up with things in general. I heard that they were passing out mail and I couldn't wait until I got mine! One of my buddies came down the stairs and told me he was sorry but I hadn't received any, and believe me, I was ready to sue for a separate peace and go home: then he handed me a stack of letters that would stagger the imagination! For the next three hours, I didn't know what went on around me; they could have taken the place and I'd never known. Since that time, I've reread those letters a dozen times and still I don't tire of them. I'm sure glad you had such a wonderful Christmas; guess Old St. Nick hasn't forgotten where we live. I just knew what was happening all the time and could see you going after the tree, decorating it, putting packages under it, etc. It sure is a wonderful

THE WHISKEY BOTTLE CONVERSATION

holiday! I received the pictures from Jean; and Ricky sure is a good-looking kid. I had to show everybody, of course, and even then, they don't believe Jean and Rick are mine! Guess I don't look like the marrying kind (just a kid, you know).

You've sure been having an old-fashioned winter! Seems pretty wonderful to me, but I suppose you're getting a little tired of it.

Did you receive my last two letters? This is the third one I've written; thought maybe you'd like to keep track. Don't seem to be in a writing mood today, guess it's because all the things I want to tell you about are secret for the time being!

Well, kids, and that goes for you, too, Grampap—until the next time, take good care of yourselves and don't worry about me; if this is war, you ought to join the Army for a visit. "You poor civilians!"

I love you all very, very much and miss you in spite of myself. The time won't pass too quickly to suit me.

Your loving son,
Dick

P.S. The last letter I received was dated December 30.

Dick looked very relaxed and happy, sitting in his chair, taking an occasional sip of his Scotch.

"This letter is about you and some of the boys going into Bombay."

Dick laughed. "What a shithole that city was! There were dead bodies everywhere, beggars, prostitutes, and just about anything else you wouldn't want to see!"

Hello Folks:

Well, another week has slipped into our memory books, and all our mountains have become molehills, at least for the present. Know approximately where I am going. If I only knew exactly where, I might be satisfied. Don and I are going to the same Air Force but probably not to the same field; that's asking a little too much. War news sounds pretty good, maybe they won't be needing me, I keep telling myself.

Visited Bombay a short time ago and had quite a time. Wrote Jean about it so if you have been reading her mail again, this is old stuff; but for the relatives, friends, and customers I'll relate, once more, my experience.

Had seen a little of India, but this was my first big city and I felt like a farm boy getting his—well, that's another story. We and I shall use the plural. because there were about twenty of us armed to the teeth, left our post around two o'clock (thirteen hundred, Army time), and after a short trip entered the portals of enchanting Bombay. The first sight that greeted our eyes was the line of taxis all tooting their horns and hollering, "Taxi! Come, see the city. Take you to see pretty girls." Already we felt at home. We decided to walk a little ways just to get the feel of

THE WHISKEY BOTTLE CONVERSATION

things but soon we were convinced it was much easier to ride, and may I add, much safer! We only had gone about a block and the taxi drivers were in close pursuit; rather annoying but a little later on they looked very good indeed.

You see, the streets in this particular section of town weren't too wide and you were forced to hobnob with the rank and file; this in itself wasn't too bad, but then all of a sudden, out of nowhere, charged hundreds of street vendors. Well, it was a surprise attack and not being prepared for it, our ranks were split wide open, and each peddler had singled out his victim. I was confronted by a swarthy-looking bunch of rags which I surmised hid a human being. I shall never really know, because before I had a chance to examine them closely, a bony hand was thrust toward me and with a snap, a six- to twelve-inch knife blade flashed in the sun. Superman couldn't have moved faster! I was in a taxi with one leap and my brave friends all ran close second.

When the confusion was quelled, we decided to go to a nice quiet place, have a drink, and plan our counter attack. We had heard that the Taj Mahal Hotel was where the elite meet, so we asked to go there. The trip was eventful as everyone was recuperating and the only thing I remember was seeing the Gateway to India. The only thing I can think of to compare it with is Gateway into Collegetown, Ithaca, N.Y. or overhead crossing, Salina Street, Syracuse, N.Y. Very Impressive!

We soon discovered that it was necessary to eat in order to drink up until six at night. A very depressing thought, but after pondering at least thirty seconds, we decided to go all the way. We were ushered into a very lovely room about the size of the main dining room at the Hotel Syracuse and were shown a large table near the window or perhaps should I say a window. The view was very nice; we could see The Gateway to India with a large bay dotted with hundreds of tiny white sails as a background. A cool breeze was fluttering through the window and everyone was soon at peace with the world. We later found out that the sailboats belonged to native fishermen. Our friend also informed me that the beach patrol picked up the remains of a hundred or so seafaring men every day. Guess they don't go much for swimming over here.

Let's get back to the meal: to begin with, the service was astonishing! It took at least four men to do the work of one healthy blonde in the states. One was an interpreter, another in charge of silverware, another in charge of service and supply and still another in charge of finance! It was really quite an organization. To make it as simple as possible, we all ordered the same thing. A big bowl of chicken soup (cold and jellied)—no one ate this. Next came cold meats, vegetable salad, bread and butter, and of course, we had something to drink. All in all, it wasn't too good and this included the Indian whiskey and gin. A whiskey and soda tastes

THE WHISKEY BOTTLE CONVERSATION

a little bit like floor varnish. In short, we were very disappointed and so decided to tour the city instead of drowning our sorrows!

We grabbed a cab and told him to show us the sights. We were very fortunate in finding a respectable-looking chap with a Forty Dodge sedan who spoke fairly good English so off we went with a constant honking of the horn.

Cabdrivers are alike all over the world. They keep their feet on the throttle, one hand on the wheel and the other on the horn. These chaps are experts at "pedestrian polo," but of course, the streets being so narrow, gives them quite a handicap over our own professional men. If some poor fellow doesn't move, he is a cooked goose and here again a special patrol picks him up and carts him away. Strange as this may seem to you, it's the truth.

Our tour started in the better part of town. Here we saw very modern apartment buildings and some real nice homes. Our first stop was at the famous Hanging Gardens, never heard of them before but that doesn't make them less famous, I guess! The gardens are built over the city reservoir. It covers several acres, both the garden and the reservoir, and the latter holds thirty million gallons. The garden is really beautiful; there are hedges clipped to resemble every living thing, and all of them are produced to their living size. There are open pulling carts—driver and all, elephants, giraffes, lions, tigers, dogs, cats, snakes, and any other creature you might be fond of. There are all types of flowers and vines and even a few fountains scattered here and there. Looks like Dexter's Rock Garden!

This beautiful spot overlooks the home of the richest man in the world. I won't go into how much he has, but I do know he doesn't own two or three homes in Syracuse. It also overlooks the Temple of Silence. This place is operated by the Persians, or Porsie, as they are called over here. The temple consists of four walls, a grated floor, and no roof. Confusing, isn't it? I know it was to me until our guide told us the story. When a kid gets tired of it all and cashes in his chips, they bring him to this temple. Here he is strung up, just how, I didn't find out, but that's really a very small matter. It can be noted from a distance that the sky is black over the temple and this we learned was caused by thousands of vultures. As you have already guessed, the vultures just hang around for a meal and when a juicy corpse is produced, it takes them only twenty minutes to make him a gleaming heap of bones which in time falls through the grated floor into a large pit. Finis—they have three partitions in the temple, I'm told one for women, one for men, and one for suicides. So as we left this picturesque spot, we felt sadness in our hearts and hoped someday we might never return! Our next stop was a Hindu temple; our driver insisted we visit this and as he was a pretty good fellow, so we obliged. It seems that all these jokers use their temples for is to get rid of corpses. As we entered the door, a huge pile of wood greeted our sight and our friend informed us that this was for the pyres.

When one of the Hindus makes his bid for eternity, the family carts him to the temple, buys some wood, builds a pyre, lays the deceased on top, and then turns the service over to professional mourners while they all go down to Joe's for a short beer. When we entered the cremation chamber, there were several bodies on the fire and there were several in line waiting. We saw the pyres in all stages of completion; a very interesting sight but a little hard on the constitution. So as this place was a little too dead for us, we decided to seek romance. In Bombay, this is a cinch.

They have a little section of town called The Cages. This consists of several blocks of cages lining both sides of the street, and a very narrow street it is too. In these cages live prostitutes; each to her own cell. In this covey, they have all their worldly belongings and their professional equipment—a cot for the higher class joints, a mat for the lower class or for those who thrash around too much! If Vanity is the Spice of Life, this place leaves a lot to be desired. There are fat ones, skinny ones, some that aren't too bad American Standards, and for those that like a masculine touch, they have their fairies.

This is very confusing because with a sheet and a turban wrapped around them, the only way you can tell is to stand them on their head and that isn't considered the best manners on this side of the *world. Guess the only thing to do is take a shot in the dark! Fortunately, we Americans are only allowed to ride through this part of the city. I don't know who is more fortunate, them or us! They have a standard price which I think is rather chubby, no use outdoing your neighbor; for one person (one anna $.02) for two or more (two anna $.04)! You might think this would make it hard for high-class customers to determine whether their quail were as tidy as they might be. It would seem to me, not being a man of the world, that if you had to pay a little more for one than the other, you might at least feel in your own mind that she was pure. But once again, they have jumped this hurdle and as you pass down the street looking over the girls, they have this unique way of showing they are lily white. They take one hand (I noticed they prefer the right one) and pass it between the legs, in the vicinity of the solar plexus, and then into their mouth. The moral of this story being, quote Dr. Warbois, "If you feel athletic, go to bed and sleep it off." In this country, I would advise you to recline "solo" and let nature take its course. (Amen)*

It was with great feeling we left the city of cages and returned to The Great Eastern Hotel, where we paid our cab and withdrew to the top room. A cool Tom Collins was enjoyed by all.

We did a little shopping after this but soon gave this up. Enough is enough! I am personally happy to have seen Bombay (past tense).

THE WHISKEY BOTTLE CONVERSATION

Well, kids, it's dinnertime and I'm always ready to eat. Say "Hello" to Mexico, give my best to relatives and friends, take care of yourselves, and believe it or not, "I sure would like to be home."

Your loving son,
Dick

Dick and his buddies in Bombay India

I said to Dick, "You weren't kidding about Bombay. It must have been quite an eye-opener for a kid from Mexico, New York."

"It really was, Dave. To see crews of men walking around the city with their little carts, throwing dead bodies on them, was unbelievable! The value of life over there meant nothing. Every place I went made me realize how fortunate I was to live in a free society and the accomplishments that could be achieved when men had the right to choose their own destiny."

"I have another letter here, Dick. You want me to read it?"

"Sure, Dave. Read on."

I know he was enjoying his experiences, the descriptions, and the anecdotes he had shared with his family fifty years ago.

My Dear Parents:

Last night, they killed a snake two tents away and after finding out that its bite kills in thirty seconds, I'm really ready to leave this place. This creature, although it reminds me of some of my friends, was only about twelve inches long and had much the same appearance as that of a copperhead. When the monsoons arrive (only a few months away), they say the king cobra, kraits (snake that was killed), and all the other chummy reptiles come out of hiding and life isn't too valued around here. I'm being convinced more every day that this is nooo place for me!

THE WHISKEY BOTTLE CONVERSATION

Am still enjoying our little lake and am getting as dark as the natives here. Just yesterday, I was going to the shower with a towel wrapped around me, when one of the natives came up and started giving me hell for shirking my job. Even though I couldn't understand what he was saying, I felt badly because even I have to admit, I'm not doing a damned thing to win this war! Yesterday another kid and myself made a little bet and swam the lake—both ways without stopping! The distance was? Oh, only about four miles! I'm so lame today I can hardly wield this pen; doesn't improve my writing, does it?

We have some British troops a short distance from here who persist in shooting in our direction. Don't know what the idea is, but for the past week, shells have been bursting all around us, some as close as a quarter of a mile. I don't mind them hitting me, but this scaring me to death has got to go—I just can't stand it! If they'd let us shoot back, it wouldn't be too bad, but guess we Americans have got to be diplomatic (someday, I hope we smarten up).

Hope to leave here soon. I'm getting too healthy for my own good, and with only two Red Cross girls for several thousand men, you can see things are really tough. Natives are getting whiter every day; in fact, some of our Black GI's have already indulged in a dalliance with some Indian girls. They almost caused a breach in America-India relations. They also got hold of some marijuana and really went on a bender. This inactivity is a breeder of trouble for anyone. Often thought a little dope would come in handy myself.

Have been on several hikes and the country is very similar to New England. Not as woody, in fact, the mountains are quite barren, but the lakes and lowlands could be interchanged—snakes not included in this transaction. There are several native temples around this area, but they seem to lack the glamour of storybooks. No diamond-studded statues, no carved pillars, nothing except a poorly built shack with no furnishings or decorations at all. When a temple is completed, it is turned over to the Gods and after that, it's his baby. No repairs are made by any human hands and from all appearances, the Gods aren't craftsmen or else they're lazy as Hell. That's an awful thing to say, but facts are facts.

Speaking of religion, your son ate ravishingly of soul food yesterday—Sunday! Heard a very good sermon on the "Lord's Prayer." We had the service out of doors, and the setting was quite... quite...! We reclined on the ground and with the sun in our eyes and the flies in our hair, we sang the praises. Can't unbutton your vest and lean back here, HK—you sit up and take it like a man!

It's getting close to dinnertime and although the food isn't delicious or even appetizing, it's filling, and if your imagination is good, you have some variety! Chicken fried Spam, Spam and dehydrated eggs, Spam gravy on toast, cold cuts Spam, now and then some dehydrated potatoes, peas or sweet potatoes. Yesterday we did have fowl. First we had a cockfight, then we ate the loser!

Love,
Dick

"How long were you in Bombay, Dick?"

"We were there for two weeks. Basically, it was a recuperation period from our two and a half months aboard ship. After we left Bombay, Don and I, along with all the other boys who came over with us, got aboard a train headed for Calcutta. Calcutta, I would say, was a thousand miles away.

"The train cars weren't like regular trains in this country. They were more the size of a trolley car. Each car could carry about fifty men. There were just simple bench seats along the outside walls. The tracks were narrow and would run for four or five hundred miles. At that point, we would have to get off the train and march to another location where we would board a different train. In fact, I wrote a letter home about our trip. Why don't you see if you can find it, Dave. It will give you a firsthand description."

I opened the box and pulled out the folders containing Dick's letters. After looking for a few minutes, I found it and began to read…

My Dear Parents:

This letter, strange as it may seem, is to be read in the breakfast nook. I can just see the happy faces gathered around the table all wondering if the old boy has really gone off the deep end. I hope you don't mind the hard bench, but like everything else, without atmosphere, you have practically nothing.

No doubt, you're all interested in knowing why I chose the nook. Well, do you remember a long time ago when Herbert Knox Smith told the story about the fellow who was reading either "Igloma" or Dr. Grenville's "Afloat on an Iceberg" and in the dead of winter, he threw open all the doors and windows, and with snow and cold blowing through the room, he sat huddled close to an oil lamp enjoying his book and eating dog biscuits? Crazy—perhaps—but he believed in getting the full benefit from his reading material and man can't be condemned for that! For the same reason (atmosphere), I'm having you gather in this particular spot.

You'd better take rations for several days, because we're going to take a trip and the food is scarce. In the original trip, we started with a full pack and after a three- or four-mile hike, boarded a train. This I will spare you because I couldn't ask my own parents to go through that torture. Your trip starts as we board the train. Picture, if you can, a crowded railroad car, easy, isn't it? Now stop and think how hard those seats you're sitting on really are. Well on this bench, you're going to eat, sleep (sort of), and enjoy, if you can, an extensive trip through India. The journey starts at night so if you care to lay down for a couple of hours (any longer is not recommended), you're entirely welcome. I'm sure we're all ready to get up by now and start the day

THE WHISKEY BOTTLE CONVERSATION

with a smile. What! You want to brush your teeth, wash your face and hands, and your hair? Well, if you want to, you can, but your water ration is only one canteen per twenty-four hours, and it may get hot at little later on. Let's just pretend we're taking a shower—feels good, doesn't it! Strange, no gleeful song is coming from the shower room!

Now that we have finished our toilets, let's have breakfast. How would some ham and eggs go (sunny-side up)? GREAT! O.K. Well, have some K-rations. In case you aren't up on K-rations, I'll describe one to you. First take a can of soup (vegetable beef) a few rye krisp biscuits, a package of cocoa mix, and a few hard candies. Open up the soup and eat it out of the can, cold. Now take your cup, fill it three-fourths full of water, and add to your cocoa, cold. "Sure is a wonderful breakfast!" someone says. Well, we won't have any more remarks from him! To clean your mess gear, all you have to do is lick off your spoon and wipe it with a piece of toilet paper. You can wipe out your cup if you want to. Now that we have completed our breakfast, let's take stock of our surroundings.

Looking out the window, we see acres and acres of beautiful fertile land and for a background, tall wooded peaks. What are those things all over that field? Why, they're Natives all hunched over in sort of a squat. Wonder what they're doing? "Don't you know?" says some smart kid. "Why, they're taking a shit!" Sorry, I almost forgot myself. But on close inspection, if you care for such things, we find he *was right. Well, it's a beautiful outfit anyway. After seeing this it reminds you of your duties so with the paper under your arm, off you go to the latrine. Oh, yes, we do have one. I saw the sign on the door. Opening the door, I'm surprised to see nothing at all in the room except a clothes hook and a funnel-shaped hole cut in the floor. Right away, I decide to put it off for another day or so! So with my heart or something heavy, I retrace my steps and quickly sit down. Soon my troubles are forgotten, for the train has come to a stop and millions of derelicts are outside the train hollering, "Bakshesh" which means gift. A cracker or piece of candy tossed in the center of them causes a riot. Are you enjoying this sight? You might just as well get used to it because we still have a ways to go. Here and there, perhaps one out of ten, you see cripples of all kinds. No use of their lower legs so they scuff around on their knees. Over there is one with no hands and only a stump for a foot. Sort of quells your appetite and makes you thank God you're an American and you have your health.*

Enough of that, let's learn something about the natives. Well, after questioning a few of the intellects, and there are a few, we find that a well-paid government employee makes around twenty-five dollars per month. The middle class makes seven to ten dollars per month, and the majority as we can readily see, makes what he can beg or steal!

The clothing (if they are fortunate enough to have any, and many of them are nude, especially

THE WHISKEY BOTTLE CONVERSATION

children) is a sheet which is filthy, and a turban which is also dirty. Shoes are practically never worn and only occasionally are sandals seen. They certainly aren't very good-looking. Remember those pigpens we saw along the track a few miles back? You remember they were about twelve feet square with mud walks and thatched roofs? Well, they weren't for animals at all; they are respectable homes—I have to admit the animals: sheep, goats, chicken, and cows certainly gave it the appearance of a shed. I'm told whole families live in the little huts. Most of them have one room with one opening which is used for a door, window, and chimney. Certainly is a time saver for the construction engineer.

Let's stand up and stretch for a minute, sort of hard to get up, isn't it? Okay, look at that vendor with those big oranges; let's buy some. What—only a rupee (.30) for two dozen? Give us a couple dozen. Loud voice—"What in hell are you men doing?" (Lt. Col. M.D. of the train)

(Small voice)—me—"Nothing, sir, just buying a few oranges."

(Loud voice) "Don't you know those skins are liable to be highly infected with any and every type of disease known to man?"

(Small voice) "No, sir."

(Loud voice) "Well, they are, and when you peel them, those germs get under your nails and will contaminate everything you eat!"

(Loud voice) "Now, throw those G.D. things away!"

(Small voice) "Yes, sir."

Well, that cures us of buying eatables from vendors! Here comes one of the fellows from the latrine and he says it ain't so bad—so here I go. Well, I'll wait until the train gets out of the station, but it isn't necessary, people do it whenever and wherever nature calls! I'm still a little modest.

How are you enjoying the trip, folks? No, damn it HK, you can't wash your hands and waste the water, you've just got to get used to it! Whew!—I'm glad to be out of that city! Boy, doesn't that air smell good? Why even that click, clack of the wheels sounds like music. They sure aggravated me last night. I'd have sworn this damned thing has square wheels. Look out this window; as far as you can see human beings with their hands outstretched and if you listen closely, you can hear them hollering, "Bakshesh, Bakshesh." Feel sorry for them? A little perhaps, but even that is wearing off now. Look—acres and acres of unplowed fields just begging to be planted and cultivated! Now and then you see an industrious man with a stick and a couple oxen or water buffalo turning over a couple of inches of top soil. He's only barely moving. He and the water buffalo go well together. Neither of them want to get anything done. The only time you see anyone run is when someone is throwing or giving something away.

Gee whiz, here it is two o'clock. Let's eat! What—you aren't too hungry? Okay, we'll wait until four and have dinner and supper together. We're coming into another station and I heard we

THE WHISKEY BOTTLE CONVERSATION

can get off and stretch for about fifteen minutes. Hate to get off and mingle with all those natives; guess I'd better get used to it. (Come on, HK) Boy, someone had turned on that boiler water filler. Let's make a dash and maybe we can crowd up and get enough to wash our hands and face. Got pretty wet all over but it sure feels good. Does your hair feel like mine, just like wire? Just look at the dirt and I only ran the comb through once. Oh, there's the whistle—let's get back on.

Everyone is a little tired of looking, no doubt, so let's play a little gin rummy or poker. The next couple hours passed rather quickly, didn't they? How do you feel after your first twenty hours? Yeah, I feel sort of numb myself. My poor cheeks feel as though I had the mumps.

Getting a little hungry now so what do you say we have some supper? Not hard to plan a meal, anyway. What do you say to some c-rations? Sure you don't mind? Strange as it may seem, the food tastes the same as breakfast. Personally, I'm hungry enough to eat anything and so won't even think about the taste.

With the dishes done and the sun setting, it's pretty nice just to sit here by the window and look at things far, far beyond the horizon. Pretty easy to forget the hard bench, the poor unhealthy souls, and all the troubles ahead and behind. They can take you away physically, but never spiritually. Everyone seems to be quiet about this time, but as the sun drops beyond the horizon, someone starts to sing and after a couple hours of both old and new, dirty and clean songs, the fellows are ready for the sack. A couple blankets spread on the bench floor, a jacket for a pillow and the night of twisting and turning starts. First, one hip hurts, then the other, then your spine kills you and finally you lay on your stomach until your ribs crack and your neck kills you. After this, the cycle starts again and so forth into the night.

Well, folks, that's a train ride through India. Hope you enjoyed it!

Give my best to all.

*Love,
Dick*

"That's quite a story, Dick. It gave Mimi and Gramp a real feel, so to speak, for what you were experiencing."

"That was a tough ride," Dick said. "We were on the train for over a week with the never-ending sound of clickety-clack, clickety-clack, no showers, and the toilet being a hole cut in the floor with a wooden crate over it."

He began to laugh.

* * *

At one point we were changing trains and had to cross this river that was maybe a quarter of a mile wide. The Army had built a pontoon bridge that was held together by two wire cables that were attached to the riverbanks. There were about two hundred of us on the bridge when one of the cables snapped and then the other one let go. The

THE WHISKEY BOTTLE CONVERSATION

bridge split in two, and down the river we went. The cables anchored on the banks held, so it just swung the section around to the banks. A couple of the boys got dumped. The river was moving quite fast, so it was a thrilling ride.

They tied another long cable to each section of the bridge and hooked that to two jeeps on both sides of the river. The jeeps drove along the riverbank and pulled the two sections back in place. Once in place, they reattached the cables, and the rest of the men came across.

When we arrived in Calcutta, we were put in a holding area where they had a camp set up for us. It was much the same as the one in Bombay. The officers and men were split up, and from there, we were on our own. Don and I spent a couple of days in Calcutta. It was a lot like Bombay, except it seemed to be a more active city. It appeared to be a community that was growing. There were busy parts that had big markets. In the open-air markets, you could buy almost anything from clothing to food, hardware, guns, and dope. The streets were narrow and filled with people. Many dressed in Western clothes while others wore traditional Indian attire. We spent two days in the Green Hotel. There was a jewelry shop in the lobby where I bought Jean a big blue opal, which she had made into a ring. That was the only thing I ever sent home. Really, it was the only time I had an opportunity to buy something.

We had been at the holding area a week when Don and I received our orders. We were going to be flown to Kunming, China, a B-24 base run by General Clair Chennault.

CHAPTER TWELVE

You Want to Build Runways?

Don and I left Calcutta aboard a C-54 and were flown to one of our bases in Northern India. It was a supply base with four squadrons of C-46s. The C-46 was the workhorse of the Air Corps. They were used to transport supplies—such as, gas, ammunition, parts, and food—to the different bases around China. We were there about a week.

One night Don and I were in the outdoor theater, watching the *Sound of Music* with a couple hundred other GIs. About halfway through the movie, they called us over the loud speaker, and we were told to report with our gear to an airplane at a certain area of the base. We boarded the plane about eight o'clock with twenty other men and were flown over the hump into China.

The hump was the Himalayan Mountain Range between India and China. I would say the altitude of some of those mountains is between twenty and thirty thousand feet. We couldn't really see anything because it was night. It was a rough flight because of the turbulence over the

THE WHISKEY BOTTLE CONVERSATION

mountains. We all were strapped down pretty good, but some of the boys got sick.

The plane touched down in Kunming about midnight, and all of us were given barracks assignments. The next day Don and I had to fill out paperwork. It was required of each soldier to sign a document, which swore us to secrecy about whatever we experienced in China and also that we were guests of the Chinese government. We didn't have any duties for about a week. Our time was spent checking out the base and talking with different personnel.

The base was located on a flat plain surrounded by mountains. There was one runway, and another one was scheduled to be built in the near future. The base had four barracks that each housed around two hundred men. Two large hangar buildings that could accommodate five planes each were used for repairs. Others were under construction. Another large building was used to store incoming supplies. Approximately two to three hundred planes a day were landing with supplies. They were all C-46s. The planes would land, be unloaded, and get back in the air within an hour.

About a half mile from the base was an area where tanks were kept. I would say there were a thousand tanks and a full contingency of troops to guard and maintain them. These tanks were under Chennault's command and were to be given to the Chinese. Chinese military personnel were trained in their use, and then the tanks would be turned over to them for fighting the Japanese.

At the end of the first week, Don received orders to report to Chic Yang, a supply base in the mountains about two hundred miles from Kunming. I was to report to General Chennault.

His office was in a building located at the center of the base. As I walked in, there were four Chinese women working at their desks in large room. All of them spoke good English and seemed to be quite busy. There was a door to the right that had "Gen. Chennault" written on it. I knocked, and a voice from inside said, "Enter."

I opened the door, stood in front of his desk, and saluted. "Lieutenant Leonard reporting as ordered, sir!"

He saluted me. Chennault had the nickname "Old Leather Face," and I could see it was well deserved. His facial features seemed to melt together, and his skin was ruddy with pronounced crow's feet around his eyes. He always seemed to be squinting and had the nose of a man that liked his whiskey.

As I stood at attention in front of his desk, he said, "Welcome to Kunming, Lieutenant. You will be in charge of flight operations here. According to your file, you've had considerable experience in operations at Biggs Field, so I shouldn't have to stand around and mother you. Take some of the men working on the new hangars, and build yourself an office. Set up operations any way you want, and report to me when necessary. You're acting as my second-in-command, so don't go screwing anything up. Dismissed."

I saluted, turned around, and walked out without getting a word in.

I went back to my barracks and drew up some plans for my office. It was just a simple twenty-by-twenty-five-foot building, but I wanted windows on the front and two sides so I could see out on the field. I went to a first ser-

THE WHISKEY BOTTLE CONVERSATION

geant in charge of hangar construction, gave him my plans, and took him to the spot in the center of the field where I wanted the office built.

He said, "Shouldn't be a problem, Lieutenant. I'll put some men on it, and in a couple of days, you'll have yourself an office."

I said, "See if you can find me a few filing cabinets, a desk, and some chairs, Sergeant."

"Yes, sir! Will do, Lieutenant!"

Two days later, I was in my operations office.

Claire Chennault

* * *

"How did Chennault end up in China, Dick?"

* * *

Chennault had been a captain in the Air Corps before the war. He was a well-known pilot and was in the first authorized fighter squadron in the Army. He helped develop the characteristics of battle and how to train pilots for combat. Chennault believed that the future of warfare was in the airplane.

The problem he had was that most of the top military brass at the time weren't about to relinquish their authority to the airplane.

Chennault continued to work with his fighter squadron. He picked a group of his best pilots and formed the Blue Angels. They flew all over the country, putting on shows in their P-40s, which were a single-engine fighter. The Angels would fly in formation and do stunts. During this time, he had been turned down on all his promotions and grew disillusioned with the Army. He decided to retire.

After Chennault left the Air Corps, he got sick and spent some time in the hospital. While there, one of his Army buddies told him about the Japanese invasion of China, what role China would play in the war, and how they didn't have any real facilities, or way of communicating from different parts of the country. He left the hospital and went to Washington to meet with some of his friends. He told them he was going to China on his own and survey the situation. Once he found out what was going on, he was counting on their help.

THE WHISKEY BOTTLE CONVERSATION

After arriving in China, he began pinpointing all the places where the Japanese were fighting. He gradually got to know Chain Kai-Shek, who at first didn't pay much attention to him. Apparently, however, Chain's wife took to him. She arranged for him to meet some Chinese generals in various parts of the country. Chennault gradually put together his own assessment of the war and after a year was given permission to set up a base at Kunming.

Chennault, the civilian, returned to the United States and arranged for the sale of P-40 fighter planes to China. He also contacted the pilots of the Blue Angels and others he had flown with in the Air Corps. He returned to China with a ragtag group of 112 pilots. Chennault and his boys were mercenaries paid by the Chinese government. They received between six and seven hundred dollars per month plus a five hundred–dollar bonus for every plane they shot down. All had bogus passports, which listed them as salesmen, teachers, tourists, musicians, bankers, and baseball players. Their planes had chilling eyes and jagged teeth of a shark on the nose of the plane—hence the name Flying Tigers.

They had to brave overwhelming numbers of Japanese planes, including Zeros that could turn and climb more than twice as fast as the P-40s. In February 1942, the Japs dispatched 166 planes to bomb and strafe Rangoon. The Tigers met the attack with nine P-40s and downed twenty-four aircrafts, losing only three of their own. The next day, the Japs sent two hundred planes back to Rangoon. This time eighteen enemy planes went down, and all six Tigers returned to base.

The success of the Flying Tigers lay in the unorthodox tactics taught by Chennault. His was a hit-and-run strategy. He'd instruct his pilots to use their speed and diving power to make a pass, shoot, and break away.

The newspapers in the States were getting reports on their successes and started a comic strip, naming the group "The Flying Tigers." They were getting so much press that the Army brass back in the States felt that they had to get involved. In March 1943, they made Chennault a major general and formed the US-China Air Task Force's Twenty-Third Fighter Group. That's when the US government began building bases to bring in B-17s and B-24s. By the end of the war, the Flying Tigers were credited with destroying more than 1,200 Japanese planes with seven hundred more probable. Their own losses came to just over five hundred.

Tigers scramble to meet Japanese Kunming base

Crew repairing a P-40

* * *

I said to Dick, "So Chennault, by his own initiative, vindicated himself in the belief that air combat was the future of air warfare!"

"That's true, Dave. Old Leatherface made his point!"

I threw some more wood on the fire, poured us both a drink, and sat down.

"Tell me more about the base and your duties as operations officer. Were there any towns nearby?"

* * *

Kunming was a little town of about twenty thousand a few miles from the base. I would consider it one of the resort areas of China. There were a number of lakes; some of which were well populated with nice homes, and others were just wilderness areas.

When I arrived there was one ten thousand–foot runway, which was dirt and rock covered with some sort of pavement similar to asphalt. There weren't too many P-40s, but there were a lot of Transports landing night and day, bringing in supplies from India.

My duties were to oversee all the planes coming in and going out. If a plane had a flat tire or engine trouble, I would have to get a crew to fix it quickly so they could take right off again. Different crews were designated for various jobs. One crew was in charge of plane maintenance, another unloaded and stored supplies, while the parts crew handled that aspect of the operation. Each group had a person in charge of keeping the records. At the end of a shift, the crew chief would bring me the paperwork, and I would record, file, and make a master report of the day's activities.

Every five days I went to Chennault with my records—when he was available. Chennault wasn't a well man and spent a lot of time in the hospital in Kunming. I never did find out what was wrong with him, so in his absence, I pretty much ran the base.

* * *

"After spending some time there, what was your impression of him, Dick?

"Well, to be honest with you, I think he was a man who was overwhelmed. I mean, he had been a pilot in the Army, and when he came to China, he had a group of one hundred men. After, he was made a general and given the responsibility of a thousand tanks, two thousand men, and a resupply base—plus being sick. I think it was bit much for him. I mean, I never saw a piece of paper on his desk when I was in his office. As far as the tanks and men stationed outside the air base, I don't think he gave a shit about them. I felt his real interest was in the three or four P-40 bases he had around China. They were his top priority.

"For example, at one point, the Japanese were going to attack Kunming. The Burma Road that runs from India into China was the only way to transport their men and materials. Chennault's reconnaissance reported that the Japs were on the move, so he fitted six P-40s with bombs. They weren't designed to carry bombs, but he mounted some makeshift devices on the planes to attach the bombs.

"Much of the Burma Road is surrounded by high cliffs, so there's really no way to turn around. When the convoy got to this one point where there was a gorge, the six P-40s strafed the road and dropped their bombs on the cliffs. The rocks and debris came crashing down on the convoy, burying much of it and blocking the road. If Chennault hadn't done this, the Japs would have come right into China and attacked Kunming. He was a genius when it came to that type of warfare. As far as the rest of it, I think he felt that it was someone else's worry."

As Dick was telling me about Chennault, I looked through his letters and found one written soon after he arrived in China.

"I've got a letter here, Dick, that you wrote after arriving at Kunming."

He took a sip of his Scotch and leaned back in the chair.

My Dear Parents:

Guess it's been a week since I've written to you, but circumstances have delayed me. First, I've been moving again and am now in China; second—I've been sweating out a permanent assignment but as yet, have received only a temporary task; third and not the least, the gang has been scattered all over China and I've been feeling rather low. Guess the anticipation of adventure, the thrill of traveling and seeing new country is wearing off, and the realization that all war is not exciting and full of glory has sort of left me down in the dumps! In these

THE WHISKEY BOTTLE CONVERSATION

few short days, I've been at work, trying to learn about China Operations, the fact that some people have to stay out of the limelight and take the shit has impressed itself deeply on me. I have been assigned to the "China Air Service Command" and will act as a Base Operations Officer somewhere in China. I sure had hopes of getting assigned to a combat squadron; even offered to go as a copilot in a 24. But I was informed that I came over here as an Operations Officer and would remain as one. I sure hate the thought of sitting behind a desk for a couple of years, but as the Classifications Officer said, "Someone has to!" I was pretty bitter for a few days but have come to the inevitable conclusion that "Life is what you make it" and have settled down to work.

Now that I have told you my troubles, I'll tell you a little about China—what I've seen so far hasn't impressed me too much. It's similar to India in respect to filth and smell; the people are just as dirty but look a little lighter in complexion and they all wear clothes of some type. I'm near a fairly large city and have had the pleasure of a couple steaks. I won't go into how good they were, because anything I get my hands on, tastes good, so I'd be prejudiced. Don and I paid four thousand Chinese dollars apiece for a steak. The exchange is five hundred to one! Boy, you walk around with a roll that would stagger the imagination. They have rickshaws to ride around in—cost about a hundred and fifty bucks for one, or ten miles—they also have some wine, gin, and brandy made out of second-grade motor fuel which gives you a hell of a hangover—experience is a great teacher. When Don and Andy left, we decided a party was called for, sooo—and Oh! (A bottle of booze cost two thousand bucks). I won't tell you the grim details of our party, but I assure you that it was quite—quite!

I'm pulling a night shift at the present time, so if this letter wanders a little, it's because of the numerous interruptions. Someone is always blowing a tire and blocking a taxiway or something similar and it's my job to rush out and get things straightened out.

Received a nice letter from HK and Harriet. How's Grampaps doing these days? Seems to me he's getting pretty high class having Earl Moore come down to cut his hair! Tell him I said for him to use some of his stand-up or stored-up energy and write me a letter. Boy, what a wonderful surprise that would be! You all seem to agree that the snowstorm is the worse on the history of New York and with no coal on top of that, I would say things were pretty tough. Glad you are all well and are weathering the storm—just continue to stay that way and I'll be happy.

Met a doctor tonight from Utica who interned at Crouse Irving Hospital and knows Carl, Dr. Dick, and says he has met Sussie. His name is Capt. Ameduri. We had supper together and really had a swell time talking about Syracuse and vicinity. It's sure great finding someone who has interests that

THE WHISKEY BOTTLE CONVERSATION

correspond to your own. He seemed to think a lot of Dr. Dick but still doesn't agree on his ideas on milk. I never have written Dr. Dick thanking him for that twenty dollars for his help in packing and sending our things to Texas. Why don't you send me his address and I'll be sure to do it. By the way, how is Carl and Sussie and their family? Give them my best, and I sure hope Carl can get a discharge. Tell him I said it's evident he can't get anywhere in the Army, so he might as well be home. Guess we Mexico kids are just civilians at heart.

It's getting close to the end of my shift and I'm getting pretty weary, so I guess I'll say good night. Take care of the home front and yourselves and don't worry about me; it looks like I'll always have a desk to crawl under!

Your loving son,
Dick

"Sounds like you were pretty disappointed about your assignment," I said.

"I joined the service to fight, Dave. I could have stayed in the States at Biggs Field, but I wanted to get into a combat outfit. Having listened to my letter reminds me how disappointed I was when I got to China. That's military life. Do what you're told."

"So you were pretty much stuck at your desk, Dick?"

"Well, a lot of my time was spent on paperwork, but when they began building the second runway, I did manage to get involved in that whenever possible."

* * *

You remember we all had to sign the documents saying we were guests of the Chinese government? Well, the Chinese were supposed to be building this runway. They had a Chinese station master, who was like a superintendent, and several thousand Chinese laborers called Coolies. The laborers would break rocks into small stones with hammers then haul them to the runway in little carts pulled by a horse or donkey. Or some would carry the stones in baskets on their heads. It was really archaic. They would pile the stones, and another group of laborers would shovel or push them around with boards. The Americans were just there to supervise.

One afternoon the engineering officer came to me and asked if I wanted to help him.

I said, "Sure! What do you want me to do?"

He said, "After the Chinese go home, meet me down on the runway."

That evening I met the engineer, and he had three bulldozers and another enlisted man with him. We got on the dozers and started leveling off the stones and dirt the Chinese had piled up during the day. We worked late into the night and leveled off about two hundred feet of runway.

The next night we did the same thing. When the Chinese came back the following morning, all the rocks they had piled up would be leveled off. After the third night, we had finished about five hundred feet of runway, and Chennault found out what we were doing. He called me into his office and chewed me out.

THE WHISKEY BOTTLE CONVERSATION

He said, "We are guests of the Chinese government, Lieutenant! It's their job to build that runway, not the Americans! I don't want to hear any more about our bulldozers out there again! Do we understand each other, Lieutenant?"

I saluted and said, "Yes, sir!"

A couple of weeks later, when he was in the hospital or off at another base, we would get the dozers out again and make some more runway. When he returned the station master would go to him and complain. Chennault would call me in his office and give me hell.

He said, "Are you building runways again?" He would get so excited that he would start to lisp while he was chewing me out.

I said, "General, at the rate those Chinese are going, that runway will never get done!"

He said, "I don't care! It's their job!"

I said, "Yes, sir!" and walked out.

The next time he was off the base, we got the bulldozers out again. When he returned, I was called to his office for another reprimand. The last time he called me in, he was madder than hell!

He said, "Goddamn you, Leonard! You want to build runways? I'll give you a goddamn runway to build! Dismissed!"

I didn't know what he meant until three weeks later.

Building runways at Kunming

* * *

I said to Dick, "It seems like you hadn't been in any trouble since leaving Biggs Field. Must have felt pretty good, getting reprimanded by the general!"

He laughed. "Yeah, it was kind of invigorating."

He picked up the folder of letters I had on the table and began looking at the dates. He stopped at one and gave it to me and said, "Here, Dave, read this one."

I took the letter.

My Dear Parents:

Your son is getting settled for a change and is working (Strange as it may seem) quite hard.

THE WHISKEY BOTTLE CONVERSATION

Seems a little peculiar to have a room of my own, a place to hang my clothes, and a desk to write on and throw junk into. Having a little trouble getting operations set up, but people are beginning to cooperate somewhat and have made up their minds that there has to be such an office. There hasn't been one here before, as I have mentioned, and people have been running things just about as they see fit. Can't say I blame them for feeling a little belligerent toward a mere First Lieutenant telling them how things are going to be run; I imagine I should feel the same way.

We're having a new office built and it's going to be really "Ding How"—means okay in Chinese. "BooHow" means "No good." That's the extent of my Chinese! I hope to have a regular stateside operations before I'm finished.

I have also been doing a little flying around the countryside. I have ten hours in already this month—pretty good, eh? I'm now a C 47 pilot—it's just like flying a kite—only more so! The thing cruises at what a B 26 stalls out and its maximum speed is what a B 26 merely flies at. A little discouraging at times, but nevertheless, it's flying. I now have the total flying time, in China, of twenty-three and one half hours—ten hours being logged as "combat." That means in a combat area, not necessarily over enemy territory. I only need around six or seven hundred hours to come home or two years, so you can start looking for me December 29, 1947—what a future!

The food isn't too bad, but nevertheless it's far from being good. From all reports, we eat seasonally, For instance, black beans, turnips, and spinach are now in season, so every meal except breakfast, we can expect the above. A little monotonous, but filling. Every morning we have eggs of some kind and a side order of hot cakes, occasionally, a little bacon, and now and then some toast. Have coffee every meal or hot water. The water tastes like hell, so I've become a confirmed coffee drinker; two or three cups per meal. Hard to believe, isn't it?

We got our monthly rations of PX supplies Tuesday. It consists of the following: two boxes of cookies, four boxes of candy, one box of hard candies, three cartons of cigarettes, seven cigars, one bottle of ink, two writing pads, two packages of razor blades, and a box of matches. When the above is gone, you go without. Oh yes, we got a can of chocolate milk, which I devoured as soon as I got my hands on it.

I tried smoking cigars for a while, but one night—after about two weeks of it—I tried to smoke two in a row and drink a little China Gin; boy did I get sick—I tasted those damned cigars for three days—Finis—I then took up smoking cigarettes for lack of something to do. Well, I did fairly well the first week, must have smoked two packs with the able assistance of my friends. I then gave two cartons away and since that time have smoked three or four cigarettes—in a period of about two weeks. Guess I just ain't a smoker!

THE WHISKEY BOTTLE CONVERSATION

Received two letters from home; one dated January 20, and one dated the 26th. I'm glad you realized the necessity of "atmosphere," but I'm sorry it took so much out of you all. That skiing trip you took tired me out, but your description of the lake sure made me feel a little empty; but to be truthful, Harriet, I like those little scenes you paint. It does my heart good and sort of gives me something to look back on and forward to.

I'll bet it was good to have Carl home. I sure wish he could stay. Mexico needs a guy like that around. Hope the big wheels can do him some good. He was bringing the Mexico batting average for births up, in more ways than one! But I always say—what's a business without advertising and what's a better advertisement for a doctor than a big family of his own. If they'll give both of us a choice, we may be able to save civilization yet! While on the subject, give Sussie, Mrs. Allen, and the kids my best. Say hello to "Tiger Lil" also and tell her to lay off the old man. He ain't as strong as he used to be no matter the big ideas he has.

Went to church Easter Sunday and took communion. First time since I've been in the Army, I'm ashamed to say. We had a very impressive service and I sent Jeannie a copy of it. I could only get one and I instructed her to show it to you, so remind her of it.

The days seem to go pretty fast, but the nights are really long. Your letter of the twenty-sixth mentioned something about me writing a book and it gave me an idea. Easter Sunday I started writing an account of different incidents of my life and have spent several hours since writing what came into my head. When I get two or three hundred pages, I'll send it home and you can make corrections, additions, etc. Maybe between the two of us, we can make something of it, eh, Harriet?

Tell Old Grampaps I think of him often and miss him very much. I sure wish he'd find something worth living for, but I guess I'd feel the same way if I were in his shoes.

Well, Folks, it's once again chow time and although I complain about black beans, black bread, spinach, turnips and coffee, I'm always there when they're handing it out.

Your loving son,
Dick

"You mentioned you were flying C-47s. What were you doing with them?"

"Whenever I got a chance to fly supplies to one of the other bases, I would volunteer. Much of the time it was transporting gasoline. We'd load up a C-47 with ten to twelve fifty-five-gallon drums of gas and fly them to a designated base. Usually the runways were just long enough so we could get in, unload the gas, turn around, and get the hell out.

"One time I was flying ten drums of gas to one of the advance bases. The drums were supposed to be strapped down so they wouldn't move around. On a C-47 there's a rear cargo door on the side of the plane. I came in to land at this little strip, and after touching down, I realized that I was running out of runway. I locked up the right wheel brake and spun the plane around. Two of the drums broke loose and went right out through the cargo door, taking the door with them. They landed on the ground and rolled off the side of the runway."

Dick laughed. "Jesus, it was a miracle they didn't go off. Of course, all the boys at the base got a big bang out of it."

I said, "They were lucky there wasn't a big bang, Dick!"

We both laughed.

Dick said, "The things we went through! Probably, if the truth be known, someone forgot to strap the drums down. They were just sitting in there. I probably made a dozen flights like that. Running the base, I didn't get to fly much, but whenever an opportunity arose, I took it. You know, just a chance to get off base for a while. I really enjoyed it."

"So where did Chennault send you to build a runway?"

"He sent me about thirty miles north of Kunming to convert a fighter strip to accommodate larger planes. I was assigned an engineering officer, by the name of Lieutenant Perkins; a doctor, Major Selingman; and about seventy-five Seabees." Dick laughed. "What a crew of misfits. Chennault also gave us enough bulldozers, trucks, and equipment to build the strip. There were a few Chinese who did the cooking and built mud adobe huts for our sleeping quarters. The Seabees were American boys who built bridges, runways, or anything else that needed to be constructed. They really knew how to do things. We had all the natural material right there."

* * *

Before I left, Chennault called me into his office and told me where and what the assignment was.

He said, "You're runway happy, Leonard, so now you've got one to build. Dismissed!"

I saluted and said, "Yes, sir! Thank you, sir!"

To my knowledge, Chennault never saw the runway. I don't think he gave a good goddamn what we were doing so long as we weren't in his hair—as long as we were away from him doing something but not fighting the war.

Our new home had been a fighter strip for P-40s. It was dirt and just long enough to handle the small planes. That was it… no buildings, just a little runway. Chennault wanted it big enough to handle C-47s. I broke the seventy-five Seabees into three groups. One group ran the bulldozers and dump trucks. The second was in charge of surveying and construction of the flight tower, and the third would relieve the boys in the first two. We worked almost around the clock. When someone would get tired, another boy would take his place while he slept. When that fella got up, he'd replace someone else. We were like a team. One player would come out, and another went in.

Our living quarters surrounding this new runway were pretty basic. They were adobe huts made of dried mud bricks with a thatched grass roof. Usually, there were four men to a hut. We each had a cot and some mosquito netting. A little mat on the cot served to tuck the netting under. After being there for a couple of weeks, these foot-long rats would come in the adobes at night and scurry around. After a time I got used to them, but I made sure my netting was tucked in good before I went to sleep. Every once in a while, one of the boys would get pissed off and start blasting at the rats with his .45. The next morning there would be four or five holes in the wall.

Major Selingman took care of the medical needs of the base. He was about thirty-five, tall, had dark hair, and wore glasses. The doc was a real happy-go-lucky guy. If someone needed medical attention, he'd see to their needs; otherwise, he was usually down on the runway, riding a bulldozer or driving a dump truck. He just kept busy so he wouldn't go stir-crazy. He thought he was the world's greatest cook. Almost every morning he would make scrambled eggs with something mixed in to give them body—like fruit, vegetables, meat, or a combination of things. They were usually terrible, but nobody said anything.

* * *

I asked Dick what kinds of things they did to entertain themselves.

"Every couple of weeks, I'd plan some type of party for the boys just to give them a break. On one occasion, I put in an order for three- or four-gallon cans of number 10 fruit cocktail. The doc ordered four or five gallons of medical alcohol. He and I got three washtubs and filled them with the fruit cocktail and the grain alcohol and let it set overnight.

"The next day I told all the enlisted men to meet at the mess tent at five and bring a cup with them. 'We're going to have a party!' Everyone showed up and was filling their cups with the juice, but nobody seemed to be catching a buzz. Then I noticed this GI over in the corner all goggle-eyed. I went over to him and saw he just had fruit in his cup. He couldn't even lift it to his mouth; he was so drunk. Doc said the fruit must have absorbed all the alcohol.

"Everybody started eating fruit, and we all got hammered! What a party! Some of the boys got in the dump trucks and were having drag races up and down the runway. Another bunch built a big bonfire and danced and hollered like Indians. Others took off and wandered aimlessly into the night. One thing is for sure… we all had a ball! The next day, however, there were some sad cases walking around in a daze. That grain alcohol was tough stuff!"

"Did you ever have any trouble with the men, Dick?"

"For the most part, they were all pretty good guys. There might be a fight, or someone would get drunk and raise a little hell, but they were pretty well behaved. There was one time when one of the sergeants came up missing. He had a Chinese girlfriend that lived with her family not too far from the base. He had been gone all day and returned to base around midnight. One of the enlisted men came to my hut and woke me up. He said, 'The sarge is back, and he's got a knife! He's drunk too and says he'll kill anyone who tries to take it away!'

"I got the doc up, and he filled a syringe with a tranquilizer. The GI took us to the sergeant. He was a big, muscular kid about six three and well over two hundred pounds. The doc tried to talk to him, but he waved his

THE WHISKEY BOTTLE CONVERSATION

knife and said, 'I'll kill anyone of you bastards that try and get me!'

"While the doc talked, I got around to his side and tried to tackle him. It was like hitting a tree. He picked me up and threw me like I was a rag doll. I said to the GI, 'Go get some big boys and hurry back!' He came back with three men, and while one distracted him, the rest of us grabbed his arms and legs. One guy got the knife out of his hand. The four of us wrestled with him for a good ten minutes. He tossed us around like we were little kids. Finally, we got him down, and the doc gave him a tranquilizer. In about a minute, he was in lala land.

"Some of the boys carried him to his hut. The next day one of the Chinese men that cooked at the base told me that the sergeant's girlfriend and parents had been murdered... stabbed to death. The doc filled out a report and sent it down to Kunming. That afternoon, two MPs arrived in a jeep and took the sergeant away. That's the last I ever saw or heard about him. The boys who knew him on the base said he was the nicest, happiest guy you could ever meet."

"Did you think they put him on trial or court-martialed him, Dick?"

"I don't think so, Dave. They probably interviewed him and transferred him somewhere out of China. There wasn't any system of justice in the countryside of China. The average Chinese Coolie had a life expectancy of twenty-five to thirty years. There wasn't much value placed on human life. That's not to say that the sergeant should have gotten away with murder, but that's just the way it was back then."

"How long did it take you to complete the runway?"

"It took us a little over a month. After we finished, planes started coming in. They were mostly fighters, but some C-47s would land with supplies. One afternoon, a P-51 fighter had just touched down when his landing gear collapsed. The plane came sliding down the runway, stood up on its nose, and then flopped back down and stopped. There was a fire, and it was leaking gas. I ran down to the plane, climbed up on the wing, and tried to get inside to get the pilot out. I was leaning over headfirst in the cockpit, which was filling with smoke, and I couldn't find him. He must have jumped out on the other side of the plane.

"Finally, the smoke was too much, so I jumped off the wing and started running when the plane blew up. The force of the blast knocked me over, but I wasn't hurt. Major Selingman witnessed the whole event and wrote a report, recommending me for the Distinguished Service Cross. I never got a medal or heard anything more about it. I imagine when it got to Chennault, he filed it in the waste paper basket. I didn't deserve a medal anyway. I was just doing what I was trained to do. We took care of our own when there was trouble."

Dick pulled up a handful of the letters off the table.

"There should be some letters here I wrote home when I was at this base."

He looked for a couple of minutes while I put a log on the fire. He picked out two and set some pages on his lap.

"Here, Dave. Read these to me."

I felt that he really enjoyed having his letters read to him. He would sit back in his chair, usually with his eyes closed and a little smile on his face. I'm sure his words stirred up many different emotions for him. I know it was a

THE WHISKEY BOTTLE CONVERSATION

pleasure for me to be sharing Dick's private thoughts written so long ago.

My Dear Parents:

Another payday has rolled around and it finds your son as well as could be expected. The war news certainly sounds wonderful, and it looks as though Germany was or is all ready to say "uncle." The Japs are still giving us a bad time, but if Russia and England will give us a little hand, I think we can dispense with the pests. Just heard the news and it's too bad, but rumor of an unconditional surrender couldn't have been the truth.

My last letter from home was dated April third, just thought you'd like to know where we stand. I was really surprised about the light typhoon that struck your area. That isn't like good old northern New York! I should like to say, while it's on my mind, that I enjoy and appreciate all your letters very much. Guess I'll never get over being a home boy! That's what you get for treating me so swell—now you can't get rid of me, in fact, I've moved my whole family in!

This kid has really been working hard the last couple of weeks, but now I'm beginning to see some results. Looks as though I'm going to have the best damned setup in China. You probably think I'm bragging—well, you're right!

Received a swell letter from Helen Rose Kelly and a note from Little Anne Rose Kelly, which I enjoyed a great deal. Helen says her "Tommy Boy" can't catch up to Rick as far as weight goes, but she still will bet me that Tom will out hang Rick—that I've got to see!

My Gal Jeannie keeps the mailbox full with her letter a day. Sure keeps the sun on the right side of the heart. She tells me she is doing pretty well in school. Are you still giving two bucks for A's, HK? If so, see that my wife gets properly reimbursed for her studies.

I suppose Old Gramps is still holding down the upstairs. Give him my love and tell him that one of these days, I'm going to surprise him with a letter that just won't wait.

By the way, kids, how would you like to send your son a few necessities? I should appreciate very much some vitamin pills (any brand—we are lacking in everything but sunshine), some calcium pills, a couple tablets of Vitamin C, some of Jerry's hair tonic (getting a shiny spot), a bottle of shampoo and anything else you've got. Some type of sweets would be great! You know if you'd like to send me some canned stuff—sardines, shrimp, fruit juice, or any type of food at all it would be deeply appreciated. I'm not kidding a bit when I say "the food situation is critical, except for nice old beans!" Whenever you feel in the mood, just type out a letter for me and take it to the P.O. with a box. I had all of the film developed that I had taken on my trip and none of it turned out. It seems as though the lens of the camera was shot. Made me cry a little, but I've written

THE WHISKEY BOTTLE CONVERSATION

to all the kids that came with me and asked them to send me some copies of their pictures. I sure hope they come through.

Well, folks, guess that about winds up the news of the day. I think of you all a great deal and needless to say, love you all very much, even you, HK

Take care of yourselves and my family,

Your son,
Dick

Dick had reclined his chair and was staring into the fire as I continued to read...

My Dear Parents:

The monsoons have arrived. Boy, is this place a sea of mud! A few days ago, the weather was perfect and then for no good reason, it started to rain. From all reports, boots and raincoats are now standard equipment for several months to come.

Last Sunday was one of those perfect days and your son, R.P., sacrificed a whole twenty-four hours to posterity. For the first time since March 19, I took a day off and did I have a good time!

It seems the Colonel likes to fish, so he had a boat made and a very nice boat it was. I use the term nice for a specific reason, which you shall presently hear about.

I have a very good friend, Dick Thum, from Baltimore and like Hank, he says "wooder" for water. Well, this kid is a mechanic and has access to an outboard motor. Put the Colonel and his boat, Dick and his motor, together and what do you have? Right—a motorboat. Well, Sunday morning, Dick and I fixed a motor mount on the good Colonel's boat and right after dinner, loaded motor and boat on a truck and headed for the lake. We took a few guests along for the outing and for your information, I'll give you their names, rank and duties. One was Major Selingman, the base First Lieutenant Surgeon, and a fine fellow. He and I fly together all the time—we're pretty good buddies. Number two was Captain Scully, an Air Transport Control Operations Officer from Rochester, N.Y. Third and last was Dick Perkins, Engineering Officer for the 68th Service Group, who is also a neighbor from Warsaw, N.Y.

We arrived at a nearby lake around one o'clock and after a minimum of trouble unloaded the boat, motor, and several blankets and pillows, also other accessories such as gasoline, tools, and a few refreshments. When everything was properly stowed away, we set sail.

As mentioned at the start of this letter, it was a beautiful day! The temperature was around eighty degrees, there was a cool refreshing breeze from the southeast, and the sun had a warmth to it that made body and soul glad to be together! The lake itself was just choppy enough to make boating fun, and just blue enough to reflect every object in its surroundings. The sky was a misty blue and white cumulus

THE WHISKEY BOTTLE CONVERSATION

clouds hovered over the surrounding mountains. In short, it was just one of those days!

We had no sooner left shore than yours truly, disrobed and naked as a jaybird, assumed a horizontal position on the bottom of the boat. What a life—a candy bar in one hand, relaxation in the other, and a mind as vacant from worry as it usually was from sense! The first hour of the voyage was truly out of this world but then, my friends, things began to happen.

At first it was only minor engine trouble. Being an old mechanic, I soon had the problem taken care of, just a little water in the carburetor. But it wasn't five minutes that the damn thing stopped again with the same trouble. Once again, I took action and once more enjoyed success, at least for a short time. This happened several times and was becoming a little monotonous when other worries were added. We were in the middle of the lake, a very lovely place to be under proper circumstances, but in our condition, it was quite depressing. You see, our situation was soon to become a little desperate. Now this wouldn't worry the average boating party in the least but we were not the average group. In the first place, we had probably the only outboard motor in China, accompanied by the Colonel's boat, undoubtedly the only one of its kind in the Orient. Now with all this scarce and vital equipment you would think that we should have along a little more of the ordinary accessories. For instance, a set of paddles. This, I am sad to say, was not the case. The best boat in the world isn't any good without propulsion, and the best motor in the world won't run without fuel constantly, so "we were up the creek without a paddle."

Our position seemed to be closer to the opposite side of the lake than from the home side and as the wind was from the port, we decided on this plan of action. It was a known fact that a Chinese factory was located on the far side of the lake and that there was the possibility of getting some gas. There was only one possible solution… to head away from home and pray! This we did and the closer we got, the farther away it looked and the lower went our gas supply. It was soon evident that we wouldn't make shore and I daresay the prospect of a happy ending seemed very doubtful. Approximately one mile from shore, the engine sounded that antagonizing and fatal sound, "chug, chug, silence."

Being good soldiers, a little thing like being out of gas ten miles from home and in China where gas sells for eighteen dollars per gallon if you can get it; also, the fact that we were one mile from the nearest land with no means of propulsion didn't bother us. Do you know what we did? Of course not—a civilian wouldn't be expected to cope with such an emergency, but an Officer faces little things like this every day, so it was no problem at all to hold up a blanket and sail ashore.

We arrived at land some two hours later where we were greeted by several dozen gabbing Chinese. None of them had ever heard of gasoline let alone

THE WHISKEY BOTTLE CONVERSATION

have any of it, so you can see we were really up against it. All the time this unintelligible conversation was going on, yours truly was standing on sharp jagged rocks to keep our canvas boat from being ripped to pieces. I must have presented quite a spectacle to our allies. I had on a leather jacket, a pair of blue shorts, and that's all. The waves were up to my expectations and I was afraid they were going to tear my shorts right off as one poorly sewn button was the only thing between my self-respect and total unconditional shame! Under ordinary circumstances, I would gladly have matched any and every Chinaman there, inch for inch, but after being submerged in that cold water, I'm truly afraid I would have lost face!

We finally decided to beach the boat and go in search of that precious fluid so after a terrific struggle, we successfully accomplished this feat. During the entire operation, there was only one casualty. I was nearly mortally wounded. A large, one-eighth inch, laceration of the left foot almost spelled doom. If a Doc hadn't been onboard at the time, I might have bled to death. Luckily a "Band-Aid" was applied immediately.

After completion of this task, the good Doc and Skully went on a reconnaissance mission. Dick Perkins and myself remained to guard the boat. This proved quite amusing. Our boy, "Dick the Engineer," managed to communicate with the Chinese very extensively. He's been overseas two years and so knows a little Chinese, consequently, he struck up quite an interesting conversation which amounted to "Japanese BooHow" and "No Japanese." This means first "Japanese No Good" and secondly, "You're Japanese." The Chinese men all got a big kick out of this. I thought they were going to finish us right off there but Dick said, "Meg Wa, Boo-How" which means "American no good, and this brought the house down. The Chinese laughed, clapped their hands and stomped their feet. After this, we received the keys to the city.

In the meantime Doc and Skully were winding their way through the countryside and found a hotel. Finally, they entered a palatial suite and were doing everything but standing on their heads trying to get over to the Chinese that they needed gas. They called the man behind the desk a dumb so-and-so, and a no-good Chink. He got up from his chair and said, "I'm Chin. I spent several years in America, going to MIT; won't you be seated?" The Doc and Skully were embarrassed as hell and apologized to the Hotel Manager. He was very gracious in accepting their apology and got them a gallon of gas.

Hurdling this barrier, we were greatly exhilarated and ready for practically anything that could happen and as usual, it did! The first problem was launching the boat and attaching the motor. You are familiar to this process. First, I launched the boat and this usually proves fairly simple—in fact, all I did was lift the boat into the water, but when the waves start pushing us around it became a real

THE WHISKEY BOTTLE CONVERSATION

challenge trying to keep the boat from banging on the rocks. Once the boat was in and my three mates had it secured I dashed towards shore to get the motor all the time banging the hell out of my shins. Unfortunately, the motor was heavy, and naturally I couldn't afford to drop it, so I staggered drunkenly from one rock to the other, all the time cursing like mad. You would think that from here on out, it would be (figuratively speaking) smooth sailing, But we Marines know better, don't we HK?

Everyone was settled in the boat and anticipating a lovely ride, but what happened? The (blankity, blank, blank) or the G.D. S.O.B. wouldn't start—I'm speaking of the motor. I was sitting in the middle seat and then—whack—the starter rope caught me behind the ear. That was the last straw. I vaulted out of my seat, grabbed the starter rope, wound it around the fly wheel, and with full choke pulled it through a couple of times. Then I opened the throttle, opened the choke, and with a wild streak, a loud groan and flexing on my many well-defined muscles (like my father used to have) pulled the rope. Results, negative! In short, it didn't start.

Well—that just about did it; but remembering "Patience is the virtue of all great men." I tried again and again, and finally got the damned thing started.

It was a beautiful sunset that evening. Probably it was just average, but it's so seldom one really set-

tles down and enjoys the glories of mother nature, but when you do happen to notice her handiwork, it's quite impressive!

The sky was tonsillitis red and the setting sun was a mass of red-hot coals. As our little craft skipped from wave to wave, I was sort of lost within myself. Those happy days at "Leonard's Retreat" flashed through my mind and I even went so far as to taste those delicious hot dogs, potato salad and other delicacies we used to enjoy on the front porch, just as the sun was setting for the night. When I came back to everyday existence, there was an empty feeling in the pit of my stomach and as the sun bid us good night, the chill of the evening began to settle in my bones. All my clothes were wet, consequently affording little warmth. My companions were all in the same fix.

Things went quite well for a while. It was a lovely night and if I'd had my love to keep me warm, I would have classified myself as one of the fortunate; but circumstances were different and all I could think about was heat and warmth. Even this soon left my mind when a horrible, scraping noise attracted all of my attention. No doubt you have guessed it; we were aground! Well, we couldn't run the motor, but we slowly made our way to deeper water, but alas, this was full of seaweeds, and as soon as we would start our motor, it would clog up and we'd have to shut it off. Then one of us would lean out over the back and untangle the weeds from

THE WHISKEY BOTTLE CONVERSATION

the prop. This became routine and after an hour, a little monotonous but as all things come to an end, so did the weeds, and once more we encountered smooth sailing.

The next thing I remember (you see, I had laid down on the bottom of the yacht and took a nap) was someone was saying, "This doesn't look like the place!" And never truer words were spoken—we were lost.

After a lengthy discussion, we chose a direction and headed our trusty craft for the spot we had chosen.

The boat touched shore exactly at 11:30 and I went to get the jeep. I planned on backing it into the lake so as to load the boat and motor. I climbed in, turned on the switch, and hit the start button, but nothing happened. Our Chinese friends evidently had been blowing the horn, turning on the lights and in general, running down the battery. I tried the truck next and found it to be in the same state. By this time, I was in an ugly mood (and my friends were in even a worse frame of mind). We finally pushed the jeep and pushed the truck, thus bringing them to life. The rest of the trip was the same old story—you know—just having a good time!

We finally arrived home around one o'clock in the morning and after a hot shower and a cup of hot cocoa, things began to look brighter. Here's a word of advice—if you have insomnia, spend your Sunday boating!

The next day I woke feeling a trifle lame but otherwise none the worse for wear. A few days later, the Colonel wanted to know how the holes got in the bottom of the boat and may I say my public speaking came in handy!

That is how yours truly spent his first day off in two months. Believe me, I'll take twenty before I take another, although truthfully speaking, it was a lot of fun!

Well folks, hope you love it, and now that you're up to date, I'm going to hit the sack!

My love to the whole family and may God grant me the privilege of frolicking once more together—at Leonard's Retreat!

Your loving son,
Dick

Dick was laughing and shaking his head. "What a day that was! A crew of land-lovers, and anything that could happen did."

"Sounds like a good time to me, Dick."

"Aside from a few glitches, it was, Dave. Things always look a little better in hindsight, I guess."

"What did you do when the runway was finished?"

* * *

About the time we completed the runway, this new colonel comes in with a group of forty or fifty men in their

P-51 fighter planes. They had flown in from India and were going to be stationed temporarily at our base until they received their assignments.

When he arrived, he came up to me and asked, "Who's in charge?"

I said, "I am."

All of us who worked on the runway just wore cut-off shorts, boots, and T-shirts. I didn't require any military protocol. I didn't care how the boys looked as long as they got the job done.

The colonel started chewing me out. "Why aren't you or your men in uniform? You're in the Army Air Corps, mister, and there are rules! I want your name, rank, and serial number! You're on report!"

I just stood there, and when he finished, I turned and walked away. He had just come over from the States and didn't have a clue what it was like to live in China. He and his boys set up tents a few hundred yards from the runway.

I still wanted to join a combat outfit, so I figured this was a good time to fly up to Looyang, which was a B-24 base about one hundred miles north of us. When I got to Looyang, I talked to the CO.

I said, "I'd like to join your outfit, sir. I've been operations officer in Kunming and am eager to see some combat!"

He said, "Well, Lieutenant, your chances are pretty slim. We're getting ready to leave for the Pacific in about a month, and I've got all the pilots I need. Give me your name and where I can get ahold of you. If something changes, I'll see what I can do."

I flew back to our base, very disappointed.

A week later, a B-24 landed at the base. This major gets out of the plane and asks for Lieutenant Leonard. One of the boys found me, and I reported to him.

He said, "Get whatever clothes you've got and climb aboard. You're assigned to my group now."

I went and collected my gear and asked him if everything had been approved by Chennault.

"Everything's taken care of, son. You're now a member of the 373 Low-Altitude Bomber Group."

I got in the plane, and the major said, "Climb in the pilot's seat, Lieutenant, and fly us back to Looyang."

I strapped myself in, took off, flew us up to the Looyang base.

The major said, "Okay, Lieutenant, you're all checked out. One of our copilots came down with a case of the nerves. He's going back stateside. I guess today's your lucky day!"

I said, "Yes, sir! Thank you, sir!"

The major said, "Report to Captain Comerford at Operations. He'll fill you in on your assignment."

* * *

As Dick told me this, I could see that he was still excited about being transferred. He was smiling and seemed a little restless as he moved around in his chair.

"Well, Dick, I guess you got your wish after all."

"I was one happy SOB that day, Dave." He handed me the letter he had in his lap. "Here, Dave. Read this."

THE WHISKEY BOTTLE CONVERSATION

373rd Bomb Squadron
308th Bomb Group
APO 30

My Dear Parents:

Above is my new address; it is only temporary but my mail addressed as such will get to me much quicker than if the old one is used. As you can see, I'm in a new outfit; a bomb squadron. You are probably wondering why the transfer, but all I can say is "I believe sincerely it was for the best." Just before I left the 68th GP, I was made GP Operations Officer and had been promised a Captain's position, if I would stay. But, after much deliberation and advice from several wheels of the GP, I made up my mind that this was it. There are a swell bunch of fellows in this squadron, and it has a reputation of being the best of its kind in China. As yet I haven't done anything, but undoubtedly, I'll have to start at the bottom. You probably think I'm crazy and perhaps I am, but I'm well satisfied with the change and in a couple of months, I'm sure I'll be on my way to the top of this outfit (let's hope so).

Today, Sunday, has been a beautiful day and I spent the afternoon playing softball. First time I've really enjoyed sports since my arrival in China. I'm getting a little lame, but it's exactly what I need. For two days, I've been sleeping and getting sunburned. You'll never know what a relief it is to get out from under Operations. For the first time since I started in Operations here in China, my mind is perfectly blank of ideas and worries. In fact, I've had time to get a little homesick and even that feels good! I never realized how much I missed home until I spent a couple of days thinking about it!

I'm sitting on the porch of the barracks at this time and the scenery is quite beautiful. The sun is just going down and the colors of the nearby mountains are really showing. There are pretty big, white clouds just doing nothing but hanging and everything seems quite peaceful. This could be beautiful country if it wasn't for the poverty, the ignorance and the conflict. I'm afraid there's not much hope for this part of the world.

Well, folks, guess I'll relax in the quiet of the evening and think of home. Be good children and take good care of yourselves. I love you all.

Dick

P.S. Please get Jean some flowers for our anniversary. Enclosed is a ten. Spend it all.

CHAPTER THIRTEEN

The Lucky Leprechaun

I reported to Captain Comerford at Operations headquarters.

I introduced myself, and he said, "Nice to have you aboard, Lieutenant. You'll be flying copilot with Joe O'Connor and his crew. They're a good group of boys. Joe's a little on the wild side but one of our best pilots. He's in A barracks. Why don't you go see if you can find him, and he'll fill you in on the details."

The base was located in the mountains about five thousand feet above sea level. There were six barracks, five large maintenance buildings, a control tower, and an officers' club to accommodate the B-24 squadron. Fifty planes were equipped with special radar gear, which allowed the bombardier to take control of the plane when making a bomb run. It was the only low-altitude bomber group in the Pacific. The payload was delivered at about three hundred feet above the target.

* * *

"Nothing like getting close to your work, Dick," I said.

He took a sip of his Scotch. "No kidding, but it was exciting as hell!"

* * *

I went to the barracks and asked around for Captain O'Connor.

One of the boys said, "If he's not here, he's probably over at the officers' club, doing shots and beers."

I walked to the club, and there were several men sitting at the bar and a few tables of boys playing cards. I asked the bartender if Joe O'Connor was there.

"Who wants to know?" came a loud voice from the other end of the bar.

I walked around the bar, where I saw a big redheaded Irishman. He must have weighed at least 250 and had what looked like a three-day growth on his face. This had to be Captain O'Connor.

I saluted him and said, "Lieutenant Dick Leonard reporting as your replacement copilot, sir."

He looked at me and said, "Get your hand off your forehead, Dick, and do something useful with it, like wrap it around a glass."

He called to the bartender and said, "Hey, Billy! Give my new copilot a shot and a beer, and I'll have the same!"

Billy brought us our drinks, and Joe raised his shot glass and said, "Well, Lieutenant, I hope you've got balls as big as pickle jars because where you're going, you'll need 'em!"

THE WHISKEY BOTTLE CONVERSATION

All the men at the bar started laughing as we tossed down the whiskey.

The fellow next to me smiled and said, "He ain't kiddin' either!"

I asked Joe what type of missions we would be flying.

"We're mining the Yangtze River," he said. "But don't worry about that now. Tell me what you've been up to, Dick."

Joe and I sat there and swapped stories for a couple of hours and got drunk.

When we left, he said, "All my crew is in barracks A. You come and bunk with us."

"Are you sure there's room there, Joe?"

"If there isn't, we'll throw some kid's sorry ass out." Then he slapped me on the back. "I think you're going to fit in just fine, Dick!"

* * *

"It sounds like you and Joe were a match made in heaven."

* * *

I can't tell you how much it meant to me to be with his crew. As operations officer, I was always under the gun. I had to keep the planes flying, maintain all the records, build runways, and try to satisfy the brass. Now I was just one of the boys, and all I had to do was fly. I felt like a free man, and to be copilot for someone like Joe was just the frosting on the cake. I was a tremendous feeling of relief.

The next morning, Joe introduced me to his crew. They were a good group, always laughing and kidding around. They thought the world of Joe. After meeting the boys, he took me over to the plane. As we got close, I couldn't help but laugh. On the side of the cockpit was a big leprechaun holding a bomb with a shamrock painted on it. Underneath, it said, "The Lucky Leprechaun."

Joe gave me an elbow in the ribs. "What do you think of my bird, Dick?"

We did our preflight check and got in the plane. Joe told me to take the pilot's seat.

He said, "I'm just along for the ride."

I fired up the four Pratt and Whitney's and taxied out on the runway. When the control tower cleared us, I pushed the throttle forward, and we took off.

We flew up over the mountains, and Joe gave me a heading to follow. It was a beautiful sunny day, not a cloud in the sky. I flew in a southwesterly direction for about an hour when Joe pointed out the Yangtze River.

He said, "When we go to work, Dick, that's our office down there. Okay, turn the Leprechaun around, and let's head back to base."

About fifty miles from the field, I was cruising at fifteen thousand feet, and Joe said, "Put her in a dive, and level off about two hundred feet above the deck."

I did as he asked, and in no time, we were screaming across Chinese countryside, like an eagle swooping down on its prey.

"Okay," he said. "Pull her up, and let's land this thing."

I pulled back on the wheel and climbed to five thousand feet. Once the control tower cleared us to land, I

THE WHISKEY BOTTLE CONVERSATION

brought the 24 in and made a smooth landing. We taxied to the parking area, and I shut her down.

Joe said, "You've got a nice touch, Dick. Glad to have you aboard. We aren't going to be making a run for a couple of days, so just relax and enjoy yourself. I'll meet you after mess for a drink."

I spent the next two days sitting in the sun, reading and playing softball off with some of the crews from the 24s. I started to feel like a normal human being again. The lack of pressure and responsibility was a welcomed change. My evenings were spent in the officers' club, drinking beer and playing cards. I felt a real sense of camaraderie among the pilots.

On the morning of the fourth day, Joe and I went to Operations to get instructions on where to drop the mines. We carried twenty mines or "pills," as the crew called them. After checking the plane out and making sure our payload was secure, the Lucky Leprechaun lifted off the runway. Joe took her up to fifteen thousand feet, flying over the mountains. The navigator gave us our heading.

We flew at that altitude for about an hour when the navigator called up and said, "We're in position to make our run, Captain."

Joe said, "Open the bomb bay doors, Dick."

I flipped the switch and called on the intercom, "Bomb bay doors open."

Joe said, "Hold on, boys, we're going down. Push those pills out on my mark."

My heart was pounding as he put the plane in a dive. When the plane reached 150 feet, we leveled off, flying down the center of the Yangtze.

Joe said, "Okay, boys, let 'em go!"

One by one, two of the crew in the back pushed the mines out the bomb bay doors. About halfway through our run, one of the side gunners called up.

"We've taken some machine gunfire on the port side, Captain."

Joe laughed. "Goddamn peashooters. We'll take care of that after we dump our load."

After all the mines had been released, Joe pulled up and circled around to make the same run. He called back to the side and belly gunners.

"When those little nip bastards start firing, give them a taste of those .50 calibers. Don't hit 'em, just give them a little scare."

Joe took the plane closer to the shore at one hundred feet above the water. All of a sudden, I saw the muzzle blasts from what looked like about ten Japs on the shore. Then the boys started shooting with their .50 calibers, hitting the water and beach in front of our attackers.

Once they opened up, it was assholes and elbows heading for the underbrush on the riverbank. Everybody onboard was laughing.

Joe called back on the intercom, "Nice shootin', fellas! It will take them at least an hour to clean their pants." He threw his head back, slapped his knee, and gave a big Irish belly laugh. "Let's go home, men. That's enough fun for one day."

We continued our river-mining delivery route for about two weeks. On some days, when we weren't scheduled, Joe and I would fly gas to different bases around China. If we had a chance to get in a plane and go someplace, we took it.

THE WHISKEY BOTTLE CONVERSATION

During my third week at Looyang, orders came down that our B-24 LAB group was headed to Clark Field in the Philippines. From there we would be working our way through the islands to Okinawa. The push toward Japan had begun.

* * *

"What was the mood of the men, Dick?"

* * *

Everyone was real excited about leaving China and finally getting into some real combat situations. We had three days to get the Lucky Leprechaun ready.

The morning we left, it was Friday the thirteenth, with thirteen men onboard and a ton and a half overload on the plane. We were the last B-24 out of China, so they loaded everything they could on the plane. What couldn't be fit in was just left behind. There was one major challenge left: trying to get the plane off the ground.

The runway was ten thousand feet, and Looyang was five thousand feet above sea level, so the air was thin. It would be a challenge at best. We lined up as far back on the runway as we could get and checked everything out. Three of the props were wide open to take a big bite of air. The fourth prop was in a fixed position, which would be normal for flight. There was a malfunction, so we couldn't adjust the pitch on that prop. In the open position, it changes the RPMs of the engine to give more power, which helps get the plane off the ground.

On a multiengine plane, if one engine isn't in the same position as the others, the rpm have to be cut back until all the engines sound as one. To make a long story short, we took off with a ton and a half more weight than the plane was designed for, and the engines running at a lower rpm necessary for a normal takeoff.

Joe called back on the intercom, "Okay, men, cross your fingers and say a prayer. Here we go! Dick, lock the brakes."

Joe pushed the throttles all the way forward. As the engines maxed out, the plane began to shake.

Joe said, "Dick, release the brakes, and let's see if this bird will fly."

I let off on the brakes, and slowly the plane began to crawl down the runway, gradually building up speed. The plane took a hop as we pulled back on the wheel, but it came back down. Joe and I pulled back again, and we were airborne for about five seconds and back down again. The end of the runway was now in sight.

Joe said, "This is our last try, Dick. As soon as we pull back, you raise the landing gear. If we don't make it, it's been fun!"

Joe and I pulled back on the wheel, and the plane came off the runway. I flipped the switch for the landing gear, and we both were pulling with all our might on the wheels. The plane skimmed just above the ground at about twenty feet over the end of the runway. Then we began to gain altitude, and all the boys let out a cheer. Joe and I looked at each other and began to laugh because the sweat was just rolling off our faces. We climbed to our altitude and adjusted the engines for a nice, long flight. Joe got on the intercom.

THE WHISKEY BOTTLE CONVERSATION

"Settle back and relax. Next stop… Clark Field for some wine, women, and song."

Another cheer arose from the back of the plane.

* * *

"You always were one for making a grand exit, Dick. Did you have any regrets about leaving China?

"None at all," he said. "In fact, I wrote a poem about China when I left. It might be in with my letters."

I picked up the folders and began looking while Dick stoked the fire and poured us another drink. I found a two-page poem entitled "China" and read it to Dick…

"China"

If I were an artist with nothing to do
I'd paint a picture, a composite view—
Of historic China—In which I'd show
Visions of contrast, the high and the low.

There'd be towering mountains, a deep green sea,
Filthy brats yelling, "Ding How" at me.
High-plumed horses and colorful carts,
Two-toned dresses on hustling tarts.

I'd show Chinese coolies, seemly merry,
Dejected old women with too much to carry.
A dignified old gent with a Fu Manchu beard,
Bare-bottomed children with both ends smeared.

DAVID LEONARD

Temples and graves and houses too,
Houses on mountains, a marvelous view;
Homes made of wood, brick, straw and mud;
People covered with crabs, scurvy and crud.

Poverty and want, men craving food,
Picking through garbage, practically nude.
Stately Temples with high-toned bells,
Thatch-covered shanties with horrible smells.

Mounding catacombs, a place for the dead,
Noisy multitudes clamoring for bread;
Grass-fringed "paddies" swept by the breeze,
Goats wading in filth up to their knees.

Revealing statues, all detail complete;
A sensual lass with sores on her feet.
Creeping highways, a spangled team,
Alleys that wind like a dope fiend's dream.

Rice paddles set on the side of a hill,
A sidewalk latrine with privacy nil.
Two-by-four shops with shelving all bare,
Gesturing merchants, flailing the air,

Narrow sidewalks, more like a shelf,
Butt-puffing youngsters scratching themselves.
Lumbering carts hogging the road,
Old nondescript trucks, frequently towed.

THE WHISKEY BOTTLE CONVERSATION

Diminutive donkeys loaded for fair,
Man-drawn rickshaws seeking a fare.
Determined pedestrians courting disaster,
Walking in the gutters, where movement is faster.

Chinese drivers all accident-bound,
Weaving and twisting to cover ground.
Homemade brooms (weeds tied to a stick),
Used on the street to clean off the brick.

Rickshaws and pushcarts blocking your path,
Street-corner coolies needing a bath;
Soldiers galore, with manners quite mild,
Prolific women all heavy with child.

Arrogant wenches picking up "snipes,"
Miniature flats of various types,
Listless housewives with bound-up feet,
Washing and cooking right out in the street.

The family wash of tattle-tale grey,
Hangs from a cord blocking the way.
Native coffee—Ugh! What a mixture!
Dirty buildings with nary a fixture.

Families dining from one common bowl,
A farmer taking a honey-bucket stroll.
Chinese "zoot-suiters," flashily dressed,
Barefooted beggars looking depressed.

Mud-smeared children clustering about,
Filling their jugs from the community spout.
A dutiful mother with a look of despair,
Picking the lice from her small daughter's hair.

Capable craftsmen, skilled at the art,
Decrepit old shacks falling apart,
Intricate needlework out on display,
Surrounded by filth, rot, and decay.

Elegant caskets, carved out by hand,
Odorous shops where leather is tanned.
A shoemaker's shop, a black-market store,
Crawling with vermin, no screens on the door.

I've neglected the war's scars, visible yet,
But those are the things we aren't trying to forget;
I'm glad that I came, but anxious to go;
Give it back to the Chinese! I'm ready to blow!

"Judging from the observations and sentiments of your poem, I'd say you were happy to be off on another adventure."

"I really was, Dave. Finally, I was going to do what I joined the service for—to fight!"

"So did you have any problems getting to the Philippines?"

* * *

THE WHISKEY BOTTLE CONVERSATION

When we were a couple hundred miles from Clark Field, our fuel was getting low. With all the extra weight, we were using a lot more gas than we normally would. Joe and I both agreed there wasn't enough to make it to Clark. I checked the maps and found a little fighter strip on a small island not too far from our present position.

We located the island and radioed to the tower that we had to make an emergency landing. The man in the tower said the runway wasn't long enough to handle a B-24.

I radioed back, "We're out of options. Clear the runway, we're coming in!"

I called back on the intercom and told the boys to hold on tight.

We made our approach and dropped in over some large rocks at the beginning of the runway and hit the brakes. Both the rear tires blew as we skidded a couple hundred feet off the end of the runway. Joe spun the plane around, got it back up on the pavement, and cut the power. We all got out and kissed the ground.

One of the boys said, "The Lucky Leprechaun saves our asses again!"

The operations officer on the field ordered us some new tires. He also called in a C-47, on which we loaded all the materials we had onboard our plane. Our crew flew to Clark on the C-47, and Joe and I followed once we had our new tires on.

When Joe and I landed on Manila, we located the crew, and all went into town. We ended up at a big dance hall. There were probably three or four hundred soldiers, and Philippine women there. All of us got drunk. I think I had a good time, but I don't really remember.

After being in China and drinking medical alcohol and fruit punch, the real thing did me in. We all danced and told stories to the other soldiers about our exploits in China. I think someone slipped me a Mickey Finn, and I woke up the next morning in an alley behind the dance hall. All my money was gone, and I had a terrible hangover.

I pulled myself together and went out in the street and bummed a ride with a military jeep. He took me back to the field. I got there about twenty minutes before we were scheduled to take off.

* * *

Dick laughed. "I was a wreck, and so was Joe and the rest of the crew. We were a sad group. I don't know how the hell we ever flew that plane. My vision was blurred, and my head was pounding. Joe didn't look any better."

* * *

We got the plane off the ground and set our heading for the Mariana Islands. Whatever recollection I had of two short days in the Philippines would be indelibly burned in my memory.

Our seven-hour flight to Saipan seemed like seven days! We had been instructed to avoid certain islands because they were still occupied by some Japanese. We were in the first group of B-24s to land on the island, which had been recently secured from the Japanese. Three thousand Americans and about ten thousand Japanese were killed in the Battle for Saipan. Three hundred Jap planes were also lost in that battle.

Once we taxied to our parking area and had the plane secured, Joe and I checked with flight headquarters and were given our tent assignments. After we had our gear put away, we were greeted by the nicest, wildest bunch of Australians you ever wanted to meet. They were glider pilots. Their gliders were still created up in preparation for the invasion of Japan. Each glider could carry about fifty men. The idea was that they could be towed over Japan and then released for a slow, quiet descent into the Japanese countryside.

They were a hell of a good bunch of guys, asking us all sorts of questions about America and what our duty in China had been like. All of us were amazed at the bracelets, earrings, and necklaces they had made from stones—which they polished and made into jewelry for all their ladies. They probably hadn't seen their wives or sweethearts for a couple of years, but I'm sure they had pleasant memories of them.

Before we left China, we exchanged American for Chinese money. It was one American dollar for five hundred Chinese dollars. All of us had barracks bags full of this funny money. We couldn't take any gifts of any size or weight, but the barracks bags could be stuffed in spaces in the plane. We figured it would be good barter, and it was.

We would trade money for the Aussies' jewelry and use it to play poker.

* * *

Dick laughed. "We had wads of it! Our stay on the island was a nice vacation."

* * *

Our crew flew missions at night, sending back weather reports. Occasionally, we'd spot an enemy ship and make a pass and drop our bombs. We were equipped to fly low-altitude bombing missions; however, we carried a weather observer to analyze and send back weather reports.

When this B-24 outfit was formed in China, they were equipped with radar, and the bombardier would have a radar sight that was tied in with the bomb sight. Once we started our run on a ship and leveled off at three hundred feet, the bombardier would take control over the plane. This was new technology, and we were the only group in the Pacific with this low-altitude bombing equipment. It was much more efficient bombing at low altitudes, particularly when you were flying at night.

The Japs were sending supplies to various ports day and night. At night they thought they had the ocean all to themselves.

The Australians were always eager to go with us on our missions, so we took as many as possible along. They enjoyed the flights, and although we weren't supposed to have unauthorized personnel onboard, who knew? They were good company.

We spent two weeks on Saipan before we were given our next stop: the Ryukyus Islands. They were about one thousand miles northwest of the Marianas and three hundred miles south of Okinawa.

THE WHISKEY BOTTLE CONVERSATION

* * *

I remembered reading one of Dick's letters about his first air raid, which occurred on Ryukyu. I looked through the letters and found it.

"You want to hear about your first air raid, Dick?"

He started to laugh. "I'm not sure I want to or not. It was pretty embarrassing!"

My Dear Parents:

Arriving at our present location (A.P.O. 903), a little island in the Ryukyu, we were welcomed with the same stories we'd heard every other place, and they all went something like this:

"How in hell did you ever draw this place? The food here is terrible! No one knows what's going on and things are really screwed up!" Then some new recruit always comes up with this question: "Say, is it true there are Japs around here?" To this question the old veterans really settle down and you can expect at least a thirty-minute oration on "The Life and Love of the Japanese." Their stories usually go like this:

"JAPS? you're goddamned right there are Japs here! Why, just last night, a thousand of them surrounded a moving picture area and wiped out every man there! They're all over the place! I wouldn't go outside the camp area for a thousand bucks!" About this time everyone swallows hard and starts wondering why in hell they ever did come to this dam-

nable place. This gives our storyteller more courage and he starts telling about things that would scare Orson Welles.

Eventually, the stories come around to air raids and the fiction they create concerning this subject makes cold chills run up and down your spine. They tell about suicide planes loaded with T.N.T. that dive out of the clouds onto the target with unbelievable accuracy. Then there's always the tale of how last night it was reported that fifteen thousand paratroopers landed near the prison camp and set all those devils free; and they're supposed to be right up in those hills now just waiting for darkness to try to retake this air strip. Everyone is alerted! After about an hour of this, you're so scared that if anyone even sneezes, you freeze where you are sitting.

We'd been hearing these stories ever since we got to the South Pacific area, and I might add we were retaliating with even worse stories about China. A good soldier is never outimagined, especially if he's been somewhere none of the listeners have been. At least he hopes they haven't been there! So far, none of their stories had come true and we were starting to take them with the usual grain of salt. After three weeks, the stories got a little stale and we would give them a big laugh whenever they'd start their wild stories. We'd had a few alerts, true enough, but the only thing that scared me was the sound of that weird fire whistle. The first time it blew, we all went outside to see what was going on; we didn't

THE WHISKEY BOTTLE CONVERSATION

even have our helmets on. The second time we still went outside and even the third; but after that, we'd just stay in bed and go back to sleep. The next day there would be all sorts of stories about how such and such an island was raided and how we shot down from five to five hundred Jap planes. After the first couple times, these tales also got pretty dull and as time passed, our helmets, helmet liners, gas masks, and foxholes became neglected. Then came the dawn!

It was around two o'clock one morning; the usual time for an alert and according to schedule, the old fire whistle gave three long, mournful sighs, and according to schedule, I rolled over and went back to sleep. The next thing I remember, I thought I was in a boiler factory. I never heard so much noise! It sounded like blasting on a construction job, a thunderstorm with lightning all around, and the Fourth of July at the World's Fair all combined! Well, big brave Richard P. started shaking so, I thought I had the St. Vitus Dance! I rolled off on the floor, felt around for my steel helmet, found it and pulled it on my head. Unfortunately, the liner had fallen out of it and when that hard cold steel hit my skull, I was sure I'd been hit! Recovering somewhat, I grabbed my bed and pulled it over on top of me, and there I lay shaking like a leaf, saying my prayers, and cursing myself for not getting into a dugout when the warning was sounded.

After what seemed like an eternity, the noise died down somewhat and I heard one of the fellows *say, "Well, that's that!" so I proceeded to replace the bed, but still kept my helmet on and stepped out the door. The search lights were still following a Jap plane which was moving away from the island and occasional bursts of flames could be seen exploding very near. I watched for a few minutes more and then, exhausted, I headed for the sack. However, the all clear hadn't sounded, and why I didn't recall it, I will never know. I had no sooner climbed into bed that that horrible blasting started again and once more, I rolled to the floor but this time I gently put my steel helmet on and mustering a little courage, I decided to find the helmet liner. I remembered that it was in my duffel bag, so I found my pants and took the key from my pocket. Well, I was shaking so hard I couldn't get the key in the lock. When I finally did, the guns were starting to fade out. This didn't keep me from getting the liner, though, and I made damned sure it was in my helmet! Then I went outside and watched the remaining fireworks.*

That was my first air raid but not my last. The rest were similar, but when nothing happened to me the first couple of times, I became bolder and near the last, I would sit by the tent, still with my helmet on, and still shaking, but watching the whole show. It's really a very beautiful sight to see the shells bursting close to a tiny object gliding through the air, the tracers leaving their mark all through the heavens, but no matter how beautiful, you always shake a

THE WHISKEY BOTTLE CONVERSATION

little, at best. In the back of your mind is the fear of getting hit with falling flack or an evening bomb. I've seen very little of real war, but what I have witnessed has convinced me thoroughly that Sherman wasn't fooling when he said, "War is Hell!"

Well, kids, there's another chapter in R. P. at war. I've still got a couple more to tell, but that won't be possible for a time at least. Perhaps in a couple of months, and this is being optimistic, I may be home telling you about them verbally. Until that time I expect you children to take care of yourselves, be rather good kids, and to keep an eye on my family.

My love to the whole tribe.

Your loving Son,
Dick

I put the letter down and laughed. "You're quite a character, Dick. I'll have to give you credit, though. You always seem to maintain your sense of humor and a positive outlook."

"That's what keeps men alive in tough times, Dave. If you aren't scared, you're a fool. If you panic, you're dead."

His words brought to mind a statement made by an old watchman who worked at Dick's factory some years later. I had become acquainted with him one summer when I worked at the plant. He had been a sergeant in Patton's tank crew. One evening he was telling me some of his stories about the war.

At one point he said, "You know, Dave, it was the strangest thing… The men who ate fast and rushed through their meals were always the first to die in battle."

I guess his observations lent themselves to Dick's words.

I asked Dick about his activities on Ryukyu.

"Well, we were there about three weeks, and there was a lot more activity than on Saipan. Being that much closer to Japan, you've seen in the letter that we experienced air raids and threats of Japanese invasions."

* * *

The pace of the planes taking off and landing was constant. Our crew in the Lucky Leprechaun flew at night up into the Inland China Sea, which boarded Japan and sent back weather reports. The reports would be used to schedule bombing missions on the Japanese mainland by B-29s the following day. So there was a lot of activity on Ryukyu and much anticipation about our next stop, Okinawa.

The Battle for Okinawa had been a costly one. Estimates ran as high as twenty thousand Americans and sixty thousand Japanese killed. Chester Nemitz was commander of the Pacific fleet. When the fleet closed in on Okinawa, they were attacked by two thousand kamikaze planes. The pilots were young and relatively untrained. They flew planes loaded with explosives and believed that dying for the emperor was the highest honor one could achieve. They dove their planes into American ships. Nemitz lost thirty vessels and had 160 more damaged.

THE WHISKEY BOTTLE CONVERSATION

The Japanese knew that Okinawa was their last stand. If the Americans captured it, they could bomb Japan almost at will. Although you could consider their efforts valiant, they were no match for the determination and might of the Allied Forces. After our third week at Ryukyu base, we received our orders to fly to the YonTan airstrip on the southwest corner of Okinawa. The Lucky Leprechaun and its crew were off on their last flight as a single unit.

CHAPTER FOURTEEN

Freedom, Equality, and the Army Latrine

Dick had written a letter describing Okinawa. I leafed through the remaining pages and found it. I thought hearing his firsthand description might stimulate his recollection. He had gone to the bathroom, and when he came back, he put some wood on the fire.

"Since we're near the end of the war, Dave, I think we had better have one more drink."

I walked into the kitchen and got another bucket of ice and fixed two bowls of chocolate marshmallow ice cream. When I returned, Dick was looking at pictures.

He said, "Here are Gus and me in California when we were flying missions on Patton tanks. This one here is of the B-26 I flew Congressman Costello around the country in. Here's Don Oaks and me in Bombay. I'm not sure who this other fellow is."

I spent about ten minutes kneeling by his side, looking at and listening to the explanation of who or what the pictures he showed me represented.

THE WHISKEY BOTTLE CONVERSATION

At one point I said, "We'd better eat our ice cream before I have to get us two straws."

Dick had put at least four logs on the flickering fire. By the time we finished our ice cream, it was roaring.

As Dick took a sip of his Scotch, he said, "Now that's what I call a fire!"

I moved my chair back a few feet.

The wood Dick had stacked by the fireplace that morning was almost gone. It was now ten o'clock. I asked Dick if he was tired.

"Hell, no, Dave! I feel good. I want to finish my story before I call it a day."

I saluted him. "Okay, Lieutenant, you're in charge! I've got a letter here you wrote, describing Okinawa. You want to hear it?"

"Certainly, Sergeant. Read on."

My Dear Parents,

You asked me about a description of Okinawa. Well, other than being a body of land entirely surrounded by water, it's something like this. It's a long, narrow island approximately eighty miles long and varying in width from five miles to twenty miles. It looks very much like the top of a small mountain and the terrain before the engineers leveled it off, was very rough and covered with the usual lush vegetation. It has numerous small rivers and several excellent harbors. Approximately a quarter a mile offshore, the bottom just seems to drop out of sight, so large boats can practically come up onshore anywhere around the island. As you have no doubt read, the Japs took advantage of the rough terrain and honeycombed every cliff and hill with artillery. It's a wonder how we took the island without losing even more men than we did.

From the air, Okinawa is a series of landing fields surrounded by harbors. I'd hesitate to say how many fields there are, but it must run into the twenties. Then there are the numerous cemeteries; each outfit has its own and they are all very neat and nicely located. They usually rest on the top of a hill overlooking the ocean; each is surrounded with a white picket fence and at the entrance is a huge plaque telling the name of the outfit. Most of them have their own little altar and have some very nice monuments inscribed with the name of the outfit, its history, and accomplishments on Okinawa.

The people of Okinawa are very small, intelligent, and very poor. Their homes are grass shacks and their livelihood comes from what they grow and the ocean. I would say they were lost brothers of the Japs. I have visited Naha, their largest city and harbor. It was about the same size of Mexico and the remains of its buildings looked fairly modern. I say remains because the city is entirely flat except for a couple of buildings which were pretty well gutted. Naha harbor is strictly the handiwork of Mother Nature and before the war, a large ship was probably a yearly occasion.

Not a very good job of explaining but the best I can do, at least for the time being. When you said,

THE WHISKEY BOTTLE CONVERSATION

"to us, it's just a battlefield," you more than expressed my feelings toward it. If you weren't fighting Japs, it was the elements you had to contend with. I'm afraid Okinawa will be a haunted island in years to come. I hope it's by friendly ghosts and not bitter ones!

Lots of love to the family,
Dick

"So what was it like when you arrived in Okinawa, Dick?"

"Well, we landed at the YonTan Airfield. We were one of the first groups to arrive. I'd say there were maybe fifteen to twenty planes on the ground. That number grew to about four or five hundred within a month. Ours was the only low-altitude bomber group on the island. Many of the other bomber groups had gone to other islands before us. All the planes at YonTan were B-24s. The B-29s were stationed at Tinian, farther back in the island chain.

"On the west side of the island was Buchner Bay, and soon after we arrived, it was full of ships—hundreds of them. On the north end was another natural harbor that was also full of ships. Before the American ground troops invaded, the Navy ships had pummeled the island with their big guns. They destroyed everything. I mean, there wasn't anything left! When the ground troops attacked, they found the Japanese were all underground. They had the whole island tunneled, and their guns were camouflaged. The Japs could go from one end of the island to the other in their tunnels. As you know, it was a bloody battle to secure Okinawa.

"The base consisted of a single runway approximately twenty thousand feet in length. At the end of the runway was a sheer cliff that dropped off about one hundred feet into the ocean. If you didn't get off the ground, you went for a swim. Usually, one or two planes a day took the plunge. With probably five hundred planes taking off each day, there were bound to be some accidents."

I asked Dick what caused them not to make it.

"Some didn't have enough speed. Perhaps a tire would blow or pilot error would cause the plunge. A lot of boys died off the end of that cliff."

* * *

The living conditions compared to China were beautiful. Our quarters were tents with four men assigned to each one. Joe O'Connor and two other pilots were my mates. The pilots were big camera buffs, so we built a ten-by-ten dark room on the side of our tent where they could develop their film. The boys would barter with sailors on the ships to get the chemicals they needed. They were pretty handy bartering with the ship's personnel.

Our tent was on the side of a hill and generally kept in pretty good shape. It was sort of a hangout with different GIs bringing their film to be developed. Inside our "studio" were shelves, cutoff barrels to hold the chemicals, and other equipment for developing film. In the living quarters, we had four cots and a footlocker for each man. There were personal items, such as pictures, books, and some small

THE WHISKEY BOTTLE CONVERSATION

items of war booty. The tent looked damn good, and the cot felt likewise.

Once I got settled in on Okinawa, I began to fly missions. We always took off about five or six at night. When I got airborne and looked down, I was always amazed at the number of ships in the harbor. They were building up the fleet for the invasion of Japan, and from the air, it looked like there were at least a thousand ships.

I was a substitute pilot, so my days with Joe and the Lucky Leprechaun were over. The boys on the Leprechaun used to say I was nuts. I flew missions with different crews I'd never met before. Usually, every other night, I would grab a flight with a crew that needed a pilot or copilot because somebody was sick or frightened to death so they'd call me. They stayed together as a crew with their plane, but I was just a pilot that filled in for that mission. I loved to fly, and the Lord was good to me. Because we were the only low-altitude bombers on Okinawa, when new crews came in, they would assign these crews to fly with our LAB group. Our twenty planes were the only ones equipped with LAB radar. All the other B-24s that came in were the regular type of bombers. Their missions were always during the day, dropping bombs on Japan. Our LAB boys were known as a renegade group—always flying at night and dropping our load at low level. We were shown a lot of respect by the other crews.

While I was in Okinawa, there was a typhoon. They took all the ships out to sea, away from the island. They figured they'd rather fight the storm at sea than be washed ashore. Word came down for all pilots to report to the Operations shack. Each of us was assigned to a B-24, so all five hundred planes were manned. They figured the planes would be wrecked in the storm if left tied down on the runway.

We were instructed to get into our planes, start the two inboard engines, and keep the nose into the wind. As the wind—which was blowing around one hundred miles per hour—shifted, I turned the plane with the wind. I kept the wheel forward, which kept the nose down and the brakes on. Some of the planes were tipped over when the pilots didn't respond quickly enough. Most of the tents and light equipment were destroyed, and a lot of men were killed by flying debris. I was in my plane for ten hours, fighting the wind.

* * *

"So it was really like flying the plane on the ground, wasn't it, Dick?"

"That's basically what it was like, Dave. It was quite an experience maneuvering five hundred planes every time the wind changed. When there was a shift in direction, I would let off the brakes, and the wind pretty much turned the damn thing for you. After I got the feel of it, it was kind of fun."

I laughed and shook my head. "You're really something, Dick!"

He smiled.

"What were your missions like?"

* * *

THE WHISKEY BOTTLE CONVERSATION

We'd generally take off from Okinawa about 6:00 p.m. with a full crew. Each man had his special task. I'd fly to the blind bombing line, which ran from Pusan to Hiroshima. Everything past this line was considered enemy territory and a good place for the bombardier navigator to begin looking for enemy ships. He'd make a list, and on our return trip, he'd select a target. The engineer would continually check all components, making sure the equipment was operating all right. The copilot and I had to check the engines and make sure flight operations and our direction was in order. We were also responsible for overseeing the members of the crew.

The weather officer was the topman on the crew. He would make his analysis and send back reports every half hour, giving Operations the data they needed for the next day's bombing mission.

When we crossed the blind bombing line, the main thing we had to worry about was enemy fire. Naturally, everyone's adrenaline was flowing and all crew members were at their jobs. Our altitude was generally about ten thousand feet. Finally, when we were ready to head back to base, I'd call down to the bombardier and have him give me a heading for the target he had selected.

Once given the heading, I would fly a pattern so I could line up with the target. My focus when starting into a dive was on the airplane, getting into good position and making sure everything was running smoothly. I'd put the plane in a dive about 120 mph just above stalling speed. To control the speed of the dive, I'd drop the flaps like I was coming in for a landing.

When we reached three hundred feet, we were on our bombing run. At that height, with the throttle full boar, the plane was going like a bat out of hell… probably three hundred plus miles an hour. I kicked her in the guts, pushed the throttle all the way forward with flaps up, and turned the plane over to the bombardier. Then the bomb bay doors were opened. He flew the plane to the target and dropped the nine 500-pound impact bombs in trail. As soon as the bombs were away, the control of the plane was turned back to me, and I would make evasive maneuvers to get out of the range of the ship's guns.

* * *

"Were you able to see any explosions when the bombs blew up, Dick?"

"Not really. As the pilot, I wasn't looking for explosions. All I wanted to do was get the airplane and my crew the hell out of there. My focus was on the instruments, my altitude, and maneuvers to get away from any shots. The tail gunner would have the best view of whether we hit anything. At that altitude, though, there was a good chance of making contact. Every night we flew, we dropped our bombs on some poor bastard. Our flights usually ran about seven hours, so we got back to the base around one or two in the morning.

"After landing, I'd report to the Operations shack where two officers would review my mission. They'd want to know where we flew, the condition of the airplane, the number of enemy ships, and things of that nature. The pilots were given coffee and usually some type of snack to

THE WHISKEY BOTTLE CONVERSATION

help us unwind. When I satisfied the Operations staff, I'd return to my tent and go to bed."

"What did you do when you weren't flying?"

"Well, as a rule, I got up about lunchtime. After lunch, I'd go over to Operations to check on flight schedules and any other notices on the bulletin board. Mail call was of particular interest, and a letter from home was always a joy to receive. I'd take my letters and climb a little hill, sit on the grass, and daydream for an hour or so. A letter from back home always brought back fond memories. Sometimes I'd take a hike down to the waterfront and look out over the ocean. If I ran into someone, we'd have a conversation. A good book would pass the time of day, and swapping books with other men was something to look forward to.

"Almost every day, there would be a plane that didn't make it back. The nonreturns would be posted, and if I knew any of the boys, I'd go to their tent and see if there was anything I could do. It was more a token visit out of respect for a fallen comrade than anything else. That was pretty much how my free time was occupied."

"Were there any missions where you got shot up?"

Dick stared into the fire. He sat quietly for a couple of minutes.

"There were two occasions when we got into some trouble… serious trouble," he said.

* * *

One night we took off and flew up into the Inland China Sea. We flew back and forth across the sea, sending back our weather reports while the bombardier was looking for ships.

We had been flying practically all night and were on our way back to base when the bombardier picked up this good-sized ship. I brought the plane into position and put her in a dive. I leveled off at about three hundred feet and turned the plane over to the bombardier. When he signaled, we opened the bomb bay doors and on his mark, dropped the bombs.

This time, however, I think we were lower than the three hundred–foot level. We might have been as low as one hundred feet. The bombs were released, and one of them skipped off the water, came up, and hit the left wing between the first and second engines. It made quite a noise, but for some reason, it didn't explode. Impact bombs are supposed to go off when they hit something. I don't know why this one didn't. I guess the good Lord was with us this night. The ship began shooting at us, so I took it off automatic pilot, made my turn, and began to climb. We took some hits, but no one was hurt.

As we gained altitude, I smelled gas. When the bomb hit the wing, it ruptured one of the fuel tanks. The wings on a B-24 are above the cockpit, so gas started running out of the left wing right behind the cockpit door inside the plane.

One of the crew called up on the intercom and said, "Lieutenant! Gas is running down inside the plane! What the hell are we going to do?"

I called back and said, "Calm down, don't anybody touch any of the switches!" One spark, and that would have been it.

THE WHISKEY BOTTLE CONVERSATION

The gas was flowing out in a heavy stream. It was hard to breathe with the fumes, so I left the bomb bay doors open. The gas was running down the aisle and out the doors.

B-24s have a pumping system where you can pump the gas from one wing to another. I told the copilot to switch the system on and begin the transfer. The gas ran into the cabin for about twenty minutes before the transfer was complete.

* * *

"Christ, Dick, were you scared?"

"I was damned scared! I think all of us did a lot of praying that night!"

"How much gas do you think went into the plane?"

"I'd guess maybe a couple hundred gallons dumped inside and was sucked out the bomb bay doors. Finally, we got the remaining gas transferred, and when we were practically out, I called on the emergency channel, gave our approximate position, and told them if we made it, it would be on a wing and a prayer. I know there were some scared boys on that plane. We made it back with very little fuel. When the crew got out of the plane, they all kissed the runway. So did I. There was one hell of a dent in the wing!"

Dick started to laugh. "I'll tell you, Dave, when you land after something like that, Old Mother Earth feels pretty good!"

I said, "I would certainly think so!"

* * *

The next day, Operations reported that a good-sized ship had been hit and was listing badly. I guess we got her!

About a week after that, I was going up with a different crew and a different plane. We all introduced ourselves. The copilot's name was Jim Martin. They seemed like a good group of young boys. It was a similar mission. We took off at about the regular time on a beautiful night. It was clear as a bell with a full moon. I took us past the blind bombing line into the Inland Sea.

The thing that impressed me was, the B-29s had been bombing Japan around the Inland Sea with incendiary bombs. Every place I looked, there were flames. I just couldn't believe the fires! City after city lit up the night sky. There aren't really words to describe it. It was a sight I'll never forget! A beautiful night with all the ships at work around the sea. It was just like day with that full moon.

I flew around for a while just to look at the devastation. There weren't any discernible buildings because I doubt there were any left. Everything was on fire, and I was low enough to see that there was a hell lot of people suffering. The boys in the crew were just as amazed as I was.

A voice would come over the intercom, saying things like, "Jesus! Look at that! I can't believe it!"

One of them said, "Those poor bastards! I'm glad I'm up here!"

I took the plane back up to ten thousand feet and continued with our mission, sending back the weather reports. The bombardier was looking for targets, and apparently there were plenty of ships down there going every which way.

After about five hours, I decided to head back to base. I was still over the Inland Sea when a Japanese ship shot an antiaircraft gun, and I could actually see the fire around the shell coming up toward us. It hit the plane in the nose section.

I called on the intercom to the engineer, "Go up front and see if the bombardier is all right!"

A minute later, a voice came over the intercom, saying, "He's dead, Lieutenant! Bill is dead!"

There was a lot of flack bursting around the plane from the antiaircraft fire coming from the ship. I got back on the intercom and said, "Does anybody know how to run the bomb sights?"

The engineer said, "I do, Lieutenant."

I said, "All right, get into position. We're going to make a run on that bastard!"

In a few minutes, the engineer gave me the coordinates, and I brought the plane around a put her in a dive.

I said to Jim, "Open the bomb bay doors," and I turned the plane over to the engineer at two hundred feet. I could see the ship as we were coming up on her. They were shooting at us with everything they had.

We were taking hits all over the plane.

The engineer said, "Bombs away!"

I took the plane off automatic pilot and made a hard right bank.

As I banked, the tail gunner came on the intercom, "We hit her, Lieutenant!"

A cheer went up from the crew.

"We got her, Lieutenant! We got her!" he said again.

As I gained altitude, other ships were shooting at us.

A voice came over the intercom, "The radio operator has been hit! He's alive, but he's hurt bad, Lieutenant!"

I pulled up to ten thousand feet and headed back to the blind bombing line. I tried to call on our IFF, but it had been shot out.

* * *

"What's an IFF, Dick?"

"IFF stands for Information Friend or Foe. It's a radio frequency, or code, that's changed every day. When a plane was coming back into the blind bombing, or American-controlled zone, we sent out a message on the IFF so the ships would know we were one of them.

"When we got to the blind bombing line, we couldn't send out the code, so the American ships opened upon us. They hit us and took out the left inboard engine, so I had to feather back the two engines on the right wing to stay on course. Jim was calling, 'Mayday, Mayday,' and giving our number, but it didn't have any effect. They kept shooting and hit the right inboard engine. I saw a shell come off one of the ships right for the cockpit. I can remember thinking, 'This is it, Richard! It's over!' The shell came through the cockpit right under my legs, passed under Jim's legs, and out the other side."

I said, "You're kidding me, Dick!"

"That's the God's honest truth, Dave! There were two holes about a foot in diameter on both sides of the cockpit just below our knees!"

"What did the copilot say?"

THE WHISKEY BOTTLE CONVERSATION

"He didn't say anything. He was speechless, and so was I. There was just this big rush of air coming in. Besides, we had other things to worry about.

"All of a sudden, the plane lurched to the left, and the wheel got light. The top gunner called on the intercom, 'Lieutenant! We've lost our left tail section! They shot off the left tail! God, Lieutenant, I don't want to die!' I called back, 'Hang in there! We're gonna make it!'"

"What was going through your mind, Dick?"

"I don't think I was thinking about anything except trying to keep the plane in the air. There wasn't time to think... only respond as best I could. I mean, we still had two hours flying before we got back to the base."

* * *

Jim kept up with his "Mayday" calls. Some clouds had formed, so I got the plane up into them, hoping they would provide some cover from our own ships shooting at us. Fortunately, it did. When things calmed down a little bit, I called back on the intercom to ask how the radio operator was doing.

A voice came back, "He's bad, Lieutenant. Real bad! And the tail gunner's been hit! He's got some shrapnel in his shoulder!"

Just then the engineer came up into the cockpit and said, "Lieutenant, one of the bombs didn't release. It's hung up in its hangar."

I told Jim to take over and keep on course. "I'll go back and check it out."

I went back to the bomb bay, and there was the bomb, just as the engineer had described! I grabbed an ax and, with tile bomb bay doors open, tried to chop the metal hangar free.

I can remember thinking, "One slip of the ax, and this thing is going to go off, or you're going out those bomb bay doors!"

I worked for a good ten minutes, trying to get it to release. I couldn't break the metal hangar. So finally, I said, "Screw it!" and went back to the cockpit.

Once back in my seat, Jim said he received an acknowledgment to our Mayday from a Navy seaplane that had been looking for us. They reported that they had a visual and sent the code on the IFF so we wouldn't be shot at.

A call came over the radio, "We'll follow you back to base. Your plane is in pretty rough shape. If you have to ditch, we'll be right behind you to pick you up. Good luck!"

* * *

"Believe me, Dave, those were welcome words. I thought we might just make it, but we still had an hour left to get back to base."

* * *

Somehow we managed to keep the plane in the air. About fifty miles from YonTan, I told Jim to put the landing gear down. He flipped the switch, and the indicator light showed that only the left wheel was down. I told him to put it back up. We'd be better going in on our belly

THE WHISKEY BOTTLE CONVERSATION

than with just one wheel. He hit the switch, but it wouldn't retract.

So I called back on the intercom and told the boys to secure themselves because we're going in on one wheel.

The engineer called up, "What about the bomb, Lieutenant?"

I told him there was nothing we could do about it now.

I brought the plane in, and when the left wheel hit the runway, I kept the nose up as long as I could, trying to keep the plane level. Then the tail dropped and started to drag on the runway. Three of the crew went right out through the bottom of the plane. The nose and the right wing dropped, and we skidded probably two or three thousand feet before coming to a stop just off the right side of the runway. I cut the power, got out of the plane, and ran back to the boys lying on the runway.

* * *

"Were they dead, Dick?"

"No, but they were in tough shape. Two of them had all their clothes torn off, and chunks of skin and flesh were just hanging off different parts of their bodies. The third boy apparently had rolled, so he wasn't as bad as the other two.

"An ambulance pulled up, and I helped get them in the truck and rode along to the medical tent. We carried them inside, and I held the tail gunner down while the doctor worked on him. Two other doctors and nurses were attending the other two. The doctor gave the tail gunner a shot to put him out, and after about ten minutes, he thanked me for my help and told me to go get some rest.

"As I walked out of the tent, I saw a B-24 coming in to land. When they hit the runway, the right rear tire blew. The pilot lost control and skidded into my plane, detonating the bomb. There was a huge explosion and fireball. I ran over, and Jesus, Dave, there were bodies everywhere! Some of them had arms and legs missing; others were on fire. It was a horrible disaster! I did what I could to help with the boys who were still alive. Seventeen men were killed in that explosion. Some were from the plane that hit mine; others were emergency crew working on my wrecked B-24."

Dick stopped talking and sat quietly for some time, looking into the fire. I didn't say anything. To be honest, I was speechless. I didn't know what to say. Eventually, he picked up the bottle of Scotch and poured himself a shot. Without saying a word, he raised his glass to the fire then drank the Scotch. He was staring into the fire and said something in a whisper. I asked him what he had said.

"'Attitude is altitude.' In flight school, some of the instructors used to say that."

"What happened after that?"

* * *

I went to my tent, got a bottle of whiskey out of my footlocker, and walked up to the grassy hill where I read my mail. I sat there, looking at the sea, drinking my whiskey, until I fell asleep. The next morning Joe O'Connor woke me up.

He said, "God, Dick, I heard about what happened last night! We were all worried when we couldn't find you! Are you okay?"

THE WHISKEY BOTTLE CONVERSATION

I said, "Yeah, Joe, I'm all right."

He picked up the bottle and took a drink and said, "They're going to have a service this afternoon for all the boys who were killed. Why don't you and I go over to the mess and get some coffee."

"You go ahead, Joe. I think I'm going to take a shower. I'll see you a little later."

He said, "Okay, Dick. If there's anything I can do, you know where to find me."

I thanked him and lay back down in the grass for a while.

That afternoon I went to the service for the men who had died in the explosion. The minister started by reading some passages from the Bible. Then he began to talk about the dangers every time we went up.

He said, "I have flown many times with crews in combat, and I know what you men go through."

I got really mad because I knew he had never been in a combat situation and, for that matter, probably never been in a plane! He didn't know what it was like, and I felt he was being a hypocrite saying he did. I was so upset I walked out. That was the only time during the war that I recall being that upset.

I took the jeep and just drove from one end of the island to the other on some of the new roads that the Seabees were building all over Okinawa.

* * *

"After that incident, Dick, did you feel like you'd had enough?"

"No, Dave. The ordeal of being shot up, losing those boys, bothered me, but it didn't deter me from my flying duties. I had done everything I could in that situation, and there were no feelings of guilt—only loss. I went up on another mission a couple of days after that. That's what I joined for. That's what I did. I also felt that we were getting near the end of the war."

* * *

The last time I flew a combat mission, I was a copilot. Operations advised us that there was a big Jap battleship that was camouflaged near Tokyo.

They said, "If you want to make a pass on it, go ahead."

I said to myself, "No way am I going to attack a battleship!"

The pilot felt the same way. We flew up into the Inland China Sea and sent back our weather reports. I can't even remember where we dropped our bombs. We just dumped our load and flew back to base.

A few days later, they dropped the atomic bombs. They told us the bombs were dropped on Hiroshima and Nagasaki. Apparently, the plane would be climbing when the bomb was released, causing it to go straight down. Harry Truman was thrilled about how well the bombs worked, and they had brought an end to the war. Their effect, as you know, was devastating, but thousands of American lives would have been lost if we had invaded Japan. On August 15, 1945, Japan surrendered.

Just before the surrender, MacArthur flew into YonTan, and a transport landed right behind him and lowered the

THE WHISKEY BOTTLE CONVERSATION

ramp in the rear of the plane. Out came a black Cadillac sedan. MacArthur got in the car and toured the island. After about three hours, he came back to the base, loaded his car on the plane, and took off. He was a real showman and knew how to travel in style.

* * *

"How did you feel when the news came that Japan had surrendered?"

Dick sat there for a moment. Then he said, "I suppose I felt good—sort of happy. I didn't really believe that it was over, I guess. Having been away from home for so long, being involved in fighting to defeat the enemy, and mainly being focused on that end of it took awhile to realize it was over."

There was a letter Dick had written at the end of the war. I looked through the folder on the table and found it.

I said, "Dick, I've got another letter I want to read to you."

Lt. R. P. Leonard
373rd Bomb Squadron
494th Bomb Group
A.P.O. 903 %
P.M. San Francisco, CA
8/18/45

My Dear Parents:

It's a beautiful day here in Okinawa: no doubt you've heard the name before, and while sitting here in the cool of the afternoon, I started reminiscing. While my thoughts were wandering and my vision was taking in the beauties of another nature, I happened to see a small insignificant building a way off by itself: and after pondering for some time the merits of this necessary but rather frowned-upon shed, I decided that I really owed it a vote of thanks; consequently, I immediately set to work jotting down its points which have been of so much help to me in my Army career. Knowing your keen interest in my Army friends, I thought you might like to hear about every soldier's friend, be he Private, Sergeant, Lieutenant, Colonel or General.

I'm going to tell you about this friend, in a strong form, and as all stories should have a name, I have decided to call this one, "Freedom, Equality, and—The Army Latrine!"

He laughed and took a sip of his drink.

"All men are created free and equal," so says the Constitution of the United States. This, I am told, is the foundation of American Democracy and something we all believe in whether we realize it or not!

In the Army of these here United States, it is rather difficult at times to see yourself as a free and equal man. This is not too hard to visualize even if you know very little about the Army. From my first moments in the service of my country, I have remembered that I was no better than any other

THE WHISKEY BOTTLE CONVERSATION

man and vice versa, but also from the beginning, I have been compelled to do business with fellow mankind, whom I'm sure had forgotten the Constitution of the United States and what they had started out to fight for—namely Democracy!

It was a very dismal day when I entered the gates of "Nashville Classification Center," in more ways than one! First—Mother Nature wasn't her usual cheery self, and persisted in throwing down buckets of rain and intermittently cloaking the earth in a sheath of heavy, dense fog. Secondly, it was my first and so far last entrance into an Army post in civilian clothing. Third, I was dressed in my Sunday best in order to make that good first impression—and to be met at the gate by an acting P.F.C. really made the bottom drop out of the world.

As soon as my rear extremities had passed the gateposts, I was ordered by this acting P.F.C. to board a truck very much exposed to the weather and he then climbed into a nice comfortable cabin. After riding just far enough to become thoroughly saturated, he stuck his head out of the window and told some poor kid to march us into a nearby building. So the poor fellow, a new recruit like myself, told me in a very weak voice to get off the truck, and I quote, "Forward march into that building over there!"

When they finished with us in "that building over there," I started to lose my feeling of being created free and equal. They asked us numerous questions and had us sign dozens of forms. Then, after satisfying themselves that we weren't spies and were quite trustworthy, they entrusted us with one blanket, one cot, and a space in a very cold barracks. Here we stayed for one week—a casual barracks they called it—it sure was casual, all right. It being September in Tennessee, the nights were extremely cold and with only one blanket and our very filthy civilian clothes, it was rather depressing. In order to keep warm at night, we would take turns sleeping and standing by the fire. This gave us two blankets and warmth enough so that we didn't freeze entirely! As the days progressed, I was really wondering if we were fighting for democracy, and had just about decided that freedom and equality were a thing of the past!

Every morning that damned P.F.C. came in and blew a ten-cent whistle, but I don't think he got any real satisfaction out of it because we were usually all up and dressed (never took our clothes off anyway), and were just waiting (huddled around a stove) for him to march us to breakfast, which none of us enjoyed!

After a filling, but far from appetizing breakfast, we were lined up and given various assignments such as K.P., cleaning the area, sweeping and mopping the barracks, or cleaning the latrines! You are all familiar with the first three duties, but the latter has been rejected for reasons of decency, I suppose, therefore, for the sake of furthering your education, I will tell you about it!

THE WHISKEY BOTTLE CONVERSATION

You may think, "cleaning the latrine," a rather unsavory subject; but I assure you, it is not. I'll admit it has its unfavorable aspects, but so does every other job. From the first I have always had a soft spot in my heart for the Army latrine, because here a man's soul is his own, even on a cleaning detail! After being assigned to this particular job, you are left alone to do your duty as you see fit. There's no P.F.C. or Corporal to lord over you; the job is quite simple and how you go about it is left to your own discretion: here you may regain yourself respect, and your feeling of freedom and equality.

Dick started laughing again.

If you want to wash the bowls, clean the mirrors, wash out the showers and then mop the floor, you may do so; or if you want to mop the floor first, you are free to do so! That was the first job in the Army where my own judgment was considered adequate, and it was here that I realized that perhaps, even in the Army, you could be considered free and equal—a son of Democracy!

At Nashville, I received my Army clothes, learned to drill, did seven straight days of K.P., and received my classification as a pilot. These were the trying days, full of unpleasant duties, interviews, and tests. Men ranging in rank from Privates to Colonel screamed and hollered at you; they told you, you were lower than a bitch dog, you were a bundle of nerves, and then in the same breath they would say, and I quote, "Gentlemen, you are the pick of our country's men or else you wouldn't be here. You have been chosen because you are mentally, physically, and morally fit!" Five minutes after this little speech, some fellow who could barely write his name, was on limited service, and undoubtedly had the morale of a passionate cat would be supervising your existence! What a life! But—no matter what the day's trials and tribulations, there was always one sanctuary where all the men gathered some time to think their own thoughts, feel their own feelings, or if they desired—to discuss politics with their next-door neighbor be he Cadet, Private, Lieutenant, or Colonel. The Army latrine was a haven where free men gathered! Not even a lowly acting P.F.C. would disturb a man who was communing with nature.

As my training continued, there were new problems to be solved and instead of enlisted men hollering at me, there were officers ranging from the lowest to the highest rank bellowing orders at me. The first thing they taught me to say was, "Yes, sir!" "No, sir!" and "No excuse, sir!" Does this sound like a land of free and equal men? You bet your sweet life it doesn't. Many are the times while thinking things over at the end of the day in my secluded spot, I would say to myself, "Dick, are you a man or a mouse? Don't let those damned 'Gravel adjusters' (what we called guard officers) brow beat you! You're just as good as they are and know a hell of a lot more about getting along with the average man than they do." Then, trying to square myself

THE WHISKEY BOTTLE CONVERSATION

with myself, I'd say, "Dick, it's your duty to mankind to go through with this thing—to become an officer—then you can show these 'sand pounders' (gravel adjusters) how an officer should treat his fellow men!" You see in this atmosphere, I straightened myself out through good, clear, undisturbed thinking. Once again, I owed myself respect to that part of the Army which is frowned upon by those who do not realize the important part it plays in everyday life.

Finally, that day arrived when the Colonel pinned my wings on, gave me my gold bars, and shaking my hand, welcomed me to the realm of officers and gentlemen (the latter by an act of Congress). Overnight, I became a man among men; I was no longer a protégée of the First Sergeant or a no-good "Pencil Pusher"—I was a Flying Officer—my troubles were over! I could speak as a free man and for the next ten days, I did exactly that... I was on a ten-day leave!

My first assignment as an *Officer* was at Loughlin Field, Del Rio, Texas, a B-26 Transitional School. Believe me, I felt like Somebody! I arrived at Del Rio with my wife, and checking in at the Base Adjuncts's office, I informed the Sergeant that I would be living at a hotel in town with the Mrs.! The next thing I knew, I was confronted by the Captain, politely but firmly informing me that I would live at the post and would visit my wife only when issued a pass! Needless to say, I objected...

"I'm an Officer," I informed him. "I'm entitled to live with my wife. Regulations say so."

"Well," said the Captain, "If you would care to discuss this with the Colonel, I'm sure it can be arranged." I called Jean and told her the bad news. Then I remembered my friend and to her (or, it, if you must), I sought comfort and seclusion.

Assuming one of the most comfortable positions a human can assume, I began to think once more. "I'm free and equal and an officer. I will go see the Colonel. I'll tell him a thing or two. I've got my rights." I cussed myself, the Captain, the Colonel, and the Army. Then the atmosphere, so peaceful and quiet, got the better of me and I began to take both sides of the question into consideration. Going over the plans carefully, I decided perhaps I was a little hasty, maybe the Colonel was right. "Del Rio," I said to myself, "is a small town with limited housing facilities and a limited amount of restaurants. It wouldn't be fair to the town's population if the whole of Loughlin Field infringed on their hospitality and privacy. Perhaps it is best this way." So for the hundredth time during my career, I owed my self-respect to "an Army Latrine."

Leaving Del Rio and Loughlin Field, I proceeded to El Paso, Texas and Biggs Field. Here I was permitted to have my own home and here I began to live as a man. I had regular hours, an airplane to fly, a wife to come home to... consequently, I was very happy and content. For these reasons, I forgot my old friend and it wasn't until nearly a year and

THE WHISKEY BOTTLE CONVERSATION

a half later, that I took shelter in my Army sanctuary, in China. You can see by this that I really had a staunch friend. Even to the ends of the world, she was there to comfort and coddle me.

The first part of my tour overseas was full of new things. Lots of travel and excitement and so my moments of seclusion were spent thinking of the joys of the past and the possibilities of the future. I relived many a happy moment in the peace and quiet of My Old Friend. Even in the worst of Army Latrines, where eventually, your legs go to sleep, I found I could spend many happy, contented hours. Why, I can even remember a few times when I have been aroused by tingling legs just in time to make an important engagement. Is there any wonder why I hold this friend in such high esteem?

Eventually, life in China became rather boring and quite unbearable. The food wasn't too good, unless you consider rice and buffalo meat a delicacy; and after a year and a half of the same type of work, most of it on the ground, I longed for new country and new thrills. But the lust for a promotion and the idea of being a big wheel in a small machine kept me imprisoned.

Then one day, while taking refuge from the drab outside world in a nice, clean, shiny, Army latrine (my respects to the last engineer), I decided to attempt a break and this is how it happened. There had been a big shake up on the field and another outfit was taking over my job. They were taking my equipment, my ideas, and my men, all of which I had worked many, many hours to perfect. This in itself made me a little bitter.

I'll have to admit, I'd stolen most of my equipment and men, but that was the only way I could accomplish the job and for that reason, they were that much closer to me! Consequently, I was in the depth of despair, and therefore I should seek comfort in my usual abode.

Looking around at the white walls, the clean floor, and the sun streaming through the windows, I began to feel better and the spirit of freedom and equality started to flow through my body and the desire to see new things and experience new problems overwhelmed me. I had long desired the opportunity to be a part of a "combat team," and the more I thought about it, the more determined I became to attempt the change. Finally, the yearning to be free once more, to fly every day, and to bring destruction and defeat to the enemy got the better of me, and I dashed from my retreat to the Colonel's office!

My life in the bomb squadron was very enjoyable and to my liking in its entirety. I had no sooner become a member of a combat team than the whole outfit was whisked out of China to the South Pacific. The trip alone was worth the break. Arriving in the Philippines, we were treated like heroes. Boy, they figured we really had it tough in China and our stories didn't portray anything different. From the Philippines, we went to the Molucca Group and Morotai. Here, we lounged for several days and then returned to the Philippines. Then things got really

THE WHISKEY BOTTLE CONVERSATION

serious and they shipped us to the Ryukyu Group and Okinawa. Here I got my first and last taste of combat; here I experienced my first and last air raid; in general, here my desires (thirst) for thrills and excitement were squelched (quenched.) And to think if it wasn't for "The Army Latrine," I'd have still been in China.

Then one night, in a valley of fireworks, the likes of which has never been seen before, or will probably never be seen again, the war was over. From here on in, all I had to do was bask in the sunlight and wait for a trip home and a discharge.

It was during this lull, as I mentioned at the beginning, that it dawned on me that I owed a great deal to that inconspicuous, lovely "Army Latrine," and so decided to pay my respects to a real friend, the only way I know how.

In closing, let me impress upon you that even in the Army, men are free and equal. I have shown through actual experiences that a man can be himself if he so desires, therefore, in the name of democracy, let me offer a toast, and I do this with a feeling of gratitude and good fellowship, to the only place in the Army where free and equal men gather to cuss and discuss their own individual problems... "The Army Latrine"!

Well, kids, hope you approve of my friend and agree that my respects are warranted. If I haven't made any particular point clear, I'm sure a note dropped in your nearest mailbox will lead to a quick and satisfactory answer!

I started this early this afternoon and here it is chow time—sometimes I wonder if you really had your minds on what you were doing when you begot me!

Your son (if you'll still have him),
Dick

I put the letter down and looked at Dick.

"Well, that certainly puts it all in perspective."

We both began to laugh.

"Yep," he said. "That was my sanctuary."

"What did you mean by 'a display of fireworks the likes of which the world has never seen'?"

"Well, you remember there were hundreds of ships in the two harbors at Okinawa waiting for the invasion. When they announced that Japan had surrendered, it was about nine at night, and all the ships began firing their guns into the air... tracers, big guns... everything was going off! It was an unbelievable show that lasted for at least an hour! Later on, it was referred to as the million-dollar blunder because that's how much they figured it cost in spent ammunition! All the personnel on Okinawa had their helmets on because of the falling flack and shells. Some boys were actually killed or wounded from falling debris."

I said to Dick, "That's a hell of a way to end the war... being killed by friendly fire."

"Yeah, it was, Dave. I don't suppose the families of the boys killed ever knew the real circumstances of how they died."

"So what were your duties after the surrender?"

THE WHISKEY BOTTLE CONVERSATION

"I was on Okinawa for about a month after the surrender. I was assigned to flying crews that were going home. I had to make sure their records were current and that they checked in all their equipment. Everybody knew that I had a list of their military issue and what they were supposed to have. I was responsible for a couple hundred men. For example, everyone had a revolver, and I had to make sure they turned it in. A lot of them wanted to keep souvenirs. I told them that if they could fit it in their barracks bags, to go ahead and take it home. It's awfully damned hard to turn a man down after he's put his life on the line for his country. When they got aboard ship, they were checked again. If they were going to fly home, I suppose they were stricter than if they took a ship. The activity on the island was greatly diminished when I left."

"Did you come home after that, Dick?"

"I could have, but I volunteered to go to Japan."

"Why?" I asked.

"Because, Dave, I wanted to see what we had fought for. I wanted to see Japan, or what was left of it, and have the chance to talk to some of the Japanese people. I had fought too long not to take that opportunity."

I sat there for a few minutes, trying to understand his perspective. After giving it some thought and reflecting on his life and love of adventure, I realized it was the only decision he could have made.

I asked Dick what he did.

"I got aboard a C-54, a mail-carrying plane, and flew to Tatchakawa, Japan.

CHAPTER FIFTEEN

I Wanted to See What We Fought For

Tatchakawa was a research and development base for the Japanese Air Corps. It has taken its share of bombs. It was a real industrious-type base with aircraft and transportation facilities still intact. Many of the hangars were in rubble, but there were a few that we could operate out of keeping the planes in service and flying.

My duties were to fly mail and pick up personnel on the outlying islands. When assigned, I took a plane, usually a C-47, and flew around to the islands… just a guy out for a ride. I was flying a couple of times a week. In fact, they had so many pilots that wanted to take a trip someplace many times I'd just go along as a passenger. Everybody was relaxed and happy not to have someone shooting at you or worrying about the next mission.

After a time in Tatchakawa, I decided to go to Tokyo. They had an electric train that was one of the few left. Once out in the countryside, it took my breath away. Every place I looked, it was like driving through a garbage dump. All

THE WHISKEY BOTTLE CONVERSATION

the way to Tokyo, I didn't see a single building standing… not one building. It was total devastation!

When the train finally arrived in Tokyo, I reported to this communication center for soldiers coming into the city. The men in the center were really nice guys. They were happy that the war was over and went out of their way to see we got everything we wanted. They told me where I could go to have some fun and see generally what our bombing had done. I was assigned a jeep and went into the city alone. There was only one building standing intact… a hotel built by an American. It was designed to withstand an earthquake, and that's where MacArthur set up his operations.

The Japanese people had no direction at that point. They were basically wandering around, trying to find food. On the outskirts of Tokyo, people were working in the fields, trying to raise food. Most of the activity was underground in basements connected by tunnels. There were little stores and shops. It was an underground city. I spent some time there, looking at what they were selling. Of course, the prices were out of this world!

* * *

"How did the Japanese people react to you, Dick?"

"None of them ever bothered me. I had a sidearm on. For the most part, they were just as relieved as we were that the war was over. In war, it's always the civilians that suffer the most. They had no part in starting the conflict but were the ones, in reality, that suffered and sacrificed the most. I wrote a letter home when I was in Japan, Dave. It gives a pretty good description of what life was like. Why don't you see if you can find it?"

I looked through the remaining letters and found the one Dick was referring to.

Lt. R.P. Leonard
56th Troop Carrier Squadron
375th Carrier Squadron
APO 704 %
P.M. San Francisco, CA

My Dear Parents:

Living off the fat of Japan and doing nothing in particular, except trying to get home; and I'm not really doing well with that project. This outfit I'm with flies all around the Pacific and is known as the "Tokyo Trolley." They were the second troop carrier squadron in the Pacific and the second to get to Tokyo. Most of the fellows are new kids with only a couple months' overseas time, consequently, they don't have that defeated expression that we "old-timers" have. They're a nice bunch in spite of their "eager beavering" and I'm satisfied. We just moved out of a factory and into, of all things, a Veterinarian laboratory. The smell makes me homesick, but aside from that, I can't complain. This was apparently a Vet College; it consists of a dozen or so very large buildings, half of which are still full of supplies. If you need anything, HK, let me know and I'll go on a moonlight requisition.

THE WHISKEY BOTTLE CONVERSATION

Tokyo was quite the city! Apparently, it was as beautiful as prewar descriptions, but now is just a mass of destruction. There are very few buildings left standing and most of these are badly damaged. I live in a town called Tatchakawa, which is located approximately fifty miles southwest of Tokyo. It is on the main line as far as transportation is concerned, and trains run about every fifteen minutes. It's about like a New York City subway at five o'clock and the smell is that of a fish market, but it's a pretty good little train. It takes around an hour and twenty minutes to get to Tokyo station—I mean, what's left of the station. I think the boys used to drop a load on it every day just for good measure. The whole trip is just one picture of devastation; both sides of the track are a mass of debris, as far as the eye can see. People are living in anything they can throw together and those that can't throw things together are just out in the cold. It's purely "the survival of the fittest" and will continue to be so until next summer rolls around. By that time, it will be the "survival of the fittest-fittest"!

The Emperor's Palace is still intact and people still bow very low when they pass within four or five miles of it. I was talking to a Commander in the Navy who was employed by the Japanese government before the war and I asked him his opinion of Jap feelings toward the Americans. He said that next to the Emperor, the Japs thought MacArthur was the greatest man in the world! Every day, thousands wait in front of the General's headquarters to see *"Dugout Doug"* come out. I even waited an hour the other day to see him. My commander friend also said that America's occupation of Japan was one of the greatest things in Jap history. The people are so tired of being bullied by the militants that this is really a honeymoon. They figured the Americans would really run rampant with everything, but when they saw American guards protecting the Emperor and everything else of any value in Japan, they changed their minds. Now the terrible Americans are giving them chocolates, nylons, cigarettes, and paying their high prices. They're really happy... at least for the time being!

The other Sunday, I went to a baseball game between the Japs and the GI's. It was held at the Meiji Stadium which was built for the 1941 Olympic games. The game started at two and by ten in the morning, the place was crowded with Japs who, after being deprived of all sports for five years, weren't taking a chance on getting a poor seat. The stadium is just a small part of the Olympic Center; it has everything from Judo rings to swimming pools, and they were once really modern and beautiful grounds. Now it is run down and all available space is producing something to eat.

The Imperial Hotel is nice, but compared to American hotels, it is average. It has a club atmosphere but to me, anything with a tablecloth is considered very elite! The service is excellent and the meals all come in courses; the second always consisting of fish! The price is quite reasonable due to

THE WHISKEY BOTTLE CONVERSATION

Army supervision and for extras, which are limited, an American cigarette will work as well as a five spot in America.

Geisha houses—don't be shocked—I have visited one! There are two types of Geisha houses and Geisha girls. One type is strictly monkey business, if you know what I mean, and I'm sure you do! This is called Yardo or Gero in Japan. This is a low-class Geisha house. The true Geisha house is altogether different. It is strictly a place to be entertained by young ladies who aren't selling what they used to give away. The one I visited had been modernized to meet American standards. You didn't have to remove your shoes, in fact, it was quite like a small restaurant. There were approximately twelve to fifteen girls there; half were dressed in Western styles and the other half were dressed in traditional Japanese dress. All the girls I met were quite well educated and spoke understandable English. You can sit and talk, dance, sit and drink, or just plain sit. They had an electric Victrola with American and Japanese records, and I might add, the girls danced quite well. The prices are high, naturally, and the sake is strong. No doubt you have read of this kind of whiskey. In the States we call it "White Lightning" or in better circles, "Panther Piss"! A true Geisha girl, to get back to the subject, is trained from childhood to be an entertainer. They are usually purchased by a rich house at an early age and are trained until they are mature and they can properly take care for a lonely man who isn't amorously inclined, if there is such a dull creature. In short, it was amusing, but personally, I'll take a ham sandwich and a ride on a streetcar.

I've been souvenir hunting a few times but have about given it up as a bad job. A kimono sells for around ninety bucks, that's one worth looking at, and an obi (that little job they wear on their back) sells for forty or fifty dollars. I'd like very much to buy a lot of junk, but it ain't worth it to me, and I don't think it would be to you. So unless I really get a bargain, I'll save my shekels and throw a party when I get home, or else buy Rick an apple stand!

Speaking of getting home, I still don't have the slightest idea when or how. I'm not doing anything constructive here or anything destructive—but it's an idea. I'm still hoping to deck the halls with bows of folly—and no one realizes more than I that, "It can't happen here!"

Well, Dear Parents, it's taken me three days to finish this letter. You can see where my mind is, so I guess I'll bring this epistle to an end. My love to the whole tribe, and may God grant us a very Merry Christmas—together!

*Your son,
Richard Pressure Leonard*

I asked Dick, "Why do you think they didn't bomb the Emperor's Palace?"

"I would say that they felt it was of historical significance and revered by the Japanese people, so they left it

THE WHISKEY BOTTLE CONVERSATION

alone. In war, the idea is to defeat the enemy, not totally obliterate the foundations of their culture or civilization. You know, there is life after war, and some standards had been established in the Geneva Convention about treatment of prisoners and things of that nature. The Japanese, for the most part, didn't adhere to the rules established, but that didn't mean that we were going to follow suit.

"In fact, it was MacArthur that was responsible for rebuilding the Japanese economy and really, the entire country. The United States poured billions of dollars into Japan to get them back on their feet. He did a hell of a job and was admired by the Japanese people. It's rather ironic, isn't it, that first we destroy the way of life and then go in and restore it? That's not to say, of course, that we weren't justified in what we did."

"How long were you in Japan?"

"Well, when I went there, it was with the understanding that I would fly or do some sort of job. Mostly, I wanted to see the country and what we had fought for.

"After about two months, they were having a tough time finding things for me to do. Most of the boys I knew all wanted to get home. I didn't really think that way. As long as I was busy flying, I felt that I should stay. However, when I started having a lot of free time on my hands, I decided, what was the point? I put in to be sent back to the States.

"Soon after my trip to Tokyo, they sent me home. I can't remember how I got back to the States—whether it was by ship or plane. Of all my war experiences, I draw a complete blank when it comes to that. Strange, isn't it?

You'd think that would be the one thing I'd remember… how I got home."

Dick sat there for a moment, looking at the flickering fire.

* * *

The first thing I recall is being in San Francisco. I was at a discharge center for all the boys coming back from the Pacific. There were a lot of men there, so we were given a day to report when we could get our mustering-out pay and our discharge papers. I had about a week.

On my scheduled day, I walked into the office, and there was this major sitting at his desk. I saluted and gave him my name. He pulled out my 201 file and looked it over.

He said in a very curt tone, "Do you want to be discharged, Lieutenant, or remain in the service?"

I said, "Well, sir, I'd like to have some time to think it over."

He looked up at me and said, "You're either in, or you're out!"

I couldn't believe that little prick was talking to me in that tone. He'd obviously been stateside during the war, and I'd just returned from two years overseas.

I glared at him and said, "I'm out!"

He stamped my papers and said, "Pick up your check at the disbursement office."

I turned around, walked out, and slammed the door behind me. Jesus, I was mad!

THE WHISKEY BOTTLE CONVERSATION

I picked up my check, got my gear together, and grabbed a slow train back East. I wanted it slow. I hadn't called Jean or my family to tell them I was back in the States.

* * *

"What went through your mind on the trip back home, Dick?"

"As the train took me from state to state, I thought about the beauty of this country and the freedoms we fought to protect. My thoughts about my personal life were another matter. I would say I was quite confused. Having had a career in the Air Corps, being designated where to go and what to do, and all at once not having that career anymore was very confusing to me. I was in the service for four years and had only spent about four months with Jean and Rick. After spending all that time in training, fighting, trying to stay alive, not really thinking about anything but my next mission, and then to come back to the world of everyday life was very unsettling. When I arrived in Syracuse, I got a room in a hotel and stayed a week before I called home."

"Why did you wait a week before you called?"

"I think I was scared, Dave. I wasn't ready to see my family. I needed some time to try and put things back in perspective."

* * *

When Harriet answered, I told her I was in Syracuse and would appreciate it if they all didn't come to get me. I just wanted someone to come pick me up and bring me home. Of course, they all came… Jean, Rick, Harriet, and HK. When I saw them, we all started to cry. Jean hugged and kissed me. Rick was three and cried and squirmed when I picked him up. He didn't have a clue who I was and put his arms out toward Jean.

After not seeing your family but for a few months over that period of time, you would think it would be a tremendously elated feeling. It wasn't. Not for me. The first feelings I had were wondering what I was going to do tomorrow. Instead of being on the move all the time, knowing that I was on my way to someplace, living with soldiers, I was suddenly thrown back to my family expecting me to get right up and find a job. It was a terrible, confusing feeling. I would say that I struggled with the reintroduction to civilian life for the better part of a year.

Jean, Rick, my parents, and all my relatives and friends were everything a man could ask for. They gave me help, friendship, and of course, the love that I needed to once again rejoin civilian life.

* * *

Dick and I both sat quietly for some time.

Finally, I said, "That's quite a story, Dick. I want to thank you for sharing it with me."

He looked at me and said, "I want to thank you, Dave, for giving me the opportunity to relive that part of my life. I haven't thought much about the war in the last fifty

THE WHISKEY BOTTLE CONVERSATION

years. It was an exciting time in my life—the challenges, the adventure, fighting for a cause we all believed in. Many of the men I was associated with never came home. Their sacrifices, however, made the world a better place—not only in the preservation of our own ideals and principles in America, but for all the countries we fought to protect, and those we defeated, it was a noble cause."

As I listened to his words, I felt some tears roll down my cheeks.

Neither of us said anything for what seemed like a long time.

Eventually, Dick said, "I think I'd like a cup of tea with some honey, Dave."

I went into the kitchen and made a pot of tea, put it on a tray with two cups and a jar of honey. When I got back to the study, Dick had his chair in a reclining position and was asleep.

I sat down and drank my tea. I decided to put the letters and pictures back in the box while Dick slept. As I was doing so, I saw a brown manila envelope in the bottom of the box that I hadn't noticed before. I took it out and opened it. Inside was a document and a newspaper article. The document had the White House seal on the top of it. It read:

DAVID LEONARD

RICHARD P LEONARD

To you who answered the call of your country and served in its Armed Forces to bring about the total defeat of the enemy, I extend the heartfelt thanks of a grateful Nation. As one of the Nation's finest, you undertook the most severe task one can be called upon to perform. Because you demonstrated the fortitude, resourcefulness and calm judgment necessary to carry out that task, we now look to you for leadership and example in further exalting our country in peace.

Harry Truman

THE WHITE HOUSE

THE WHISKEY BOTTLE CONVERSATION

The newspaper article was written for a business journal in 1955.

As Business Leaders See It...
Scientific Research Is Termed Key to the Nation's Future

R. P. Leonard, Sales Manager
Cyclotherm Division
National—U.S. Radiator Corp.

The man in the laboratory is the man of the hour, the decade and the century. Scientific research more than any one thing, has created modern American. It is responsible for its prosperity, its way of living, industrial and military strength. Today, more than ever, it holds the key to the nation's future and survival.

The rise of scientists and the technicians dates back only to World War II. During the war, research made possible such developments as nuclear fission, proximity fuses, sonar and rockets. It helped to win the allied victory. Since the war, much of the emphasis has been on industrial research again with spectacular results.

The men at the drawing boards and with the test tubes have been responsible for thousands of products, making the transformation from laboratories and testing grounds to production lines in an unending stream. Now they have created new industries and opened up new job possibilities. They have also helped to build stability into an economy that was formerly at the mercy of sharp business cycles.

My company, definitely a product of World War II, was formed in order to produce package steam and hot water generators commercially. It has since grown through a series of rapid developments in the field of steam generators. Recently we introduced a hot water boiler which is the result of three years of extensive work, design and testing.

The scope of this development is worldwide. This boiler is a packaged fire-tube type designed for modern forced circulation systems for both high and low temperature operation. Previously hot water boilers were in actuality steam boilers redesigned and reequipped for hot water use.

Our faith and confidence in our industry's long future are shown by an ever-increasing research and new product exploration. With automation on the increase, the optimum employment of the working force hinges in new and improved products continuously flowing from the drawing boards.

No expense will be spared on our part in making the finest package generator money can buy.

THE WHISKEY BOTTLE CONVERSATION

I looked at Dick sleeping so peacefully in his chair and thought that he had fulfilled the wishes of his president in both war and peace. I also thought about the legacy he had left—not just a legacy of a father to his son, but he represented the legacy of an entire generation to their country.

Children of the Depression who grew up in hardship and want, yet always maintained a firm belief in America and the principles that it stands for. When it came time to defend those principles, they joined by the thousands. It was also this generation that catapulted mankind into the new age of technology. As a result of the need for more and better weapons and machinery, technological advancements were made in years that otherwise might have taken decades.

They were men and women who believed in themselves, their country, and the ideals of duty and honor. I knew that from this day forward, I would never forget the examples they have left behind, and I hoped that mine and future generations would reflect on and use their legacy as a principle to live by.

I poured myself a little Scotch and walked out to the solarium. The storm was over, and the clouds had dissipated, giving way to the bright full moon that hung over the mountains. The snow shimmered in the reflection of the moon's light with the dark silhouette of the mountains in the background. I felt very happy and content as I walked back into the study. I looked at my watch. It was twelve thirty. The fire had burned down to just a handful of glowing embers, and our bottle of Scotch sat almost empty on the table.

I gently shook Dick. He opened his eyes slowly, and I said, "It's time for bed."

I helped him out of his chair, took his arm, and walked him to his room. I waited until he climbed into his feather bed, and I covered him with the down comforter.

I said, "Is there anything I can get for you?"

"No, thanks, Dave, but some other time, we'll get another bottle, and I'll tell you about after the war."

I smiled and said, "I'd like that, Dad."

As I walked back into the study, I felt a sense of pride. I was proud to know Richard Leonard, the man, but even more proud that I was his son.

David Leonard

THE WHISKEY BOTTLE CONVERSATION

Richard P. Leonard
1920–2000

CPSIA information can be obtained
at www.ICGtesting.com
Printed in the USA
FFOW03n1948160517
35718FF